❀
Clover

Published in 2017 by Lisa Jade via lulu.com
Copyright © Lisa Jade, 2017

All rights reserved
No part of this publication may be reproduced, stored digitally, or transmitted in any form without prior permission of the copyright owner.

This is a work of fiction. All characters, locations and events portrayed in this novel are products of the author's imagination.
www.lisajade.net

CHAPTER ONE

I bring the axe down hard, aiming for the centre of the log. It splits cleanly and a smile plays on my lips. A perfect hit. I place another log on the stump, repositioning my fingers on the handle of the axe. Sunlight glints at me, reflected from the rusted blade.

I pause. I'm bathed in the warmth of a late summer afternoon. Sunlight filters through the trees around us, turning into shining speckles on my hands and face. I wipe the sweat from my brow.

"Tired already, girlie?"

The Guard stands behind me. He's a large, balding man with a permanent scowl and a shoddily-designed shock baton clutched in one hand. He taps it gently in his palm, his eyes narrowing. I shake my head.

"No, Sir. Sorry."

I lift the axe overhead and swing downward again, this time missing the log and cutting some bark off instead. An anguished sigh escapes my throat and I aim again, this time revelling in the weight of the tool in my hand. It hits. The wood splinters down the grain with a satisfying crack.

I glance at the Guard, but Wirrow's already moved on. He's pacing the line, watching the other workers now.

We're lined up in our hundreds, chopping wood together. The next time I swing the axe, the movement aligns flawlessly with everyone else's – we work in surprising harmony here, each of us used to the rhythm of things.

The person next to me groans. I steal a glance his way; the poor thing is young, only fourteen or so. He's clearly not used to the physical exertion of life at the Mill. His clothes are soaked with sweat. It drips from his face, which grows paler by the minute. He leans forward, hands on his knees, and gulps down what little air he can.

"Oi. You!"

It's Wirrow. He's walking this way, ferocity in his eyes. I busy myself with chopping again. I'm not keen to be on the receiving end of a scolding – or worse. He stands over the boy, twirling the baton in one hand. The boy stares blankly; he doesn't recognise the tool. Doesn't realise the damage it can do.

"What's your name?"

"Kane," the kid says – but there's a little too much bravado in his voice. If I hadn't been sure of his immaturity before, I am now. Only an idiot talks to the Guard like that. Wirrow leans down until his eyes are level with Kane's. The kid stares at him, warm brown eyes meeting Wirrow's beady, black ones.

"How long have you been working, Kane?"

"At the farm? About three weeks."

I wince. You never answer that question honestly. You always lie. Wirrow glances at me and I look pointedly away, making sure I swing extra hard at the next log.

"You."

I freeze, the tool still mid-swing. Wirrow wanders over and places a heavy hand on my shoulder. My knees almost buckle from his weight and I drop my gaze to the ground, a motion borne partly from submission and partly from a desire to avoid a beating.

"What's your name, girlie?"

"Noah."

He smirks.

"And how long have you been working the farm?"

I bite my lip.

"Three years, Sir."

He laughs – a big, booming noise that makes my skin crawl.

"See, Kiddo? Three years here and she's not complaining."

"But..."

Wirrow waves a hand at him and he falls silent.

"You keep working. I don't care if your hands drop off or you go blind. You keep working until I say to stop."

Kane's eyes dart around, and I can tell he wants to run. But then his gaze slides around the paddock, following the loop of barbed wire keeping us in. The Guard towers, the electronic locks. The occasional Guard-marked Hoverbot circling the perimeter. Defeat worms its way into his expression.

"Yes, Sir."

He throws his axe down hard. It splits the log flawlessly, but I can tell it wasn't intentional. He just wants to take out his anger on something. Just wants to release the pent up frustration in his chest. Wirrow chuckles.

"Good lad."

We keep working until the sun is gone and it becomes hard to see. The floodlights help a little, but once the stars become our main light source, we finally reach our limit. A whistle blows, and everyone heads inside.

I lean the axe against the nearest block and gingerly run my hands up my arms. They feel bruised and achy, and I can feel new blisters forming on my fingers and knuckles. I sigh. Okay. Pity time over. I shrug away the pain and turn to head inside.

Kane stands motionless, axe still held loosely in one hand. I pause.

"We should head inside."

He shakes his head sadly.

"Why did you do that?"

"Do what?"

"Tell him you'd been here for three years? You could have lied for me, you know."

I laugh - it's a dry, humourless noise, unusual for me. Laughter is a waste of energy.

"Kid, I did lie for you."

"Y-you did? Then how long have you been here?"

I shoot him a wry smile.

"Hmm, let's see. About eight years? Ever since I left Homestead."

He gapes. I clap him on the back as I pass and he immediately follows, his eyes still wide.

"How old are you?"

"Nineteen," I mutter, "When I was a kid, they put you to work at ten or eleven. It's different now. I think you have to be thirteen, right?"

He shakes his head.

"Ten or eleven is ridiculous. Starting work that young stunts growth."

I consider this for a moment.

"Yeah, I can see that. You newbies are all so tall!"

We join the crowd as it lumbers through the Mill. All around are stations set up for different types of work; miles and miles of crop fields, huge facilities with animals kept for food and milk and leather. In the distance I can see the shadow of the Power Plant, where we generate electricity. Further, the Factories. Beyond our vision, under a seemingly ordinary hill, sits the Mine - but I hate to think about the prison built within the tunnels. The memory alone makes me shudder.

"I know you're having a tough time of it," I tell Kane, "but don't worry. One more week and we shift over to the fields."

"What's that like?"

I shrug.

"The work itself isn't that different, but it's shorter hours because there's less light. It's practically a holiday."

He hesitates, and I can tell he has more to say. There's a redness in his cheeks, a rebelliousness in his eyes that's both familiar and unnerving. I throw out an arm and stop him in his tracks.

"You're angry."

He clenches his fist.

"Of course I'm angry! This isn't what I thought it'd be like at The Mill."

"You thought it'd be like Homestead? Spending time with Mummy? Learning farming theory? If you feel disillusioned, that's your own damn fault. Just get on with it."

He pouts - the expression is so adorable and ridiculous that I bite back a chuckle.

"I should have had a choice," he grumbles. I pat his back, but my attempt at comfort comes off far more patronising than intended.

"It's all about balance, kid. If you're selfish about it then sure, the Mill is pretty bad. How about looking outside your own wants for a change? Look."

I reach out and point, towards the fields and far, far past them. Past the Docks, over the sea, far beyond anything we can see, feel or imagine.

"The people in Thorne depend on us. Without us, they'd have nothing. If we all acted selfishly, the world would be in anarchy. Do you really think that having your own way is worth risking all those lives?"

Kane stares at my outstretched hand. His face is a picture of conflict. I get it; there's a strange disconnect between the Mill and the City of Thorne. I know that as well as anyone. But we still have a responsibility to help them. He puffs out his cheeks.

"But I don't want to be here."

I shrug.

"Then try not to think about it. This is the way the world is. You need to stop questioning everything. Bad things happen when you start asking questions."

Hurt briefly crosses his face, but I don't care. I turn and walk away. That may have sounded like a threat, but it wasn't. It was a warning, a lesson. I had to learn the hard way; and I wouldn't wish that on anyone.

CHAPTER TWO

Evening is when we're supposed to gather in one of the larger shelters for food, but I'm exhausted. I know I'll suffer tomorrow if I skip dinner tonight, but I need a few minutes to lie down. I head straight to the living area and wheel open the door to one of the large, metal bunkers.

Beds line the room. Most are small, black camp beds with shredded blankets, but some people have to sleep in hammocks. One or two sleep on the floor. There's a single bulb hanging down in the middle of the room, casting a pale yellow light. The Mill has stringent rules on energy use, and it's not considered worthwhile to waste electricity on the workers. I grab a bottle of water and gulp it down. We collect the stuff whenever it rains so it tastes stale and warm, but it does the job.

My bunk is in the furthest, darkest corner of the bunker. I sidle over and peel off my dirty clothes until I'm in just a tank and shorts. The clothes I toss aside are all standard issue stuff – grey vest, jeans, hooded jacket, heavy leather work boots. I reach up to wipe the dried sweat from my face. My fingers come away dirty. Somehow, I always end up coated in muck, even when I'm not in the fields. I idly attempt to pick it out from under my bitten nails, but quickly give up. Who cares.

After an hour or so, people start to trickle in. The bunker is all girls; we're never supposed to be alone with a member of the opposite sex, though there are those who give in to their more primal urges. Their exhaustion seems to radiate across the room. Within minutes all I can smell is sweat and muck and terrible, terrible breath – but at this point I'm so used to it that it barely registers.

"What are you doing here?"

I look up to see Nel standing in front of me. She's got her hands on her hips and her lips are pursed. I smile; it's good to see a somewhat friendly face after a long day's work.

"Hey, Nel."

"Don't 'hey Nel' me. Where were you at dinner?"

I point at my legs.

"They didn't want to move. I just needed a break."

She sighs and rubs a hand over her head. Like many workers, Nel keeps her hair buzzed close to her head - but it's started to grow back recently. Patches of carrot-coloured hair are showing through, matching her orange brows. Beneath them are clear brown eyes and a long, sloping nose dotted with freckles. She narrows her eyes at me.

"What are you staring at?"

"Nothing. Just thinking."

"That's dangerous."

She slumps down next to me and pulls her knees up to her chin.

"I am so fed up of working in cow waste. I wish I could chop wood already."

I chuckle. Nel's always a cycle behind me, so we've never had a full day together. I suppose it's for the best.

You think differently of someone when you see them struggle.

"I will gladly switch with you," I tease, "look at my hands!"

I stretch out my fingers and notice that one of my knuckles is cracked and bleeding. I watch the blood pool around the crease for a moment before sucking it clean.

When I lower my hand, Nel's staring at me in disgust.

"That was revolting. I just want you to know that."

"You seem surprised."

We sit like that for the next few hours. Some of the others try and stay up too, occasionally dropping a bit of information about their day, but eventually they, too, succumb to the day's exhaustion. Eventually it's just the two of us tucked away in the corner of the bunker, barely able to see by the light of a single bulb.

"I spoke with someone today," I say softly, "A kid called Kane. He was on chopping duty too."

Nel lifts an eyebrow.

"You spoke to a newbie? Since when are you so friendly?"

"I wasn't, really. He was threatening to play up so I gave him some advice."

We lie down now, each curled up in our bunks. We're facing one another, but I'm having trouble seeing Nel's face in the darkness.

"Play up?" she asks, "What do you mean?"

"I don't know, exactly. He was just... angry, I guess, and I reckoned he was going to snap any time. I didn't want to be around for that."

She doesn't respond, but I see her eyebrows furrow. I know. It's hard when someone snaps. It's not very often it happens - most of us quickly learn that it's easier to just get on with things - but it's not unheard of. It's usually someone who's just come from Homestead. They haven't had to work a day in their lives, and the prospect of physical labour scares them. They lash out, they try to convince others to think like they do. They attack the Guards or try to run, but they eventually get dragged away. Taken to the coal mines, where they're allowed to let out as much of their anger as they like on the rock. If they're especially resistant, the Guards will slip a needle into the back of their neck in something they like to call a 'fresh start'. Nobody's ever the same after that.

"Y-you shouldn't be getting involved," she says, and her voice sounds strange.

"What are you talking about? It's better that we try and stop them..."

"That doesn't matter. It's none of your business, Noah. Some people have issues they need to work through, so just let them. Whatever happens... it's up to them to decide. It's one of the few things we can actually control."

Her voice sounds choked, filled with uncertainty. I reach out a hand, but she simply rolls away from me.

"Hey. Nel."

She ignores me. I don't know what I could have done to annoy her.

"Nel. Talk to me."

"Sorry, Noah. I don't mean anything by it. I'm just... really tired. Tomorrow we need to separate the calves from the cows and I'm already dreading it."

I hesitate – there's clearly more going on – but she's right. It is getting late. I look toward the door, but there's no light coming through the crack underneath. Not even the floodlights are on tonight. Discomfort stirs in my gut, but there's not much I can do about it. Just like I told Kane earlier. Don't think too deeply.

I roll over so I'm staring at the corrugated metal of the bunker and close my eyes. Sleep should come easily to me – it does to everyone else. The aches and pains in my body and the heaviness in my eyes should help me drift right off. But instead I lie motionless for what seems like hours, staring at the inside of my eyelids and waiting for sleep to come.

Eventually, it does.

It seems like mere minutes before the door to the bunker flies open, the metal bouncing back with a crash. We wake instantly - you'd think I'd be used to it after so many years, but no. I still startle awake every morning.

A Guard stands in the doorway, but he doesn't stick around to wake any stragglers. He keeps walking, and after a few moments I hear the door of the next bunker over being thrown open, too.

I sit up and yawn, stretching my arms over my head to feel the familiar, and slightly painful, cracking in my limbs. Nel sits up too, rubbing her head all over and letting out a tired growl.

"Ugh, I hate when they do that. You'd think a bell or something would be easier, but no. That would make too much sense."

I hesitate at the joke, but her eyes are wide and demanding, so I let out a laugh. I don't really get why it's funny, but it seems to be the affirmation she was looking for. She gives a satisfied nod and climbs to her feet.

We dress in silence, and most of the girls file out. The two of us hang back a little and I sit on the bunk, trying to tie my shoelaces into something resembling a knot. My hands still throb a little and the task is fiddly. Nel sits nearby, mimicking me. She doesn't need to tie her boots. She's just taking the chance to hang back and have an extra minute with a friend.

Suddenly, the door opens and Wirrow strides in. He's got that expression on his face again; like there's something delicious in the room and he wants it. I busy myself with my laces.

Wirrow's greedy little eyes slide across the room, finally settling on a figure in the corner. It's still somewhat dark in here, but I recognise the tight black curls and olive skin. I think her name is Sayla, though I could be wrong. She stands as he enters.

"Are you the one?" he asks. I watch her closely. I haven't seen or spoken to Sayla in a long time, and she looks somehow different. Her body looks rounder, her face fuller. It's a change so minor that most people probably couldn't tell, but I've known her for years.

She nods.

"And has it been checked?"

Another nod.

"And they're sure?"

She smiles, then places a gentle hand on her stomach. It's bigger than before, more rounded. She caresses it softly and my gut twists.

"Alright then," says Wirrow, "come with me. We'll go to Homestead."

She follows immediately, and I can sense excitement radiating from her. There's a bounce in her step, a light in her eyes as she's led away. Wirrow glances my way for a moment before walking out. The door swings a little, lighting up the room.

We sit in silence, stunned by what just happened. Nel lowers her head sadly, and I suppose I can understand why. It's not every day someone leaves us. But my own reaction is much less kind.

"Ugh, Breeders," I snort, "it's so lazy. Taking the easy way out."

Nel raises her head.

"Really? You don't think it's just a normal part of life?"

"No way. The rest of us have no choice but to work until we drop. We have to accept that. Choosing to become a Breeder means you leave everyone else behind. Like you're better than them."

She bites her lip.

"I'm not so sure. Hearing some of them talk, I think sometimes it's just an accident."

"No way! The Guards have always kept men and women apart. You have to make a special effort if you want to end up pregnant. It doesn't just happen! It's just... ugh. Selfish."

I stand and reach for my jacket. It's always good to keep one nearby, even when it's hot. You never know when it's going to start raining, and this has been a particularly wet summer.

"Have you never considered it?"

Nel's voice is so small, so hushed that for a moment I wonder if I actually heard it.

"Considered what?"

"Having a kid," she mutters, "just to get out of here."

My chest tightens.

"No. Have you?"

She rubs idly at her scalp.

"Yes. No. I don't know. Sometimes I wonder if it's the only choice I have."

I don't reply. There's nothing to say. So I just sit down and wrap an arm around her shoulder. The closeness is uncomfortable and strange, but it's Nel. She's harmless.

"You think I'm crazy, don't you?" she chuckles. I shake my head. I do - but I'm not about to tell her that.

"Of course not. People always go through a phase when they think about other things."

"Did you?"

I consider this.

"Well, yes and no. I went through a phase, about four years back, where I just wanted to break out of routine. Didn't want to snap or anything, but I needed some kind of change. I was going mad."

"What did you do?"

I heave a pained sigh.

"Well, I uh... I signed up for six months in the Mines."

She gapes, and suddenly I think maybe I'm the crazy one.

"What? Why would you do that?"

I shrug.

"It was something I hadn't done before. Something new, but not permanent. I didn't want to do something stupid and throw it all away, but I needed to see what could be different if I did."

"And what happened?"

I shake my head. I don't like to talk about the mines. I know the whole experience was self-inflicted, so I can't expect much sympathy, but the memory of tiny caverns and the pitch black still set my heart racing.

"The work itself was fine, if not a bit boring. The people were a bit off, though in all fairness, I guess I should have expected that. They were always whispering, always sneaking around. But I could have lived with that. At least it was a change of pace. The worst thing was the pain."

I reach up and rub at the back of my neck. It aches just remembering.

"You spend all day crouching in the dark. You get plastered in dirt, head to toe. It's in your eyes, in your throat. And even if you're used to chopping wood, mining is a whole new world."

My hand finds its way to my shoulder and I remember the way the muscles there had burned after every movement, the heat burrowing into my flesh. Like I was being ripped in half.

"By the end of it, I was actually so messed up they took me off-work for a few days. But that's just the physical reminder."

Nel's hand finds mine, but I move it away and grin.

"Hey, it's fine. I'm back, aren't I?"

"So that was enough for you?"

"Of course it was. What you know might not be perfect, but there are worse things than the farm. It's not worth killing yourself just to try something new."

She nods, and although it's not what she wants to hear, she seems to accept it. I'm not an idiot - if I warn her, she'll listen to me. She's just lucky I'm not telling her about the true horrors of the mines. The endless darkness, the claustrophobia. Even now, I feel a little unnerved to be alone in the dark.

"You're right," she says, "What was I thinking?"

"Hey, don't worry about it. Now come on, the Farm awaits."

There's a gentle rain today. It breaks over the field and fills it with a cool, light mist. While it's refreshing and rather pleasant, it makes the handle of the axe slippery. I reach for my jacket, using the sleeve to dab it dry.

"Nice thinking. Mind if I borrow that?"

I toss it over to Kane. He's smiling today. The slouch in his back has gone, and he's standing taller than ever. There's even colour in his cheeks.

"Thanks."

I swing the axe overhead and chop the wood cleanly, then take a moment to look around. Wirrow and the other Guards are nowhere near us, giving us some freedom to talk.

"You seem happier today," I say, "did something good happen?"

"Not really. It's just a good day. You know?"

I gaze up at the cloudy sky and grimace.

"If you say so."

He just chuckles and swings the axe even higher. A smile plays on my lips.

"I'm glad to see you like this," I say softly. He knocks the chopped wood off the block and turns to me, eyebrows raised.

"Like what?"

"I don't know – less angry, I guess. Doesn't it feel good to have accepted things?"

His lips tighten.

"I suppose so."

"It's so much easier when you're not trying to fight everything."

He hesitates, and for a long moment I think he's going to disagree with me. But then he leans down to put a new log on the block.

"You know what, you're right. It is easier. No point fighting it."

My chest aches. I'm so happy. If nothing else, at least I managed to stop him kicking off. He may not know it, but I've just saved him from a lifetime of torture in the mines.

We work in silence for the rest of the day. When the floodlights finally burst into life and the whistle blows, we throw down our axes with a strong sense of relief.

I glance across at Kane. He's rubbing his shoulder, wincing from the pain.

"You alright?"

He pulls a face.

"I hurt... everywhere."

I slap him playfully on the back.

"You'll get used to it. Come on, it's time for dinner."

"Isn't it too early?" he asks, waving a hand at the sky. It's not as dark as it was yesterday, and there's a good reason for that.

"It's our turn to cook dinner for the masses," I tell him, "we go in an hour early so that the food's ready for everyone else."

He seems to brighten up at that, and as he walks alongside me, there's an added bounce in his step.

"I am absolutely starving."

"Don't get your hopes up. We get whatever's left after everyone else has eaten."

His face falls.

"Ugh. Great. Cold potatoes and sludge."

I laugh. It's a deep, throaty sound that echoes across the paddock. A couple of workers pause and turn around, but their blank stares just serve to amuse me.

"Looks like I'm not the only one in a good mood," Kane teases.

"Don't you try and pick a fight with me, Kid. I've got five years and fifty pounds on you."

It's true. He's much taller than I am, but as I shift muscles flex on my arms, legs and shoulders. His shoulders, though, are tiny, hunched and pale. His arms are so thin I could probably snap them if I wanted to.

"Yeah," he mutters, "when do I get my abs?"

"Your what?"

He points at one of the other men in the group. I don't know his name, but I've seen him around. He's usually shirtless, and rather arrogant about his bulging, rippling muscles. He stretches one arm overhead and a nearby girl coos.

"You want to look like that?" I ask, incredulous, "the guy looks like a thumb."

"Who cares? That's what girls like."

I snort so loud that people stare.

"Kid, no. It's not. And you shouldn't be worried about what girls like, anyway. You've got more important things to worry about than girls and romance."

The kitchens are always a fresh kind of hell. Hot, claustrophobic, and always inexplicably filled with steam. I wipe the sweat from my brow and slam the oven door shut with a clang. The others mill around me, chopping vegetables, boiling potatoes. A girl with blonde pigtails shouts over.

"Noah, how's the stew coming along?"

I frown. I've always felt it's a stretch to call it stew. Gruel would be more appropriate. We're only allowed to use the waste parts of the animal, so all the hooves and ears and bits of inedible gristle go into our evening meals. The result is a grey-pink sludge that retains its heat for all of thirty seconds and can't be touched more than a few minutes later.

"It's as good as it's ever been. So.. terrible," I reply. She tosses her head back and laughs.

I take advantage of the brief reprieve and lean back against one of the industry-grade fridges. My eyes glide across the room, and somehow my gaze falls upon a pot. It's metallic, considerably battered and only slightly rusty. It sits on the stove, the water inside just starting to boil.

I take a step forward, glancing around to make sure nobody else can see me, and lean down.

My own face stares back at me from the shiny surface.

My skin is burnt brown from the sun and covered in freckles. There's a smear of something black across one of my cheeks. I wipe it away and push a lock of hair from my eyes. It's dirty blonde and hangs around my shoulders. Most people either tie it up or buzz it, but neither way has ever appealed to me.

We don't get to see ourselves very often. There's no rule against it; we just have no reason to keep mirrors around. My scarred fingers find their way to my brow, sweeping over the dark circles on my cheeks. My eyes are blue, and I suppose they'd be pretty on a different face, but on mine they look dusty and grey.

"Noah?"

I whip around – blond pigtails girl stands behind me, one eyebrow raised.

"What are you doing?"

I instinctively shrink back. I might be bigger than her, but I'm not the best at confrontation.

"N-nothing. Sorry."

She sighs.

"Whatever. Look, go out and get serving."

I obey immediately, grabbing a tray of sludge and carrying it out into the mess hall.

It's only in the mess hall that I ever really consider how many Mill workers there are. Thousands of figures fill the room, forcing the inedible mush down their throats. In one corner I can see the old guys; the ones who have been here for decades. Their hands shake as they spoon the food into their mouths, but they smile as they do so. I wince at the dark brown spots on their skin, and the creases at the corners of their eyes and mouths. Not everyone grows to be that kind of age here. There are plenty of occupational hazards so generally people don't live to become fragile.

The newbies sit nearby, perhaps soaking up some comfort from the old guys. They all look the same, pale and thin and quaking. Some rub at their shoulders or hands, grimacing at the fresh cuts and bruises. I stand with the hot tray in my hands, unable to feel through the thick scar tissue on my fingertips, and smirk.

They'll get used to it soon enough.

One of the older men approaches me, holding out a dirty plate. I grab a ladle and dish some more out for him. Technically we're not supposed to give out seconds, but there's an unwritten rule that it's okay to do it for the old guys. He winks as he takes the plate and I feel a small rush of respect.

He wanders back to the table with the others and I watch for a moment, the feeling building in my chest. Something about the old guys has always motivated me. A small part of me wants to be them someday, softer and more weathered but solid as a rock. Someone the others look to with respect, and maybe even a small amount of admiration.

I'm so lost in my thoughts that I don't bother to look at the next person who approaches. I take their plate and scoop a spoonful of slop onto it.

"Yuck! So, what? I get all the gross bits and none of the veggies?"

I glance up. Nel is frowning at me.

"Sorry about that."

She leans over the counter.

"What are you staring at?"

Blood rushes to my face. Great. Was I just standing here and gaping like a moron?

"Nothing."

Her eyes narrow.

"Oh no. I know you better than that. Ooh, it's a boy, isn't it?"

My face falls and I heave a sigh. This again. Nel has convinced herself that I'm like some of the younger, tittering girls around here, only able to see the opposite sex and nothing else. But I've never felt even the slightest twinge of attraction. Not to men, women, nothing. I briefly wonder if that's even something my brain knows how to do.

"Of course it's not a boy. You know that."

"I don't know everything about you, Noah. Somewhere under that hard shell, who knows, there might be an actual teenage girl!"

I let out a playful growl and she chortles.

"Okay, okay. Fine. Don't tell me. I'll figure it out for myself."

Tonight, we don't bother staying up to talk. My eyes are heavy and I collapse onto the camp bed the moment I reach it. Nel lies down too, stretching her arms overhead.

"Night."

"Oh, I almost forgot," I mutter, rubbing at my eye, "You had to split the cows and the calves today, right? How did that go?"

Nel seems to hesitate.

"I don't want to talk about work."

I roll onto my stomach.

"What are you talking about? It's literally the only thing we can talk about."

She remains silent, her eyes fixed on the ceiling. I follow her gaze. There's a hole in the roof where the metal has rusted through, revealing the tiniest sliver of the night sky. It's an absolute nightmare in the winter – but she's always enjoyed the sight. I don't mind it myself.

But tonight she stares up and out of the little gap, her eyes filled with an emotion I can't quite place. It resembles sadness, but it's somehow different. Her eyes glisten, and I find myself wondering if they're wet with unshed tears.

"Nel. Nel, I'm sorry."

She rubs her face, and when she speaks, her voice wavers.

"It's nothing. Sorry."

We lie quietly for a minute, and I'm not sure if I should try to comfort her or not. Nel's always had this thing about family. About splitting up. I guess, now I come to think about it, she usually projects it onto the animals.

I bite the inside of my mouth so hard it hurts. I want to tell her not to get so emotional about it. That none of us have parents and you don't see anyone else complaining. But that's just it. I never complain. I've never taken time to consider what it would be like to have a family - nor what it would be like to be ripped away from them. I can't imagine what it would be like to love someone else that much.

My chest pangs with guilt. That's not entirely true. I don't know what I'd class Nel as; a friend, a fellow worker, a neighbour. But there's something there, in that I'd feel sad if she was gone or if I could never see her again.

But family? That's a whole other ballpark.

We all have parents. It's a biological fact. But that's where the ideal of 'family' stops. Once we leave Homestead, our parents forget about us. They move on to the next child, dedicating the next twelve or thirteen years solely to them. We're sent to the Mill and put to work. Slowly but surely, we all forget them. Forget their faces, their names. The fact that they even existed.

I don't remember anything before coming to the Mill - and that's the norm around here. If we don't forget things straight away, the Guards have a cocktail of injections they can use to wipe the last few days, weeks or months. It's not a pleasant experience. In fact, it's mostly used as a punishment. That feared 'fresh start' they always talk about.

"Nel?"

My voice is soft, but it echoes across the now quiet room. For a moment she's silent and I wonder if she's asleep, but then she turns her head.

"Yeah?"

I reach an arm across the alleyway between our camp beds. It takes a moment, but then she reaches out her own. We grasp hands in the darkness. We lie like that for a while, eyes closed, room silent around us. When she finally lets go and rolls away, her expression seems to have brightened. My hand hangs off the edge of the bed, and I don't bother to lift it back up. Instead, I just bury my face in the pillow and wait for sleep to come.

The next few weeks fly by. We shift from the wood blocks to the fields, which is easier work. It involves a lot of carrying, and pulling massive, heavily-laden carts around the Mill. My legs ache afterwards, but it's a pleasant change from the constant pain in my shoulders.

Each day seems to be a tiny improvement on the last. Kane seems brighter every time I see him, and it's not long before he starts joining me and Nel for dinner. She seems to like him well enough. She laughs at his pointless jokes and teases him about his height and naiveté. He takes it all in good humour, and surprisingly there are a few occasions where I catch myself chuckling along with them.

But Kane's behaviour still isn't normal. Initially I dismiss it; he must be missing his parents. But since he never seems to mention them, I eventually stop guessing. He flickers from relative happiness to boundless excitement that threatens to boil over. He bounces on his heels a lot, and when he smiles he bares his teeth like a worked-up animal. Granted I never knew him before, but I get the distinct feeling that this isn't how he normally is.

Still, each time I catch sight of something odd, I ignore it. Whatever's going on with him, it's none of my business. Maybe he's caught the eye of some girl. Maybe he's discovered a newfound passion for serving warm gruel. Perhaps he's just grown accustomed to the sense of satisfaction that comes with a hard day's work. I simply don't know.

CHAPTER THREE

I wake up drenched to the bone. It's rained in the night - and not just a late summer shower. It's the type of heavy, torrential rain that hammers on the rooftops and bounces off the floor. It must have been falling sideways last night, because it hasn't just fallen on Nel. I lift my thin pillow and squeeze it, grimacing as rainwater streams out.

The other girls sit up too, their beds and blankets sodden and stinking. A few complain loudly, but most just heave a sigh and start shaking out their belongings. It happens often enough that we're used to it - though apparently, not often enough for the Guards to do anything about it. As we hang our bedding up to dry, I know it'll probably be fine by the time we return tonight. If it's anything like last time, the whole bunker will smell like mildew for a few days, but that's all.

Nel pouts and throws her blanket to the floor. Her bed always gets soaked the most, so I toss a spare blanket her way.

"Did you manage to get any sleep at all?" I ask. She rubs the blanket over her face.

"Of course I did. At this point I could sleep in a thunderstorm."

I smile.

"Well, at least we're clean. No ice shower this week."

She licks her thumb and rubs at my cheek. I cringe a little, but she just shoots me a motherly look.

"What? You had dirt on you."

I wipe the spot with the back of my hand.

"I always have dirt on me. I live on a farm."

She pokes her tongue out at me.

I turn away and start tugging my clothes on. The usual - jeans, grey vest, and my grey hooded jacket. I pull it on, half wishing it had longer sleeves. The ones I have barely reach my elbows and flap around as I move, letting the cold air in. I shudder, but none of my other clothes are dry enough to wear.

For a brief moment, I attempt to create some kind of order in my hair. You'd think it would be easy enough to maintain, but it seems to never lie flat. I rake my finger through it like I'm tying it back, but it's too short. Come to think of it, I don't think I ever cut it to this length. It just doesn't grow. I settle for pushing it behind my ears.

I glance back; Nel is still trying desperately to dry off some clothes before heading out.

"Need help?"

She shakes her head.

"Nah, I'm fine. I'll only be a minute. You go ahead."

The rain has stopped by the time we reach the crop field. That's a small relief, but it's been raining for hours and the ground has turned into mud under our feet. One girl takes a particularly large step, sinks into the muck and loses her boot – much to the entertainment of the people around her.

"Here."

I turn to see Kane reaching up to his shoulder in the hole, pulling out the girl's shoe. It's caked in mud but she pulls it back on regardless. She blushes a little as she meets his eyes.

"Oh. Thank you."

He gives her a thumbs up, spots me and jogs over.

"Morning."

"That was pretty nice of you," I tease, "You like her or something?"

"Never seen her before. Don't even know her name."

"Then why did you do that?"

He shrugs.

"Someone needed to."

He turns his head, clearly looking out for something. I don't ask what. It's none of my business. But as we take our places in the field, he keeps catching my eye. His body shudders with something akin to excitement and I start to feel uneasy. He's been so doing so well lately. I don't want that to change.

A few hours later, Wirrow calls for volunteers to take some loaded carts back to the storage unit. Instantly Kane's hand goes up, and a second later I feel him grab my hand and lift it, too.

"We'll do it!"

I wrench my hand from his grip and glare.

"What was that for?"

"Trust me."

I stare the cart down. I really don't want to do this. But there's no point in fighting it, so I put myself in front of the cart, where the horse used to go back when we had horses, and lift. It's surprisingly heavy and takes a couple of adjustments to steady my grip. Kane stands at his own cart, a smug look on his face.

"Take them back to storage," says Wirrow, "then get back here. If you don't come back soon, I'll send a Hoverbot after you."

I nod; I've done this job before. Even if I hadn't, the thought of those strange, drone-like contraptions following us is enough to make me uneasy. I sneak a sideways glance at Kane. He stands calm, the weight held firmly in his grip as he waits for me to move.

Like he has a plan.

It's at least a twenty minute walk back to the Mill from here. Not too bad until you consider the strain on our backs. I stare at the back of Kane's head as we walk, my eyes narrowing. What does he want? What could possibly happen on the half-mile of empty road? And what, out of all that, could he possibly need me for?

An idea presents itself and I push it aside. He might be a kid, but he's not stupid. It wouldn't be something ridiculous like a love confession. He knows better than that and besides, he's just a child.

But then he stops dead, and I promptly collide with the back of his cart.

"H-hey!" I snap, rubbing at my nose. He waits for a moment, surveying the area with caution, then lowers the cart. He's walking toward me now, a strange expression on his face.

"What are you..."

But it's too late. He's already here. He's too close for comfort – so close that our noses almost touch and I can smell his breath.

"I need to give you some advice."

I shuffle back in a desperate attempt to generate some space between us.

"Is that advice anything remotely to do with 'personal space'?"

He shakes his head, his expression deadly serious.

"Noah. Do what I do."

My heart hammers in my chest. I shake off the feeling of growing dread and try to seem nonchalant.

"Why? What are you going to do?"

"I can't tell you."

I raise an eyebrow.

"So I have to do what you do, without knowing what you're going to do or why? Gotcha."

He shuffles uncomfortably at that, and I can tell he doesn't want to tell me. There's no point, anyway. I'm not going to do anything except my damn job.

"Just... you'll know it when I do it. Please. This is important. Do what I do."

I stare him down.

"No."

"Why not?"

I sigh heavily.

"The fact you're doing this on an empty road means that you don't want anyone else to know. That you're not telling me means that you don't even trust me to know. That tells me you're about to do something stupid. I'm not about to do something stupid, kid. Especially without knowing what it is."

He stamps his foot, sending up a small cloud of dust from the now-dry road.

"I'm serious. I need you on my side."

"Well, I'm not. And if you have any sense of self-preservation whatsoever, you'll rethink this little plan of yours."

Suddenly, I don't want to speak to him anymore. He's just dropped in my estimations. I'd thought he was growing up, learning. But he's still just a reckless, hormone-fuelled teenager.

I push past him and keep walking.

We don't speak a word as we unload the carts. I dare to glance at him just once; but he stares ahead, biting his lip. He's not even paying attention to the movement of his own hands. A part of me wants to reach out to him. To reassure him that what I'm doing, I'm doing out of friendship. But I can't. Anger stirs in my chest. I can't bring myself to show such kindness to someone who's prepared to do something blatantly stupid.

I don't say anything else once we've returned to the field, and I keep my head low as I grab a shovel and start to dig in my part of the new seeding line. He digs silently beside me. I can feel his eyes on me while we work and every so often his lips part a little, as though he's desperate to speak to me. I ignore him.

I can't really explain why I'm so mad. Nel would say it's because I care, but something about that doesn't sit right. I don't especially care about the kid. Besides, I don't even know what his moronic plan is yet. I expect it'll involve trying to steal something he wants, or perhaps creeping about at night. Maybe it'll involve a daring 'escape' plan - all of which will end with him doing double shifts, time in the Mines, or God forbid, on the receiving end of a nasty memory injection.

"Oi."

Wirrow walks over, his stern gaze fixed on Kane. The kid's just standing there, shovel dumped on the ground, a moody expression on his face. I resist the urge to roll my eyes. He's sulking, all because I didn't entertain his little idea.

Wirrow takes a step forward, fingering the shock baton in his belt.

"I remember you. Little weakling, right? Been here how long - two months?"

Kane doesn't reply. He just stares hard into the distance, like he's trying to focus on some minor detail on the horizon. Wirrow steps even closer.

"Brat. I'm talking to you."

Still no reply - but I suddenly notice Kane's hands clenching and then unfurling. The motion is slow and steady, like he's building up to something. My heart sinks.

"You trying to be smart?" demands Wirrow, his fury skyrocketing, "or are you playing dumb? Get back to work!"

Kane turns his head, and his eyes find me. He doesn't move. His expression barely changes, but his eyes seem to plead with me. I know without words what he's asking.

Join me.

Suddenly his fist balls up and – before I have time to react – he throws his whole weight into a punch aimed squarely at Wirrow's jaw.

I jump back, more from surprise than fear. The punch itself is unspectacular, the obvious result of a scrawny teen hitting a guy who's easily twice his size. He swings again, but this time his knuckles graze air as Wirrow easily steps aside. With one swift movement, the Guard throws his body weight through his elbow and into Kane's ribcage. It floors him in a second and he rolls in the mud, the wind knocked out of him entirely.

The whole conflict lasts about ten seconds.

There's a brief moment where we all stand motionless. Wirrow glares down at Kane on the ground. I stare blankly at the both of them. Everyone else is frozen, clearly horrified. Kane rolls onto his stomach and stares at me, wide-eyed.

Pleading.

CHAPTER FOUR

My gut clenches, and I consider what would happen if I helped him now. My eyes trace the lines of Wirrow's body. If I throw myself at him just right, I can probably pin him for a good ten seconds. I'd likely get a few shots in at his ribs or maybe even wind him. But the final result would be the same. I'd be pinned by him or one of the other Guards nearby, and we'd both be thrown into the mines for life - standard punishment for such blatant insubordination. The memory flashes by of dark tunnels and pain all over and for a moment I can't breathe.

I stare Kane down for a moment, then take a pointed step back. I can see the sense of betrayal in his eyes. It almost physically hurts, but I know I've made the right choice.

Then the moment is gone. Kane is dragged to his feet and held by two Guards. He fights furiously against them, kicking, biting, scratching. Doesn't he know it's useless? The other workers start to shift away, unnerved by what they've seen. Wirrow pulls himself up to full height and marches over, grabbing Kane's face in his hand.

"I should have known you'd be one to snap. Ever since that first day, you've been too weak."

He spits the last word, and both Kane and I wince.

"What do you have to say for yourself?"

Wirrow squeezes his fingers, pinching Kane's chin hard enough to make his eyes water. But Kane doesn't respond with words – instead, he wriggles his lips and spits hard into the older man's eye.

The response is immediate. The Guards throw him to the ground and he curls into himself, desperate to block some of their blows. Wirrow wipes the spit from his eye and scowls.

Panic flits through me. I stare at the kid sprawled on the ground. I wish I could find the strength to form words. What was he thinking?

They haul him to his feet and Wirrow takes a shot at his nose. There's an audible crunch as the bone breaks. I cringe; it looks like he might pass out, and I can feel my hands shaking. A part of me wants to run forward and prise them off him. I want to tell them to stop, to explain everything and scold him and try to reason with them. But I'm rooted to the ground by fear, my blood running ice cold.

"To the Mines."

Wirrow leans towards him now, so close that I can no longer hear Kane's shallow breathing.

"Say goodbye to the sun, kid."

Kane's face is an image of neutrality. There's no anger in his eyes, no grief. No regret for what he just did. He stares blankly ahead, totally oblivious to Wirrow's taunts. They pull at his shoulders but he strains towards me. I step back, unsure of what he might do. Hatred is coming from him in waves.

"Noah," he tells me, "you are going to regret this. Believe me. One day, you'll wish you joined me."

I stare at him. His youthful face is now covered in cuts and bruises, his body beaten and broken. The Guards drag him away in the direction of the mines, and we maintain eye contact until he's gone from my sight.

Then, silence.

My stomach swirls. Why would he do that? I thought I had finally got through to him. A large hand reaches around my shoulder. I gaze up into Wirrow's beady eyes. They're narrowing at me, suspicion playing on his face.

But then he smiles.

"Well now. Noah, was it? I'm sorry you had to see that."

I nod.

"But it's what has to be done," he continues, "You know that."

Another nod.

"We can't allow dissention here."

"No, Sir."

"But it seems to me like he was up to something. And not just that - seems to me he believed that you were part of it. Any idea why he would think that?"

I can feel my body shaking all over.

"No."

He leans down close to me, until I can feel his breath on my face. He stinks of sweat and booze and especially strong cigarettes.

"Are you sure? He didn't tell you anything?"

My lower lip trembles. Why bother lying? He's already been punished.

"He told me... he told me to join. But he didn't say what with, what he was going to do, or why. I swear I had no idea."

He hesitates, but then he seems to decide I'm telling the truth.

"Alright. If you're sure, then you wouldn't mind if I carry out a small precaution, would you?"

I close my eyes and try to think of the mines as a pleasant memory. It doesn't work.

"No, Sir. Go right ahead."

He pushes me through the office door and I stumble, catching myself on the wooden doorframe. I look around. I've seen the tiny building out by the fence before, but haven't ever given any thought to what it was like inside. It's cramped and dirty-looking, but warmer than I would have thought. Desks and bulletin boards line the walls, and the far corner is crammed with large blocks of computer-like contraptions. I can't even imagine what most of it does.

"Rian," says Wirrow, "got a guest here for you."

Suddenly, I notice another Guard on a nearby chair. He's wearing the familiar black uniform, but he seems somehow different from the others. He's younger, smaller. He has a pointed face and dark hair, and as I watch he puts on a pair of round spectacles and looks me up and down.

"Oh, great, another one. What did this one kick off about? A broken nail?"

I cringe. From the way he's talking, I feel about three inches tall.

"Actually, she's not done anything. Yet. But one of the newbies just had a tantrum in the fields, and she seemed to be in on it."

Rian grimaces.

"So, a stint in the Mines, you think?"

My reaction is instant. My heart pounds in my chest and my eyes fill with tears. I can't imagine anything worse. Wipe my memory for all I care – just don't throw me into the Mines.

"Nah. I need you to give her a job that keeps her out of the way for a few weeks. Something menial and far away from her usual workmates."

I heave an audible sigh of relief. Rian raises an eyebrow, but he doesn't say anything. He watches me with a strange curiosity. Perhaps it's because I've never been

37

brought in here before. He can tell I'm no newbie – which probably makes me look even more suspicious.

"Sure, I'll find something for her. But maybe you should go and see to yourself, Wirrow. Your left side looks a bit red."

I glance over. He's right. It's only very slight, but I can see where Kane hit him. The area is pink and slightly swollen, and there's a tiny graze where his fist connected. A small rush of something akin to pride rushes through me, but it's quickly replaced by worry.

What are they going to make me do? If not the Mine, then maybe the Power Plant? Shovelling their hard-earned coal into a furnace is physically exhausting. From what I hear, it often involves overnight stays to make sure the fires stay red-hot. Perhaps they'll have me carrying stuff, loading up the massive trucks that come to collect supplies for Thorne, or working at the Dock filling up the cargo ships. That last one doesn't sound so bad, actually. I've never been beyond the chain-link fence; the ocean might be a nice change of pace.

Rian sits down, takes off his glasses, and starts to clean them on his uniform. He seems unusually calm for someone who's now alone with a supposed troublemaker. I stand uneasily, shifting my weight from one foot to the other and tugging at the bottom of my jacket.

"Ah, sorry."

He waves a hand at the empty seat. For a moment I'm unsure of the command, but then he waves again and I sit. I've never sat in something like this before. It's part metal, part cloth, and it seems to rotate under my weight. There are bits holding up my back and even things to the sides, which I assume are for tying peoples' wrists to. I opt to keep my hands folded in my lap.

"So," he says, "what happened out there?"

I bite my lip.

"I-I'm not exactly sure. One of my friends snapped. He attacked a Guard for some reason. It was stupid. It was like he wanted to get in trouble."

Rian looks over his glasses at me, one eyebrow raised.

"And why would he want that?"

I shake my head.

"I don't know. Maybe... maybe he wanted to go to the Mines?"

"Why would he want that? Do you think that maybe he knows someone down there?"

I fall silent. I hadn't considered that. If one of Kane's friends were in the Mines, no wonder he wanted to go after them. Even so, it wasn't worth the risk. They could have wiped his memory blank and tossed him into the Mines to work as a brainless drone. They still might.

"Maybe. I'm sorry, I just... I don't know."

Rian presses his finger together and leans towards me.

"And how do you feel about what he did?"

My hands clench. I could describe how I'm feeling in a million different ways. Angry. Confused. Betrayed.

I open my mouth, and a word falls out.

"Conflicted."

He watches me, his face carefully blank, and I realise what I just said. I clear my throat.

"Um. Sorry. It's not..."

"Hey, it's alright. You're not in trouble. It's normal to be a little unnerved."

I nod, happy that at least I'm not making things worse. He lifts a pen to his mouth and chews on it. He's clearly thinking something over.

"Alright. I think I've got something for you. Are you alright with pulling loaded carts?"

I nod.

"Good. I think I know the perfect thing."

I follow Rian to the loading bay, my stomach still a little uneasy. I should have known. I'm going to be put on loading duty. I suppose it's the best punishment I could have hoped for; it might even be easier than working in the fields. He turns around and points into the road, where a number of trucks are pulling into the Mill.

"These guys are taking supplies into Thorne."

"Okay. So I'm loading the vehicles?"

There are a lot of them – I hope I don't have to load them all alone. But he shakes his head and gestures over my shoulder.

"Not quite. I've got something smaller for you."

I follow his gaze to a cart. It's different from the ones I'm used to; it's made of sturdy metal rather than wood, and seems to be adorned with all kinds of fiddly-looking straps and fastenings.

"The cart?"

"Yep. You're going to load that up with everything on this list..."

He hands me a scrap of paper and I stare at it, fighting to make out the words. Reading isn't exactly a useful skill around here. We learn how at Homestead, but it's been years and I fear it'll take a while to decipher Rian's spider-like scribbles.

"You're going to take it to Thorne for me."

I gasp.

"Do you want me to take the cart to the Dock?"

"Nope. This is a month-long, there and back trip. You need to load the cart here and not leave its side until you get to Thorne. Then take it to the place marked on the back of that paper."

I turn it over to see a crudely-drawn map. Thorne seems to be laid out in a perfect circle built around three points. A red arrow points to something close to the edge of the city, though there are several other areas marked with question marks. I don't ask what those are for.

"Loading it up isn't a problem," I wonder out loud, "but how do I get over the sea?"

"You'll be going over on a boat. But keep in mind it's a long journey. Find a good boat to take you there. Once you reach the Dock on the other side, you'll need to walk the cart into Thorne through the main gate. There, they might ask for a delivery pass, but you don't need one. Just say you're here to see Pan. They should send you right through."

I clutch the paper tightly, not wanting to ask the question. What happens if they don't send me right through? What then?

"What's the delivery for?"

I feel rude just asking, like I'm daring to question the Guard, but he doesn't take offense. Instead he just glances around, like he doesn't want anyone to hear.

"It's just a small group that has some high-need individuals. They require a surplus of supplies every month, so we send them separately."

I can't help but smile at that. It's easy to demonise everything the Guard does, but thinking of some tiny family getting their surplus of supplies every month is pretty nice.

"So what do you think?" Rian asks, "Can you do it?"

I consider it for a moment. I've never been all that interested in the city. Sometimes I would spot the luminescent glow in the distance on a particularly dark night, but I never gave any thought to what it meant. But I suppose it's an easy way out of my punishment. A whole month of just walking. It's positively luxurious compared to a month of chopping wood or digging holes. My stomach still twists nervously at the thought of Kane in the Mines, but I put the feeling aside for now. He made his choice. Time I made mine.

"Absolutely, sir. I'll be back before you know it."

He smiles, but then his expression falters a little and he lowers his voice.

"There are a few important things you need to know before you go. First of all, this is not a regular delivery. Do not let anyone other than Pan take ownership of the goods."

"How will I know who Pan is?"

"She's... just trust me. You'll know her when you see her. But don't let anyone else know what it's for. If they ask who you're taking it to, you don't know. If they ask what's in it, you don't know. If they ask who sent you..."

"I don't know."

He seems satisfied by that.

"Precisely. As far as they know, you're just a Millchild. Okay?"

Millchild. It's a name I've heard thrown around a few times in the past. A snobbish title given to Mill workers by city folk. I always found it somewhat patronising, not that I care all that much. Something doesn't sit right about sneaking around. But this isn't Thorne; I don't answer to their laws. This is the Mill, and the only orders I have to follow are those of the Guard.

Rian holds out a hand, and I grasp it without hesitation.

It takes a few hours, but eventually I finish packing the cart. I push the last wooden crate onto it and sigh. Rian steps up behind me.

"Looks good. Now then, I suppose you'd best be off."

Something stirs in my chest. I want to go back to the bunker for one last night and tell Nel what happened, not to mention where I'm going. I want to sit together in the dark. I want to feel her hand reaching over to comfort me; because suddenly, I feel like I'm actually in need of comfort. But I can see the trucks are finishing up, their heavy metal doors pulling shut with a clang that echoes across the Mill. I gulp hard.

"Yeah. I, er... I should be back soon."

"Best of luck," he smiles, "there are regular boats back so just come back whenever you're able. Though keep in mind that if you're gone more than a month, we'll assume something happened and you died on the way."

He says the last bit a little firmer, and I feel nervousness prickling up the back of my neck. Though he's been fairly nice to me until now, I'm still in trouble. A strange urge flickers in my chest but I shake it off. I'm not going to try and run away. I'll do this delivery, get back here, and eventually, I'll forget that any of this ever happened.

I'll forget that Kane even existed.

CHAPTER FIVE

I take off with the cart behind me, suddenly grateful for all the straps and ties securing its weight to my shoulders. The trucks take off too, but they're much faster than me so they speed out of sight almost immediately. I approach the gate. It's massive, a huge wire fence with Guard towers on either side. As I near, one of the Guards lifts a gun and cocks it in my direction. He watches me for a second before lowering it. Just an intimidation tactic.

A lone Guard stands at the gate, clipboard in hand. He looks bored out of his mind. As I approach, he barely bothers to meet my eyes.

"Who's sending you?"

"Um... Rian."

He signals for the gate to open, and an alarm sounds overhead. Slowly but surely the gates' crossed wire splits apart and the path opens up to me. I incline my head a little as I pass the Guard and take a step outside.

The road ahead of me is nothing but dust, golden brown and surrounded by dirt and the occasional patch of grass. The road itself stretches out of my view and over a hill. I don't know where the Dock is. It could be an hour away. It could be three days. But the direction is clear enough, so I start walking.

The cart isn't used to these roads; the paths in the Mill are worn down over time and are surprisingly smooth, but this road is uneven and filled with potholes and rocks. They knock at the wheels of the cart, tilting it this way and that, and I realise why this cart is so different. A normal wooden one wouldn't be able to survive this road.

As I walk, I make a conscious effort to keep my mind blank. Every so often Nel's face comes to mind and I feel a pang of guilt – so I force it down and stare at a point on the horizon instead. Kane's voice floats over me. You are going to regret this. I try to shake it from my head.

Suddenly I stumble, breaking from my binds and collapsing to my knees in the dust.

Believe me, one day you'll wish you joined me.

I stand up, ignoring the graze on my leg and the ache in my ankle. I don't want to hear him. I don't care anymore. I bite back hard on the lie and keep moving.

It's about an hour to the Dock. Once I reach the precipice of the hill I stop dead in my tracks.

I've never seen the sea before. I knew that it was a large body of water, and figured it would be like the lake at the Mill, or the well in the crop field. Before now I've stolen a moment to stand by the lake and watch the liquid shift. I've seen how the light seems to dance off its surface, and how it's somehow both clear and blue-green in colour.

But this – this is something else entirely.

All I can see is blue. It's in every direction, as far as the eye can see. It shimmers in the sunlight, crystal clear and neat and perfect. Buildings lie somewhere below me, and I pause to watch the water pull inland, then push back out again. It seems to do it every few seconds. It takes me a minute before I remember the word for what I'm seeing. Tide.

My eyes glide across the horizon. If I look closely enough, I can see where the surface of the Earth curves away from me, and the ocean sinks from my sight. Something warm stirs in my chest.

It may be the first time in my life that I've ever felt curious.

I want to know more. I need to know what makes the sea move, what draws it to the land and then pushes it away again. I have to know how the large, metal boats are somehow able to float serenely over its surface, calmer and steadier than any vehicle I've seen.

I take a step forward, and as I walk down the slope I find myself picking up speed. As I get closer I can smell... something.

I can smell fish being pulled from a net on a ship half a mile out to sea. I can smell salt and sand and rocks. I can smell fresh, clean air that's unsullied by the filth and dirt that's always filled my lungs.

It's amazing.

I approach the Dock. There are people everywhere - mostly older men, bearded and rugged looking. Each one wears what seems to be standard issue Mill clothing, but as I get closer a metal gate opens in front of me, and I see hundreds of Guards wandering around too.

"Where are you going?"

The Guard at the gate lifts a clipboard. He looks fed up, too; if I didn't know better I'd assume it was the same guy from the Farm.

"Thorne," I reply, "taking some supplies."

He reaches back, lifts the tarp momentarily, and then lowers it.

"All clear. Go ahead."

He moves on and I breathe a sigh of relief. One of the men approaches me, wiping his brow with a dirty scrap of cloth.

"Hey. Can I help you?"

My instinct is to say no, that I can handle it, but I hesitate.

"Do you know which boat I need to get to Thorne?"

He just laughs. It's a deep, booming sound that echoes across the Dock, but unlike at the Mill, it doesn't draw any attention. Everyone's too focussed on what they're doing.

"Are you trying to be funny?" he grins. I notice that most of his teeth are gone, rotted away into black stubs in his mouth. My own teeth immediately hurt.

"N-no."

"There's only one destination here. We send things to Thorne, then we get the empty bits back, along with any waste. We don't go anywhere else."

I can't help but feel a pang of sadness at his words. Looking at the vast ocean makes my throat ache. A tiny, tiny part of me wants to know what else is out there. Not to see it for myself, of course, but just to know that others go there would have been enough.

He sees me staring and gives a dismissive wave of the hand.

"Look, any boat will get you there. Just head for the Dock and someone will show you where to unload. Although, if you ask me..."

He leans in close and I can smell his putrid, rotting breath.

"I'd avoid the bigger boats. More Guards. Might get you there a bit quicker, sure, but you'll be set to work right away. Pick a smaller vessel and it'll give you a day or so to relax."

I thank him for his help and walk away. As I head off, I spot him grabbing what looks to be a giant spool of rope and throwing it over his shoulder. My strides are long as I walk the cart down the Dock. I'm a little nervous to be this close to the water. I can hear it all around me, like unnerving background music. I take a hesitant step onto the boardwalk and immediately pull my foot back. The wooden slats creak under my weight. I don't think they can handle the cart as well.

But then a man twice my size jogs by, onto the walk and out of sight. Confidence flares in my chest. If it can hold him, it can hold me. My first steps are slow, and I freeze when I realise that I can see the water rippling underneath me. It takes a fair bit of strength to keep walking, knowing that I could fall in at any minute.

I'm not scared of heights. Even the idea of falling from a height doesn't set my heart racing. But I've never been swimming before. It's a recreational activity, irrelevant at the Mill. The closest I've got was working the crop fields after a flood. Pacing through waist-high muddy water, trying desperately to find something that looks halfway edible in the sludge... it isn't quite on the same level as this. The water is crystal clear below me, but I can't figure out how deep it goes. But I do know I would probably drown – especially with the cart strapped to my back.

I'm surprised how much attention I seem to be drawing. Perhaps my diminutive stature marks me out more than I'd expected, but I can feel other workers' eyes trailing after me as I walk.

I wander for a little while, and then my eyes settle on a boat. It's metal like the others, but smaller and far less crowded. There are patches of rust but it's still somehow afloat. Two men sit by, one carving something out of a bit of driftwood. The younger glances up as I near and waves.

"Hey. Need a ride?"

"I'm going to Thorne," I tell him, "I need to get this cart there."

"We have a decent luggage hold," says the older of the two, lowering his carving. His whole face is covered in wispy white hair; it looks like he has whiskers. He reminds me of the badgers we sometimes hunt at the Farm.

"It needs to stay in the cart, sorry."

"We can do that," says the younger, "No problem. By the way, I'm Darus. This is my Dad."

"I'm Noah."

We set sail from the Dock just as evening begins to fall. I stand at the edge of the boat, both scared to fall overboard and scared to stay put. The floor of the boat lifts and dips with every movement of the waves and I feel my stomach tightening.

"Relax," Darus tells me. He indicates to a chair towards the back of the boat. I shake my head hard and he laughs.

"Oh, come on. This is a full day trip. You can't stay clutching the edge for the whole journey."

I tighten my grip. So says you.

"You'll feel better if you relax."

I glance up at where the older man is steering the boat. Despite his age he seems to be an expert, working the advanced computer with total ease.

"He's pretty good with that thing," I tell Darus. He shrugs.

"Dad's always had a gift for computers. Can't say I've ever been that good with them myself."

There's that term again. Dad. I clear my throat.

"You keep calling him Dad."

"Yeah, I know it's not true. But he's been like a Dad to me. The guy practically raised me - I messed up about eight years back and got given a 'fresh start'. Damn injection. I didn't know my head from my ass. He was the only one who looked out for me."

I feel a pang of warmth at that. How nice. A family dynamic between strangers. There's something reassuring about it. I grasp hold of the chair and force myself to sit down. The sea is mostly calm now, but I still wince at every wave. Darus laughs and leans back in the chair next to me, folding his hands behind his head. I watch him for a moment. He looks nothing like a Farm worker. He has the muscles for it, but his face is round and full and his hair sits in wiry twists along his scalp. He moves easily, and seems to have a permanent smile on his face. I suppose it's hard to be miserable with such a beautiful view.

"So, what are you taking into Thorne?" he asks.

"Just a few supplies."

"Have you been to the city before?"

I shake my head and he leans forward.

"I've been... once. Years ago, because of understaffing."

I mimic his movement, shifting forward to hear him better.

"What's it like?"

"It's like... nothing else you've ever seen," he breathes, "I still get breathless when I think about it. What kind of buildings do you have at the Mill? Anything with stairs?"

I nod.

"Not any of our buildings, no. But the Guard towers have a few floors to them."

"Well. Picture the towers, only five times the size and made of glass."

I stare blankly.

"Yeah, I can't imagine that."

I close my eyes for a second, but nothing comes to mind. I heave a sigh.

"Sorry. I'm just not the imaginative type."

"In that case, maybe it's best to just leave you to see for yourself. Believe me, you'll be blown away. Now then, do you want to help with dinner?"

"Dinner?"

"Yeah," he tells me, "with Dad steering the ship, I do the rest of the work. That includes cooking for us, as well as any guests on board."

The word doesn't sit right with me. Guest makes it seem like I'm different from them, better somehow. But technically, we're exactly the same.

We dig into a dinner of roast fish and vegetables. I've never eaten fish before, but even though it looks far from edible, once I try it I realise it's a hundred times better than gruel. I tell Darus and his Dad about the sludge we eat at the Farm and they gape, horrified that we don't eat all fresh food like them. Supposedly, we're the only ones that don't. Darus tells me that the people in Thorne have high standards for everything. Everything has to be done by hand. Organic. Free range. They condemn the use of machinery for anything beyond their own walls. I suppose that's why we have to do all the farming by hand when a machine could do it quicker. Turns out, thanks to their demands, even Darus and his Dad struggle. All fish has to be wild, caught seasonally and even then, only certain ones are deemed good enough. Apparently, it's a nightmare just to keep up with demand. His Dad tells me in no uncertain terms that the people in the city are selfish. That they care only about themselves and nothing else. I wince as he says it. I'm not an idiot. I know that they're raised differently from us. Maybe they don't really know what they're asking. Maybe they don't realise how much work is involved.

Maybe they just don't care.

As soon as the sun begins to fall, I'm ushered to bed. What they call 'bed', however, is nothing more than a tiny hammock, not unlike the ones back home – only this one tilts and wobbles with every wave. I lie back and try to force my eyes closed, but then comes a particularly sharp jolt and I find myself standing.

Sleep is just not going to happen tonight.

I climb back onto the deck and look out. At night, the sea is even more beautiful. The moon is high overhead, and I can see its silvery light bouncing off the waves around me. I look both ways; but I can't see the land anymore. We're too far out. Still, the sea air seems to calm me. My gut is still swirling, uneasy with all that's happened and my refusal to think about it, but I can ignore it more easily now. For a brief moment, I wish I could stay here forever. It sounds perfect. Sailing, fishing. Maybe even learning how to swim in those crystal depths. No more crop fields or wood chopping. No more raising cattle.

A sigh escapes my lips and I lean down on the railing, my eyes locked on the horizon. It's been so long since I've seen the sky like this. So broad, so endless. At the Farm there are always buildings, towers, fences. They block my view and keep me from seeing the stars fully. But now, I see them clearly. Like paint splatters across the sky. Every so often one of them winks, and I feel the strange urge to wink back. My hand reaches up and I feel like I could almost grab the moon.

"What are you thinking about?"

I jolt. Darus is standing behind me, his arms crossed, and for a moment I wonder if I'm in trouble for coming out here. But then he steps up beside me, leaning on the railing too.

"Nothing."

My voice sounds weak, almost like a whisper. He shoots me a disbelieving look.

"Noah, come on. I might be clueless, but nobody comes out here at night unless something's weighing on their mind."

I shrug.

"I guess I'm just nervous."

"About the city?"

I drum my fingers on the railing and nod.

"I guess so. It must be that."

"What do you mean, it must be? Surely you know if something's bothering you."

I shake my head. Maybe for most people, that would be true. But not for me. I'm never entirely sure what I'm feeling, or why.

"Not really," I mutter, "I don't really do worry."

He narrows his eyes a little.

"Obviously there's something. What were you thinking about, just before I came over?"

"Not much. Just how nice it is here."

He raises an eyebrow.

"You like it here?"

"Of course I do. The fresh air, the good food, the feeling of being clean. It's amazing. A part of me almost wishes I didn't have to go home."

I bite back on the words, but it's too late.

"Sorry. I didn't mean that. It's nice here, but I do want to go home. I want this to be over with so that I can start to forget about it."

He stares into my eyes and I'm momentarily taken aback by his forwardness – they seem far more liberal with their attentions here.

"Noah."

"Y-yeah?"

"Why are you here?"

I bite my lip so hard I taste blood.

"I shouldn't say."

"Look, tomorrow evening we'll drop you and that cart off at the Dock on the other side. After that, we won't ever see each other again. I don't know anything about you except your name. It wouldn't hurt to tell me."

I turn around so my back is against the railing. He's right. It's not like he's going to do anything to me once he finds out.

So I tell him everything. About Kane on that first day, how I had warned him. About how Nel had told me her worries. The story of my stint in the Mines. How Kane had asked me to join him, then kicked off. How I had taken a conscious step away from him, right when he was pleading with me the most.

Throughout the story Darus listens in silence, his expression unusually calm. He's an excellent audience, nodding when I need him to, furrowing his brows whenever the story calls for it. When I'm finished, he waits a couple of minutes before speaking.

"So this Kane kid, he just flipped?"

"Yes."

"Just like that?"

"Yes."

He frowns.

"And you have absolutely no idea why he did it."

"No. Not a clue."

Darus leans back on the railing and stretches his arms over his head.

"If you had known why he was doing it, would you have joined in? Assuming it was for a good reason, that is."

I pause. I hadn't considered that. Honestly, the thought hadn't occurred to me that he might actually have had a valid reason. What if it was important? What if he had no choice? What if he had a plan, but that plan depended on me following blindly?

My gut clenches. What if I'm the reason he's in the Mines?

"I... I don't know. I mean, I would never betray the Guard. But..."

I stop mid-sentence. But what? But I would have if I'd had a reason to? If I knew he absolutely needed me? What situation would he have had to be in for me to abandon everything and help him?

"What's wrong?" Darus asks.

I stare at the wooden deck, dread building in my throat.

"I didn't think."

This whole time, I've only been focussing on what's happening to me. But Kane's no fool. He didn't have a death wish – if he had, he would have just tried to run. The fact that he hit Wirrow means he wanted to be punished, and in a certain way. He must have had some kind of plan.

"What if he needed me?"

My voice seems to crack as I say it, but I don't care.

"What if he's stuck in the mines, being punished all because I didn't help him?"

Darus shakes his head.

"Sounds to me like he made his choice."

"I bet he hates me."

Suddenly my voice breaks, and something hot pricks the back of my eyes. He looks down, staring at my now-shaking hands.

"Noah..."

"I bet he feels like I betrayed him."

I don't say any more. The damage is done. I know what the next sentence is. I did betray him. By not trusting him. By not helping him. By not even jumping in to talk Wirrow round once he had Kane pinned. By stepping back and pretending that I wasn't involved, I abandoned him.

A droplet of water hits the floor below me and something snaps - before I know it, I'm doing something I've never done before.

I'm crying.

CHAPTER SIX

Darus' reaction is instant; he jumps away from me, panic in his eyes.

"Hey! Why are you crying?"

I wipe my face with my arm and take deep breaths in an attempt to calm myself. Great. I bet I look like a total mess right now. How humiliating.

"I'm sorry," I whimper, "just ignore me. I'm being stupid."

He grimaces, then holds out both arms. It takes me a second to realise what he's asking - and when I do, I pull back and shake my head hard.

"No. No, I'm fine."

"Come on."

"It's okay! Besides, we aren't supposed to..."

"Like I just said. You and I will part ways tomorrow and we'll never meet again. It doesn't matter if I give you one stupid hug."

His face has settled into an easy smile, and he stretches his arms a little, inviting me in. Tears drip from my chin but I force a smile onto my lips, and take a deep breath before stepping into the embrace.

I've never been held before. It's peculiar. Darus' arms are warm and strong; I can feel years of steadily built muscle holding me tight. I rest my head on his shoulder, and after a few seconds I raise my hands and place them on his back. I can't tell if the whole embrace is supposed to be comforting, or if it's just so awkward it breaks through the grief.

We stand silently for a few minutes, and then I clear my throat.

"I... can hear your heartbeat."

Blood rushes to my face and suddenly the moment has passed. We pull apart and take a couple of steps away from one another. He smiles warmly.

"There. That wasn't too bad, was it?"

I simply twitch. No. No, it's wasn't bad. Not exactly. Just strange, and in my books that's enough of a reason to never do it again.

"Anyway," he coughs, "I, uh... I hope you feel better. You'd better get some sleep now."

I nod, striding past him without a word. As odd as it was, I do appreciate what he just did. People like us aren't encouraged to touch, even within our own gender. It's not banned exactly, but we're warned against it. Contact leads to affection which leads to intimacy. But as I climb into my hammock, I don't feel any of that. Just a nice guy who's trying to help.

I can still feel everything shifting around me, every tiny wave pushing up against the side of the boat and tipping me this way and that. But as I close my eyes, the tears drying on my cheeks, the movement doesn't bother me. It's almost comforting now, like a child being rocked in the arms of a parent. I allow myself to forget where I am, and soon enough I forget everything.

It's about midday before I finally spot land on the horizon. The sight both excites and terrifies me, and I can feel blood pumping hard in my veins as I stare at the dark line in the distance. I'd never stopped to consider what Thorne might be like – but here it is, so close I can almost smell it behind the salty sea air. A flicker of something akin to curiosity flits through me. Huh. That's been happening a lot just lately.

"There it is," says Darus. I push myself up against the rails and gaze out across the sea. Excitement buzzes in my head and I bounce on my heels. The boat shifts and I lean with it; it's only been a day, but already I've grown used to the way the sea moves. I've adapted to the salty air and the constant sound of waves, and the sound of birds overhead. So different from the bees and farm animals at the Mill, but somehow just as reminiscent of home.

"You nervous?" he asks. I nod.

"A little. I've never been completely alone before."

"Thorne is full of people. More than you could ever count, apparently."

My heart jumps a little, and I press my palm to my chest in a vague attempt to still it.

"That's pretty scary. Are you trying to frighten me?"

"Just helping out."

"Like you haven't done enough for me?"

We share a smile. It's true. He didn't do anything more than listen and be present, but it feels like a weight is lifted. I'm not stupid. When I return to the Mill, all my problems will still be there. I'll never be able to escape them entirely. But right now, there's nothing I can do. I have a job to do. There's no point moping.

Suddenly, he lifts his hand and places it on mine. I jump, unused to the physical touch that seems to come so naturally to Dock workers.

"S-sorry."

"It's okay."

I stare down at his hand on mine. His knuckles are folded around my fingers, sending a rush of something unusual through me. Closeness? Camaraderie? Friendship? I don't know. But then he moves away and the moment is gone.

"Come on," he says, "I'll help you unhook your cart."

The Dock on the other side is practically identical to the first one. As the boat pulls in several men run forward, throwing out rope and steps to help us depart. As I strap myself into the cart and pull it across the deck, I notice Darus chatting with a couple of younger men. He smiles, his mouth wide, and they respond in kind. I feel a pang of jealousy. That must be nice.

When it's finally unloaded I pull the cart onto the loading dock and turn, looking back up at where Darus and his Dad stand, now on the boat. They lean over the railing and wave down at me.

"Aren't you coming down?" I call. Darus shakes his head.

"Nope. We don't come down unless we're loading or unloading. And since you're our only cargo..."

He points across the sea.

"...we're heading back to the Dock to wait for the next load."

"Oh. Well, thank you for bringing me here. And thank you, Sir."

His Dad seems surprised at bring called 'Sir', but he doesn't seem unhappy with it. Even from down here, I can see his eyes sparkling.

"It's been a pleasure, Miss."

I stand and wait for a little while, watching in silence until the boat finally begins to move away. Darus stands at the rear of the boat, perching on the railing and looking back at the Docks. He waves. I respond in kind, and he cups his hands around his mouth.

"See you around, Noah!"

My smile falters; but I replace it instantly and keep waving. Once I start, I can't stop. I wave until I can't see his face anymore, until the boat has faded from my view. Then I lower my hand, a feeling of unease building in my gut.

I guess I'm really on my own from here.

The cart seems to get heavier with every step as I walk through the Dock. Here, the atmosphere seems different. Though everyone mills around in the same grey clothes, it seems much more still and solemn. There are more Guards here, too. One steps directly in front of me, Hoverbot accompanying him, and I shrink back instinctively. I haven't done anything wrong, but somehow I already feel guilty.

"Name?"

It takes a second to register he's asking a question. He taps his pen on the clipboard and growls.

"Name."

I open my mouth, but somehow the words don't come.

"Do you know what I'm asking, you little buzzard? Name. What do people shout at you when you fuck up?"

"Noah."

He sighs.

"They give you lot some stupid names over at the Farm."

I decide not to ask how he knows I'm from the Farm. Perhaps I look the part. He jots something down and indicates toward the cart.

"What's this?"

"Supplies," I croak, "I'm supposed to take them to the city."

He strides past me and lifts the tarp. He glances at the boxes, and I suddenly remember Rian's warning.

"Additional... they're additional supplies!"

I blurt it out, and the Guard pauses.

"What?"

I clear my throat and try again, this time trying to make it sound like I'm not terrified.

"The, uh, the supplies in Thorne dwindled a little too quickly so this is a ... supplementary delivery."

He stares for a minute, then signals to the Guards in front.

"Alright. Go on."

I hesitate.

"Um. How do I get there?"

"God, you kids from the Farm really are stupid. Look here. See that road?"

I look past the gate, and I can just about see a sliver of road outside.

"Yes."

"Well, it's the only damn road for about two hundred miles. You follow it, you reach the city. Simple enough for even you to understand, don't you think?"

"Yes, Sir."

"Good. Then go."

The second the gate slides shut behind me, a chill shudders through me. All I can see is dirt. Not soft, brown soil, perfect for crops, or glowing white sand like the beach. Just sickly, rocky mud as far as the eye can see. The word 'moor' comes to mind, but I'm not sure if that's quite right. But it's cold, and empty, and very, very big. I'd been shocked by the size of the sea, but at least it moved. The light shimmered off its surface, making it feel alive. But this is so flat and plain that I feel tiny. I take a few steps out, but the further I get from the gate, the smaller and more lost I feel.

I accidentally kick up some dust and start coughing. I wipe at my streaming eyes and sigh. Darus mentioned this. He said it would take days to get to the city. For a moment, I wonder what it would be like to have to sleep out here. No bed, no shelter. If it rains, I'll be soaked. If it's hot, I have no water to quench my thirst. Maybe I should have thought this through.

I glance back at the gate, wondering if maybe they'd be willing to give me a bottle or two to get me across the moors, but it's sealed tight. Any Guards have wandered away, their attention drawn by more important matters. I briefly consider rapping my fists on the chain-link fence to get their attention, but the move seems too bold. So instead I turn away, my eyes focussed on the horizon, and start to walk.

CHAPTER SEVEN

The sun begins to set much sooner than I'd have expected, and a part of me wonders if I should stop to rest. But I hear something in the distance, a steady thumping, and suddenly the idea of being out here alone in the dark makes my heart hammer in my chest. The rational part of me knows that the thumping is probably just one of the Factories, or something back at the Dock. Maybe it's one of the Oil Rigs in the distance. There are places like that everywhere. I laugh at my own paranoia. What am I thinking? It's a noise – not a monster.

Something roars, louder than before, and I jump. It takes several minutes before I find the strength to move again.

The sun has well and truly set now. I can just about see the road ahead of me, a dark shadow in a mass of other dark shadows. The cart clanks and thuds with each step and I find a strange kind of comfort in the sound, the way it pierces the near silence. I try to time my feet to the noises, my left foot timed with the cart and my right with the thudding in the distance. It's mind-numbingly boring, but it keeps me moving.

I barely register when the sun finally begins to rise. I feel like I've barely moved, though I've been walking for hours. I'm suddenly grateful for the height of summer – the nights are mercifully short and not too cold. I glance back. The gate is long out of sight, but nothing seems to have changed ahead of me. I slow to a stop, and the moment I do I realise it's a mistake. Forcing myself on, and detaching from my body was the only thing keeping me going. Now I've stopped, the exhaustion catches up with me. My legs burn, the muscles screaming. I move to wipe the sweat from my face and am surprised by how little comes away. My mouth is just as dry, my throat sore and burning.

Maybe this is the ultimate punishment. Lost in the middle of nowhere, my body stalling and whining at me to rest. Knowing that if I do, it'll only delay the inevitable.

Perhaps the Mines would have been better. For all my fear of the dark, there's something equally awful about this; being somewhere infinitely large that shows no sign of ending no matter how much I walk.

I try to steady my breathing and lean heavily against the cart. Maybe this was intentional. It didn't make any sense for the Guard to send me away as a punishment. But sending me out here to die is a good way of making sure I never cause trouble.

Then, a sound.

A different sound from before. Not the steady thump-thump of the Factories, or the sound of the wind growling over the ground. No, this sound is familiar. Recognisable.

I rip free from the cart and dive into the road, staring wildly at the road behind me. It's an engine. An engine!

Eventually, it arrives. A heavy grey truck pulling an open trailer behind it, and a dull-faced man behind the wheel. I wave desperately and it slows to a stop. The man leans his head out of the window, cocks his hat and stares.

"Wow. What the heck are you doing out here?"

I point at the cart, gasping for air. Relief and exhaustion compound in my head, making my limbs feel heavy and my tongue feel thick in my mouth.

"I have... a delivery."

"Did you walk all this way?"

I gulp hard and nod.

"That's ridiculous," he gasps, "The Guards at the gate never seem to arrange transport anymore. They keep sending folks out into the wilderness with nothing. Can't tell you how many bodies I've seen on the side of the road."

"H-how far is it to Thorne?"

His head falls back and he laughs.

"A week, if you're walking. Only a few hours in the truck though. Hop in, I'll give you a ride."

Today must be my lucky day.

The man – who tells me his name is Eagen – helps me load the cart into the back of his truck. Despite my shaking limbs I try my best to help out, but I'm half-asleep and probably not much use.

The moment I'm seated in the cab, he hands me a bottle of water.

"Reckon you need this. It's stupid how long you've been out here."

I take it gratefully and gulp it down. It's warm and stale, but I couldn't care less. I save a little and splash it on my face and neck, washing away the dust. It's a few minutes of silence before I'm finally able to speak again.

"Thank you. I didn't know what I was going to do."

"Not your fault," he says, running a hand over his thinning hair. He's an older man, wizened but strong. He idly chews on an unlit cigarette, letting it stick out of the corner of his mouth. I don't ask how he got hold of it.

"What did you mean, the Guards haven't been arranging transport?"

"They're meant to have a load of trucks on hand, just like this one."

He taps at the steering wheel, and I feel the vehicle shudder beneath us as we pull away. This truck looks different from the ones I'm used to - he drives with his feet and his hands, rather than by ordering the sleek computer on the dash. Maybe it's an older model?

"But they never use us," he pushes on, "they can't be bothered with any of the smaller deliveries. Anyway, you seem a little young to be out here alone. Where are you from?"

"The Farm."

"That'll explain it. You kids don't last too long out here, though you made it further than most. Actually saw one of you out here last month, you know."

"You did?"

His face falls.

"Yeah. Poor kid, probably not much older than you. Nobody found him and he gave up the ghost halfway."

I feel a pang of sadness. That was probably the person who usually makes this delivery. No wonder Rian was so eager to replace him.

"I was given a month to deliver this. Why would they say that if it's only supposed to take a few days?"

He shrugs.

"Don't know. But don't question it. Just be happy. You'll have time to see the sights."

I stare at my lap for a moment, then up at the road.

"Have you ever been to the city?"

"A few times. Gotta say, not my cup of tea."

"Why not?"

"Us Mill workers do all the hard work for them. Everything's given to them on a silver platter and most of them haven't worked a day in their lives."

"Oh."

"At first glance, it's amazing. But without any work to do, people go a little crazy."

I want to ask more, but at the same time I'm not sure I really want to know. I wring my hands together, watching the bend and flex of my fingers.

"Thanks for telling me."

We drive for hours under a blaring hot sun. Initially he tries to make small talk with me, but inevitably we discover that neither of us are any good at it and fall silent. The heat and the comfort and the exhaustion in my body make my eyes feel heavy, and despite my best intentions, I start to drift off. Sleep doesn't come easily. I can feel my fingers twitching and sweat dripping down the side of my face. I go through horrible phases of awareness and unconsciousness.

"Noah?"

Eagen snaps his fingers in front of my face and I bolt upright.

"Did I fall asleep? I'm sorry!"

He just laughs.

"No worries. You were probably exhausted after that walk!"

I start running my hands through my hair, wiping at my face, trying anything and everything to keep myself awake and looking somewhat presentable.

"How long have I been asleep?"

"Don't know. Few hours. Didn't want to wake you. You seemed so peaceful."

Peaceful? It sure didn't feel peaceful. But I stretch my arms over my head and smile anyway.

"Thanks. I really needed it. But if you don't mind me asking, why did you just wake me? We're not in the city just yet."

His smile broadens.

"Not exactly. Just thought you'd like to see this."

"See what?"

"Look."

Thorne.

It's massive. As wide as the ocean and higher than I could have imagined. I can't believe how tall the buildings are. They shine in the sunlight – it must be the glass I was told about. It's miles and miles away, but even from here it looks formidable. Huge. Unending.

Exciting.

I put my palms on the windscreen and press my nose against the glass. I look at the city from end to end, drinking in every detail. Some of the taller buildings are darker. Some have massive blocks added to them, and others have walkways or stairs built between them. Blue screens light up every surface, visible even from here. Three skyscrapers catch my eye; they're taller than any of the others and perfectly, flawlessly circular – like the city itself. I feel a shiver through my spine.

"That's amazing."

My voice comes out breathy, fogging up the glass. Eagen laughs.

"You really haven't been here, have you?"

The closer we get, the higher and more towering the buildings seem to be. I shrink back from it; I hadn't expected to be made to feel so small on this journey.

"Now then," he says, lowering his window, "When we get close, we're going to need to unload your cart. See, I'm only able to take you as far as the first checkpoint. After that, since it's a small delivery, you need to walk the rest of the way yourself. It's only a couple of miles, mind."

"Okay. Thanks."

He pauses, one hand resting on the wheel.

"Kid. Can I give you some advice?"

"Sure."

"Best I've got," he tells me, "is to keep your head down. Most folk are good enough people, but some are only out to hurt you."

"What do you mean?"

"Just... stay out of the darker corners of the streets. Don't talk to anyone strange. It's no guarantee of safety, but you'll thank me when you get out in one piece."

"You don't make it sound very appealing."

"Maybe that's misleading of me. It's a great place. Colourful. Bright. So long as you watch your step, you'll be just fine."

Eagen helps me unload the cart about half a mile from Thorne. Here, there are a series of smaller gates. They're unmanned, which strikes me as odd, but it's nice to not have to worry about it.

I strap myself to the cart as Eagen climbs back into the cab. He doesn't say a word as he starts up the engine, only raises a hand in farewell as he vanishes from my sight. I look at what's left of the journey. I suppose I should just be grateful I didn't have to walk all the way.

My feet seem to find purchase more easily on the road leading up to the city. It changes here, from a dirt track to something black, made of many tiny stones stuck together with something shiny. A single blue line is painted down the centre of the road, splitting it cleanly. I imagine it's so the trucks don't collide, but I have no idea which side I'm supposed to be on, so I just walk in the middle. I can feel my heartbeat in my throat. It seems to pump harder and harder with each passing minute, and I can feel sweat dripping down the back of my neck. I'm not hot. I'm nervous. Every time I learn something new, it sets me on edge. Can I really do this?

The moment I reach the gate, I find myself staring down a group of Guards. Five stocky men stand in a row in front of me, each clutching a strange device – I recognise them as shock batons, though they're nothing like the clunky ones I'm used to.

"Um..."

"Name. Location. Task."

This time, I know what to do.

"My name is Noah, I've been sent from the Farms to bring supplementary supplies."

"Who do you need to see?"

"Um... Pan."

They exchange looks, and then one of them wanders off. I bite my lip and swallow hard. I hope Rian told this 'Pan' that I was coming. A Guard takes a step towards me, his eyebrows raised, his movement curious. It's like he's looking for something, searching my face for tell-tale signs of something much more extraordinary that I'm capable of.

A few minutes later, the Guard returns. He waves down the others.

"Confirmed," he tells them, "Pan's waiting for the delivery."

One of the Guards turns to me.

"Do you know where you're going?"

I nod. No. I have no idea. But I want to get away from you, and soon.

He signals someone overhead and finally, the gates begin to slide open. I stare straight ahead and try not to step back as the city is revealed to me.

Of all the things I'd expected from Thorne, I hadn't considered how loud it would be. I have no clue how that gate is able to keep it all in. It's deafening. Motors and music and what sounds like the speech of a thousand people fills the air, making my ears hurt and my head pound.

The second thing I notice is the colour. Growing up in the Mill means that I've only know certain colours - browns, blacks, greens. But here, there's every colour I could imagine. Red banners fly overhead, as bold as the apples in the orchards back home. Blue and yellow Hoverbots trawl after people, beeping their assent at the orders they're given. A surprising amount of people are adorned in nothing but pure, satin white.

And there are so many people.

I stand frozen. I can't even see the road. There are so, so many people, and judging by the size of the city, this is only a tiny fraction. Panic courses through me - but a hand finds the small of my back and pushes me forward.

"Come on, Millchild," says the Guard, "you're holding up the line."

I swallow hard, wanting to point out that there is no line, but it's too late. The gates start to pull shut, and I'm forced to grab the cart tight and run at the gap between them before they close.

I barely get through in time, and the gates shut behind me with an almighty clang.

Wait. Did he call me a Millchild?

I guess there's a first time for everything.

The streets themselves feel claustrophobic. Cramped and noisy and sweaty. I feel like the people who live here probably seek some kind of comfort from it, but not me. I'm terrified. People pass by as if I'm not even there. As I walk steadily down the road, most don't even stop for the cart. They just stride past, talking to one another or to their Hoverbots.

We have Hoverbots at the Mill, but they're Guard equipment. Small, floating, blipping things that seem to obey all sorts of orders. They're mostly for surveillance, from what I've seen – but the people here seem to use them like personal assistants, making them carry hot coffee on thin platforms or map out routes on strange, holographic screens.

The buildings around me are like nothing I've ever seen. Most have no doors to speak of, huge glass windows and a seemingly endless number of floors. I crane my neck to look at the nearest building, but no matter how far back I lean, I still can't see to the top.

My knees shudder as I work my way through the streets. Every so often something soars overhead – I don't know quite what it is, but it's large and metal and roars as it goes by. I imagine it's some kind of transport system, only somehow they've made it fly rather than roll along the ground. Very unlike the trundling ATVs we use back home.

I pull out the scrap of paper that Rian gave me. It's got a rough idea of where I need to go on it, so for now I just head in that direction. Every so often I consider stopping and asking for directions, but then I make eye contact with someone and lose my nerve.

The people here look so different. At the Mill, everyone is fairly strong. We're all burnt dark from the sun. We all wear the same shades of grey and russet brown. But here? Everyone is tall, slim, pale. They wear modest clothes in block colours, though white is by far the most common. Some women wear bizarre shoes that have spikes at the back, forcing them to walk on their toes. I can't fathom why anyone would wear something like that. But every so often, someone breaks the pattern. They wear darker clothes, more revealing. They have jewellery in their nose or ears. They have brightly coloured hair that can't possibly be natural, and what looks like pictures etched into their skin. Others eye them curiously, like they're unsure what to think. And everyone stares at me like I'm an alien, a strange, short, dark creature they've never seen before.

I suppose it makes sense. We have different priorities at the Mill. Any of these people – these fragile, paper-thin people – would snap under the pressure of a single day's hard labour. Fashion and vanity simply isn't a factor back home. You can be as beautiful as you like but that won't help when you're knee-deep in mud, trying to capture an escaped bull before it destroys two years' worth of work.

Still, it feels odd. Eagen warned me about the dark, told me not to catch anyone's attention. But that's easier said than done. While nobody dares approach me, their eyes linger as they pass. They watch me closely, tracing the way my arms and legs shift, how my muscles tense. I suppose I must seem pretty strange to them. I wonder if they're even half as scared of me as I am of them. I tell myself they're more scared. That they see me as a threat. Like a spider afraid of a bird.

The streets are complicated. I had assumed it would be like the corn fields where, though you can't see where you're headed, there's at least a clear sense of direction.

But here – nothing. The buildings are too tall and look too similar, and when I look up I can't even find the sun to follow. This is strange. I can feel it in every step, every breath. My little outburst on the boat has worked to ease my nerves, to distract me momentarily from the concern twisting in my gut, but now that worry has been replaced by an unusual sensation. Something akin to curiosity, intermingled with fear and resentment. I want to know everything about this place; but I also want to run away and never come back.

"Excuse me."

Someone steps in front of me, and I stumble to a stop. The girl in front of me is around my age, her body swathed in a white summer dress. I find myself wondering how well the garment would hold up against mud, but I shake the thought away.

"Yes?"

She bats her lashes at me, reaching back to toy with a strand of straw-coloured hair. I notice that her eyes are blue, like mine, but somehow completely different. Hers are bright, piercing, a little unnerving. When she smiles, there's a gap between her front teeth.

"I couldn't help but notice that you're not from around here. I thought I'd come over and see if I can help."

I pause. In truth, I would love to ask directions. It would help to know that I'm at least headed the right way. But then I remember what Eagen said, that look in his eye as he warned me not to trust anyone in the streets.

"Thank you, but I'm okay."

"Are you sure?" she asks in a singsong voice, "I'd be more than happy to help."

I bite back a scowl. This is exactly what Eagen warned me about. Since I've got here, I've been looked at in much the same way that a hunter looks at its prey. Mildly threatening, suspicious. It's alarming that this girl should suddenly be so friendly.

"I'm fine," I say, more firmly this time, "I know where I'm going. I've been here before."

Somehow, despite my smile as I speak, the words still come out sounding like a lie. Still, she seems to accept it as she steps out of the way.

"Well if you're sure. Please, go ahead."

There's definitely something wrong. Her voice is just that bit too high, her smile a tad too broad. There's something sickeningly sweet about her that doesn't suit anyone else here. Still, there's nothing I can do, so I simply smile and walk past her, taking care to match her sweetness when I speak.

"Have a great day."

Have a great day. Ugh. I'm such an idiot.

I stop in my tracks and stare down at the floor, my breathing shallow. I've been walking for hours in what I had assumed was the right direction. I yank the map out of my pocket and examine it, once again staring at the arrow Rian marked on the paper.

I don't get it. I'm exactly where I should be. I've followed every cue, tracked every turn. I should at least be close by now. But the streets all look the same to me, and as I glance overhead I can see the sky growing dark. I've been here all day. My stomach grumbles and I let out a frustrated growl.

At this rate, I'll be here all night, too.

Oddly, I find myself thinking about Nel. Night is falling, so she's probably wrapping up right now. Is she on dinner duty tonight? Am I? I can barely remember. What has realistically been only a few days feels like a lifetime, like I've been away from home for years. I'm starting to miss it.

I miss falling asleep and waking up in a room full of people. The familiar breathing, the warmth of their bodies. I miss serving up dinner, sneaking the older guys a little extra food out of respect. I especially miss staying up at night, or hanging back in the morning to spend a minute or two with Nel before another day's work.

I wonder if she misses me. This wouldn't be the first time we've been apart, but how much does she know? Knowing Nel, she's got mixed feelings about it. She's probably angry at me for not helping Kane. She's probably also mad at Kane. I feel my hands clench at the thought of her wrath. I wish I could speak to her.

The streets are quieter now, nearly abandoned, and I find myself on edge. This is precisely what I was warned about. This isn't me. I'm not the type to wander in the dark, confused and afraid. Frustration flares in me and I turn, heading down an alleyway.

Eagen's voice rings in my head as I pull the cart down the narrow, winding alley. I still remember the way his eyes had widened as he warned me, the hush in his voice when he told me about those who would want to hurt me. It's enough to make me quicken my pace a little.

It's not me. I don't cower and hide, and I certainly don't allow myself to be beaten back by fear. I have no reason to be afraid. I'm bigger and stronger than anything I'll meet in these parts.

"There you are."

I freeze. Someone steps out from the shadows just ahead of me, and immediately I recognise the form. The slow movement, the way one hand lifts to twirl a lock of hair.

"I've been looking everywhere for you."

I tense at the sound of that sickly sweet voice.

"Y-you know, a girl like you shouldn't be out here alone in the dark," I reply, "who knows what could happen."

She flips her hair and lets out a high-pitched giggle. I briefly consider running; but the alley is too small to turn the cart. I would have to reverse out. I take a moment to remind myself of her size. She's about my height, but seems to suffer from that common city issue of being slim and frail-looking. Unless she has a gun, I've nothing to fear.

"Please don't worry for my sake," she smiles, "I have my friends."

As if on cue, multiple somethings shift around me. Several shuffle forward, and suddenly I'm surrounded on all sides.

These people don't seem like they belong. They're big and tough, all scowling, all wearing dark colours. The girl stands out like a sore thumb, and suddenly I realise that's the point. If, earlier on, I had accepted her help, she'd probably have led me here. Perhaps reading my mind, she tilts her head and bats her lashes at me.

"I should have known," I sigh, "So what do you want?"

"Whatever you have in that cart."

That's it. No nonsense, no quibbles. The time for phony politeness and falsehoods is gone. Good. It was making me sick.

I cross my arms in front of me, flexing as I do so. I'm not stupid. I know I won't be able to beat them all. I don't have a violent bone in my body. But the fact remains that I cut an intimidating form. In all seriousness, I'm the one you wouldn't want to meet in a dark alley.

"Sorry. Not doing it."

She smirks again, and now I can see beyond the wide eyes and helpless expression. Now I can see the cruelty in her smile, that ruthlessness that separates her from civilised society. I feel my body tense. I'm not the type to fight. But if I return home without having made this delivery, I can look forward to another stint in the Mines. I remember the heat in my skin, the pain throughout my body. I remember seeing fire and darkness, and watching my own skin grow pale and paper-thin from lack of sun. If I have to choose, then I choose to fight.

One of the men lurches forward and my body moves instinctively. I tense and swing hard, feeling my knuckles collide with the side of his jaw. He's floored by the blow, but now the alley is filled with yells. They come at me from all sides and I lash out again, more confident this time. Years of hard labour have worked in my favour; as I strike, I can feel all of my strength coiling in my arm. Their blows may hurt – but mine send them sprawling.

In the midst of the fight, I find myself panicking. There are too many – and even if I could fight them, I don't want to. My chest swirls with the same horror I felt when Kane hit Wirrow. It's too similar. The starting blow, the overwhelming numbers.

The inevitable end.

In only a minute or so I find myself pinned to the ground, staring at the cobblestones. Several of the men nurse bruises – and with a hint of pleasure, I realise that one figure is still motionless. My face is sore and swollen, and I can feel the familiar sensation of a developing bruise across one eye. I can vaguely taste blood.

I hate this. I hate where I am and what I'm doing, and I hate that it's come to this. I don't know these people. I don't care about them. I feel no sense of loyalty towards Rian. I'm just reacting out of fear. I remember the look in Kane's eye just before he snapped, that ferocity and strength. I don't have that. I don't have a reason to fight.

"Let's move this out of the way," says the girl, striding past without a word. She doesn't even look my way. As far as she's concerned, I'm one of many victims. Suddenly, a part of me looks forward to being dumped here. Maybe I'll scrape a few hours of uneasy sleep before I have to face the shameful walk home.

I hear a scuffle, and dismiss it. They're probably having trouble moving the cart. I find that funny; they can pin me without too much trouble, and then can't shift what I've spent three days carrying. I resist the urge to scoff.

But the sound seems to get louder, and suddenly it's punctuated by yelps. Another fight. I close my eyes a little, desperate to block out the sound. I don't want to see or hear this. I'll just sit here, pinned against the cobbles, and wait until it's over.

The two men holding me shift away and I gasp for air, taking advantage of the brief reprieve before sitting up and shuffling back against the wall. I make an effort to sink into the shadows.

There is a fight going on – but it's not one-sided. Shadowy figures seem to lurch from the darkness, and I can't tell who's who. But they do. There's a general sense of chaos as a dozen people fight; and over all of it, I hear a voice. It's bored-sounding and sarcastic, but there's a youthful vibrancy to it that strikes me as somehow exciting.

"Oh come on! Guys, this is overboard. Just quit it."

As if on cue, the fighting comes to an abrupt end. The tension is still there, though, so thick in the air that I can nearly taste it.

Someone hops down over the cart, and I find myself staring.

CHAPTER EIGHT

The woman in front of me is gorgeous. She's tall, with a body the shape of an hourglass and a shock of fire-engine red hair. She has a sharp face with bright green eyes and a number of metallic piercings in her ears and nose. Her brows are thin and high, making her seem permanently surprised. She's unlike anyone else I've seen - but somehow, she exudes wit and charm. Her hips wiggle as she walks, and I can see the men around her starting to weaken.

"This is ridiculous," she continues, again in that vibrant voice, "Luse, you promised you wouldn't mug people around here anymore."

"I can conduct business anywhere I want," scowls the blonde girl.

"No, you can't. Look, we don't agree with what you're doing here, but we're not going to report you to the Guard because you sympathise with the cause. But this isn't helping anyone. It draws attention to the area, and that's the last thing we want."

Luse takes a pointed step back – and suddenly, all the cruelty is gone from her face. She gives a small, sad nod, and turns away.

"Fine. We'll spread it out a little. Can you tidy up this mess for us?"

The red-haired woman smiles.

"Sure. Just go."

She waits until the group is out of sight before moving again. When she does, she heaves a long sigh at the sight of the cart.

"Great. Look what they took this time. Where the heck's the owner?"

"Probably long gone," a male voice replies, "we'd better just move this out of here."

"Hold up. I'm going to have a look round."

She turns her head, and our eyes meet in the darkness. I find myself standing. It's strange. The way she looks at me both unnerves and encourages me. Those shocking green eyes, that easy expression. It's like the whole world is hers – and damn it, that doesn't even bother me.

"Oh, damn," she grimaces, "I take it you're the owner of this cart?"

I can feel the bruise still blossoming over one eye, but with a quick movement I wipe away what little blood was still smeared across one cheek.

"Yes."

She looks me up and down, curiosity in her eyes. I know what she's thinking – who am I? What am I doing, and why here of all places? But then she seems to relax, those tadpole-like eyebrows settling into position.

"You're from The Mill, aren't you? What's your name?"

"Noah."

"Hey. Listen, I'm sorry about those idiots. They do this all the time. We've asked them to stay away from this area, but... ooh, you're bleeding."

I give a dismissive wave of the hand.

"It's fine. I've had worse."

It's true. As I draw myself up to full height, I can barely feel it. It's painfully familiar, the pulsing under my skin, but it doesn't bother me. Accidents happen when chopping wood or digging holes - I've given myself enough black eyes in my time to not be bothered by a minor bruise or graze.

"It's not fine. Come on, I'll clean you up."

"I'm okay."

"Where are you headed?"

I shake my head.

"I shouldn't say."

She purses her lips, but seems to accept it.

"Fine. Well, if you're sure. I wish you'd let me patch you up though."

I open my mouth to refuse just as someone reaches for her shoulder.

"Pan. I don't know if we should..."

"Pan?!"

I say it louder than I intended to; they both stare.

"Sorry. It's just that... this delivery is for you."

Her face breaks into a smile. It's a strange expression. People don't smile and laugh like this at the Mill. Not to say we can't, just that we don't smile so easily.

"Really? Wow, now I really am glad we recovered it! I don't think Rian would be impressed if we had to ask for this a third time."

I blink a little, confused that she would know Rian directly, but decide not to question it. Everything's easier if you don't ask questions.

"Well, now you definitely have to come in," Pan smiles, "You've come so far to bring this to us, I couldn't possibly let you leave in that state."

I hesitate for a moment, sucking at my lip. While it's true that the pain is minimal, I can't say I feel confident to walk back out into the street. I glance down; my grey jacket is stained and torn from the scuffle.

"I suppose it wouldn't hurt to get cleaned up a bit."

Pan and the others lead me to an alleyway across the street. For some reason, none of the others bother to engage me in conversation, or even look my way. I can't say I blame them – they're city folk and I'm just a farmhand... or as they might say, a Millchild. It makes sense that they wouldn't want to lower themselves by talking to someone so far below their station.

Still, Pan is wonderful. Even as we walk in silence, she takes care to glance my way. Her eyes glitter with a confidence and intelligence beyond her years, and when she smiles it's like I'm a child again, watching the Guards go by. Respect fills my chest. I don't imagine she's more than five years older than me, if that – and yet she's unlike anyone else I've ever met.

We eventually reach a metal shutter door embedded in the wall of a building. I glance up. The structure itself is unspectacular, at least compared to those around it. Tall and glass and twisting up into the clouds. But as Pan raps a strange melody on the corrugated metal, there's a little spark in her eye. Like something exciting is about to happen.

When the shutter door opens, I find myself ushered in. Someone pulls the cart away and a firm hand finds my back in the ensuing darkness. I stagger as we reach steps, but those around me seem to float down them with ease. I suppose it's second nature to them.

Briefly, I wonder who these people are. It seems strange that in a city full of glass and open doors, this particular group would need to have a lock, let alone a secret knock. But again, questioning it would be far more trouble than it's worth. I'm here to clean up, unload, grab the empty cart and go. The remnants of the fight are still flickering in me. I never wanted to hurt anyone. I just wanted to get the job done and hurry home. I fight to keep my hands from shaking.

Lights flicker on overhead, and I find myself standing in a strange, metallic room. I blink in the harsh fluorescent light, gazing around at the space. Everything is metal – the floors, the walls, even the ceiling. The room is lined with computers that whir and beep. A large metal door blocks entrance to the rest of the place. Everything seems to be locked and protected, heavily defended for some unknown reason.

A young man stands on the other side of the room, ticking something on a clipboard. I'm surprised to see he's not much older than me – he has a small, sharp face with close-clipped dark hair and nearly-black eyes. An advanced-looking blue Hoverbot lingers nearby, as though monitoring his every action. He nudges his glasses up his nose and gasps when he sees us enter.

"What the – Pan? Who is this?"

Pan gives an idle shrug, rolling her eyes and tugging off her jacket. The outfit she wears beneath is hardly deserving of being called clothes, and I can feel her drawing the gaze of the men who follow us into the room. Something churns uncomfortably in my stomach.

"Calm down, Jensen. This is Noah. She's from the Mill."

Jensen scowls, first at me and then at her. The others scuttle from the room, as if sensing the rising tension.

"You can't just bring people in here. Do you even know who she is?"

"I just told you. Noah."

He slaps one hand to his forehead and sighs.

"That's not an answer. She could be a spy."

Pan scoffs.

"Come on. Does she look like a spy to you?"

"No. That's the point."

Pan turns away and reaches for a small box. She pulls out a rag and dampens it with something – she pushes it against my eye and I jump back, surprised to find that it's cold.

"She got hurt looking for us, Jensen. The least we can do is help out."

She nudges the rag a little closer, and I'm pleasantly surprised by how nice it feels. It's strange; we never treat these things at the Mill. I've had black eyes before – but they've been left to nearly close up from the swelling before healing on their own. This seems much more gentle.

"There," she smiles, "is that better?"

I give a small nod. I wish I could say more, thank her for her kindness – but then Jensen catches my eye and the sides of his mouth draw down in a grimace. He regards me like someone might regard a bug or a rat, or perhaps a particularly stinking pile of manure.

"I don't trust her. We need to do something."

Pan sighs again.

"What do you want me to do, Jensen? Tie up and cross-examine every person who comes near us?"

"I don't mean that. But maybe we should run her DNA through the public database, just in case."

"Fine. If it's the only way to get you to drop it, we'll do that."

She pulls away, passing me the rag. I take it to dab at the bloodstains on my jacket. While it wouldn't be the first time I've walked around covered in blood, it probably wouldn't look great if I returned to the Mill like this.

"Noah," Pan says, "I was wondering if you wouldn't mind us doing a test."

I pause, lowering the rag to my lap. Any other time, I'd say no. I'd pull away and refuse. But there's something about her, about the way she holds herself, the way her smile is both gentle and gutsy at the same time – I can't help but trust her.

"Sure. What test?"

"It's a blood test. We just want to check that you are who you say you are, by checking your DNA against the Citizen System."

I don't bother to ask what the Citizen System is. Instead I draw back, suspicion building.

"Blood test?"

She nods.

"Yep. Just one prick of your finger with a needle, and we can check it. Takes thirty seconds and won't hurt a bit, I promise."

"What are you hoping to find?" I ask, finally garnering the confidence to raise my voice a little.

"Simple. The System has the stored DNA data of everyone in Thorne. If you're from the city, when we check your DNA you'll show up, and we'll know exactly who you are."

"But I'm not from the city," I point out, "so I won't be on your System."

She seems to mull this over for a moment, chewing idly on her bottom lip.

"True. I suppose that'll prove it."

"Fine. I don't get it, but sure. It's just blood, right?"

Jensen sits me down on a metallic bench and prods the very tip of my finger with a needle. I find it hard to hide my surprise that he does it so easily – my hands are thick with scar from years of physical work, and it seems strange that a needle could pierce my skin so well.

As Jensen steps away to fiddle with something on one of the many computers, Pan takes a seat next to me.

"Do you mind if I ask something?"

"Sure."

She tosses her head back, nudging a crimson lock from her face.

"You don't seem fazed by any of this. I think that's why Jensen is so on edge. You didn't seem scared when you got attacked by Luse and the others, or when we brought you in here and took your blood. It's kind of suspicious that you would be so relaxed about this when none of it makes any sense to you."

I give a small shrug. I don't feel like explaining life at the Mill to her. I only care about getting this over with and leaving with the sunrise.

"It's not that I'm not surprised," I mutter, "I just figure it's easier not to freak myself out by questioning things all the time."

She watches me closely, and there's a strange expression akin to sadness on her face.

"You never question... anything?"

"What's the point? It's easier for everyone if we just get on with it."

At that she looks away, breaking the strange eye contact she's been holding with me. I don't know what she's thinking. Perhaps she's looking down on me with pity or sorrow, full of sympathy for the poor, stupid farm girl who doesn't understand the world around her. Maybe she's annoyed. Perhaps I've done or said something that's offensive to her. Frankly, I don't care. I'm looking forward to getting out of here.

I toy idly with my thumbs, grazing them over one another. I can feel the ridges in my skin, the scars on my knuckles that are so familiar at this point. Although it's hard work, there's a strong sense of satisfaction that comes with manual labour. I can feel a rush of anticipation. I can't wait to get home. Back to the Mill. Back to my crappy little camp bed right underneath that hole. I don't care if it rains for a week once I get back. I'll happily lie in the rain-soaked bunk without a word of complaint.

I've only been gone a few days, but it feels like much longer. There's an odd feeling in my stomach, a swirling, churning sensation that I now recognise as homesickness. I just want to get back and see Nel and Kane –

Oh.

My hands tighten as I remember his face. Stupid kid. He could have done well. He could have learned the joy that comes from a hard day's work. But for whatever reason, he threw it away.

That night on the boat hasn't completely wiped away my fear. There's nothing I can do about it now, no reason to look back and dissect his actions from that day. The guilt's still there, though, filling me like smoke, mixing with the homesickness to become something black and foul-feeling.

"So," Pan continues, "What's it like at the Mill?"

"It's okay. Hard work."

She puffs out her cheeks. Typical. Here, they can afford the luxury of being unimpressed by my lack of conversational skills. But if I don't need to say it, then why should I?

"Oh my god."

Jensen's standing over the console, his eyes fixed on the screen. I can't see what it says; I don't think it would make much sense to me anyway. But his eyes are wide, and his jaw has dropped, and suddenly my stomach shifts. Something's wrong.

Beside me, Pan groans.

"Calm down, Jensen. What is it?"

He turns, his eyes shifting from the console to me. I can feel his face travelling the length of my body. It's uncomfortable, and I shuffle away a little. Eventually his eyes settle on my face, and he finally manages to pull his mouth shut.

"I should have known. Same eyes."

Pan huffs.

"What the hell are you talking about?"

When he speaks, his voice is unsteady, unsure, like he's both scared and happy at the same time.

"This girl... it's Ada."

Pan gasps and jumps to her feet. Her face is the picture of shock, and she pulls away from me like she's scared I might bite her.

"No way. That's impossible. Are you messing with me?"

Jensen gestures towards the console.

"Look for yourself, if you don't believe me."

She does as she's told, scurrying over to the console where she stands frozen.

"Damn. You're right."

He sits next to me, one hand reaching over and grasping mine. The motion is so far removed from what I've seen from him that I wrench my hand from his grip.

"What? What's going on?"

My mind races. What could they have seen when they ran the scan? What's Ada and what does it mean to be one? Is there something wrong with me? Are they going to attack?

But then I look at Jensen. His brows are furrowed, his eyes filled with concern. He leans forward, and when he next speaks, his voice is soft.

"What's your name?"

"Noah."

"And your second name?"

I shake my head, and he frowns.

"You don't use them?

"No."

His mouth tightens.

"Have you ever been here before? Does the Cull mean anything to you?"

I consider this.

"I've not been here before. But the word Cull means something to me. We often go through and do culls on the vermin animals at the Mill. Foxes and the like."

"Nothing else?"

"No."

He falls silent, and now it's my turn to stare.

"Why are you asking me all this? I'm just here to drop off this delivery. As soon as I unload it, I'll be going."

The two exchange confused looks, and Pan takes a hesitant step forward.

"A... Noah? Do you have any siblings?"

I shrug.

"Probably. I wouldn't know. My parents and I aren't exactly on speaking terms. Haven't seen them since I was about... eleven?"

Another exchanged look.

"What are your parents' names?"

"No clue. Don't really remember them."

She opens her mouth, then closes it, then repeats like she's not sure what to say. I lean forward, placing my elbows on my knees and setting my jaw.

"Enough? What's with all the probing?"

Pan bites her lip so hard that I swear I can see blood pooling around her teeth.

"We have our reasons. This is big and it's really not down to me to say. I need to introduce you to someone. Will you come with me?"

I hesitate. I don't want to. I don't care about these people and their problems, and I certainly have no interest in making friends. I just want to go home.

Still. There's something about the way they're talking, the renewed interest in their eyes, that draws my attention. Concern and shock and relief all rolled into one. I can't just walk out of here now. Not after seeing their reactions - I have to see this through.

So instead, I heave a weary sigh and stand.

"Fine. But if I come with you, then you owe me an explanation. What this place is, why you're so secretive. Everything."

If I'm going to do this anyway, I may as well try to get something from it. A good story to tell Nel when I finally get home. Pan gives a small, satisfied smile.

"I'd say that's fair. Come on."

Pan and Jensen lead me through a maze of long, metal tunnels. They weave together, twisting this way and that, endlessly confusing. I try to remember every turn we make in case I need to find my own way back, but I quickly lose track.

"This can't be inside that building," I mutter, "are we underground?"

"Something like that," she replies. Behind me, I can feel Jensen shuffling. His Hoverbot lurks behind me, now watching my every move, and I'm sure he's instructed it to do so. Even now there's some strange tension between us, like he's not quite sure of me. I'm probably not helping the situation with my own suspicions, either.

As we walk, I start to doubt my own decision. I'm supposed to be gone by now. The journey here was horrendous; the journey back will likely be worse. I remember the sound of the ocean, the way the floor of the boat had swayed beneath me. The endlessly long road into the city. I don't even want to think about how difficult it will be to find my way home.

This is a good distraction, if nothing else.

Pan glances back at me. There's something new in her expression now – an excitement, a sense of anticipation. I swallow hard and hope that her amusement doesn't come at my expense.

What am I doing here? These are total strangers, and they could be crazy. I could be walking into a trap. This is ridiculous. Not to mention that Wirrow would beat me over the head if he knew I was straying from my instructions for even a moment.

But the way she looks at me, I feel something akin to respect. She's like Nel, if only she were harder and braver. For some reason, I trust her. I can't help it.

Pan throws out a hand to stop me as we reach a heavy steel door. There's a small window inset into it, but it's blacked over. She looks me up and down, pursing her lips.

"Listen. I know this is confusing. Fair warning, this is going to be intense. But you can trust me."

I cross my arms and look pointedly away.

"Thanks, but I don't especially trust you."

The lie feels awful on my tongue, but it has to be done. There's no reasonable way to explain blind trust of a stranger. I barely understand it myself.

She doesn't seem to mind, though. Most would be offended. There are few who would stay silent at that insult, even back at the Mill. If I'd said that to another farm worker, I'd expect a snide response and the cold shoulder for a few weeks. But Pan just shrugs it off.

She taps a code into the keypad on the wall, then nudges the door open.

"Brace yourself."

It's another room. Just like the others it's made entirely of metal, but there are some homey touches. There's a glass door across the room, and through it I can see a mass of other floors, areas and open-topped spaces. This place must be as big as the Farm – perhaps even bigger.

There are sofas in the corners, a large mahogany desk and leather chair, and a small white machine propped up against one wall which I recognise as a coffee maker, just like the ones the Guards have back home. What always seemed like a very minor luxury has always confused me; what's so great about bean water?

My pondering is suddenly interrupted when someone turns around. I hadn't even noticed him as he had stood motionless by the glass, watching over the goings-on outside his little shell. But now he moves, and my eye is immediately drawn to him.

He's a stocky man, a few years older than me. He sports dirty blonde hair and dusty blue eyes, and there's a spike-like piece of metal through one ear – a fashion statement, I can only assume. He's heavy-browed and broad-shouldered, giving off a definite air of authority. His eyes meet mine and he stiffens.

"Who the hell is this?" he snaps at Pan, "will you stop bringing randomers in here? And Jensen, you and that

Hoverbot of yours are supposed to be the second level of defence. Why didn't you stop her?"

Jensen shuffles uncomfortably.

"T-there's a good reason for this, honest."

Pan clears her throat. A moment later I feel her hand on the small of my back, nudging me forward and into the centre of the room. Suddenly, I feel very exposed under the fluorescent light.

"Jay, this is Noah. She was sent from the Mill to bring us those supplies we asked Rian for."

The man looks me up and down, his expression a mix of suspicion and utter boredom.

"And let me guess. You found yourself taken by our way of life, and want to join the cause?"

He pauses, rubbing at his head with an exasperated sigh.

"Well, I suppose you wouldn't be the first. Still, this isn't something you should be bothering me with in the dead of night. You should have just taken this girl down to Nate."

With that he turns away, a hint of disgust on his face. Confusion fills my chest. Is this why I was brought here? What's this 'cause' they keep talking about?

"Well, about that..."

Pan steps forward and smiles, wrapping an arm around me. It's an uncomfortable motion, one that suggests familiarity – I fight the urge to pull away.

"What?"

"Luse and some of the others tried to rob her on the way here. We explained everything and got things settled, but I brought her in to get cleaned up."

He growls.

"What did I just say about bringing in randomers? This is kind of a covert operation."

Jensen pipes up now, his voice suddenly less harsh.

"I wasn't happy either. So I ran her through the system."

That makes him stop. He looks at me with renewed interest, his eyes travelling the length of my body. His mouth contorts into an uneasy grimace.

"Do I need to call for backup?"

I tense, somehow finding the confidence to speak up.

"No, you don't."

He raises an eyebrow at that, and I feel like I should flinch away. There's something about him that demands respect, a certain ferocity burning behind those hazy eyes. There's an awkward moment as we size each other up, but then Pan and Jensen exchange an excited glance.

"Jay. This is Ada."

Jay's reaction is instantaneous. He stares at me, wide-eyed, his body tensed like he thinks I might tackle him.

"D-don't be ridiculous," he blurts, "is this some kind of joke? Because if it is, it's not funny and I have half a mind to kick you both out of here."

Pan shakes her head.

"It's not a joke. We checked her blood against the database. See for yourself if you don't believe us."

He looks me up and down again, but this time he seems to be looking for something in particular. It makes me a little uncomfortable to be stared at like this. It's been a good many years since anyone's paid me this much attention.

"B-but this doesn't make any sense. It isn't possible. It must be a trap."

"No trap here," I answer, "I have no idea what I'm even doing here."

His eyes narrow, suspicion building.

"What... who are you?"

"I know who I am," I bite back, "clearly it's you who can't figure it out."

I glance back at Pan and set my jaw.

"Is this it? Can I go now?"

She ignores me, instead talking to Jay.

"See? Rian must have figured out who she was and sent her. He must have known this would happen."

"Seems unlikely," Jensen interjects, "we don't normally test everyone who comes by. Rian couldn't have known that we would this time round."

The two begin to bicker over some strange technicalities, but the man in front of me just stares. Those dusty eyes take me in slowly, my stocky build and dark tan, my flop of unwashed, dirty blonde hair.

He does look familiar. Maybe it's the eyes.

I clear my throat.

"I hope you don't mind if I ask, but…who are you?"

His face falls at that. He glances back at Pan, who's fallen silent.

"She doesn't know me."

"It doesn't look like it."

With that he takes a step back, then turns away.

"I don't know what to think. Jensen, rerun the test. I need to see this with my own eyes."

Jensen takes more blood from my finger, and this time it's significantly more than just a drop. Whatever they're looking for, they apparently want to be certain.

As it runs through the system, though, the blonde man - Jay - watches me closely. His expression is a strange combination of delight and fear, like he's hoping for good news but simultaneously terrified of the results.

This time when the screen lights up, it's large enough that I can see it. The words themselves don't make an awful lot of sense to me - literacy isn't exactly an important skill back home - but there's a picture, too.

The girl on the screen is tiny, no more than two or three. She's got blonde hair scraped behind her head and a sweet smile. She's skinny and pale, and completely typical of the people I've seen in Thorne. Bright, pretty eyes stare from the screen.

Familiar.

Suddenly I'm standing, and as I walk towards the screen Jensen moves aside to let me see. The girl smiles back at me through the screen, unnervingly gentle. There's an undeniable air of innocence about her.

"W-who..."

It's familiar. But that doesn't make sense. There's nobody like this back at the Mill. I don't even think there's anyone like this back at Homestead. But I know this kid, even though I can't, even though it's impossible.

"Who is that?"

It's Jay who replies, his voice low and soft as he does so.

"That's Ada. That's my little sister."

"But... you said I was Ada."

To my surprise his eyes fill with tears, and he clenches the console behind him.

"Exactly."

CHAPTER NINE

I have to get out of here.

This is too much. I don't know who these people are, or what they want from me. This could be a lie – in fact, it has to be. Because there's no way they're right. These people must be crazy if they think I'm anyone other than Noah. Anything other than a Mill worker. Unless...

"Y-you don't look like the Mill type," I choke, "did you leave young?"

"Not exactly."

"Well, I...I mean, it's always nice to meet relatives. Like I said, I've known for years that I could have siblings in the Mill. We don't stay in touch with our parents, so..."

I falter at that. It's a somewhat feeble attempt at redirecting the conversation, but I'm convinced that this must be right. Because what they're suggesting is impossible.

He shakes his head sadly.

"Ada. What have they done to you?"

I stamp my foot.

"I-I'm not Ada! My name is Noah. Now, if you'll excuse me, I'm all cleaned up now. So I'll just go. Pan, thanks for the help."

"What?"

With that I'm gone, hurrying down the hallways that led me here. I don't really remember all the turns and twists we took, but I'm sure I can find my way out.

I just have to get away from them. Away from their new, scary ideas.

"Wait up!"

I hear footsteps behind me. They're approaching faster than I'm moving, and I don't have the confidence to run. I simply walk faster.

"it's fine," I lie, "I'll just get out of your way."

Suddenly there's a strong hand locked around my wrist, and I'm pinned firmly against the metal wall. Jay stands over me, both hands holding me in place. His face is a picture of conflict.

"Ada. Don't go. Just... listen to us."

"I'm not Ada!" I scream, "Let me go!"

"No. Not until you've heard me out."

I struggle against his grip, but he's got the advantage and my will is fading fast. Pan and Jensen stand by, and suddenly all the joy is gone from their faces. Their expressions are full of pity and sorrow, and I could swear that Pan brushes away a tear.

My chest hurts. Why won't they let me go?

"Please."

The room they place me in is dark. My vision's pretty good, all things considered; early mornings have allowed me to grow used to dim light. I've been in a place without any natural light only once before – but just thinking about the mines makes me shudder. It's about an hour until someone finally comes back.

The door behind me opens, then closes, and as the person steps up beside me I snap my eyes shut. I don't want to see them. Don't want to hear what they have to say.

"Noah."

They used my real name. I allow my eyes to slide open by the tiniest degree. Pan sits next to me, and on her face is that same confident, kind expression she greeted me with.

"I just want to talk to you. I think things got out of control."

"Oh, really? What gave you that idea?"

I bite back on my sarcasm, but it's too late. I shouldn't speak that way to my captors. Luckily, she doesn't seem to notice.

"I'm sorry. We dropped it all on you at once. We didn't explain."

"I don't care. I've done my job, now I just want to go home."

"Earlier, you asked to know everything. What changed?"

I laugh.

"Typically, when you tackle someone and trap them in a dark room, they're not so receptive to new ideas. I'm done with this. Please let me go home."

She sighs, then rests a warm hand on my arm. The motion is undeniably comforting; though I'd never admit it.

"Let me explain. Once I do, you'll be free to leave. Just give me a chance."

"There's not much to explain," I tell her, "you all seem to think I'm someone else."

"System's never been wrong before. As far as it knows, you're a citizen. Specifically, you're Ada Young. Age nineteen."

"But that's not my name."

She considers this.

"I suspect the Mill - or whoever took you there - probably designated a new name to you. Changed it. Along with whatever they did to your memories."

"My memories are just fine. The reason I don't remember him is because he's a stranger. I remember everything about my life upon leaving Homestead. If there was something before that, especially something important, I would remember."

She clearly disagrees, but I ignore her. It didn't happen. Nobody could take my memories away. Sure, the Guards back home have that technology, but they would never use it on me. I'm a model worker.

"Why would someone want to erase my memories, anyway?"

"That, we don't know. But there's a whole story here, and you need to understand that first. Once you do, we can try to find the answers to your questions. Are you willing to listen to me?"

I heave a sigh.

"I'm not getting out until I do, am I?"

"Not really, no."

"Fine."

Pan sits opposite me, hands folded in her lap. It's so quiet that I shuffle a little in my seat, eager to make any kind of noise to break through the silence.

"So, who are you?" I ask. Sympathy crosses her face briefly but she pushes it aside, drawing the corners of her lips back into an understanding smile.

"We're called the Clover. We're a protest group - or at least, that's how it started. These days we mostly work underground. There have been warrants out for our arrests for years now."

"What are you protesting?"

"The Cull."

That word, again. We have culls at home. I've lost track of how many times I've been sent out, battered shotgun in hand, to destroy the excess bulls or hunt down some foxes when they've broken into the pens one too many times. I can't say I ever liked doing it; it always felt wrong, unfair. They don't even stand a chance. But it's necessary, especially the bulls. They require too much care, too much attention. We simply couldn't spare all that they needed.

Pan's hands tighten a little, her knuckles turning white.

"The Cull is carried out by Thorne's three leaders. It's... well..."

"Population control, right?"

"How did you know?"

I shrug.

"We do them at the Mill. Too many animals. So we trim the fat, get rid of a percentage of them."

She leans back in the chair and sighs, seemingly pleased that she didn't have to explain it to me.

"That's about right. But the Cull here isn't with animals."

"It's not?"

"No."

I meet her eyes, expecting her to continue, but instead she stands and begins to pace.

"Thorne is drowning under the weight of its own people," she explains, "just like at your Mill. Too many people. Not enough of anything. There were all kinds of methods to begin with, tricks our leaders used to try to control it. Nothing worked. Eventually, they reached breaking point."

My gut clenches. I'd thought hauling away useless animals was bad enough. But to do it to people - who likely weren't useless at all - makes my stomach churn.

"That's sick."

She nods sadly.

"Exactly. Every year they remove a percentage of the population. Specifically, those who are three and under. They're taken away and killed."

I don't know what to say to that. Her face is creased with grief and anger, and though I understand why, I don't know how to react. So instead I settle for staring at my hands, examining the scars there.

"That's why we're fighting. That's why we're hidden away underground, too. We're trying to figure out how to stop the Cull."

"Why does it happen in the first place? Why does everyone let it happen?"

I can't imagine having a family. It's not something that's ever mattered to me, not even for a moment. But when I think of Nel with her sparkling eyes or Kane with his eternal bad attitude, something hot burns in my chest. If someone pulled them away from me, tried to kill them... I like to think I'd stop it.

Kane's betrayed expression flashes in my head and I shake the thought away. No. Maybe I wouldn't, after all.

"They tried," Pan says, "to begin with. But those people were killed, too. Publicly. Eventually, people just learned to accept it."

"I don't understand. Why?"

"Because we're helpless. We don't have any choice in the matter anymore, and it's what we know now. It's been going on for so long. Nobody knows any different."

I suck on my teeth.

"That's a poor excuse, if you ask me."

"Precisely."

"So what does this have to do with me?"

She stops her pacing at that. Her expression is suddenly reproachful.

"You were taken."

Her voice is so soft that for a moment I'm not certain that I've really heard it. But there they are, the words hanging in the air between us. An idea so preposterous that I have to bite back on a laugh and remind myself that this is serious.

"I think you might be wrong about that."

"I'm not," she insists, "you were born here, to your Mother, Father... you had an older brother called Jay. But at the age of three, you were taken during the annual Cull. And executed."

"But... I'm alive."

She laughs out loud, and the sound is gorgeous and infectious and magnificent, but I find myself cringing away from it. Terrified by it.

"That's the point!" she cries, "that's why we were so shocked!"

In an instant she's sobered up, regarding me with a renewed sense of curiosity. I could swear I see the glimmer of tears in her eyes.

"Jay was told you'd been killed sixteen years ago. Your parents... it's what inspired them to fight. That's why they... oh, but that's not important right now. The key thing is that you're back. You've returned home."

My head spins. She sounds insane – but there's something in her voice, a sweetness, a sincerity, that feels like her words could almost be true. Even if they're not – and they can't possibly be – I can't help but think she believes them.

I'd love to shout her down and run away. It'd be easy; she's taller than me, but I outweigh her. I could wriggle from her grip easily and race off before they could catch me. I could forget everything she's told me and go back to the Mill. Pretend this never happened.

It would be easy.

Instead, I find myself leaning forward.

"But... why wouldn't I remember? If I were three, I'd remember something. A face, a name. Something."

"I don't know. But you don't remember the people who raised you, right? Maybe it got wiped somehow."

"The Mill Guards do have a way, but it can't wipe everything. Only a few weeks."

"They could have found a way to make it stronger."

"I just don't know. Besides, the Mill is where I belong. Look at me. I'm not city material and you know it."

"You were once."

She's keeping her distance, but I can still feel her eyes on me. I sigh.

"What do you want from me?"

"Just stay. Reconnect with Jay. Maybe join in on our little cause."

The thought of returning to Wirrow later than normal, or not at all, is unnerving. I'd rather not imagine the beating I'd receive for even trying to escape. Besides, I had my chance to piss them off. I decided against it then, so why would I change my mind now?

"I have to go back."

"You have a month, right? That's normally the rule. I have allies in the Guard on the city limit. We can arrange a safe passage back for you, it would only take two days to return. So you still have over three weeks spare."

I almost laugh at the notion of 'spare time'. The luxuries of city folk never cease to amaze me.

"I really should go back."

"Don't you want to get to know your brother?"

"Listen. I always figured that I had siblings somewhere. That's not some big revelation - my parents are back at Homestead, as far as I know. I don't care about getting to know them or even trying to remember them, so why would I be interested in a brother? Besides, doesn't your little theory all rely on one computer system's say so? That doesn't prove anything."

"Oh."

Pan seems visibly crestfallen at that, and though she opens her mouth to object she shuts it again, considering what I've said.

"So if we can prove it, you'll stay for a little while? You'll give it a chance?"

"I'm not interested in family."

"But you'll try?"

I bite my lip. Family means something different here, doesn't it? Just like Nel always said. I remember the sadness in her eyes when she had to separate the calves from the cows, the way her fingers clenched at her side when the other girls were taken to Homestead.

Outside of the Mill, family isn't just a stranger you happen to share genes with. They raise you, care for you, love you. If what they're saying is true, did I have that kind of family? Jay doesn't seem much like the loving type. Even so, who cares? But then Pan looks at me with those pretty eyes, pulling her face into that pretty smile.

It won't hurt to stay a few days.

"I suppose I can't head out tonight anyway. It's too dark to unload things and I don't know my way back to the gate."

I don't even know if I could find my way home. The likelihood of stumbling across another truck willing to take me back are slim to none, and when I think about wandering the city streets in the darkness, something akin to fear shivers through me.

"We can help you get back," Pan tells me, "the return journey will take a day, two max. So stay. Just for say, four days. That's all."

I consider that. Has Nel started to worry about me yet? Has she been told why I'm gone? It's dark out; is she lying on her crappy little campbed, surrounded by gentle snores, wondering where I am?

My chest hurts at the thought.

But if she knew what was going on, that I may - potentially - have found a family, she'd be furious with me for even considering leaving. I don't want to imagine what she'd say if I told her I'd come back early and passed up this chance, however small it may be.

"Four days. That's all."

She nods.

"That's all I ask."

Pan doesn't force me to talk to anyone else. She leads me from the room and through yet another darkened, metal hallway. I glance behind as we walk, but there's nothing and no one behind us.

"Where are we going?" I dare to ask.

"It's late. It was late when you got here, and now it's about..."

She steals a glance at her watch, then grimaces.

"...Never mind. It's late, let's just leave it at that."

She yanks open one of the heavy steel doors and I wince as it squeals against its frame.

"This place is definitely underground, isn't it?"

"You figured that out right away. How?"

"I've been underground before. It's a similar feeling."

That's only half-true, though. The Mines were cold and dark too, only much, much colder and nearly impossibly dark. It's hard to break through rock and dirt with only the strength in your arms – it's even harder to do that when you can't see anything, not even your own hand in front of your face.

The room we step into is unlike the ones before. Sure, it's dark and dank and metal-clad, but there's something different. Two beds are nestled in the corner, and while one is empty and not dissimilar from my familiar campbed, the other contains a mass of brightly coloured blankets. Strings of beads hang from the ceiling, looping around the buzzing fluorescent lights overhead. In the corner, there's a rickety table and chairs, a small wooden cupboard, and an electric fly killer that crackles as we enter.

"Homey."

I bite back on the words, but it's too late. Whoops. Her living space is still a hundred times better than mine, and a thousand times better than anywhere I've slept in the past two days. I close my eyes and remember trying to lie back in a hammock, only to shudder and tumble at every movement. Anything's better than that.

"You'll get used to it," she smiles, "for tonight I've promised to keep an eye on you. Tomorrow, Jensen will find some more efficient way to monitor you but for now, you're my guest."

I clear my throat.

"Why two beds?"

"I just kind of ended up in this room. I used to have a roommate, years ago, but..."

Her expression falters.

"But they're not around anymore."

Ouch. I should really take my foot out of my mouth. Luckily she seems indifferent to my blatant rudeness, and simply tugs at her shirt. I look away as she pulls her clothes off – while I'm not offended by the sight of a naked body, I know that has different ramifications here. Staring is impolite; and heaven knows I've already filled my quota of that.

"Oh, sorry," she mutters, "do you mind?"

"No. Go ahead."

"You should probably take off those dirty clothes. I don't know if you'll fit any of my stuff - you're a little broader than me - but I might have one of Jay's shirts lying around here somewhere."

I decide not to question why she'd have his shirt in her room. It's none of my business what they get up to. But as she digs around and passes me a grey scrap of cloth, I wonder about it. I'm not great at picking up on social cues, but I hadn't felt any spark between them.

But then again, I was a little distracted.

That thought echoes in my head again, that preposterous notion that I could be part of something much bigger than myself. That I could be something more than just a Millchild with a penchant for insulting people. I shake the thought aside.

I turn away and pull off my hoodie and shirt, surprised at just how bad the stains are. In all the commotion I'd forgotten the fight altogether. I gingerly touch my busted lip; it hurts, but it's so minor that it's easy to forget.

"Oh, my god."

I freeze as a pair of small, icy hands touch my back, sending strange chills up my spine. We don't touch each other back home - never on bare skin, anyway. But she ignores my apparent discomfort, searching my skin with her fingers. I can hear her muttering.

"Um, excuse me?"

"I'm sorry, I shouldn't have grabbed you. But your back... I can't believe it."

Briefly, I try to remember if I've ever seen my own back. It doesn't seem likely. Nel would have, but she's never commented on it. My eyes are drawn to Pan's svelte physique, the soft curves of her body. Maybe she's just not used to someone who's built like me, all muscle and edge, without that softness that screams femininity.

But then she loops an arm around my neck – gently, to my surprise, like she's scared she might hurt me – and whispers in my ear.

"What do they do to you there?"

"What do you mean?"

"Your back. It's scarred."

"Yeah, I know."

"How did you get those? Do they beat you at the Mill?"

"No..."

I clear my throat.

"Not always. Only if you break the rules, and that was a long, long time ago. They haven't laid a hand on me in years."

"So the scars?"

"Mostly old. Some are from working. When you swing an axe all day, sometimes you catch yourself, or someone else."

She bites her lip.

"And what about these 'rules'? What are they?"

"Basic stuff. Cheek, violence. Running away. Things you'd deserve a good clap around the ear for. People learn quickly."

I tug on Jay's shirt, fighting hard to ignore the masculine scent emanating from it. How did I get into this mess? Pan watches me with those eyes again, that infuriating, pitying look filling her otherwise pretty face.

"I'm serious," I tell her, "this is normal. A parent will beat a kid when they're bad, right? To show them what they did wrong. It's fine. Besides, I'm practically a baby compared to some of the guys there. Some of the old guys, you should see them. Their bodies are like patchwork."

I swallow the rush of admiration that builds in me at the thought of those workers, then shoot my brightest smile at Pan.

"So it's fine."

She opens her mouth to speak again, but I turn away. I don't want to talk about this anymore. She's making me question things I don't want to question, making me doubt things I never intended to doubt.

The bed is soft. Much softer than my crappy little campbed. My back immediately seizes. I've gotten so used to sleeping on hard, cold, and thoroughly soaked surfaces that this bed provides little in the way of comfort.

I look up at the ceiling and imagine I can see past it. The sheet metal and rivets fall away to reveal the rusted, corrugated ceiling of the bunker. I close my eyes and try to remember the sight of a moonlit sky, the gentle sound of incoming rain. As Pan settles down in the next bed over, I imagine that her snuffly breathing belongs to Nel. I'm home.

But then I breathe in, and instead of the stink of two dozen unwashed bodies, I'm greeted by the stale, empty scent of the tunnels. The dream fractures.

CHAPTER TEN

I wake out of instinct the next day, even without a Guard to scream me awake. It's like my body has adjusted to wake with the sun. Even when I can't see the sun. Pan watches blearily from her bed, and her expression makes it apparent that she's not normally up so early.

"It's not even dawn yet," she mutters.

"Sorry. Habit."

She opens her mouth again, as though to tell me to lie back down. But then something falters, and instead she simply tosses her blanket off. Oddly, she's still just as charming this way. It's weird. I don't care what people look like; it's a non-issue. If someone can do the job they're meant to do, I don't care about anything else. But Pan's on a whole new level. Even with her crimson hair in an unkempt mess around her face, and her body barely hidden by a scrap of material, she's gorgeous. Envy pangs in my chest, and I move to silence it. I'm not about to start primping.

"You don't have to get up," I tell her, but she shakes her head.

"I probably should. Jay always tells me I sleep in too late. Everyone else will already be awake. This is why I normally don't eat breakfast."

I fight to keep my face blank at that, not wanting to give her more reason to pity me. We don't always do breakfast at the Mill. Or lunch. You get one guaranteed meal a day, take it or leave it. I never cared much about that - but Pan's the bleeding heart type. No doubt she'll see an economic decision as a terrible cruelty.

I pull on yesterday's dirty clothes, much to Pan's dismay. Apparently, that's not the way they do things. The scratchy material of my familiar grey hoodie is comforting, though. It's some tiny trace of home in this big, sterile place.

"What now?"

The words slip out and I bite back on them, but it's too late. She heard.

"What do you mean, what now?"

"I mean... what do I do now?"

It's a valid question, even if I'm somewhat frightened of what the answer may be. Does she expect me to rush outside, excited to learn about their precious cause? Am I supposed to support them from the side-lines, or do they expect me to put my life on the line? I can feel the beginnings of regret stirring in my chest, the thought that I didn't make the best choice yesterday. I'd felt pressured and unsure, and I'd allowed myself to get sucked into something I want no part of. But there's no going back now.

I thought about it last night. While staring up at the metal ceiling, counting the rivets, I'd wondered if I could run. I'd formulated a rough map of the tunnels in my head, even figured a good time to make a run for it. But I don't know where my cart is. Or how many people might be here. Jay had been able to match me in strength when he pinned me; if the rest are even half as strong, I don't stand a chance of forcing my way out.

Pan tilts her head at me.

"We need to go see Jensen. While we're out, I can show you around, too. If you like."

"Sure."

I don't really care about seeing the views. But it's something to do, as well as a little bit of info to store in the back of my head. I can imagine Nel's reaction when I return to her with this, when I regale her with the stories of everything I've seen on my travels. It doesn't hurt to look.

Pan leads me through a labyrinth of tunnels, each one as dark and metal and stale as the next. It seems impossible to me that she could remember the routes through such an endless maze – but then I remember the winding pathways at the Mill, and seeing those for the first time. They'd be just as intimidating, but I memorised those. It's the same.

"Are you sure about this?" she asks, glancing back, "this might be a bit overwhelming."

"I'll be fine."

She nods, but that warm smile is gone. Her expression isn't cold or distant, though – in fact, it's just as friendly and welcoming as ever. But her smiles have been replaced by looks of renewed curiosity, like I'm a different oddity than I was this time yesterday. She waves one hand, gesturing at the walls around her.

"For the most part, the base is miles and miles of tunnels. We're buried deep under the city, too deep for scans to find us. It's the safest place to be."

"How did you put this down here?"

"We didn't. They're old tunnels that used to be used for transport a long time ago. As far as the three leaders are aware, they're caved in. But we caught them in time. Reinforced them. Used the tunnels and rooms to make a safe place. We have entrances across Thorne, each one guarded like the one you came in through yesterday."

So she wasn't just wandering the streets in an effort to save the innocent, then. She was actively guarding the entrance. I suppose that makes sense.

"The only time we ever need to go out is to take deliveries of emergency supplies... like the ones you brought. Rian usually organises that."

That name, again. Rian's the Guard at the Mill, the man who sent me here in the first place. So he's allied with these guys. Working for them. But then...

I stare at the back of Pan's head, then stop dead.

"Why are you telling me all this?"

She glances back at me, utterly confused.

"What do you mean?"

"Don't think I didn't see the way that guy - Jay - looked at me. You might trust your computers, but you still don't know who I am. Not really. It could be an error. It could be a trick. Realistically, I could be anybody. So why are you trusting me with this?"

For a moment she's silent, and my chest swells with a sick kind of pride. I've got you. There's no logical answer she can give, nothing she can say to justify her actions.

"Because," she says, her voice soft, "it's you."

"But it might not be. I don't remember this place. There's no evidence that this Ada girl is alive, much less here now. You've got one computer system and a similar eye colour to base your whole theory on. You said it yourself that it might be wrong."

"Technically, yeah. It could be. But it's not."

She turns to me now, those pretty eyes flashing with ferocity.

"You're Ada. You have to be. Because you're just like Jay. You're awkward and you're direct and you're kind of careless with your words. Just like him. You're also honest and brave, though - you're so similar it hurts. That's why I trust you. Maybe I shouldn't, I don't know, but I reckon that even if I'm wrong, even if you're not her... I still feel like I can trust you."

Any sense of bravado I had vanishes in an instant. The desire to run fades, dissipating into the atmosphere like the remains of a floating ember.

"I don't understand. We only met yesterday. How can you trust me already?"

She shrugs.

"I'm a really good judge of character."

We open the door into an area much, much larger than any of the others - it's like a huge storage shed, though when I point this out Pan corrects me, telling me it used to be an old station back when they had below-ground trains. I don't ask what that is, not wanting to seem totally uncultured.

The area is built up of dozens, possibly hundreds of platforms - any open area is taken up by makeshift shelters, shoddily-made tables, and sheer numbers of people. In a particularly large area to my right people are wrestling, surrounded by a small crowd of onlookers.

It's brighter in here, too, illuminated by a cool, blue light - and as I look up I see that instead of a ceiling, there's glass. As I watch it, small shadows flicker across its surface.

"Footsteps?"

"Yep," she smirks, "the ceiling is made of a special glass. It looks like concrete from the street, but it lets light in here. Makes it warm, as I imagine you've noticed."

Now she mentions it, there's a pleasant heat in here. Nothing compared to the scorching temperatures of a field during the height of summer, or the burning in your skin when you're shovelling coal into a furnace. Still, it's there.

"It's nice to see outside again," I mutter.

She seems surprised by that, but I don't bother to backtrack. It is nice. I hate tunnels. I hate being underground. Back when I was in the Mine, there were times I'd catch the tiniest glimpse of sunlight, when they opened a door or broke through somewhere they shouldn't have. The rush of joy I'd felt seeing that light was enormous - this ceiling has a similar effect.

"Yeah," she eventually says, "it's good for the gardens, too."

She points to a lush patch of green in the distance. Several people work the land, plucking crops from the dirt and piling them into wheelbarrows. I inhale deeply, but we're too far away to catch the scent of fresh soil. Shame.

"I can't believe how many people are here," I say, "how many of you are there?"

"About sixty. But not everyone's part of the cause. Most are volunteers and sympathisers. They just help out where they can. Protect the entrances, stuff like that. I'd say the core group is about twenty, if that."

She starts to count on her fingers, rattling off a list of names I've never heard before, but I ignore her and carry on walking. The further we move into the structure, the more I pick up on it. The sensation of lingering eyes on my back. The sound of hushed whispers as I pass by. They scurry out of my path when I near, and I can't tell if it's out of fear, respect, or something else entirely.

Of course. Typically, they'll have heard about their leader's sister returning. If Ada really was used as a symbol for the Clover, it would be a big deal if she was suddenly alive, right? But the hesitation in their eyes, and the way they shrink from my gaze makes me think otherwise. Maybe they know it's not been proven. That I could be anyone - including someone who could want to hurt them.

I've never had so many eyes on me at once before. When doing farm work, nobody looks to their sides, or bothers to pay even the slightest amount of attention to those beside them. I'm as guilty of that as anyone. So now, my skin is crawling under the gaze of dozens of strangers who regard me with a sort of reproachful positivity.

"Unnerving, huh?"

Someone steps out, and I'm relieved to see Jensen's face. His previously creased face has smoothed out to reveal a handsome, clean-cut young man. Very different from how he'd presented himself yesterday. But he still regards me with suspicion, maintaining a fair distance from me. Like he thinks I might launch myself at him at any moment.

"Y-yeah," I reply, scratching my head.

"It'll die down soon enough," he says, "everyone's very excited about Ada's return."

"But that's not..."

"I know. That's why nobody's approached you yet. Until we know for sure, nobody's going to get their hopes up about you."

"Charming."

"Don't blame them. They just don't want to be let down again."

"Again?"

Pan hooks an arm over my shoulder, making me shiver under her too-familiar touch.

"Our leaders know about us, Noah. They like to mess with our heads. It can get pretty brutal. That's why we can't rule out the whole 'trick' thing."

I nod, but inwardly I'm shouting. Wasn't it Pan who just insisted I must be Ada?

"Anyway," says Jensen, "Jay actually sent me to find you. He wants today to be a fresh start. Personally, I think he just feels guilty for pinning you yesterday."

My wrists pulse at the memory of his hands gripped around them, but I shake the thought aside.

"It's okay."

"I know. But we still gotta do this."

With that he extends one hand, and the corners of his lips curl. The smile transforms his face.

"I've been instructed to greet you formally. I'm Robert Jensen, but people just use my last name. I'm what you might call the tech guy around here. Head hacker."

"Um..."

"That means I'm good with computers."

"Oh!"

I take his hand firmly. I've seen enough visitors from the city meeting with the Guards at the Mill – so I recognise this some strange, overtly-formal greeting.

Jensen winces.

"Ouch. Good... good grip."

"Sorry."

Pan lets out a strange sound that lies somewhere between a chuckle and a squeal, then grabs my hand in hers.

"Like introductions are needed! But whatever. I'm Pan. Technically it's Penelope, but if you call me that I'll have your head. Nobody uses their full names around here. I'm Second in Command, technically."

"H-happy to meet you."

"I have something for you," Jensen interrupts.

He reaches behind himself, into the box strapped to his back. He pull something green and heavy from it - I recognise the shape of a Hoverbot and tense. They've been known to shoot at Mill workers who misbehave; and more often than not, their aim is spot on.

But as he lowers it to the ground, there are no lights on its surface. No beeping. It's off.

"What's this?" I ask, daring to look a little closer. The device isn't dissimilar from the blue one lurking behind Jensen; I wonder if he's made changes to this one, too. It's got four small blades and a series of screens, lights and scanners. I don't understand what most of them do, but it sparks my curiosity. I've never seen one up close before.

"Jay wants to make sure you're safe to be around," Jensen explains, "until we figure this out for certain, you need to be watched all the time. So he asked me to fix up this Hoverbot. We'll allocate you as the user and it'll follow you around wherever you go during your time here. If you do anything unusual, the Hoverbot will alert us."

"So I'm being spied on?"

A smile plays on his lips - it's not altogether unfriendly, but the motion is still rife with suspicion. He doesn't trust me one bit.

"If you're not doing anything wrong, then what's the issue?"

I sigh. I wish I could tell him no, that I'm not a child and that I don't need to be watched. But then I remember life at the Mill; Hoverbots watching every inch of the fence, Guards on every row, cameras closely watching nearly every corner and crevice. I've spent my whole life being watched. Why should I care now?

"Fine."

"Good. Now then, every Hoverbot has a handle – a name, that is – and you log yourself in as the primary user by saying its name while it's in stasis mode, like now. Just read the side panel out loud."

I do as I'm told, though the letters painted on its side are messy at best. I'm not the most literate of people, either; I can read just as well as the next person, but it takes a minute. Eventually, I decipher his scribbles.

"A-Atlas?"

The device immediately springs to life, launching itself from the ground with a high-pitched squeal. I leap back; but to my surprise, it circles me. The beeps and squeaks it emits make it sound almost happy – I can't help but feel it's somewhat cute as it spins in the air and fixes a light on me. I even dare to crack a smile.

"It's called Atlas?"

"Yeah," he chuckles, "I come up with the dumbest names. This blue one is called Atticus. He's my personal Hoverbot. Responds only to me."

I take a moment to size up the machine in front of me. Atlas is still spinning happily, like a puppy whose owner has been away just a few minutes too long. It's just a piece of metal, I tell myself; but I still reach out and gently touch the interface. It beeps as I do so, nestling into my hand as though it enjoys my touch.

"W-what does it do, exactly?"

"It's set to automatically watch for any signs that you're doing something you shouldn't be. If it catches you asking questions you shouldn't, or trying to download data from our systems, it'll block you and alert me. It'll also alert me if you go anywhere you shouldn't, or if you try to sneak away. But that will work in the background. It also works like any other Hoverbot. Say its name to start a command. You can ask it to show videos, play music, store data, create maps. It can scan for body heat, heart rate, pulse... and communicate with others, like Atticus here."

"Wow."

I had no idea that a Hoverbot could do all that. Atlas twirls again, its joy contagious, and I vow to see what exactly it's capable of the moment I get chance.

"Now, if you're ready, we need to go and see Jay."

Jensen's voice pierces through the small degree of comfort I've built around myself. I don't think I want to face him again. Those intense eyes, immense hope guarded by an even bigger shield. Hesitant and distrustful. It's hard to be the subject of someone's hatred while also being the subject of their greatest hope. Especially when I don't fully understand why.

But it seems I don't have any choice in the matter, as I'm swept along the pathways by Pan and Jensen. They chatter as we walk, bickering like children – and though I should find it irritating, it's actually kind of nice. They argue like siblings, Pan's arm always hooked around his in a sisterly fashion. Atlas lurks behind me, its presence actually somewhat comforting.

I allow myself to fall just a half step behind, then pause as we cross a bridge. Beneath me is a man-made river of sorts, its water far too clear to be natural. Its edges are straight and neat, unlike the rough, muddy banks of the river back home. But that's not what my eye is drawn to.

There's another small garden beneath the bridge. Small flowers bloom all over. It's much less structured than the crop garden, but I can tell that the placement is very intentional. In the centre of the clearing sits a stone statue. Two figures, abstract in form, twist around one another and lean into an embrace. The river parts around them.

I don't understand art. I never have. When Nel talked about the beauty of the sunset or the artistry in the night sky, I'd simply nod along. I never cared about things like that. It doesn't matter if something's lovely, unless its sole purpose is to be lovely. And if so, it's useless anyway.

So why can't I tear my eyes away from the statue?

"Noah?"

Pan's hand finds my arm and I jump. I'd thought they were further ahead.

"S-sorry."

"For what? We thought you'd got lost."

"I was just looking at the garden."

She follows my gaze down to the statue, and that bright, confident expression falters. It's just for a moment as she quickly replaces her smile, but it's too late. I saw her reaction.

"What is that thing?"

Her fingertips tighten around my arm.

"Pan?"

"Come on. Jay wants to see you."

They push me into the room and shut the door, leaving me standing like an idiot. There's something unnerving about the way it clangs shut. Intimidating.

"You're here."

I turn. Jay's standing in the middle of the room. It's the same room from last night – or at least, it looks similar. Perhaps this is the base of operation.

He draws his lips back in a polite smile. In the morning light, I'm surprised by how old he looks. He can't be more than three or four years older than me, but there are dark circles under his eyes, deep lines near his mouth. He looks as exhausted as I feel.

I open my mouth to speak, then realise I've not got anything to say and draw it shut again.

"Sit down," he says, and I obey immediately. He perches across from me, nudging his seat back a little, like he's afraid to get too close. He shoots a glance at Atlas, perhaps reassured that I won't launch myself across the desk.

"I'm sorry about yesterday. I think we may have thrown a lot of information at you. That wasn't fair."

"It's alright."

It isn't. But I'm not prepared to tell him that.

"I'm not sure how much Pan told you about us."

"She told me about the Cull. About Ada."

When I say the name, his face gives a small, involuntary twitch. I inwardly vow not to say it again.

"I know what your system told you," I start, "I know you think I'm her, but…"

"I wouldn't go that far."

With that he stands to pace the room, maintaining the sterile distance between us. I wish I could complain, but I'm secretly pleased he's staying away.

"You wouldn't?"

"No," he says, "I know what the Citizen System told us – but that system's provided by our leaders. It could very easily have been manipulated to include you."

"You think they're messing with you again?"

He hesitates at that.

"Pan told you about that, huh? I'm not ruling it out. Look, clearly you're clueless about all this. You have no idea who I am, do you?"

"I'm sorry."

"I don't think for a minute that you're a spy. There's nobody around here who looks quite like you. Or acts like you. And don't take it the wrong way but, you don't exactly have the makings of a secret agent. You're definitely from the Mill and I don't think you're out to deceive me. There's a chance you are my sister in which case, I'd want you to stay here. Be a part of the Clover."

"But…"

"But without knowing for sure, I can't do that. I hope you understand."

I bite my lip, relieved by the slight pain it causes.

"So what are you going to do with me?"

I want to go home. Sure, there's a tiny part of me that's screaming out for more - more knowledge, more detail. A tiny voice is begging me to absorb everything I can about this place. I'm not a fan of that voice. Of course, it might not be that simple. He might have much worse plans for me. My stomach twists at the thought.

But he simply sits back down.

"If you're her," he says softly, "then I want you here with me."

"And if I'm not her?"

"Then I'm not opposed to you staying here, if you really want. But it won't be the same. At all. You understand that?"

"Yes."

"Would you want to stay?"

I consider this. My immediate instinct is to say no, to insist they let me go home as soon as possible. I don't want to be here a moment longer than I have to be. But I sense that's not the answer he's looking for. Time to lie.

"I'm not sure," I say carefully, "I don't know much about Thorne, or about your cause. It's hard to judge when I don't know the first thing about it."

"Makes sense. Go ahead, ask your questions."

I nudge a strand of greasy hair from my face and pretend to be thinking of a question – though I already have several in mind. Better to start with the basics.

"Who are the city leaders?"

"There are three leaders that we vote in every ten years. They each take care of separate aspects of running the city. Social, Political, Financial. It's much more detailed than that, of course, but that's the basic explanation."

"But they're all involved in the Cull?"

"Yes. And there's never been anyone in power who's opposed the Cull. Because nobody ever opposes it, except us."

"Why not?"

He knots his hands together until his fingers start to resemble thickly tied rope.

"The world outside our borders – outside the Mill too – is in chaos. War's been raging across the globe for so long now that nobody even remembers who caused it."

Something stirs uncomfortably in my gut.

"It has?"

"Yes. Everything within our borders has immunity, as long as we remain completely self-sufficient and don't ever demand anything from other places. My best guess is that people are so scared of screwing up that immunity that they're afraid to speak out against the Cull. If they scream too loudly, they're frightened they'll draw the attention of less than desirable powers. Our records suggest the war may be over, but without proof, there's nothing we can do. Nobody is willing to take the risk."

"But..."

I trail off, suddenly unsure. I'd never bothered to consider what might be happening outside our little patch of the world. The Mill has been my life for so long that half the time, I forget there's anything at all past the chain-link fence and Guard towers. Even since coming here, it hadn't occurred to me to think about the space beyond their walls.

A war. I suppose I shouldn't be surprised. Humans fight over menial, unimportant things. I've seen it myself; teenagers scrapping over the last spoonful of gruel, or bickering over one more log being loaded into their wagon. Sometimes, I think humans weren't built to live in groups.

I expect Jay to tell me more but he simply watches, his eyes filled with a quiet curiosity. Waiting for me to continue with my questions.

"So why aren't you scared of the war, too?"

He chuckles.

"Oh, I am. Believe me. But I could never ignore the Cull. Just because there's greater danger in the world, doesn't mean we should forget about the danger outside our own front door."

I bite my lip. There's a certain air of pride when he talks like that. His chest swells and his voice slips into a lower octave. He's proud of what he's achieved.

"Why does this mean so much to you?"

Instantly, I regret the question. That's not fair. It means a lot to everyone here. Not just him. After speaking with Pan, I've no doubt it means a lot to her, too. But she seems to face it with a retired acceptance, like she knows change is coming but accepts it. Not Jay. He clearly hates the situation, and everything about it. It fuels his anger, motivates him.

He doesn't seem surprised that I asked. Maybe he hears it a lot.

"What did Pan tell you about me?"

For a brief moment, I consider telling him what she said. How we're too similar, too alike to possibly be strangers. But I feel like that's not what he's asking.

"Nothing."

"I'm surprised at that. She normally jumps at the chance to tell people my tragic backstory. Typical."

Jay rolls his eyes, as though he's irritated with Pan - but the motion seems devoid of any real annoyance.

"My parents weren't anything special. Just normal citizens. They'd always figured the Cull was a disgusting process, but they never questioned it. Just like everyone else. That is, until their youngest child - their daughter - was taken in the Cull."

"Ada."

"Exactly. She was just under four. Close to having survived the annual Culls - but then they took her. They carried out the normal executions in public to scare us, and then disposed of the rest elsewhere."

I should be shocked at the thought of public executions. Really, I should. It should horrify me; but then I remember watching kids get lashed to the whipping block, faces burning with pain and humiliation.

He pushes on.

"After that, something snapped. My parents realised that the Cull was wrong - even more than before. They set this place up. They gathered people and tried to use sheer numbers to overthrow the city's leaders."

He looks away from me, eyes glistening. When he speaks, his voice punctuates the silence between us.

"The next year, my parents were the ones chosen for the public execution."

Something squirms in me – the knowledge, perhaps, that they could have been my parents, too.

"I'm sorry."

And I am. It's not often I feel pity for anyone. It's a patronising, superior feeling and I hate it with a passion. But I can't help it. Family means something here, and he lost that. That's like losing a friend back home.

Kane's face flashes through my mind, a not-so-subtle reminder that for all I know, he could be dead.

"I'm... really sorry."

"That's okay. It was a long time ago. After that, I took over. Built this thing from the ground up, made it what it is today. But there's still no way to win. Every year we protest the Cull and try to get people to join us, but they're so terrified that they won't even try."

"Oh."

"But now, you're here. And that might just change everything."

"Really?"

Suddenly his face is flushed and feverish, excitement bubbling just a little too close to the surface. The feeling is almost infectious, and after a moment the discomfort in my gut settles. He leans forward on his hands, looking me up and down with a renewed sense of interest.

"You see, if we managed to find Ada, that would mean she was never killed. If she's you, that means she was sent to the Mill instead. And if she was, then maybe they all were. Maybe they're all still alive – and maybe there's enough hope in that to spur everyone into action. The hopes of being reunited with their lost loved ones."

"That's a lot of maybes."

"I know. That's why we need to find out the truth. The first step is finding out who you really are."

"How are you going to do that?"

He rubs a hand over his chin, picking at the sandy stubble there.

"I'm not sure yet. But I'll think of something. Will you stick around long enough for us to figure it out?"

I shrug. I want to go home. I want the dirty fields. I want my soggy little campbed back. I want Nel's snuffly breathing to be the sound I fall asleep and wake up to. But there's so much hope in his eyes, so much passion. Nel would never forgive me if I turned away now.

"Sure."

"Good. In the meantime, make yourself at home. Enjoy your time here. I'll let you know once we have a plan."

I nod. I step towards the door – but my path is suddenly blocked by his hulking figure. His expression is hard as he sizes me up.

"One more thing. Like I said, I don't think you're a spy. It's unlikely you're from Thorne. Even less likely that you understand anything. But on the off-chance that you are, and we find out – we've had traitors before. It's nothing new. I want you to know that I won't take any chances, if you show even the slightest inclination towards betraying us."

I gulp hard. My heart is racing suddenly, and though I have no intention of hurting anyone, the threat still unnerves me.

"I understand."

He pushes me somewhat unceremoniously from the room, seemingly eager to get back to whatever he was doing before I chose to intrude. Pan and Jensen are waiting outside for me, and as I near, they watch me closely.

"How did it go?"

I shrug.

"Fine. I got the full history."

"And what's his plan now?"

"I-I don't know. He wants to find out who I am."

Pan rolls her eyes, but Jensen gives a small, understanding nod.

"I get that. I have some ideas for how we can find out, too. I'll run them by him later."

Pan loops an arm through mine. There's a smile on her face again, like she knows something I don't. Perhaps she thinks there was some soppy brother-sister moment in there. But nothing happened. In a way, I'm disappointed. I'd thought that family meant more here. But when he'd looked at me, he'd regarded me in the same way one might regard a particularly interesting sheet of paper. With mild intrigue and not much else. There was no sense of familiarity between us, no familial affection. Maybe I expected too much.

Pan must see the disappointment on my face, because her grip on my arm tightens.

"Hey, don't worry about it. These things take time."

I nod, but the feeling persists. I've never cared if someone liked me before. Except for Nel, it never mattered if someone noticed me or not. This time? I want to impress him. I want him to be proud of me.

What a strange feeling.

As the afternoon sun blazes overhead, Pan takes me to meet Nate. He's a heavy-set man in his thirties, though he seems much older. He's got a balding head and a pair of tiny glasses perched on the end of a crooked nose. He greets me with a warm, overly familiar hug.

"So you're the mysterious newcomer. Welcome to the Atrium."

"The Atrium?"

"That's what we call this big space," Pan chuckles from behind me.

Nate looks me up and down, then laughs. The sound is deafeningly loud, but nobody looks around at the noise. Clearly, everyone's used to it.

"You really are the spitting image. The similarities are uncanny."

I smile politely in return, but I don't get it. Sure, both Jay and I are blonde and stocky, but that's where the similarities end.

"Really?" says Pan, "I don't see it. She doesn't look all that much like Jay."

"Not Jay. Alix."

He pats me hard on the shoulder, and I'm honestly a little surprised my feet haven't sunk into the floor under his immense weight.

"I'm sorry, but who's Alix?"

Pan seems momentarily alarmed, but Nate doesn't seem to notice.

"Your... Jay's mother. You're so similar."

He waves one of his oversized hands at a small photo frame on his desk. I scoop it up and squint at the figures in the picture. A wispy-looking man with a twisted grin embraces a dainty, blonde woman. Behind them, the city. These are supposed to be my parents?

"I'm sorry, I don't see it."

The woman in the photo is pretty and long-limbed, with sparkling eyes and a brilliant smile. Her expression doesn't exactly scream rebel leader – but then, neither does the man's. He looks slightly goofy, actually. Like he told a lot of bad jokes.

Nate winks.

"It's there. You'll see it eventually."

I can't help but roll my eyes in response.

"So, what do you do around here?"

"Whatever they need me to do. I tinker around with ideas a lot. I'm not a computer genius like Jensen, and my people skills are admittedly a little lacking."

He stares as though expecting me to deny it. When I don't, he heaves a sigh.

"Not one for small talk, I see."

"No, not really."

He laughs again, then turns to Pan.

"So what's she going to do while she's here? I imagine the same rules apply to her."

"Rules?" I ask.

"Yep. Everyone has a role to play here, missy. There are no free rides."

Suddenly, my heart sinks. I don't think I have any skills suitable to service people like this. I can't even read all that easily, much less use a computer. But Pan just smirks.

"It's alright. We'll figure something out."

"Are you sure?"

"Yep. But for now, how about you and I help out with dinner? There are lots of people to feed here, and nobody ever wants to cook. Hop into the shower, then we'll throw something together."

"All I heard was 'shower', so yes."

CHAPTER ELEVEN

I had no idea that one human being could smell so bad. It's shocking to me now, as I pluck my dirty clothes up off the floor of the shower room. They stink to high heaven, weeks of sweat and dirt built up to an unbelievable stench. At least my body is clean now.

Idly, I run a hand through my hair. It's lighter than I thought, a soft gold instead of murky brass. What's more, it now smells like flowers. It's been a long time since I've smelled of anything even remotely nice. We have showers at the Mill - but a few minutes standing under icy water can't compare to soap.

Pan's left me some clean clothes. I recognise them instantly as men's, but that doesn't bother me one bit. It's pretty clear the women here aren't built like me. They're tall and soft and curved - and me? I'm stocky and muscled and burnt brown from the sun. I pull the clothes on, pleased at the feeling of clean, warm material. Grey trousers, black t-shirt. Unremarkable in every sense of the word, and yet I feel a thousand times better. Pan stares as I step out of the shower room.

"Oh, wow. You've actually got a face under all that muck."

"You seem surprised."

"Don't take it personally! I'm just impressed. You're prettier than I would have guessed."

She smiles warmly at her own compliment, but though I reply in kind, I don't really care. 'Pretty' simply isn't a factor.

This time as we walk through the tunnels, the glances are different. People no longer regard me as an unwashed, scary-looking stranger. There's still that hesitation there, that fear of who I might be and what I might do, but clean skin and a pleasant smell seem to help a lot. The kitchen here is similar to the Mill's. Instinct takes over as I pick up a knife and start chopping away at the nearest stack of vegetables. If Pan's irritated at that, she doesn't say anything. Instead she just pulls up next to me and joins in. Atlas settles on a work surface, carefully filming my hands. Watching for any signs of disobedience.

"So, what do you think of the place?"

"Everyone seems nice," I say, "it's less scary than I thought it would be."

In truth, it's not. I've been cautious of everyone I've come across; the only difference is that I've been able to weigh up my chances of winning a one to one fight. Luckily I'm bigger than most people here, and I'm quietly pleased to have such a distinct advantage.

"Everyone's in a good mood," she tells me, "It's such an exciting time."

"It is?"

"Seriously? Noah, sometimes I think you forget how important this is. If you're Ada, the whole cause will take a turn for the better. We might finally be able to end this."

"I get that. I do. But that doesn't really have anything to do with me, does it?"

"Why do you think that?"

"I'm happy for you if Ada turns out to be alive. Even if she's me. But be realistic. There's nothing special about me. I just don't want you all to get your hopes up, thinking I can do something amazing when I can't. I'm just a Millchild, remember?"

She falls silent at that, and we work in silence. Aha. There's nothing she can say back to that. What I'm saying is true. It doesn't matter if Ada is me or not, not really. It matters that she's alive. But whether she's me? Irrelevant.

"I don't expect anything amazing from you, Noah."

I pause at that, arm half-stretched towards the nearest potato.

"Good. You shouldn't. I'm a Farm worker, and that's all I'm good for."

"But that's wrong. Expecting a miracle isn't fair, I know. But I can't stand to hear you say that all you're good for is working on a farm."

"Why not?" I snort, "it's true."

She slams the knife down, suddenly angry.

"It is not. You're more than what they turned you into, Noah."

I can't hold back my laughter. I feel like an ass. She's trying to be encouraging and kind, trying to support me through a weak moment. But this isn't a weak moment. I'm not down on myself. I'm realistic. There's no underestimation going on here. I just know my limit.

She stamps her foot.

"Hey!"

"I'm sorry. But you're wrong. If you need someone to trawl through mud or chop wood or carry something heavy, I'm your girl."

"You should expect more of yourself. Until last night, I had no idea how the Guards treated Mill workers. I had no clue you were slaves."

"Slaves is a bit harsh."

"But true. And what's worse, they raise you that way. So it's all you ever know, and you never look for a bigger purpose."

I scowl. A bigger purpose? Bigger purposes are for city folk. Like being able to find yourself and build your talents, or find love. They're luxuries - and she's talking about them like anyone can have them at a moment's notice.

"I don't need your pity, Pan, and I don't need you to save me either."

She winces at that.

"I didn't mean it like that. I just..."

"It's fine."

"I mean it..."

"So do I."

And I do. It's fine. I wasn't really hurt by Pan's words - just irritated.

She glances at my hands, then gasps.

"How have you cut so much already?"

I stare at the pile of potatoes next to me. Whoops. Too much.

"Sorry. Guess I'm used to cooking for a lot more people."

"No, it's fine. Very efficient."

Her smile's still a little sheepish, but I ignore it.

People come for dinner in droves, and it's to my great relief that Pan takes over. I don't want to be faced with the stares, the mutters, the barely concealed glares. Instead I hide myself away - though in my little hiding spot behind a large, battered freezer, I can still hear everything.

Everyone's curious. Some, it seems, don't know about me yet. They ask who the stranger from earlier was. Others seem to know everything and delve straight in with the most prying questions. Still others seem to have already come up with their own theories about who I am and what I want from them.

Pan doesn't try to dispel them. She just shrugs the questions off. Like they're not even worth answering. As the tenth person proclaims me to be a murderous traitor, though, I can't listen anymore. I turn away.

Standing alone in the cramped, hot kitchen, I can finally breathe. I've never been used to alone time – it's practically non-existent back home. It's a luxury to have time alone with your thoughts. After a few moments, I sigh. Apparently, my thoughts aren't all that interesting. Still, it's nice. The relative quiet of the room around me is oddly comforting after the long, chaotic day. Atlas beeps quietly next to me, alerting me of my decreasing heart rate. Apparently, I'm finally starting to calm down.

I feel like I've not thought clearly since getting here. One minute I was completing a task, eager to get home. The next, I'm backing up an inner city protest group on the off-chance I might be related to one of them. If I'd been able to think clearly, I'd have run the first chance I got. Now, it's too late. This chaos is going to carry on, and I just have to deal with it.

Something cold touches my arm and I jump; but it's just Pan, pressing a plate into my hands.

"Here. Dinner time."

I stare at the strange pile of food she's given me and scowl. It doesn't look like anything I've seen before. It doesn't even resemble the food Darus offered up on the boat. I've half a mind to pass it up – but then my stomach snarls and I pluck it from her grip.

"Thanks."

The food's good. Really good. As I pick at a slab of some kind of meat, I feel my mood lift.

"This is amazing."

"This is pretty awful compared to what you can get on the surface. What do they feed you at the Mill?"

"We make do with what we can get," I reply, eager not to give her any more ammo for pitying me, "but I can see now why you city folk are so demanding."

"Demanding?"

"Yeah. Everything has to be farmed to a really high standard, you know, because that's the expectation. It's a lot more work, sure, but this more than makes up for it."

I swallow the mouthful of food, ignoring her incredulous expression. I suppose it sounds ridiculous. Years of back-breaking labour aren't wiped out by one good meal. But I never really minded doing the work in the first place.

"Is it dark yet?" I ask. Today's been eventful, but I'm still buzzing with energy. Back home I'd still be working until the floodlights came on, so the thought of trying to sleep so early is unpleasant.

"Yeah. Why, are you tired?"

"Not really."

"Then how about we watch some sparring tonight? They always do it on Tuesdays."

Sparring? I open my mouth to ask what that is, but pause. When we stepped into the Atrium earlier, there had been people fighting down below. But it was a kind of structured, measured fighting. More like practice than a genuine, no-holds-barred fight.

I shrug.

"Sure. Sounds good."

The stranger leans down and barges towards his opponent, embedding his shoulder in the taller man's gut. He stumbles back from the blow and scowls, somehow remaining on his feet. There's a surprising grace in his movement as the taller man circles the shorter then ducks to the ground, sweeping his legs out from under him.

The crowd around me groans and cheers as he hits the floor.

"Yeah!" cries Pan from beside me, "Well done!"

But then the fight is over, and they're shaking hands. Both are a little bruised, a little worse for wear – but they exchange broad smiles and wrap their arms around one another. I'd been wrong in my previous judgement. It's organised and friendly, sure. But it's still a no-holds-barred beat down. It strikes me as odd that neither of them seem bothered by the scrapes they've received, nor angered by the fight itself. Camaraderie. I think that's what it is. I toy with the word, turning it over on my head. It's a good word. I like it.

Nate steps into the clearing now, clapping his hands. "Good job, fellas. Now, who's next?"

Nobody steps forward, though several crack jokes on who they think should step in next. Pan glances at me, her eyebrows wiggling.

"I think you should give it a go."

"Are you crazy?!"

"It's just a bit of fun. It's not often that we get into serious fist fights, but it's always good to know how to hold your own. Give it a try."

With that she grabs my shoulders and shoves me unceremoniously into the middle of the ring. The reaction is immediate. A sudden hush falls across those around me, and I can feel a dozen or more sets of eyes casting cursory glances my way. Silent judgement hits me from all directions.

Nate doesn't seem to notice.

"You want in on this?" he grins, "are you sure?"

"I-I don't want to..."

"It doesn't hurt to try. Nelson, come up here."

Someone steps from the crowd. He's a younger man with a mass of orange-red curls and a face that I might find amusing, if not for the distinct muscles flexing under his skin. I swallow hard.

"Um... how am I supposed to..."

"Just have a go. Your main objective is to not get pinned. And try to land a blow, somehow. If you knock him to the floor, you win."

Nelson takes my hand in his, seemingly proud at being picked to fight me. I wonder if that's because he knows who I might be, or if he's one of the few who believe me to be a traitor. I take the chance to size him up. He's taller than me, but even with his toned arms, he lacks my bulk. His expression is hopeful, a pleasant smile playing on those peculiar-looking features.

"Okay, then. Guess we're doing this."

As Nate shouts to start and Nelson takes a step towards me, my body freezes. All of a sudden, without any warning, I'm terrified. Nelson isn't huge – he seems strong, sure, but he's not unstoppable. I fought off several attackers in the alleyway without issue. It's not fear of fighting that keeps me rooted to the spot.

It's the face that floats ahead of me, breaking through my vision. Kane.

He fought Wirrow that day. I remember how his hand had curled into a fist at his side. How he'd aimed at the Guard's jaw. I remember being horrified – and I remember the terror I felt upon seeing the repercussions.

But that's not now. I'm not going to get thrown into the Mines for this. Right?

His first blow lands on my shoulder. Pain flits through me and I stumble back a little, still hesitant. He's circling me now, finding weaknesses. The second blow hits my back.

"Noah?"

Pan's voice breaks through the crowd. She can see me. See that I'm scared. That I don't want to fight. There's shame dripping from her every word.

I don't want her to think I'm weak. I'm not weak.

Nelson lunges forward for a third blow, but this time I'm expecting it. I twist out of his way and hunch down, lifting my fists in front of me. The crowd reacts somehow but I can't tell if it's cheering or booing or something in between. There's a strange ringing pressing in on my ears. Adrenaline coursing hot through my limbs.

When he hits again, I block his punch with my arm. He seems surprised at that; but the pain is negligible. I whip around and hit him so hard I swear I could feel bones creaking under my hand.

A moment later, he crumples to the ground. One hand reaches his jaw, nursing it – and my stomach drops. Did I hurt him?

I jump back, raising both hands in surrender.

"I-I'm sorry. I didn't mean..."

"Noah!"

Pan's coming this way. As she nears I instinctively flinch – the Guards would have my head for this. I'd be thrown in the mines, or at the very least lashed a few times for my insolence. But when my eyes slip open again, her face is awash with sympathy. Oh. Right. This isn't the Mill.

Nelson's standing now, and my hand is in his again. He's smiling, even though the side of his face is pink and swollen. There's a graze on his cheek and the start of a nasty bruise close to his eye, but he doesn't seem angry. In fact, there's something akin to pride on his face.

"Good job," he says, "you might be slow to react, but you hit like a bulldozer."

"A-are you okay?" I choke. Even as I ask it I can feel my shoulder aching from his blows, but the pain is practically non-existent. Nothing seems to hurt much anymore.

"I'm fine, it's just my ego that's bruised. My mistake for underestimating a newcomer, huh?"

He laughs and I laugh too, even though it's awkward and I don't really get the joke. I can't blame him for underestimating me. I'm not like him.

Pan hooks an arm over my shoulder, and her chest swells with pride. She's clearly pleased with me. Maybe they consider this a rite of passage or something. Those around me seem to think alike, too. The glares are now replaced by smiles. Even Atlas twirls delightedly overhead. Everyone's pleased that I won a fight.

So why does it feel so terrible?

We sit for a while longer, watching as others spar. They really are a step above; many seem to twist and hit and manoeuvre together, as though in sync. Like they've fought one another a thousand times before and by now, they can predict one another's movements.

Jay said his parents started the Clover. That would have been about sixteen years ago. It would make sense that these guys would be so flawlessly in sync with one another. When we chop wood back home we often fall into the same pace, swinging our axes in perfect harmony. That's what happens, given time.

Still, it's hard to hide how impressed I am. For the first time since I got here, it's finally starting to sink in what these guys do. It's easy enough to want to protest, to talk about it in theory. But seeing them practice makes their cause seem that much more real.

Nate and Jensen wander over to us at some point in the evening, and suddenly I'm pulled on a leisurely stroll through the Atrium. As we walk, I suppress a chuckle at the sight of Atlas and Atticus twirling together like birds. It's surprisingly cool in here - as I glance up towards the glass ceiling, though, I frown.

"What's wrong?" asks Pan.

"No stars."

"Huh? Oh, that. There's too much light pollution. It blocks out all the stars. Sure, they're there, but I've never seen them. I imagine you have."

"Yeah," I breathe, "they're... good."

Jensen snorts.

"Is that all? Just 'good'? Wow, artists and poets have sure exaggerated the night sky."

I smirk in response, inwardly cursing myself. Words can never really express how the night sky looks to me. I've never cared about beauty, sure - but there's something about a starry sky that screams 'home' to me. They wouldn't understand.

"I don't know how to describe it," I say, "but it's nice to see them. They're kind of out of place, though. Like they don't belong at the Mill."

He seems bemused by my answer. I shrug off the embarrassment and glance around. The Atrium's quiet now, most people having gone to sleep hours ago. I'm not sure what time it is - but judging by the chill in the air, we're deep into the early hours.

"So, tell us about the Mill."

Nate glances back at me with a warm, encouraging smile. I hesitate. I don't really want to talk about home. I'm having fun right now, imagining this is some kind of fever dream that I could wake up from at any moment.

"There's not much to tell. It's split into sections. Fields, Forests. There are some places nearby, like the Plant or the Mines. Factories, Oil Rigs. Further out you reach the Docks – they're part of the Mill, too."

"Sounds pretty big. How many of you are there?"

I shrug.

"No clue. Thousands. Maybe tens of thousands. That's just what I've seen, though. There are a lot more."

Nate and Jensen exchange stunned looks. It's becoming clear to me that city folk know as little about us as we do about them.

"And they're all your age?" Jensen asks, suddenly curious despite himself. I shake my head.

"No. We're all teenagers when we leave Homestead – that's where we're raised and taught farming theory. Then you work until you drop. We have some older guys who've been there for decades. They're kind of amazing."

Even now, hundreds of miles away, I feel that small rush of respect for the old guys at the Mill.

"Amazing how?"

"They're just… strong. People don't live very long at the Mill – hard labour does that to you. It's everyone's dream to make it to that age."

My voice changes a little, and I'm surprised to realise that I'm smiling. Even now, that's the dream. Live long enough to earn that additional shred of respect. Power through the hardest years.

Jensen narrows his eyes at me, but says nothing. Nate, on the other hand, laughs.

"What do you guys do for fun?"

I simply stare. Fun? How stupid is he? It's a Farm. It's for labour. Sure, the Guards play cards and drink whiskey, and sometimes on a cold night they'll take some rather questionable company back to their barracks – but for the rest of us, it's not that simple. I don't want to tell them that, though.

"A better question would be, what do you guys do for fun?"

Aha. Turned the question around. It's hard to hide my pleasure at having successfully avoided the subject. Beside me, Pan smirks.

"It's mostly about enjoying each other's company," she explains, "we play a lot of pranks, mostly on the three leaders."

"You do?"

"Yep. They're always trying to think of new ways to alienate or scare us, so we try to get our own back where we can. Just last month, they aired the video of Jay's parents being executed. The idea was to scare us into submission by showing us what could happen. It didn't work, of course. We're past the point of being frightened."

"So what did you do?"

It's Jensen who answers.

"I hacked into their live Feed," he chuckles, "and we pieced together clips of all the leaders' lies and contradictions. Broadcast it non-stop across the city for three days. The aim was to encourage people to see through the lies – but as usual, it didn't work. Funny, though."

"Wouldn't that make them angry?"

"Oh, it did. They came after us more viciously than ever. But we're faster than them, even though they outnumber us. Not to mention, we work smarter. We have spies and supporters across Thorne. We can wriggle our way out of anything."

He laughs – and something inside me is weirdly comforted by his words. I'd found it difficult to understand how they'd survived so long. Drawing the attention of their leaders seemed like a bad idea. But it's slowly becoming clear. They're smart. They know how far to push.

I guess losing your leaders would force you to learn.

The others settle down by the man-made river as the night grows darker overhead. For a brief moment I wonder why there are no lights, but then I remember. If there were, then those above ground might be able to see. Their cover might be blown.

As the others chat, I find myself perched at the edge of the water. My feet dangle into the flow, and even though the water is icy cold and moving quite quickly, there's a strange sense of comfort about it. As a kid, I'd looked at the murky river at the Mill and wish I could jump in and play. This isn't quite the same; the water here is crystalline and perfect, a far throw from the muddy embankments back home.

Pretty soon I'm able to tune out their voices, and suddenly the evening is calm. The world around me is blue and soft, and though there are no stars overhead I can at least hear the familiar chirping of insects in the grass around me. How they got down here, I'll never know. Frankly, I don't care. I close my eyes against the darkness. This is heavenly.

But when I open them again, I see it. The same statue from earlier, in the corner of the ornate garden. The same one that Pan wouldn't tell me about. Something stirs in my chest when I look at it, unsure what to think or how to feel.

What am I doing? Am I really here, knee-deep in an artificial river miles underground? Have I really been enjoying this so much that for a moment just now, I forgot all about home? Guilt pangs in my chest.

For the tiniest moment, I find myself thinking what it would be like to stay here. For every day to be filled with the same laughter and movement and camaraderie as today. It'd be nice, no doubt. To be part of something bigger. Helping fight for a cause is exactly what Pan mentioned earlier. A higher calling. My lips tighten, ready to smile, but I hold them still. No. I'd be no good in a team. After what I did to Kane, I know better. I won't allow myself to get so attached again. I won't ever put myself in that situation where I'm forced to choose between what I know to be right, and a friend. It's an impossible decision.

"Hey."

Pan and the others are suddenly beside me, stripping off their shoes and socks. They yelp as their feet touch the icy water, and in spite of myself I start to laugh. I don't think I've ever laughed so much in all my life. It's a pleasant sound. Low and throaty, with the occasional hiccup. It's the kind of sound that I'd likely find annoying if it came from someone else. But for me? It's oddly fitting.

An arm finds my shoulder for the hundredth time today, but this time I find myself leaning into Pan's embrace. Her hands are warm and her face is flushed from the cold water – but as I lean on her, she seems pleased. She doesn't say anything, though. Perhaps she's frightened of breaking the peace of the moment.

I am, too.

CHAPTER TWELVE

I'm awake before dawn again. This time, though, I manage not to wake Pan. She's still snoring, lying half-naked across her bunk, mouth wide open. We'd stayed out for a few more hours last night – much later than I think she's used to. I just don't have the heart to wake her.

Still, I can't sit around and do nothing, so I tug on my clothes and decide that it might be worth it to break the rules, just once. I shoot a small glance at Atlas. It's woken with me and is now scanning me for temperature, heart rate and a bunch of other dull, innocuous details. I don't care about that – but Atlas is supposed to be guarding me, right? As long as it's with me, I can be alone.

The Atrium is still dark when I enter. One or two people wander idly around, but it seems like most are still fast asleep, like Pan. Nobody seems to notice as I make my way down to the crop field.

It's not huge, all things considered. The fields back home are enormous, dozens of miles wide at least. This is merely a patch in comparison, only a few acres. Instantly I recognise the plants; potatoes, tomatoes, green beans. Basic stuff.

It's all so familiar to me that suddenly, I just can't help myself. I step into the field and start to work.

The sun's still not shown itself by the time I'm done. Harvested, reseeded, dug up – work so familiar to me that it took barely any effort at all. It's nothing compared to the endless hours of work back home. I hope they don't mind me doing it. Out of the corner of my eye, I catch sight of something else. Stacks of logs – for firewood, I imagine – but they're uncut. An axe lies nearby, gleaming in the dim light as though beckoning me forward. I sigh.

I swing the axe high overhead and breathe, then swing it down in a single, swift movement. The log splits cleanly, a cut more perfect than I've ever achieved before. A smile plays on my face – for once, I'm actually enjoying myself. I swing up again.

"Ahem."

I jump and the axe slips from my hand, hitting the tile below with an almighty clang. I whip around. There's a figure standing just beyond the reach of my swing, watching me with an intense curiosity.

"Jay."

He stares at the crops, then at the wood behind me. His face lingers on my sweaty face and the dirt on my hands – but he manages to keep his face surprisingly neutral.

"Did you do all this?"

"Was I not supposed to?"

"No, that's not it. You're welcome to do it if you want. I'm just surprised – this is normally enough work for a ten man team."

"Sorry. I guess old habits die hard. I couldn't resist."

Even as the words come out, I question them. I've never felt an uncontrollable desire to chop wood before. It's never been fun. If I'd been told to stop, that I'd never need to do it again, then I doubt I'd have refused the offer. But there's something of home about the work, something comforting in the feeling of wood snapping under my touch.

Luckily, he doesn't seem displeased. Again, I can't help but notice that he fights to keep a straight face. Like he's worried about showing weakness. That's a feeling I can understand.

"Why are you up so early?" he asks. I shrug.

"Like I said, old habits. I'm always up before the sun. Why are you awake?"

He sets his jaw.

"I couldn't sleep."

"Oh."

The world falls silent around us, and I inwardly kick myself. Oh? Is that all you have to say? Say something, anything. Something funny or charming or observant. Heck, just something polite. Nothing comes. We just stare at one another, awkwardness building.

Finally, I choke out a question.

"C-can I ask you something?"

"Go ahead."

"Why..." I hesitate, "why is there a garden down there? Towards your room, I mean."

At that, his expression changes. It's a tiny, almost imperceptible difference – but it transforms his face. He suddenly looks much younger.

"It's a memorial garden."

My heart sinks.

"I see."

"Have you been down there?"

"No. I've been to the river, but not up there. Not up close."

He steps back, then beckons for me to follow.

"Come on. I'll show you."

Morning's barely starting to break overhead as we step into the garden. Somehow the grass is dewy underfoot, and the flowers are still curled tightly into their brightly coloured buds. It's too soon for them to bloom.

That statue looms over the garden, making it just a little darker than it should be. I hesitate as we near, but Jay doesn't - he steps up close, shoulders back. Idly, I wonder how much time he's spent standing here. He said it was a memorial garden. I don't even need to ask who it's a memorial to.

"So this statue..."

"Yeah. It's them."

The dancing figures are carved smoothly into the stone, twisting around one another. Jay's eyes are transfixed on it. They don't look a thing like the people on the photograph Nate showed me; but that's beside the point. The bland, expressionless faces on the statue obviously mean a lot to him.

I watch it for a moment, then bite my lip.

"What were they like?"

He chuckles.

"You really don't remember, do you? They were wonderful. I know that everyone would say that about their parents given the chance, but they really were. Even before they spoke out, they had this real passion for life. They loved art more than anything."

"They did?"

"Yeah. Personally, I've never been able to appreciate it. It never made much sense to me. But it meant a lot to them, so when they started to fight back, they used art. They'd paint controversial things on public buildings, scatter inspiring sculptures across the city. They wanted to convince people to their side, but they wanted it to be a choice. I think they hoped to sway people's opinions with their artwork."

I glance back at the statue, my heart filled with trepidation. When I finally gather the courage to speak, my voice is a little too loud in the silence.

"That sounds like a lot to live up to."

"It is. And I could never do what they did. They were really wise – but all I know is brute force."

I roll my eyes.

"I know how that feels."

Suddenly his eyes meet mine, and I can sense the first, tiny strand of trust forming between us. It's unnerving. I swallow hard and shove my hands in my pockets.

"I have to say, I like it here. It's different from what I expected at first."

"What did you expect?"

"I'm not sure," I say slowly, "I guess I thought it'd be scarier. People don't fight back where I'm from. You just take whatever punishment is given to you. You learn to ride it out."

I'm staring at my hand now, turning it over. I never noticed how many scars I have. They litter my skin, marring the deep tan there.

"But here... everything's different. You don't just deal when something bad happens. I always thought that was a bad thing, but now, I'm not so sure."

He says nothing, just watches me with a hesitant glare.

"In any case," I push on, "I've had a lot of fun lately. Thank you... for letting me stay here."

"That's fine. But it's not my doing. Pan's the life of this place, as you may have noticed."

"She sure is. But you built all this, didn't you? I think your parents would be proud."

I bite back on the words, regret filling my chest. What am I saying? I don't talk like this. He's a perfect stranger; why do I care how proud his parents are? I never even knew them.

"Sorry. That was out of line."

Again, he says nothing. But as he walks forward, passing me, and his hand rests on my shoulder. It's only for a moment, so fast I don't have time to react, but as his footsteps fade behind me a smile plays on my lips.

That's the first real bit of kindness he's shown me since I got here.

It's another few hours until Pan finds me. She scolds me, both for leaving her to sleep and working when I didn't need to. But when I tell her about Jay and our talk in the garden, she softens. Her face is suddenly wistful and gentle, like she's remembering something from long ago. I don't question it; let her believe what she likes.

We spend the afternoon at the river, dipping our toes into the water and chuckling as it bubbles around us. It's surprising how easy it is to laugh now, even if it has only been two days. I feel strangely light.

At some point, I ask about my job.

"What job?" she asks, clearly confused.

"Nate said I need to work to earn my keep."

"Oh, that! I was going to ask if you wouldn't mind helping with the crops, since you know all about that stuff. But you already did it. Plus everyone's work for a week."

I gulp. Whoops.

"Sorry. I didn't think."

"Don't worry about it. Thanks to you, nobody has to work that patch for a while. It filters down, so that means everyone has a little less work to do now. You'll find people are very grateful for that. We're always so busy trying to win this fight, so chores like that are a nuisance."

And to my surprise, she's right. As we walk around the Atrium, I'm suddenly greeted by people who spent yesterday glaring at me, or shrinking back as though afraid I might bite them. Suspicion gives way to friendly smiles and cheerful hellos. I do my best to return them, trying to hide how unnerved I am by the sudden change. Even more oddly, I find myself smiling back. Waving. Grunting greetings at the same people who frightened me just a day ago.

Someone grabs my arm and I jump.

"Sorry!"

Jensen's voice floats across at me. He's standing awkwardly behind me, a lopsided smile on his face. There are straps on his arms and goggles on his head, giving him a strange, insect-like look. I'm laughing before I can help myself. He puffs out his cheeks; but the irritation is hollow. He seems almost amused.

"Laugh it up, go ahead. I've been hard at work today. What have you been doing?"

I shrug.

"I was at the river. What are you working on?"

Suddenly his face is filled with passion and joy – the excitement of sharing his interest with someone else. He clearly doesn't get asked all that much.

"I'm installing cameras around Thorne. We've already hacked into the existing ones plus a ton of Hoverbots, but the three leaders are secretive. So we've been trying to sneak into locked-out areas and install hidden cameras there."

"I didn't know you could do that."

"Yep. The key to bringing the Cull to a stop is information. We've not yet been able to hack into the leader's mainframe, but we can monitor practically everything that happens outside each of the three leaders' buildings."

Somehow, I've been having so much fun that I forgot about the low key battle raging just outside these walls. Jensen pushes on, eager to have an audience for his speech.

"Each leader has their own tower," he explains, "with ridiculous security. We have theories on how to get in but so far, it's too risky. So we just monitor them for now."

"So the straps and goggles…"

"I'm about to head out to install a new camera. It's a fairly quiet area from what I can tell, so it's fairly low risk, but I need help. Specifically, I need manpower."

"And that means me?"

"I hope so. I need someone to help with heavy lifting, and everyone's busy. You're kinda strong, aren't you?"

"I suppose."

"Good. Pan, you don't mind if I borrow her for a couple of hours, do you?"

I glance at Pan, expecting her to refuse. She's supposed to be looking after me, right? I shouldn't go sneaking off without her. But to my surprise, she nods.

"It's fine with me. But grab a jacket before you go, and keep the hood up. I know it's getting dark soon, but don't risk it. I don't think we're ready to have her face known just yet."

"Of course. We'll leave the Hoverbots here, too. Don't want them to be spotted. You coming?"

With that Jensen holds out an arm, and though I'd really rather do anything else, I take it.

The streets are quiet by the time we leave. There's a warm, reddish glow seeping its way between the buildings as the sun sets overhead – but it's too early for lights, so everything's bathed in shadow. I can almost hear the click and buzz of the floodlights turning on back home.

"So where is this place?" I ask. He simply reaches up and pulls my hood further over my face.

"Don't talk yet. Just follow me, and be quick."

He glances out of the side street and darts across the road with expert precision, so fast that if I hadn't been watching, I may not have noticed. He tugs his goggles from his head and stuffs them into his pocket, blending seamlessly with any other randomer on the street. I follow suit, though my movements are far less delicate. Unlike Jensen, there's no way for me to blend in. Any onlookers will be drawn to me instantly; my short, stocky form and tanned skin is a far cry from anything they've seen before. But with my face sufficiently covered, I'm not too concerned.

As we walk, I notice that the people around us seem... different from before. They're few and far between, but they act strangely, compared to how they do in the day. Some stumble around on the pavement, or laugh a little too loudly. Two figures are curled up in a doorway, their faces pressed together. I inhale deeply; the stench of alcohol and unwashed bodies floods over me.

What was it that Eagen told me, all that time ago? People in the city are strange. When they have nothing to do, people go a little crazy.

Jensen must notice my discomfort, though, because he allows himself to fall a half-step back, coming into line with my steps. There's no eye contact between us, nothing that would suggest we know each other. But it's enough to settle my racing heart. It's strange, but my apparent trepidation seems to be enough to make him warm towards me. That suspicion's not quite gone, but he seems to be softening.

Finally, we come to a strange, round building. There are signs everywhere that I can't quite read, but judging by the look of the suited men strolling outside, it's somewhere important.

"Follow me," whispers Jensen, his hand locking around my wrist. I follow obediently and soon we arrive at the rear of the building. Here it's dark and silent, and the general bustle at the front of the building is muffled.

He points at one of the gates. They're huge and white, made of painted metal. They remind me of the heavy gates back at the Mill. The same ones that clanged shut behind me as I left with the cart. That noise – the one that had felt so inescapably final.

"This is why I brought you. The gates are way too heavy for one person to move, but I need to get inside to install the camera."

That's it? He brought me all this way just to open a gate? Irritation flares in me, but I push it aside. I'll do it, but only so we can go back.

The gate squeals as we move it, sending vibrations through the air around us. Jensen winces; I can't help but feel like he's not used to being out here on his own.

"How long have you been doing this?" I ask. I'm not really all that curious, but as his shoulders relax, I know it helps him to talk about it.

"I've been here since the beginning. I was just a kid, really – but I'm a fast learner. Figured out how to handle the computer systems."

"What about your parents?"

We squeeze through the gap and head slowly down the darkened alley, and towards the shadowed building. Jensen hesitates for a moment before replying – suddenly, I've overstepped the boundary and asked him something he doesn't want to talk about.

"I don't know where they are anymore," he eventually admits, "I fell in with Jay and the others when I was younger, and they were against it. Our little group is considered 'bad company' by most in Thorne, even if they agree with what we're trying to achieve."

He waves towards a particularly large, metal bin and I step forward, leaning my shoulder against it and pushing. It doesn't budge. He doesn't even notice.

"Anyway, when I went to my first protest with the others, my parents were furious. They disowned me that day. Never spoke to me again. I moved away from them and never bothered again."

"Do you miss them?"

I push harder this time, finally feeling the wheels give way. Behind me, Jensen clicks his tongue.

"I don't know. Sometimes I feel like it'd be nice to see them again, but it's not worth it. I don't think I could stand to be around people like that anymore."

The bin moves smoothly now, allowing me to shuffle it over to where he points. He jumps on top of it, pulling some equipment from his pockets – including a tiny, metallic camera. As he works, I stand watch, though there's really no point. Nobody's around.

But questions still linger in the air between us, still hang from my tongue.

"What's it like? Living in the city, I mean?"

He sighs, clearly wishing that I hadn't asked.

"It's hard to explain. I make it seem bad because I'm jaded about the whole thing, but there are good things, too. Most of the time, it's amazing. We have all the time in the world and everything we could possibly need. People spend their whole lives working towards their own goals, instead of focussing on their responsibilities. Here, you can get away with doing nearly anything – as long as you find it fun."

"That doesn't sound too bad."

"It's not. Even the Cull doesn't seem too bad once you consider the alternative. It's like living in a bubble. Everything looks distorted and wrong, but it doesn't matter. Because what you can see is pretty and what's outside the bubble might not look so nice. Once you burst it and see what's really going on, there's no way of putting it back again."

With that he falls silent, and it's obvious he's done talking. I try to imagine what his family are like – as intelligent as him, I'd expect. Only less committed, less brave. Happy to look through their bubble just so long as it means avoiding hardship.

Something stirs in my chest. I hadn't expected to feel sad about this. A word comes to mind; empathy. I know what that is, what it's supposed to mean, but I never really cared about it. My life's been an endless list of things to be done, and those things take up so much time that there's never been any chance to think about something like 'understanding' other people. I didn't understand Kane. I don't even think I understood Nel all that much.

I stand in silence until he finally hops down from the bin.

"All done?"

"All done. Now, I can view this spot from my room in the Atrium."

"But, if this spot's quiet, then why do you need it?"

He chuckles.

"You never know. This is a secure back entrance. Anything could happen back here."

I don't challenge him on that. I set to work pushing the bin back to where it needs to be. As I slide it back into place, though, something cold drips onto my arm.

"Looks like rain," says Jensen, shuddering. I glance up and sure enough, the sky is darkening overhead. The sunset is well and truly gone now, leaving us in darkness.

"Should we head back?" I ask, ignoring that little part of me that would much rather wander around. He nods.

"Yeah. We'd better."

As we approach the gate, the rain begins to fall more heavily. It bounces off the ground, obscuring my vision. Water soaks through my hood and hair, dripping down into my eyes – Jensen lets out a few irate grunts as he wipes at his glasses, but I'm used to it. I'm used to finding loose potatoes in knee-deep mud with rain blurring everything around me. Used to chopping wood in a torrential downpour, even though it makes the wooden axe handle slippery under my touch.

So I usher him through the gap in the gates, then gather my strength to push it shut. It catches. The squeal is louder this time, almost deafening. Jensen's eyes widen.

"Damn! Hurry up, hurry up!"

Suddenly, I can hear it. The distant sound of barking dogs and questioning yells. Further down the alleyway, white lights swing – searchlights, looking for the intruders. How did the City Guard snap into action so quickly?

Jensen jumps up next to me and together we slam the gate shut. Then his hand is in mine, and before I know it we're running. We follow the route we came from, but then skid to a stop. I wonder why and open my mouth to ask, but then I see lights coming from that direction, too.

"This way!"

He pulls my arm so hard I wince, but there's no time to complain. I allow him to lead me down a different alleyway. This one's so narrow that we can't run side by side, so he pushes me ahead.

"Keep running!"

I obey immediately, and when I glance back he's running full pelt, head down as though he's doing his utmost to ignore the encroaching lights. In the distance, I can hear yelling. They know we're here.

Wait – who are they? Guards? Something to do with the three leaders? Whoever they are and whatever they want with us, it hits some deep-rooted fear in my chest. My heart is in my throat. I don't know what they'll do if they catch us, and I don't want to find out.

Jensen yelps behind me, slipping on the wet floor. He rolls forward, promptly and painfully colliding with a trash can. I skid to a stop, but he's already sitting up. He clutches at his leg and yelps. There's undeniable terror in his eyes.

"Come on, we have to go!" I cry.

"Y-you go. Back to the others."

"What? No!"

The voices are louder now. There are shadows encroaching on the edges of my vision. They're still some way off – but now, they know we're here. Jensen cringes.

"You know the way back, Ada. Just go!"

My blood runs cold. Then, a split second later, it's hot again – so hot it feels like it could burst from my clenched fists.

"I am not Ada!" I snarl, "I'm Noah, and you'd better use my name when you talk to me, got that? Now put your arms up."

I don't give him chance to do as he's told. In an instant I've scooped him up and thrown him over one shoulder. Jensen screams in protest, but I don't care. He's tall but skinny, his weight nothing compared to things I've hauled before.

I take off at a dead sprint.

CHAPTER THIRTEEN

I run so hard and fast that my vision begins to blur. The rain doesn't help, either, turning everything into a strange blackness that's broken by strobes of passing light. My hood's slipping down and I'm eating my own hair - but the voices are quieter now, the lights gone from my sight.

"Noah, slow down!" Jensen croaks in my ear, "they're gone, we got away."

"You don't know that."

"I do. Come on, stop in an alleyway."

I don't want to. My heart's still pounding in a way I've never felt before, and there's something boiling in my veins. Adrenaline, perhaps? I don't know. But it's painful and scary at the same time. It takes more effort than I'd expected to finally slow to a stop, dropping Jensen unceremoniously onto the ground at the entrance of an alleyway. I can barely breathe, so I sit down next to him and try to gulp down what little air I can get.

I'm still tense, but as I listen to the silence, I hear nothing. No sirens, no yelling. Nobody's coming after us. Jensen's breathless too for some reason, and it's only now that I see how puffy his leg is. I've seen breaks and sprains before. They're unremarkable, basic as far as injuries go – but I know from experience that they hurt like a bitch.

Still, as he meets my eyes, something builds in me. It pushes up from my stomach and bursts out through my mouth. Laughter.

Why am I laughing? This isn't funny. He's hurt. We're stuck in an alleyway in who-knows-where. They're still looking for us. There's nothing funny about this at all. So why am I emitting high-pitched, hiccupping laughter, like some kind of maniac?

He stares at me, and I half expect him to be angry. Instead, he laughs, too. It's low and throaty and seems strangely mismatched with my own.

"W-why are you laughing?" he chuckles. I shake my head.

"This... this is ridiculous! What was that?!"

Suddenly, he's sobered up. Those dark eyes are fixed on me, his expression unreadable.

"That was... intense. I'm surprised with how well you kept it together."

"I didn't."

"You saved me back there."

I bite back on another bout of laughter, and solemnly shake my head.

"I panicked. I'm not even sure what happened."

"The Guards. They're security for the city, especially around the important buildings. Someone must have heard the gate."

"What would they have done if they'd caught up to us?"

He says nothing, so I decide not to push for an answer.

"How is your leg?" I ask, trying to inject a little sympathy into my voice.

"It'll be fine. I think it's just sprained. A few days and I'll be good to go. It's more my pride that's wounded."

"Huh?"

"I brought you out here to help me out," he smiles, "and instead, you carry me like a baby. It's pretty embarrassing."

"Oh. Well, if you want, we won't tell the others about that bit."

Jensen's trying to stand now. He touches one foot to the ground and yelps - I tuck my shoulder under his arm and hold him up.

"Don't be silly," he tells me, "I'm telling them everything. Jay especially will need to know."

"Oh, right. He's your leader, isn't he? It makes sense. He needs to know that you got hurt."

"That's... not the only reason."

Jensen was right, as it turns out. Pan gives him a tentative once-over and declares his ankle to be badly sprained and nothing more. He's visibly relieved, and I can see why - broken bones are a pain to recover from. As she binds him up, she scolds him for his recklessness. I want to jump in, to defend him, but every time I open my mouth I'm reminded of how little I understand. It's not my right to comment.

"This was supposed to be routine."

I'm suddenly aware of Jay standing next to me. He doesn't look my way but his voice is low, like it's intended for only me. A quick glance confirms it.

"Things got out of control," I say simply.

"From what I hear, you managed to keep calm long enough to escape."

"Not really. I was scared, so I started running."

That must be the first time in a while that I've admitted to being scared. Oddly, it doesn't feel as bad as I'd have expected.

"Well, here's something exciting."

He claps me on the back, a warm, confident motion that makes my cheeks burn with joy.

"You've broken your first law. You're a criminal, now. Enjoy it."

My chest swells with pride, but inwardly, I'm screaming.

What have I done?!

Pan falls asleep before I do, curled tightly into a ball. The chaos of the day has left everyone exhausted – but the adrenaline in my veins is still there. I feel like I could sleep for a week, and yet the thought of falling back onto the pillows leaves me unnerved. The room is dark around me, and if not for the soft glow of Pan's fairy lights, I'd feel frightened of the shadows.

Today was... awful. Awful and wonderful and incredible. I've never been so scared or so happy. I've never felt pride before. I've never laughed so hard in all my life. Is this what it's like here? If I chose to stay, would this be my life? Fighting and running and laughing all day, every day? My chest swells with joy at the thought.

Wait. No. Being here isn't all excitement and action, is it? People have died fighting for this cause. Jay's parents were executed.

There's a strange, unpleasant disconnect between the fight I know and the people on Nate's photo. If they were my parents, by some miracle, then I should care. I should grieve their loss. I should admire everything that they did. Instead, they look like perfect strangers to me.

"Atlas."

My voice is low and throaty as I activate the Hoverbot, eager not to disturb Pan. Atlas beeps into life and hovers closely, its tiny flashing lights flickering as it waits for a command. It's weird; it's just a mindless machine, but I feel a sense of attachment to it already. It's hard not to care for something you spend every moment of the day with. I sit up now, pulling the blanket up and over my shoulders. Jensen said I could ask Atlas anything. That it would recognise me as a user. So it should obey me now.

"Atlas, how did Jay's parents die?"

Almost immediately, it projects a small screen into the air between us. It's somewhere between a hologram and a flat image, like whatever camera recorded it was only able to gather half the detail. Some shadowed, half-blurred figure strides across a set of marbled steps. They're holding something long and slim in one hand, and they walk with a strange sense of purpose. As I watch, the glowing screen shifts. Now it shows the view from behind the stranger; two people are chained and bound next to the glass side of the building. The video's not clear enough to show their faces - but I recognise the woman's shock of blonde hair.

Jay's parents. They're beaten and bloodied, their heads hanging as though they're barely conscious. My chest tightens, and though I try to tell myself it's not real, the sense of horror in my gut is all too real. This may have happened sixteen years ago - but it feels like it's happening right now.

The figure walks a little closer to them, and I catch sight of dark hair and a long, white coat. They look more suited to working as a doctor than anything else; but as they swing back the item in their hand, I realise they're no doctor. They're an executioner.

"No!"

I cry out loud as the shock baton collides with the man's throat. Though the blow itself is light, the electricity that jumps out from the device is terrible. Pained screams fill the air around me - and suddenly there are tears building in my eyes. I can't watch this.

"Atlas, stop!"

It obeys immediately, shutting off all light and sinking onto the table across the room. Darkness and silence once again swallows me, but I don't care. I glance across at Pan; amazingly, she's slept through the flickering light, the screams and yelling. Thank heavens. I don't think I want to explain why I was asking about that.

I force myself to fall back into my pillows now, though I know I won't sleep. My hands are quivering with fear and sadness and some strange third emotion that I can't even begin to understand. I pull the blanket tightly around myself and shut my eyes tight. The flashes of light finally fade from behind my eyelids.

Now if only I could stop the screaming echoing in my head.

The next day, there's nothing to do. Pan explains that the Cull's coming up in a few months. At this point, it's too late to try and stop it altogether. So instead, the days need to be spent watching, resting, and practicing.

"Practicing what?" I ask. The question rolls off my tongue more easily now. I've gotten used to the constant urge of curiosity.

"Fighting, mostly. We try to find out who's likely to be taken during the Cull and protect them. So that's what Jensen will be doing right now."

I nod and turn away. The memorial garden is beautiful today. The water of the river is a little cold, but I still kick my feet playfully in it. A warm summer day has caused the flowers around us to bloom, and the grass we're sitting on is greener than ever. Atlas has settled down next to me, opening up a black panel that Pan tells me is to gather sunlight. I inhale deeply, enjoying the familiar scent of soil.

It's strange. This place seemed so alien to me only three days ago. I remember feeling frightened as I walked into the Atrium, my heart in my throat. I'd been scared of everyone - what they could do to me, what they might think. Now? Nothing. Instead, it's warm and comfortable and familiar.

I tug my feet from the water and fall back, laying spread eagled on the grass next to Pan. She doesn't seem surprised. In fact, she's reaching out a gentle hand to scoop some insect from her knee.

She doesn't fit in here. Just like me, she stands out too much. Those sparkling green eyes and red hair are out of place by themselves, but more so than that, she's soft. She's not hardened like the others, though she has just as much reason to be.

"Pan..."

"Hmm?"

"How did you end up here?"

She pauses, the insect fluttering away from her. Her head sinks into her knees as she hugs them close. My chest pangs.

"You don't have to tell me, if you don't want to."

"No," she says, "it's fine. But I want to know why you're asking."

"You're different from the others. You trusted me before anyone else, and... I don't know. You gave me a chance when nobody else did."

At that, she smiles.

"I had to. I learned the hard way never to abandon someone."

Questions tug at me, but I bite back on them. Let her say what she wants.

"You know how Jay's parents died when he was young?" she eventually says. My chest tightens.

"Yeah?"

"Well, he was really young. Like, eight years old. He really wanted to carry on his parents' passion, but a kid can't do that. Nate's his cousin, though their families hadn't been on speaking terms for years. He was a little older, so he looked after Jay."

"Hmm."

"Support for the Clover vanished as soon as his parents died, so for a while it was just them. Jay didn't know what to do. Even when he got older, nobody would listen to him. He had nowhere to start."

I sit up.

"What does this have to do with you?"

"I'm getting there," she insists, "Jay didn't have a clue how to gather a following. Everyone was so willing to believe whatever they were told. They were too scared to rock the boat in case they were killed off, too. Nobody cared about what was right."

She heaves a long, pained sigh.

"I grew up on these streets. It's tough. Thorne is just perfect - unless you're a street urchin. Then, you're considered scum."

"What about your family?"

"I ran away as a kid. They were some... messed up people. I've been alone since I was about nine."

"Oh. Sorry."

"It's okay. I'm better off without them. But I was alone one night when they carried out the Cull. The city's database decided that it would Cull one of the homeless kids who lived nearby - a girl called Cady. She was a sweetheart. Sometimes I'd take her food that I'd nicked. I couldn't let them do it. I attacked a guard, and before I knew it I was being chased. Once they have you in their sights, nothing will ever stop them. I was labelled a criminal for a split second of anger, and even though I got away, I knew they'd find me eventually."

Her voice is strained now, like she's fighting back tears. I shouldn't have asked.

"Pan..."

"It's fine. I escaped. I ended up in an alleyway a few miles away. I didn't know where I was, but I knew that if I stepped outside again, they'd find me. I'd be punished. I... didn't know what to do. I was still crying when he found me."

I don't need to ask who 'he' is. The smile playing on her lips tells me everything.

"He was just a kid," she laughs, "just like me. He asked me what was wrong, but I didn't tell him. I thought he'd turn me in. But he didn't. Instead, he told me who he was. He explained what had happened to his family. What he was trying to do. It sounded wonderful. He offered me a place to stay that was safe, as well as protection from those trying to hurt me. All I needed to do was take his hand."

She stares at her own hands now, furling and unfurling her fingers.

"Of course I did, and I ended up here. Now, I'm sure that this is what I was always supposed to do. My calling, if you will. I became Second in Command and that's been it ever since."

I hesitate before speaking. To know Pan, I'd never suspect something like that had happened. She's too friendly and too sweet. Guilt swirls in my chest. What right do I have to be distant and hard, when my life's been easy by comparison?

"And you don't regret it? Giving up everything for this life?"

"Absolutely not. I know that Jay can seem distant, but that's not him. Not really. He's the best person I've ever met. I'd do anything for him."

I bite my lip.

"You really love him, don't you?"

I've picked up on the signs. His clothes in her room. The way his gaze lingers on her. How she touches his arms, leans into him – it's obvious there's something there.

She simply laughs, then pushes me back down. I'm lying on the grass again, and there's the warm air and the light feeling in my heart again. Pan stares up through the skylight, and even though I can't see her face, I'm certain she's smiling.

CHAPTER FOURTEEN

The sound of rain breaks through my peaceful sleep. I stir, half-expecting my bunk to be soaked thanks to the hole in the bunker's ceiling. Nel's probably at my side right now, growling in frustration as her bunk is drenched though.

But then I hear snickering, and my eyes snap open.

I'm in the Atrium. The rain is pounding against the glass overhead, breaking through the warmth of a summer day. I'm still in the garden, on my back, the grass tickling my face. Did I fall asleep? Pan's not sitting next to me, anymore. She's standing behind me, talking to someone. They both chuckle, and I recognise Jay's voice. Oh, great.

"Morning, sleepyhead."

Pan's voice is high and singsong as she teases me, but I simply growl.

"Please, don't say it's actually morning."

"It's not. But you've been napping for a few hours now."

I sit up, ignoring the ache in my back.

"Seriously? I can't believe I fell asleep."

"I don't blame you," Jay chuckles, "Jensen's the same. He overslept by about three hours this morning. Long day yesterday, wasn't it?"

He's talking to me differently, now. There's nothing hard or distant about his voice, and as he holds out his hand for me to take, there's an easy smile on his face. I grab his hand, surprised by the strength in his fingers.

"Ouch. Good grip."

"You, too. Listen, we're sparring again tonight. I know you probably aren't interested in fistfights, but we could do with the practice. From what I hear, you're pretty tough. Feel like helping me out? I could do with a new challenge."

I gulp hard. The idea of facing Jay is frightening. He might be shorter than the others, but he has the same stocky build as I do. My wrists throb at the memory of being pinned on my first day here. I certainly don't fancy fighting him.

Still, I push my fear aside and smile.

"Sure thing."

There's a crowd gathering tonight. They circle the sparring ring, watching as Jay paces. There's excitement in the air. They're all looking forward to seeing him fight. I suppose it makes sense. If he were weaker than his comrades then he wouldn't be the leader, would he? Even so, when I compare him to Nate and his oversized limbs, I find it hard to imagine that he's a heavy hitter. He glances my way.

"Are you ready?"

His voice is calm, patient. He's giving me an out. If I say no, he won't force me; but there's sense of hope in his eyes. I can back out, sure, but only at the risk of disappointing him. And I can't bring myself to do that.

"Yeah," I lie, "I'm ready."

He glances around, a sly smile playing on his lips.

"Lots of people here tonight."

"They're excited to see you fight, aren't they?"

My hesitation must show on my face, because he shoots me a reassuring look.

"Don't worry so much. It's just because I normally don't join in. I prefer to train in private. Besides, this isn't a fight, remember?"

I bite my lip.

"I don't understand how I'm supposed to help. I don't know how to fight - I just throw my weight around and hope for the best."

"That's exactly why I asked you. From what I hear, you're slow but strong. We're not used to that. The Guards usually use these, long, electrified batons, so it's usually speed that saves the day for us."

"Batons?"

I give an involuntary shudder. They're likely not quite the same thing, but suddenly my mind is filled with thoughts of the cattle shockers from the Mill. They're a short, sharp pain for the animal- but the Guards have been known to modify them and turn them on disobedient workers. On a human, they do some serious damage. A person's lucky to survive full contact with one; and even if they do, the scars and pain are terrible. I think of the video Atlas showed me and shake the thought from my head.

"You know about them?" he asks.

"Yeah. Kind of."

He watches quietly for a moment, perhaps waiting for me to explain. When I don't he just shrugs, then waves me into the ring.

"Okay, normal rules. Let's see how I do against a different kind of opponent. I'll try not to land any hard blows, okay? If you want to try to hit me, aim for the chest. Bigger target."

If I try to hit him? So he thinks he'll be so fast that I won't be able to lay a hand on him? Something rebellious flares in my chest and I tense, lifting my arms in preparation. This time, I'm not scared. Now I know there are no repercussions for fighting, the fear is gone. All that remains is subtle excitement at the thought of sparring again.

"Go!"

My first blow hits air. Jay dodges me easily, then twists and locks a hand around my arm. My weight shifts as he tries to throw me, but I'm too heavy - I lock my knees instead and pull, wrenching my wrist from his grip. He just laughs.

"You gotta think faster!"

I don't reply; I just lower my shoulder and barge his way. Again he steps side at the last moment, tries to catch me as I pass - and this time, it works. My knees hit the ground but I'm standing again quickly, and this time when I swing my fist his way, the blow lands.

That's it. Just like last time, I expect him to crumple from the force of the blow. But he doesn't. Instead, he staggers back, looks momentarily surprised, then laughs. My frustration builds. Is he trying to annoy me?

This time, he kicks out - and it's the last thing I expect. His foot catches my leg and sends me sprawling onto the ground. Before I can move, he's got me pinned. My body strains under his weight, but he simply chuckles.

"Give up?" he teases, delight dancing behind his eyes.

I sigh.

"Y-yeah."

When Jay finally lets me up, my face is burning. The humiliation runs deep. I'd been concerned about that match - but I hadn't expected to lose so quickly, and certainly not so thoroughly. The others cheer for him, clap his back, chant his name. In their eyes, their leader just won a match.

In my eyes, I just lost.

But then he holds out a hand to me.

"You okay?"

I take it hesitantly, a little afraid he might try to pin me again, but he doesn't. He just pulls me onto my feet.

"Pan was right. You do hit hard."

"You didn't even react."

"That doesn't mean it didn't hurt. I just didn't let you know it."

"What was that?" I blurt, "how did you beat me so easily when you didn't even throw a punch?"

"I was trying to use your weight against you. You might be strong, but you've got bad balance. I figured all I had to do was knock you off kilter and you'd be easy to pin. Looks like I was right."

I swallow back the embarrassment.

"That wasn't much help, was it?"

"No, no. It was helpful. People in the city aren't built like you. They're really tall and thin, so they're easy enough to bring down with a little force. It was interesting to spar with someone like you."

Somewhere in there, tucked away in his words, I'm sure there's an insult.

This is strange, right? He could be my brother, but we were just fighting. I suppose it could be labelled a sibling rivalry by some, except that there's no real rivalry there. Siblings tease each other sometimes, don't they? Maybe that's what it was. I suppose I can think of it positively if it's something like that.

A small voice in my head objects to the warmth in my chest.

But he might not be your brother.

I sit quietly for the rest of the evening, nursing my fresh bruises and sore ego. As expected, Jay manages to best nearly everyone he faces. He really does know how to use people's skills against them; the only person he doesn't beat with ease is Pan, and I suspect that's due to his obvious soft spot for her.

Their relationship strikes me as odd. They never outwardly show affection, but there's a sense of intimacy there. Like they understand the situation but simply choose not to act upon their feelings. Still, it's sweet. I can't help but smile as I watch them laugh together.

Even though my cheeks are still red from my loss, and my back is aching from being pinned, I'm happy. There's so much joy in the space around me and I absorb it, revelling in it.

I'm so happy here. Already, this place feels like home.

But it's not.

My joy is tinged with sadness as I watch them, and while their laughter makes me smile, I can feel a small, building sense of loss. Tomorrow, I have to go back.

That was the agreement, right? I promised Pan I'd stay four days. She clearly expects me to stay now, that those four days will stretch on forever, but I don't think they can. Things have changed so much over the past few days. If I could make the choice, I'd want to stay here forever.

But to abandon the place I call home? To turn my back on everything I've known? To never see Nel again? I can't do it. Besides, after what I did to Kane, I don't think I ever want to be that close to someone again. I'm clearly too cowardly to be trusted.

Jay throws out a hand to help up his latest sparring partner, grinning his toothy grin. Kindness and strength radiate from him in waves.

Maybe if I knew the truth, this wouldn't be so hard. Sacrificing everything for a long-lost brother makes more sense than giving it all up for strangers. If only I could be certain, I could convince myself to stay in this life. But without knowing the truth...

Suddenly, I can't watch anymore. I stand up and head back to the room, Atlas trailing after me.

I'm up before Pan the next morning. She's clearly exhausted from last night's chaos; she's sprawled across her bed, blankets entangled in her legs, dried drool on her chin.

I wonder if she noticed me leaving last night. Did she wonder why? Did she even question it? She's supposed to be keeping an eye on me, right?

My Mill clothes are crumpled and stinking, still abandoned in the corner where I left them. There are still some remnants of bloodstains on the shirt, reminding me of that fight my first day here. At the time, I was furious. But that anger is fading fast.

I run a hand through my hair, surprised at how smooth it seems to lie now. Before it was just a crusted mass, but soap and care have encouraged it to lie flat. I don't care enough to look in a mirror, but I'm sure I must be unrecognisable from the person who came here four days ago.

"Noah?"

Pan's awake now, groggily watching me from across the room. She eyes the clothes in my hand.

"What are you doing?"

"Morning. I'm just sorting things out for later."

"Later?"

Here goes.

"Yeah. It's day four, remember?"

In an instant she's awake and standing, but her legs aren't as alert as her mind and she stumbles across the room to get to me.

"W-what are you talking about?!" she cries. There's a definite touch of anger in her voice, but I choose not to point it out. Instead, I busy myself folding the clothes. They don't really need to be folded, but I can't bring myself to meet the hurt in her eyes.

"I promised you four days, that's all. If I don't head home soon, there'll be hell to pay."

"But I thought..."

Her voice breaks a little – the realisation, perhaps, that she couldn't convince me. Guilt burns through me. She did convince me. I wish I could stay, but I can't.

"Look, I don't have a choice. If I'm late, I face some pretty bad punishment. I don't fancy another stint in the mines. If I end up being really late, they might even wipe patches of memory as punishment."

She doesn't seem to hear that part – she's too distracted.

"Then don't go! I thought you liked it here."

"I do. Really, I do. It's amazing, and I love it. But I can't do this forever."

She stamps her foot.

"Why not?!"

"It's not me, Pan! You know that. I'm just not cut out for this. I'm just a Millchild."

"I thought you were finally starting to see past that. I thought you were having fun."

"I was. I am. But you don't need me around."

"Who says we don't?"

"I do," I insist, my anger rising. Why doesn't she understand?

She locks her hands onto my shoulders, forcing me to look straight into those bright, clear eyes.

"Tell me the truth. Why won't you stay?"

"I…"

I bite back on the words, but then think better of it. I'm leaving either way. What does it matter if she knows the truth? When I speak again, my voice is hard and bitter.

"Back home, there was a kid. His name was Kane."

"Huh?"

"We were close for a while. Then one day he asked me to back him up with something. He attacked a guard for some reason – and even though he asked me to support him, I didn't. He got dragged off to the mines, probably beaten stupid. They could have wiped his memory, or killed him. He could be dead right now for all I know, and it's all my fault."

My hands are shaking with barely concealed anger, the likes of which I didn't even know I was holding in. Her face falls.

"Noah, I didn't..."

"He probably had a plan, and I ruined it," I choke, "all because I didn't trust him. Now, he's paying the price. Do you understand now? You don't need me around because I'm not like you. Not where it counts. You can't trust me to stick around when you need me."

I wrench myself from her grip and turn away, clutching the clothes to my chest. I thought I'd gotten over this. I thought that moment with Darus had resolved this – but no. The guilt is there, as real and painful as ever.

"Is that why?"

Pan's voice is hushed, barely a whisper, but it echoes in the tiny room.

"Is what why?"

"You feel guilty for what you did back then. And you're trying to punish yourself by leaving when you don't even want to."

"I-it's more complicated than that. You've only known me four days. You barely know me at all. I... I could be anyone."

"But you could be Ada. You could be the key to fixing everything."

"But what if I'm not? Then I'm just a disappointment, aren't I?"

She looks away, and I can tell that she wants to deny it. She wants to wrap her arms around me and tell me she won't be disappointed, that it's fine no matter who I am. But she can't do it. Because it's not true. No matter how sweet she is, she can't pretend it's okay.

"If I knew the truth," I say, "things would be different. Maybe I could stay. But..."

"Would that help?"

"Huh?"

"If we find out who you are, would that change things?"

I hesitate.

"I... think so. If I was in a position to help you, then I'd stick around to do it. But if I'm not Ada, then as much as I love it here, I have no reason to stay."

She grabs my arm now, a sudden fire in her eyes.

"Then that's what we'll do. I know Jensen's been looking into ways to confirm your identity. I'm sure he knows a way. We'll find out the truth, okay?"

"But..."

"Please," she pleads, "just... trust me."

I want to say no. I want to pull away and insist that I'm leaving. But suddenly I'm falling into those clear, green eyes. Always so kind, so trusting. All of her vulnerabilities are out there for me to see, and I can't help but weaken when faced with them. I sigh.

"Okay. I trust you."

"You want to do what?!"

Jay's voice is so loud that I can hear it even through the walls of his little control room. My hands tighten against the railing. I'm standing on the little bridge overlooking the river and the rest of the Atrium. Pan had decided it would be better for me to wait outside, rather than be present for their conversation. As we'd walked through the corridors, she'd grabbed Jensen and explained things. The two of them went in to speak to Jay about fifteen minutes ago, and since then, nothing.

Until now.

The door to the room flies open, flung so hard that it hits the wall behind it and bounces back. I shrink back as Jay marches towards me. His shoulders are back and his jaw is set; but it's not quite anger in his eyes. Nevertheless, I take a pointed step back as he nears me.

"You want to leave?"

His voice is hard, demanding. I swallow hard.

"N-no. Not exactly."

"If you don't want to be here, you don't have to be. You're not a prisoner."

"I know."

"So if you want to go, just go."

There it is. The choice. I'd been hoping nobody would give me one. I should probably move now. Take his words as a clear signal to go. Instead, I'm rooted to the floor. My mouth is dry. An unpleasant silence falls over us.

Say something. Anything.

"For god's sake, Jay!"

Pan rushes up behind him, grabbing his shoulder. I spot Jensen sidling up behind her, watching the whole thing with apparent bemusement. He catches my eye and smirks.

"Were you even listening to me?" Pan cries, "I explained everything, didn't I?"

"I want to hear her say it."

My face is hot. I thought he might be conflicted to hear I'm leaving - maybe even a little hurt. I didn't expect anger. I take another step back.

"Why?" says Pan, "I told you everything."

Everything? Even about Kane? Her eyes suggest otherwise. Why am I doing this, anyway?

"I want to stay."

Their bickering stops at that - none of them were expecting me to say it. Jay's eyes flash with anger.

"Then why are leaving?"

"Because..."

I take a long, deep breath.

"I just... I don't want to let you down."

His face falls. My words have taken the wind out of his sails.

"What?"

He fixes me with his gaze, those dusty eyes meeting mine.

"You could be Ada."

"I might not be. I like this place, and you. I don't think I can stand to see your disappointment if you find out that she's dead after all. After everything you've been through, I don't want to hurt you."

"But..."

"I'm sorry. But if there's no way of finding out the truth, then... I can't do this."

An uncomfortable silence settles between us, and I notice that the Atrium's fallen silent, too. Even the crickets in the garden below are quiet. I wonder if they sense the mood. For a moment, Jay just watches me. His expression is unreadable, his lips slightly parted like he doesn't know what to say. Just like Pan. He can tell me I can stay no matter what, but he'd be lying if he said he wouldn't be disappointed. Guilt and sadness well in me. Half of me wants to burst into tears; but the other half just wants to go home. My hands feel empty without an axe or shovel weighing them down.

But then he glances back at Jensen, his face in shadow.

"You think this is going to work?"

Jensen shrugs.

"We've got a good chance. I'd say it's the best plan we've got."

"And how soon could we go?"

"Within a day. Maybe two. I'd need to hack some additional security systems, but I'd be able to do that pretty fast."

Jay bites his lip.

"Then, I guess we have a plan."

He turns to me, his face suddenly full of determination. He holds up two fingers.

"Give us two days."

"Two days? For what?"

He smirks.

"You're right. It's been driving me mad, too. Not knowing. So we're going to find out."

I feel my jaw drop.

"Really?"

"Yeah. We have an idea."

With that he turns away and leaves. Jensen skitters after him and the two begin talking furiously as they return to Jay's room. I watch them go, discomfort building in my chest. Pan beams.

"I'm so happy for you!"

"I'm not sure what just happened."

"I told you, didn't I? Jensen's been looking for some way of checking your DNA. Once I explained it to Jay, he understood."

"So why was he so mad?"

"Because I added it right at the end – the bit about you having to go back. How you'd get punished if you didn't get back in time. That kind of upset him."

"I noticed. Is this really okay? I feel like I've made some outrageous demand."

She laughs.

"Yeah, totally outrageous. How dare you want to know who you are? Geez."

With that she hooks her arm around my neck again, steering me back towards the Atrium. She's smiling again. It's a nice smile. It's toothy and wide, and her mouth's a little too big for her face – but it's genuine. Probably the most genuine thing I know.

I allow her to lead me away.

The following night, something lowers overhead in the Atrium. A great screen, built of dozens of smaller ones pushed together. Some only show black and white, while others are strangely bright – but the picture they form is the same.

Vast crowds of people watch a stage. It's set up in front of an endlessly tall building; one of the three skyscrapers that caught my eye before. Three people stand there, shoulders back, a dignified air about them. They're talking amongst themselves, exchanging respectful glances and friendly nods – but the noise is muffled, and I can't make out the words.

"This again?"

Jensen drops down next to me. I'm sitting on the floor near the sparring area. Nobody's fighting tonight, but it seemed like a good place to sit and rest after an exhausting day. Atlas is perched calmly by my side. It seems tired, too – I suppose that it's spent the whole day tracking my every confusing movement, scanning every change in my heartbeat and temperature. It must have been skyrocketing and calming constantly today. Jensen notices, too.

"How are you liking Atlas?"

I shrug, not wanting to let him know how much I've grown to like its presence. It's strange – it's little more than a floating computer, and yet I find myself reassured by it. Like I'm never quite alone. I hadn't expected that to feel good.

"It's alright."

He just winks. That's weird, too – it feels like the suspicion has faded.

"What's this again, anyway?" I ask. He tilts his head at me, confused.

"Wow, you really don't know anything, do you? They're the three leaders. We watch the broadcasts to gather intel about the upcoming Cull. Here, look."

He points to them each in turn – first, a tall man with a willowy figure and an expression like something stinks. He smirks and tips his hat to the camera as it passes, arrogance and confidence warring on his slim features.

"That's Cartwright. He's the Economic leader. He's a sympathiser, though he'd never admit it. We always consider him a non-risk. He wouldn't let us go if given the chance, but if we overpowered the others, he'd fall into line pretty quickly."

Next, a portly man with a shock of dark hair and a rather impressive moustache.

"Gingham. He upholds legislation for industries, Mill imports, that kind of thing. He's a total asshole, but doesn't really have the smarts to carry out a full-on attack. Most of the more disgusting laws are his idea. Personally, I reckon it's how he gets his rocks off."

"Huh?"

"You know, he's a sadist. Likes hurting people."

"Oh."

Finally, the camera settles on the third leader. She's a tiny wisp of a woman, but her presence commands the attention of everyone around her. Black eyes stare from beneath heavy brows. Black hair is scraped back to reveal a sharp face. Her slim body is swathed in white. I feel myself recoil from her glare. Beside me, Jensen shudders.

"Ugh. Her."

"Who is she?"

"Maynard. She's responsible for keeping us in line. She's basically been the driving force behind the Cull for the past twenty years. She's smug and vicious and has no respect for anyone except herself. She's a total viper."

"So, she's the main problem?"

"Absolutely," he says, "she's the only one who actively hunts us down. Sends out Guards all the time. She's also the one who sends out broadcasts to torture us. Without her, this would be a hell of a lot easier. But, and I really hate to say this, the woman's smart. Really smart. She knows exactly what to say and do to twist everything to her whim. She's vile, though. She's the one who…"

He trails off, and suddenly I realise where I've seen her before. The clip that Atlas showed me. Maynard was the figure striding around on the stairs, twirling the shock baton like a toy. She was the one proclaiming the moral high ground. She was the one who tortured Jay's parents. Their executioner. I feel a sudden urge to launch myself at the screen.

"Your patience is amazing," I growl, "If I had just fifteen minutes alone with her…"

"What?"

"Nothing."

He knows, though. His expression changes.

"We can't kill anyone, Noah."

"I know. I wasn't suggesting it."

"It's not like we haven't considered it," he explains, "We did once. We figured it'd be pretty easy to get hold of some guns from the Guards at the city limit. Kill her from a distance, before she even knew what hit her. But we couldn't do it. Couldn't even try. We hate the leaders because they kill people. If we kill them, we become no better."

I nod, regretting even thinking it.

"So, who was it that chased us the other night?"

"That was Cartwright's Guard. Each leader has their own Guard – you can tell them apart by the symbols on their uniforms. Cartwright's symbol is a tree. Gingham's is a lotus."

"What about Maynard?"

He grimaces.

"She uses a rose. I think it's supposed to be some kind of play on 'Thorne', but if it is, then her sense of humour sucks. Anyway... Cartwright might be mostly harmless, but his Guards aren't. They're armed to the teeth and they all seem to take a sick kind of joy out of hurting people. It's a common saying around here that only psychopaths join the Guard."

I sigh.

"I guess we got lucky, huh? Not getting caught, I mean."

He hesitates at that.

"About that. I never said thanks, did I?"

"For what?"

"You saved my ass back there. I never said thank you."

My cheeks burn.

"You don't need to. I wasn't even sure what I was doing. Adrenaline took over."

"That's good. It means you can snap into action. That's helpful in a tough situation. In fact if you're up for it, I want to bring you with us tomorrow. My ankle's strapped up and all, but it still hurts like a bitch. It'd be good to have you along, just in case."

"What's tomorrow?"

"The plan," he says softly, "but it's dangerous. I'd understand if you said no."

"I don't mind. But will Jay trust me to come along?"

"Trust isn't the issue. Just come with us, and let's see if he tries to stop you. Come into my room tomorrow morning. I'll explain the plan."

I open my mouth, wanting to ask more, but stop myself. He'll explain it all tomorrow.

CHAPTER FIFTEEN

Jensen's room is bigger than I'd have thought – but any useable space has been taken over by computers. Grey and black boxes fill every available surface, even the bed, and the whole place is dominated by a vast screen. He sits with his back to the door, tapping away at the keyboard.

Jay, Nate and Pan are already here, along with Nelson and another guy I don't recognise. Nobody seems confused as I walk into the room; either they were already expecting me, or are unsurprised that I'm here.

Jensen glances my way with a smirk.

"Morning. I'd have thought you'd be the first here."

"I've been up for hours," I correct him, "I've been working the crop patch. I guess I figured you'd be like Pan and wouldn't wake up until noon."

Pan blushes at that – but Jensen seems to find it funny, at least. He waves a hand at the screen.

"Gather round then, guys. I'll explain everything."

On his screen is a map. It takes me a few seconds to realise that it's Thorne, perfectly round with strong borders. I remember the chain-link fence I had to pass to get in here, and wonder if it goes all the way around the city. What a waste of the perfectly fertile soil beyond their borders. My eyes follow the lines of the roads – straight and joined from the entrance, splitting off into thousands of separate roads that worm their way into every corner, but always come back together at the closest of three points. Jensen catches me looking at them and points.

"These are the HQs for the three leaders. Each one's impossible to access. I'm talking cameras, alarm systems... they're always on total lockdown. This one here in the middle... this is Maynard's."

It's just a dot on a screen, but for some reason the thought of that woman's stern, cold face is enough to leave me shaken.

"Okay."

"Long story short, we need to break into it."

I gasp, but the others seem unsurprised. It seems they've already discussed this. Still, they exchange grim glances. This isn't going to be easy.

"I don't understand," I say, "how will this help us?"

"We think you might be Ada because our database said so. But that's not reliable because the leaders have control of the system. Maynard in particular has messed with it before. So we can't be sure that it isn't just set up to mark any similar person as a match."

My heart sinks.

"So there's no way to know?"

"Let me finish. There's no way for us to know with the access we have. I've still not been able to remotely hack their systems. They have too much protection. But if we could get in, we could use their internal database to check. Their data will be completely untouched. We could do a multi-point identity check, and confirm for certain if you're actually her. Problem is, I can't get into it from here. I think you see where this is going."

I swallow hard.

"We need to get into that building," Jay interjects, "so that Jensen can get into their computers. We won't have time to do the checks while we're there, so we'll bring a copy of the database back with us."

"But if they're really well protected, how do we get in?"

"Jensen's spent sixteen years breaking into every other system the leaders have. He can remotely turn off their cameras and security systems. He can even short the electricity, giving us a chance to get in and out while the building's using emergency power."

Jensen nods.

"They have a flawed system. If they're running on emergency power, their internal system security goes down, too. We can get in without much trouble."

They exchange small smiles, and suddenly there's a small rush of something warm in my chest. Happiness, maybe? They had a plan all along.

"So, when do we go?"

I try to inject some degree of confidence into my voice as I speak, but Jay still seems mortified.

"We? You're not going."

"Why not? You're doing this because of me. I should be allowed to help. Besides, if you're still worried I'm going to do something bad, then check Atlas' records. It's not left my side since I got here – except for when I was with Pan or Jensen."

He seems frustrated at that, partly because I'm arguing with him, but mostly because there's no good reason to keep me here. Pan gently pats his arm.

"Jay, it's alright. We'll give her a hood and scarf, keep her face covered. Just like last time."

"I don't know."

"She saved my ass," Jensen admits, "I think she'll do okay."

I just smile, my eyes meeting his. With a single glance, I issue a firm challenge. Give me the chance - and I'll prove myself. He heaves a pained sigh.

"Fine. Fine! We go as soon as it gets dark. Leave that Hoverbot behind, though."

"I thought you needed it to watch me?"

"We don't want to risk anyone spotting it. Besides, we'll be right there. I'll watch you myself."

They lead me through the labyrinth and up to one of the entrances, which turns out to be some kind of corrugated metal shed. Inside are a number of contraptions I vaguely recognise as motorbikes. They bear some resemblance to the quads we sometimes use to cross fields at the Mill, but these ones are bigger and infinitely more intimidating.

"Bikes?" I ask. Pan flashes a smug smile my way.

"We can't exactly drive a car around - and we get chased a lot. It's the best way of getting around. Before anyone even recognises us, we're gone."

"We're using these to get there?"

"Yep."

I eye the nearest one, trepidation building. They're different from the ones I've used before. Taller, less balanced. Pan chuckles.

"Don't worry. You can ride with me. I've got added stands on the wheels, so you can perch on the back pretty easily."

I shoot her a confused look, but she doesn't seem to notice.

"Ahem."

Nate steps up behind us, casting a cursory glance over the scene before him. He seems somewhat amused as he looks me up and down. I suppose I must look out of place among these glossy machines.

"You guys ready for this?"

The others nod in agreement; I stay silent, not knowing the answer.

"Remember, we're probably going to have to fight someone," says Jay, "so be prepared."

"Exactly what I was about to say," Nate replies, "that's why I've brought some gear. Just joint guards, bandages to keep with you. Things like that."

He passes them out to everyone, but stops at me.

"You alright, kiddo?"

"I think so."

"Good. Listen, I've thrown something together for you. It's not much, and I won't be offended if you don't want it, but here."

He presses something into my hand – a long, curved piece of metal and rubber with straps around it.

"What's this?"

"It's a gauntlet. I noticed when you sparred with the others that you instinctively block blows with your left arm. It's a surprising move – most people try to avoid the blow altogether rather than taking it directly like that. It's good, it'll catch them off guard. But it's still dangerous. One good blow and you could break your arm, and if you block a shock baton like that you'll go down easily."

"Oh."

He takes it from me now, wrapping it around my outstretched arm. I run a hand over it; the object is stiff and metallic, with a series of ridges and bumps across its surface.

"This is to protect your arm," he explains, "so when you block, it won't hurt as much. The bottom's insulated with rubber so it should withstand the worst of a shock baton blow – not to say it won't hurt, but it might not kill you, at least. The top's textured to make blows glance off. I didn't have enough time to make it bulletproof or anything, but it's something. What do you think?"

I look down at it, and slowly the realisation dawns on me that this is mine. Made for me, just for me. The first possession I've ever had.

"I love it. Thank you."

CHAPTER SIXTEEN

Driving through the streets on the back of Pan's bike is a wholly different experience from running down alleyways. It's strange, really - when Jensen and I came here, I'd been disturbed by the sheer number of people wandering about, acting strangely. Now? We go by too fast to see detail. They're just figures, just blurry shapes in the otherwise peaceful streets.

I adjust my hold on Pan's shoulders and blush. I'm not used to being this close to anyone. She'd tried to convince me to grab onto her waist or wrap my arms around her, but I just can't do it. Nonsense or not, the Mill's teachings are still embedded in my brain, warning me away from physical contact.

Pan checks back to make sure I'm still holding on, then tugs the front of my hood forward. I'm wearing a thick black scarf around my mouth and the light rain has soaked my hair to my forehead, exposing only my eyes. I have to admit, it feels kind of nice.

It's only now that I realise just how vast the city is. I quickly lose all sense of direction and find myself pulling closer to Pan as we venture deeper into the maze that is her home. It's not all bad, though. The speed is pleasant, fun even – I catch myself standing on the spokes and enjoying the sensation of air blustering by. There's a strange, small adrenaline rush when I feel the wind on my face, even though it's dark and cold and wet.

We cut through a street that's decorated as though for a parade; barriers line the kerb and there are bunches of flowers hanging from every streetlight. Strings of multicoloured fairy lights are strung from building to building, hanging low overhead. I find myself reaching upwards for them. The bulbs are just beyond my reach, but that's okay. Just seeing the colours flash by against my scarred hand is enough to make me smile.

Suddenly, I feel eyes on me. And sure enough when I look back, the others are watching. Most are clearly bemused by my reaction to the lights, but Pan, Jensen and Nate seem pleased by it. I suppose it makes sense. If I turn out to be her, they'd want me to love it here, right?

Jay's face is a picture of conflict. He doesn't know what to think.

My gut clenches at the thought and I sink back down next to Pan, stomach churning. I'd been so distracted by new sights and sounds and feelings that I'd forgotten why we were here. The others seem to remember, too, and a solemn silence falls over us.

We quickly approach a tall, shadowed building, abandoning our bikes just outside the perimeter. I catch sight of that awful stage from the earlier transmission, darkened in the shadow of the building. I tell myself the structure is only shadowed because Jensen turned off their electricity. The barbed wire on a nearby fence casts an unnerving silhouette in the light.

"This way," says Jay. We move slowly, hands tucked in our pockets, trying not to draw attention now we're getting close. I know, though, that they have weapons stashed away. As Pan had dressed before coming out, she'd fastened a strange item to her thigh. It looked like a gun, only it couldn't be. Guns are illegal; Jensen told me. Only a tiny fraction of the Guard have them. When I'd asked her about it she'd put a finger to her lips and warned me not to tell Jay. It was just insurance, she told me. Just in case.

The entrance to the building is still thick with Guards, and I find myself wondering for the first time why Jensen would choose Maynard's building for this. If she's really the most dangerous one of the bunch, surely her Guards would be, too. I make a mental note to ask about it later.

The other guy who came with us, a lanky, bespectacled man called Hue, pulls out a number of laminated cards. I can't read the text on them in the dim light, but they look official. Jensen mentioned this, too. He added us to the system earlier – but only temporarily. As soon as the power comes back on, the cards will stop working. We head towards an old, unused security door.

The door is rusted shut, and for a moment I doubt the cards will work. But when Jay scans his, it beeps. It takes a little combined effort to push it open, but we eventually sneak inside. I open my mouth to ask why we all needed cards even though we only used one, but think better of it. I don't think they'd take any chances – and there are more important things to think about right now.

The hallways are creepy. I'm not scared of hallways in general; if I were, living in the Atrium for the past week would have driven me mad. But these ones are different. The ceilings are too high and the floors are too white, and the way the ground dips in corners seems to play with my sense of balance. Doors line the walls on every side, and the thought of someone stepping out right in front of us is enough to send my heart racing.

Luckily, the others don't seem so unnerved. They stride down the halls with surprising ease, even though they can't possibly know where to go. There's a distinct air of confidence as they lead the way down the hallways, even daring to glance into the occasional room.

"Not here, either," says Pan as she checks the fourteenth door in a row.

"The blueprints said there was a terminal," Jensen mutters, "there has to be something nearby."

I nudge at the next door, taking a deep breath before stepping inside. It looks to be a boardroom of sorts; a long, black table dominates the room, surrounded by chairs. At the head is a large velvet throne, more suited to royalty than a politician. I can almost smell Maynard's ego soaked into the space around me.

No computer, though.

The next room over is just as dark and just as silent, but this one looks different. It's bland and empty, the floors, walls and ceiling neatly tiled. There are shadows across one wall, and as I step closer I find myself tripping on something. The familiar rattle of chains rings out and I freeze.

This is a cell. The things on the wall are shackles.

Suddenly, I can't breathe. I imagine the two smiling people on Nate's picture strapped up in a place like this. Hurt. Frightened. Wondering where their son could be. Wondering what happened to their daughter. My blood runs cold at the thought.

"Noah?"

Jay's behind me. He must have heard the chains. His eyes travel down to the shackles, then settle on me. I must look scared, because his expression softens. I fight the desire to move closer to him, to seek comfort in his presence.

"Is this...?"

My voice is weak, fragile, like I'm on the verge of tears. But my cheeks are bone dry; it's not grief that fuels my reaction.

"Is this what they do? Keep them in shackles?"

"This is their idea of justice. This is what we're fighting against."

"And they..."

I pause. I can't ask about his parents. I can't get upset. I never knew them, don't remember their faces. They might be perfect strangers to me – but to him, they're the parents he lost.

"And they think this is okay?"

"I guess so."

There's a pregnant pause as he looks me up and down, concern flickering in his eyes.

"Noah, are you okay?"

"C'mon, let's keep looking."

I dart from the room before he can say another word.

Despite my reassurances to Jay, the cell has left me shaken. At the Mill, a back-talking teen can expect a good beating. At worst, they might wipe your mind and give you a 'fresh start'. But they'd never chain us to a wall and just leave us there to rot. The thought is sickening. I pace the halls again, taking deep breaths to help slow my breathing. I don't want the others to see.

"Found it!"

We all dart towards Pan's voice – and sure enough, the office she's standing in has an active terminal nestled in one corner. Jensen sets to work straight away, telling us to stand watch. We obey immediately, and for the first time I realise how perfectly they work together. Jay might lead, sure, but they move in sync like they're parts of one body, controlled by the same mind.

The corridors are still and silent. The only sounds are our unsteady breathing and the tapping of Jensen's fingers on the keypad. Suddenly, that strikes me as strange.

"Guys."

Jay presses a finger to his lips.

"No, really. Guys?"

"Shh! You'll draw attention to us!" he hisses.

"No, I won't. There's nobody around. Isn't that strange?"

He pauses.

"What?"

"We've not seen or heard anyone," I point out, "all their systems are down. It's pitch black. No electricity. You'd think they'd be worried, maybe suspicious. But we've not seen anyone. Not a patrol. Not even a repairman. I'd expect someone to be trying to fix whatever's gone wrong."

His jaw drops.

"They know we're here."

I nod.

"I think they do. There's probably a trap set up for us."

"Damn it! Jensen, hurry up!"

"Nearly done."

Pan clears her throat.

"Wait. If they knew we were coming, why wouldn't they protect their computer systems?"

"They did," Jensen mutters, "they've put up all their security again. Fixed the loophole. I'm hacking the whole damn system this time."

Jay curses under his breath.

"So they were expecting us. Come on, get that data and let's get out of here."

It takes another fifteen minutes for Jensen to download the database, and in that time though we hear nothing, we become even more certain that they're waiting for us. He pulls the stick from the computer and jams it into his pocket, grim determination on his face.

"Let's get the hell out of here."

This time, I feel no hesitation as we head down the corridors. Knowing they could appear any moment means there's no time to wait around - we run full pelt down the darkened hallways, no longer caring about being discreet. Even so, I can feel that same panic from earlier starting to set in. The creepy halls, the 'boss' chair, the cell; it all builds to something that frightens me to my core.

Outside, the rain is getting heavier. It pounds on the windows of the building, creating a strange effect in the dark hallways.

Eventually Jay slides to a stop just around the corner from the door we used to come in. There's trepidation in his eyes as he peeks around the wall, as though expecting a hoard of Guards to be waiting there. He doesn't react so I assume it's clear, but he still bites into his lip as he turns back to us.

"I'm willing to bet there are some Guards outside that door," he mutters, "any bright ideas?"

"There aren't any other exits nearby," Jensen tells him, "but if they fixed their system security, they probably fixed the cameras, too. If they know where we are, then we're trapped."

Pan and Jay exchange worried looks, but I clear my throat.

"We need to break through."

He stares.

"What?"

"The last thing they'll expect is for you to force your way through, right? It'll take them by surprise."

"But they might have guns."

"Do you have a better idea?"

Suddenly, something shifts in my peripheral vision. It's only a moment, a tiny something – a shadowed figure, lurking just around the corner. Lurching towards Jay. An outstretched hand, clutching a long, familiar item. A shock baton.

My body moves before I can think. I grab Jay and throw him aside – the baton grazes air instead.

"H-hey!" Jay barks. I ignore him. The figure's rounding the corner now.

Some small part of me says that I should wait, that I should see who it is before attacking. But it's too late for that; just like that night with Jensen, the adrenaline takes hold. I take a half-step forward and plough into the stranger. We hit the ground hard and their arms shift as though to swing the baton – I knock their hand aside, but they're already on their feet.

The Guard steps closer to the window, and I catch my first glimpse of his face. Shrunken pupils roll in wide eyes, embedded in a creased, shadowed face. Terror flits through me.

They take the chance, swinging the baton at me again – and this time, I can feel the electricity jumping off it as I leap aside. The hair on my arms prickles as it skims past. Another swing, stronger this time, and I don't have chance to dodge. I catch sight of those manic eyes a second time and suddenly I'm rooted to the spot.

"Noah!"

Jay's voice snaps me out of it. Instinct takes over and I block the blow.

The shock is immense. The baton glances off Nate's gauntlet, rebounding back at the Guard, but it sends a flash of pain through my arm and sends us both sprawling.

"Damn!"

In an instant I've removed the gauntlet and thrown it aside, kicking it away as though frightened by the thing. I can smell burning rubber. There's a scorch mark down the centre of the metal plate, and the patches around it are starting to melt.

For a moment, silence. Then Pan heaves a sigh.

"Well, that scared me. Are you okay?"

I glance at my arm. The skin is pink and a little tender, but there's no damage done.

"Yeah," I gasp, "It's fine."

My eyes are drawn through the darkness, though, to where the Guard lies slumped against the wall. He's motionless, perhaps not breathing – and for a moment, I consider the ramifications of murder. What it means, what it changes.

Then, I push the thought aside. He attacked us. He fully intended to kill us if he could manage it. Why should I care? Suddenly, I'm glad I fought back.

Nate stares down at the still-smoking gauntlet and clicks his tongue.

"I'll, uh, make you a new one when we get home. More insulation this time, maybe."

I laugh, and the others join in. But there's someone who's not laughing. Jay watches me with an unreadable but intense expression on his face. His lips are parted like he has a lot to say, but doesn't quite know how to find the words. That's fine by me. I threw him to the ground without warning – I'd like to put off the inevitable scolding for as long as possible.

"They know where we are, then," says Pan. The mood suddenly darkens, and something aches in my chest. Is she right? Are we really trapped?

"That can't be right," Jensen says, his voice hard, "this guy's just a patrol who happened to overhear us. If they knew where we were, they'd send in the cavalry. Not just this one person."

"Unless they're playing with us," she points out.

"We can't rule it out. But once their systems started to go down, they had a good couple of hours before we got here. In that time, they might have decided to increase their system security – but they might not have realised that the cameras were down. Or they might have just not had time to fix them. We don't know. We're working blind here."

I clear my throat in the darkness.

"So they aren't waiting outside?"

He fixes me with a stern gaze.

"Only one way to find out."

A quick check outside shows nothing but darkness, and there's little noise except for the gentle rustle of the trees lining the building. Even the rain has started to ease off, leaving the concrete slippery underfoot. To my surprise, no alarm goes off as we sneak out. We exchange nervous glances. Can we really have gotten away that easily? One Guard, in and out? I'm almost disappointed with the lack of a challenge. Almost.

"Nothing," Nate breathes, "maybe they don't know where we are."

"We'll worry about that later," says Jay, "for now, let's just get back to the bikes and get the hell out of here."

We do as we're told, creeping low through the darkness until we reach that creepy staging area again. I shudder as we approach. This is where they do their speeches. Just up there, next to the doors - that's where Jay's parents were publicly killed. There's a sudden, painful ringing in my ears.

No, wait. That's not ringing.

I'm blind. Floodlights flash around us and for a few seconds all I can see is white, and all I can hear is that dreadful sound. As both vision and sound clear, though, I recognise it. It's a sound that brings out vague teenage memories - unusual noises heard in the night. I look up.

Three vast, military helicopters hover overhead, aiming even more lights down onto us as we stand frozen on Maynard's platform. I look behind; shadowed figures lurk in the darkness, holding thin objects that gleam in the light. More batons. Maybe even a gun or two.

Jay's staring at me again, only this time his expression is one of pure shock. He didn't expect this anymore than I did. Pan steps back, drawing herself a little closer to him as though to comfort herself.

"Oh, no..."

"Jay," I splutter, "what do we do?"

But his face is blank, and his body is motionless, and he doesn't know. My panic builds at the thought - how can he not know what to do? He's Jay. He always knows what to do!

"Hello, dears."

CHAPTER SEVENTEEN

That voice.

It doesn't sound familiar to me – no memories present themselves. But as the others recoil from it, I find myself doing the same. It's a cold voice, devoid of emotion or humanity. Raspy for the most part, occasionally descending into squeaks. Like some twisted caricature of a real person.

The screen behind the stage bursts into life and suddenly Jay's pushing me behind him. He signals for the others to step forward too, like he's scared of what might happen if they see me. Or maybe he doesn't want me to see them.

It doesn't work. As the picture crackles and clears, I can clearly see the face glaring down at us.

Maynard. Those beady eyes cast a cursory glance over us, counting. There's a twinge of recognition in her stern face as she spots Pan and Nate – and a moment later, her eyes settle on Jay.

He tenses. I shiver behind him. I've never seen him this mad before. His arms quake with unreleased anger. His hands are curled into fists so tight his knuckles are turning white.

Nevertheless, Maynard smiles. It's a wide, mirthless smile that sets me on edge, but it's a smile. Maybe it won't be so bad.

"What? No hello this time?"

She draws her thin lips back, contorting the smile into a grimace.

"Now then, might I ask. What on Earth are you children doing in my home?"

The others glance at Jay, but he doesn't answer. He just tightens his fists a little more. Maynard seems unsurprised by his silence, instead waving a hand at us.

"You've brought a whole cavalry this time. Even your Second in Command. Strange. This was clearly planned - but what did you want from my building? Was this some kind of brazen assassination attempt?"

"You know it wasn't," Jay finally snarls, "we're not like you."

"Then what?"

"None of your business," he says simply.

"Oh, Jay. When will you learn? It is my business. Everything here is. I'm your leader."

He emits a sound that's somewhere between a laugh and a snarl.

"If you say so. Don't you think this reception is a little overkill?"

"You children have a wonderful gift for wriggling out of even the tightest grip. So forgive me for trying to keep hold of you this time."

Pan glances back at me. Her face is pale; paler than normal. There's absolute terror in her eyes, but she still shoots me a reassuring smile. I quickly realise she's trying to keep me quiet. To stop me from revealing myself. I obediently pull the hood further over my eyes.

Damn it. What do we do now? If we run for it, they could chase us down before we even reach the bikes. I glance back. I can see the bikes from here, glimmering just beyond our reach. They either haven't noticed them, or can't see them from where they stand. That works to our advantage. If I could just get to one, I could draw some of the Guards away.

Or you could get shot in the back before you even get there, says a tiny voice in my head. Oh. Right.

What if we scattered? Run in each direction, confuse them? But no – then only one of us would reach the bikes. We all need to get there together.

The wind from the helicopters overhead brushes over us, and dread settles in my stomach. Even if we can reach the bikes, could we even get away? They could chase us, follow us all the way back. And if they ever found the entrance to the Atrium, the Clover would be destroyed.

I look at Maynard. She's still exchanging small, sarcastic quips with Jay – and there's an undeniable hint of pleasure in her eyes. She loves what she's doing. She adores it. She could have us gunned down in a matter of seconds, but she's not going to. She wants to tease Jay, just like she did when airing the video of his parents' executions. His suffering is all she cares about.

My fingers quiver. What's wrong with me? Why am I so scared?

I don't need to wait for the answer. Maynard's distraction has worked; a heavy hand locks around my wrist from behind. Another arm reaches my shoulders, moving towards my neck. My body moves instinctively; I duck out of the Guard's reach and turn back, landing a heavy punch into his gut. He yelps and stumbles back, but there are more.

"Guys!"

They're moving, now, too. The spell is broken, and the world seems to snap into action around us. Pan grabs me and suddenly we're running, ducking and dodging the Guards' blows as we race towards our only means of escape. For a moment I wonder why we're not staying to fight – but then something whizzes by and slams into a dumpster, and I stop wondering. A well-aimed fist is no threat to a loaded gun.

We reach the bikes quickly. Behind us, Maynard's speaking; ordering her Guards, directing her helicopters. Despite our immediate escape, there's a sense of triumph in her voice. And as the helicopters aim their lights on us, I can see why. There's no way out of this.

"Get on!" cries Pan as she starts the bike. I obey immediately, jumping on behind her and hoping that my broad shoulders don't make for an easy target. In an instant we're off, coursing down the roads much faster than before. We're at the back of the pack. Jay and Nate head it up, with the others following closely. We lag a little, perhaps due to the extra weight. Pan's cursing. It's the first time I've heard her genuinely angry. Her shoulders are hunched and her grip on the handlebars is so tight it looks like it might be hurting her. That shock of cherry-red hair is blustering around her as she yells into the night.

Behind us, sirens.

"Noah!" she cries, "what's going on back there?"

I look back, cringe, then yell into her ear.

"Three helicopters overhead, five Guards on bikes."

"How close?"

"Really close."

She swears again, then shouts the information forward to the others. I'm not sure how they hear her with the wind filling their ears, but they all seem to understand.

"Where are we going?" I cry.

"We can't go back to the Atrium! They'll just follow us to the others!"

My chest hurts. So I was right.

"Is there anywhere else?"

"Not with those helicopters! We could lose the bikes easily enough, but those things can follow us anywhere!"

I steal a look behind again – the helicopters are still there, spotlights aimed on us as we race through the darkened streets. The sides of the machines are packed to the brim with weaponry, but they're not using any of it. Even the bikes have stopped firing. They don't intend to destroy us, at least not yet. No. They intend to run us into the ground and take us while we're cornered.

Suddenly my throat is dry, and though I swallow hard it doesn't help. I feel desperate, terrified. I need to do something. Anything.

Pan adjusts on her seat, and a thought comes to mind.

"Hold on!" I shout at her. She asks why, but I don't answer. There's no time. Standing on the side spokes of the back wheel, I twist my hands on the seat and jump. The jolt is enormous and rather painful, but as I fall back onto the seat, it works. I'm sitting backwards now, my shoulders pressed against Pan's. She screams something indiscernible at me. I can't hear the words but it sounds like a scolding for a risky move. I elect to ignore it, instead reaching out with one hand.

"Pan! Your insurance!"

"My what?"

I point at her leg.

"Insurance!"

She glances back at me and for a brief moment, doubt crosses her face. She knows what I'm suggesting, knows what I'm offering to do. Perhaps she understands even more than I do. But when I set my jaw and ask for it again, she reaches down and slips the firearm from the straps on her thigh.

"Be careful."

As she presses it into my hand, something inside me cries out. I've never held a gun before; not like this, anyway. I'm not unfamiliar with firearms – the Mill teaches us how to shoot foxes and weasels – but this is far more advanced that some rusty old shotgun.

Still, it's with some small degree of confidence that I slide off the safety, straighten my arms and aim squarely at the centre helicopter. It's not what you'd call a smooth ride and so my aim is somewhat uneven, but as long as I hit it, that's a start.

The second I pull the trigger, though, I realise I've made a mistake. The kickback's more than I'd expected, sending me flying back into Pan. The bullet flies off to the side, hits and building and promptly explodes.

"What the... I thought this shot bullets!"

"No, it fires incendiary cases," she snaps back, "that's why I told you to be careful!"

Okay. Okay. I can do this. I sit forward, locking my knees, tensing my back. This time, I know what to expect - and though the kickback still hurts, my aim is true. Or as true as it can be, anyway. The case collides with the upper half of the closest helicopter and ignites. A split second later, the machine plummets. We reach the crest of a hill and it falls out of sight. Suddenly, I'm happy I don't have to look at the horrors that remain.

I can't stand to think about the people in the machines. Guards or not, psychopaths or not. Nobody deserves this. I push the thought aside, vowing to deal with the guilt at a later, more opportune time.

The others are shouting now, too - airing their reactions to what just happened. I don't hear their words, but I'm sure they're not all positive. Perhaps they're telling me to stop, to not sink as low as our enemies. Maybe they're warning me of what might happen. But I don't care.

If I don't do this, none of us will even be around to see what happens next.

The second shot misses, instead hitting the roof of someone's house. Whoops. I lock my knees a little harder and fire again, this time grazing the helicopter's blades and sending it down. It lands to form a massive inferno in some poor sod's front yard.

"Yes!" cries Pan. There's horror and joy in her voice, something that fills my chest with both shame and pride as I point the gun at the final helicopter. Despite the distance between us, for a moment I make eye contact with the pilot - and fire.

The case hits again, more squarely this time, blowing it up from the cockpit outwards. Victory fills my chest, but it's quickly followed by terror as the flaming helicopter comes veering down towards our small collection of bikes.

I open my mouth to warn the others, but there's no time. All I see is fire.

CHAPTER EIGHTEEN

I wake to the sound of sirens.

It takes an alarming amount of effort to open my eyes and when I finally manage to do so, all I see is dirt. I'm lying sprawled on the ground amongst a mass of flaming wreckage.

As my ears adjust to the blaring, I can hear other sounds, too. Yelling, screaming, the occasional scuffle. The sound of the others fighting off Guards.

Wait. The others. Pan!

I somehow find the strength to push up onto my elbows, where I notice that the ground below me is red. Huh. Why is it red? My forehead pulses with pain as though in answer to my question, and I take a deep breath before touching a finger to that spot. It comes away crimson.

Great. I got hurt.

The sight of my own blood-soaked finger is sickening. I'm not scared of blood, far from it – but as I stare down at my hand, my vision blurs. Other things follow suit and soon the world is spinning around me. I press my hand to my forehead to stop the constant movement, but it does little to help.

Where are the others? I was with Pan. Is she nearby? Did they already take her?

Dread twists in my stomach as I consider the alternative – that she may not have survived the crash. But no. If I'm still alive, she has to be, too.

I manage to sit upright despite the spinning. Everything seems black and charcoaled in comparison to the blinding flames around me. Pan's bike is twisted and broken a few feet away, sending panic flitting through my chest.

Please be alive.

Something shuffles to my right. A dark shape, a pair of thick-set legs, broad shoulders.

The Guard steps towards me uncertainly, his eyes narrowing as he looks me up and down. I realise with a start that my hood has fallen back. I look around; the black scarf lies near the bike, already aflame.

"A Millchild?"

His voice is uneven, like he's doubting his own eyes. I suppose he must recognise the build and dark tan. There's nobody like me in Thorne. Still, he doesn't know who I am. I'm still just a random face amongst the flames.

He watches me for a moment, then draws his gun. From the pads on his joints I'm sure he's one of the bike Guards – he must have seen me shoot the helicopters down. He must know for sure that I'm a criminal. Fear whips through me, stronger and more terrifying than anything I've ever known.

As he takes a hesitant step towards me, I recoil. Some small part of me says that I should fight back, that I should get up and wrestle the gun from him. Shoot him. I've already crossed that line once today. This would be no different.

But my body hurts, and there's blood in my eyes, and even as I look at him the world dips and sways around me.

Smoke fills the air between us, making it hard to breathe. I can't move. Not even as he comes to a stop in front of me. Not even as he raises the gun, aiming at my forehead.

Jay's there before I even hear him coming. In a swift movement he's grabbed the Guard's arm and bent it back. The snapping sound is audible even over the crackling flames. The guy screams – but Jay simply throws him to the ground, yanking the gun from his hands and firing a clean shot into his shoulder.

It seems perfectly calculated, as though he's fought off Guards in this manner plenty of times. But it's not. In his eyes is fury and rage, the likes of which I've never seen before. It reminds me of Kane when he stepped up to Wirrow; only fiercer. Much, much fiercer.

And then he's next to me, kneeling in the wreckage. A warm hand finds my head, pushes my hair back. He grimaces at the blood.

"Are you okay?"

I swallow hard before speaking, and even then my voice wobbles.

"Where's Pan?"

"She's okay. She's with us."

"I... I screwed up."

"We can talk about that later. We need to get out of here. C'mon, put your arm over my shoulder."

He doesn't wait for my answer; just grabs me and pulls me upright.

The chaos of the helicopter crash works as the perfect diversion. Nobody notices or cares as we drive away on the few bikes we have left. I glance around, noting that I'm not the only one who took some damage. Pan winces with every movement, clutching her leg as she rides behind Jay. Jay himself has cuts all over, some frighteningly deep. Difference is, it doesn't seem to bother him. His eyes are fixed on the road ahead, and nothing more.

Everything still pulses around me, moments of vibrant colour conflicting with moments of near darkness. I let my eyes slide shut for a moment, trying to calm the jolting.

"Hey," Jensen warns me, "don't pass out. I can't hold you upright and steer this thing."

I do as I'm told, leaning against him and tightening my grip on his waist. Suddenly, I don't care whether it's decent for me to be grabbing him like this. It doesn't matter. It's just skin.

Last time, adrenaline took over. And afterwards, I'd felt immense relief and started to laugh about it. Not this time. There's no rush, no intense feeling of excitement. I feel like my adrenaline is crashing, even without rising in the first place. I don't want to laugh, though. It's taking all I have not to cry.

"Nearly done... there we go."

The woman steps back, admiring her handiwork. I glance at the tiny mirror on the table next to me, counting the stitches she's spent a half hour putting in my head. Ten. Not too bad, all things considered. The spinning has finally stopped, too.

We'd arrived back in a state. Pan had started to cry the moment we stepped into relative safety, and though I'd fought to keep my expression neutral, I'd been trying not to join her. As the adrenaline rush had vanished completely I'd dropped to the ground, falling back against the wall and pulling my knees up to my chin. The relief that shuddered through me was so intense I thought I might never move again.

The others didn't let that happen, though. Jensen had offered me a steady hand to stand up again, and his comforting smile had broken through the fear in my chest. After that, we'd been pulled in separate directions through the tunnels.

The woman dabs away the last speck of blood and smiles.

"Feeling better?"

Her voice is thick with sympathy – and for once, I actually appreciate it. I touch the cut gingerly. It doesn't hurt anymore. The dizziness is gone. Turns out I wasn't all that badly hurt. Which, I suppose, begs the question; why didn't I fight back? I'd thought it was due to the blood streaming down my face, the way I was seeing double. But if it wasn't that, then why was I frozen against the ground, unable to move even to defend myself?

I don't want to answer the question, so I push it aside. The woman's face creases with concern as she looks down at my clothes – they're ripped to shreds by this point, barely covering my modesty. Another time, I'd try to cover up. Now? I simply don't care. She clicks her tongue and shakes her head sadly.

"Honestly. What was Jay thinking?"

"It's not his fault," I mutter, "it was my mistake."

"Well, it was his idea to sneak off without reinforcements. He didn't even tell us where you were all going. We heard about it through the Feed."

"The Feed?"

"The television channel. Apparently, Maynard thought it would be charming to air the whole dreadful thing."

My gut clenches. So everyone knows that I shot down the helicopters. That I froze up at the worst possible second.

"Oh."

"Yeah. I mean, it cut out as soon as the helicopters went down, but..."

She trails off, eyeing me curiously. I can tell she wants to ask about the gun, question why I did it.

"I mean..."

"It's okay," I say, my voice hard, "you can say it."

She hesitates, and I realise for the first time that I don't even know her name. We were swarmed as we came in to the Atrium, and as she'd grabbed my arm to lead me away, I hadn't even stopped to wonder who she was.

"What's your name, anyway?"

"Marla. What's yours? I mean, what name do you go by?"

"Noah."

She bites her lip.

"Well, Noah, it was pretty brave what you did back there. I don't know many people who would be willing to destroy three helicopter crews just like that."

"I didn't exactly have a choice," I snarl, "what else could I have done?"

"Darling, you misunderstand. I mean it when I say it was brave. I've often thought that if only we were a little harder on our opponents, then maybe we could win this fight more easily. Everyone here adores Jay and would have wanted you to do whatever it took to protect him. You did a good thing, Noah."

My stomach churns.

"It sure doesn't feel like it."

"Well, it was. This is war, remember? If we're too afraid to fight back, we'll never win."

She smiles again, a broad, tight-lipped smile, and I return it uneasily.

The door to the room nudges open, and a familiar face pokes its way past the doorframe. I immediately feel shame welling in my chest.

"Jay."

If he's angry at me, it doesn't show. Instead, he smiles blandly at Marla.

"Everything okay?"

"Yes," she replies, "just a bump to the head. Minor at worst."

Perhaps she senses the tension in the room, because she glances at each of us in turn before excusing herself. As the door slips shut behind her, I find myself physically recoiling from Jay's gaze. I don't quite know what to expect. A scolding? A thrashing? Some small part of me cries that this isn't the Mill, that I won't be punished. But this isn't talking back. It isn't some small trace of resistance that can easily be quashed. I took matters into my own hands and probably hurt a lot of people. If not worse.

Still, as he looks me up and down, conflict in his eyes, I can't bring myself to feel remorse. I don't like what I did, but I can't bring myself to question it. It feels terrible – but if I hadn't done it, we'd all be captured or dead by now. I'll take whatever punishment he wants to throw my way.

But then he collapses into the nearest chair, wiping the sweat from his brow, and I get my first real look at him since we got back. Jay's face is pale and drawn, and there's sweat on his lip. His body is covered in bandages and sterile patches, covering the multitude of cuts he sustained in the crash. Suddenly, despite the muscle in his arms, he looks frail. For the first time since I met him, I feel scared for him. He seems so very tired. He's not looking at me anymore. He's just staring at the ground, as though he could count the rivets in the floor. I can't stay silent a moment longer.

"I'm sorry."

He doesn't move.

"For what?"

"For using that gun. I thought I was helping, I really did. But it was a disaster. I... I never wanted to hurt anyone."

He raises his head now, narrows his eyes at me.

"What are you talking about? Everyone got out alive, didn't they? Sure, Pan's got a broken leg and I'm pretty sure it's gonna hurt for Nate to piss for a few days, but that's it. They're alive. Nothing else matters."

"Even so, the pilots..."

"Were trying to kill us. I don't condone violence, I really don't, but in doing what you did, you saved our asses. Nobody's going to hate you for that."

And he says it so calmly, so confidently, that for a moment, I actually believe him.

"Are you okay?" I ask, "you seem exhausted."

"I'll be fine. Stressed, but it's wearing off. Give me ten minutes and I'll be alright."

I don't reply; there's nothing to say. But then he looks at me, his brows furrowed in concern.

"You sure you're alright?"

I glance down at myself. I can see why he's asking. The blood's drying in my hair, my clothes are torn to shreds, and my fingertips are still shaking a little. Like him, it's taking a little while for the stress to fade. I swallow hard.

"Yeah. I'll be fine. Thanks to you."

"Don't thank me for that."

"I get it. It's just what you do for people, huh? Part of being a leader."

He laughs - but it's a dark, unpleasant sound. It doesn't suit him.

"I wouldn't have shot a guy for just anyone."

My nerves build.

"You mean because I might be Ada?"

He opens his mouth, but nothing comes out. As an awkward silence settles over the room, I consider what's going to happen now. One way or another, Jensen still got the data. We still have to find out the truth.

As if on cue, Nate taps the door open and waves at us.

"Hey. You might not be up for it yet, but Jensen's got the database working. We can check any time you want to."

With that he's gone, sending a flurry of uneasy feelings swirling in my stomach.

"Well, there's no reason to put it off," says Jay. He draws himself up to his full height and pulls back his shoulders, as though he's trying to personify the strong leader he's always thought to be. Beside him, I hesitate.

I don't want to do this.

Before, I felt like knowing the truth would be the answer I needed. If I wasn't Ada, I could just go back to the Mill and stop bothering these people with my presence. If I was, I'd do whatever I could to help them. Both answers were about causing the least harm to them. But now?

"Are you coming?"

Jay's voice is warm, inviting; but I'm too scared to reply. Instead I hang my head, tightening my grip on the sides of my chair.

"Noah?"

"I don't want to."

He pauses - and for a moment, I expect anger. I wouldn't blame him. It's my fault everyone got hurt. They wouldn't even have tried that trick if it weren't for me. To say I don't want it now is nonsensical, selfish and stupid. We can agree on that much.

"But you wanted this. You wanted to know who you are."

"It won't change anything," I say flatly, "we both know it."

"Of course it will. Listen, if you're Ada..."

"And if I'm not? Then I'll have to leave, and you'll all have gone through this for nothing."

I can't see his face, and I don't want to. I lower my head a little more, creating a blonde barrier between us. I can't stand to see the disappointment in his eyes.

"That's... listen, if you're not Ada, I still want you to stay."

"You do?"

"Of course. This is home now, right? We like having you around."

I shudder. Yes. He's right. This is home. I can't imagine ever going back now. Pretending this didn't happen.

"But if I am Ada..."

"Then there's no problem. I'll have my sister back, and you can slip right back into your old life. Pick up where you left off."

I raise my head now, meeting his eyes - dusty blue, just like mine. He's so much like me. We share the same dirty blonde hair, the same twisted smile. Heck, even the same nose. It's easy to see why we could be related.

"You barely know me," I mutter, "how do you know you can trust me? It's hardly been a week."

"You've done a good job so far, haven't you?"

"I'm not like you. I've made mistakes. I've hurt people."

To my surprise, there's heat in my cheeks. I bite back on the tears, refusing to let them out, but they're still there. They lurk behind my eyes, threatening to spill out at a moment's notice. I don't deserve to be among them. Their laughter, their kindness. All spoiled by me. I think of the pilots, hospitalised or worse. Of perfect strangers who are hurt because of me. I think of Kane, digging in the darkness, filled with anger and bitterness because of what I did.

"You're better off without me around."

He watches me for a moment, like he's scared to say what he thinks.

But then, he laughs. It's a different sound from before. It's light and airy and wonderful - and if it weren't for the sadness in my chest, I'd feel the urge to join in. Instead, I feel irritated.

"H-hey! This isn't funny!"

"Yes it is!" he laughs, "you're hilarious."

"I'm not trying to be. This is serious."

He leans over suddenly, resting a reassuring hand on my arm.

"You think you're the first person ever to make a mistake and hurt someone? Noah, I'm the leader of the Clover. When I make mistakes, people die. And I've made mistakes. A lot. Pan used to have a roommate, you know. Key word - used to. They died because I fucked up. Trust me, I know how awful it feels - but to make mistakes is human."

"I know it seems that way…"

"It is that way. Okay, you screwed up. You feel bad about it, right?"

"Yes."

"You know it was wrong, right?"

"Of course."

"And you'll never, ever make that mistake again, right?"

"No, I won't," I reply, though I know I'd do it again in a heartbeat if I had to.

He gives a triumphant smirk.

"Then why are you beating yourself up? You made a mistake and you learned from it. You can't feel guilty for the rest of your life. You've got to learn to forgive yourself."

"But I..."

"Please, Noah. Just try."

I swallow hard, pushing the feeling back. The tears pressing against my eyes seem to fade, though the pain's still there, lurking under the surface. I doubt it'll ever really go away. Still, I nod.

"Okay. Thanks."

"I am full of wisdom," he teases. I shoot him a sarcastic look.

"Let's go and see if it's brotherly wisdom, shall we?"

I'd half expected the others to still be off somewhere in the tunnels, being patched up. But no - they're waiting for us in the Atrium, bright smiles on their faces. I notice with a grimace that Pan's leaning heavily on Nate, perhaps to hide the fact she's hurt her leg. My guilt rises again, but as I meet those clear, green eyes, I realise she's not angry with me.

Instead, she looks me up and down, then laughs.

"You look terrible."

"You're not much better," I point out. She pokes out her tongue and laughs again. The sound echoes strangely through the Atrium, and I notice for the first time that it's silent.

"Where is everyone?" I ask.

"Oh, right. We asked them to head into the tunnels for a bit. Figured this might be kind of a private thing."

Jensen's sitting nearby, tapping away at the nearest console. There's a look of grim determination on his face as he types, his fingers moving too quickly for me to decipher what he's doing. He raises his head as I approach.

"Are you ready?"

I gulp.

"What do I have to do?"

"It's a three-fold test. Eye scan, blood test, fingerprints. Come here, I'll show you."

I sit obediently as he carries out the tests. The blood test is fine, no different from before. He sighs when taking my fingerprints, questioning if they'll work. I suppose I can understand that. My fingers are so calloused and worn that I'm surprised there's much print left. The eye is the hardest bit, but even that;s easy enough.

"It'll take a few minutes," he tells me, "so relax."

I nod, but I'm anything but relaxed. Nerves are flitting through me, absolute panic barely held back by reason and logic. Either way, things will be fine. It's fine.

"Hey."

Pan steps up beside me, leaning against the same railing, trying to seem nonchalant on her injured leg. She casts a curious eye across the Atrium, as though expecting something extraordinary to appear. I swallow hard. I know how that feels.

"Hi."

"Are you ready for this?"

Her voice is low and friendly, but there's a strain of concern in there. She's not just making small talk; she wants to know if I can do this. I run a hand through my hair, tugging at the root as though the sliver of pain might somehow ease my nerves.

"I guess so."

"Scared?"

"Yeah. I mean, I want this to turn out well. I do. But if it does, then that means my entire life has been a lie. It means I know absolutely nothing."

She watches me for a moment, then rests a comforting hand on my shoulder. I find myself leaning into it, towards her warmth, as though her soft voice and clear eyes might fix everything.

"You don't have to do this," she coos, "just put off the results for a little while."

"It's okay. I'm ready."

"Are you sure?"

I fix her in my gaze. Pan. Sweet, bleeding heart Pan with her endless kindness and gentle touch. Behind us, Jensen, intelligent and oddly charming. Nate, with his big smile and agile hands. And Jay, of course – his patience, his confidence. What I wouldn't give to be his family. To be a part of this.

"I'm sure."

"Noah?"

Jensen's voice rings out across the Atrium, sending shudders through me.

"Yeah?"

"It's done."

My stomach swirls. This is it. A week after arriving, I'm going to find out the truth. As I turn back, Jay's eyes lock onto mine. He stands across the platform from me, his face uncertain. There are beads of sweat forming on his head. He's just as terrified as I am. I clear my throat.

"Okay. Here's the question, then. Who am I?"

CHAPTER NINETEEN

"You're Ada."

I can't breathe. Shock and joy and delight fill me, sending shivers of electricity through my limbs. Around me, the others gasp. Their eyes light up – for them, this is the beginning of the end. Their war is finally nearing its conclusion.

My hands are shaking. I stare down at them, clenching and unclenching my fingers. It's true. I'm Ada. I'm from the city. I'm...

I look up, meeting Jay's eyes - my brother's eyes. The joy threatens to burst from my throat and suddenly I'm running, throwing my weight into him. To my surprise he expects it, locking his arms around my shoulders and spinning on the spot. Our combined laughter fills the space between us.

Eventually he stops spinning, and I bury my face in his shoulder. My brother. The last relic of a life I once lived but can no longer remember. My grip on his back tightens. A moment later, he hugs back. The laughter dies.

"I'm so happy for you guys," I hear Nate say. Jensen grunts.

"Yep. This is a game changer."

"This changes everything," Pan adds, "absolutely everything."

Suddenly, it falls silent – and I quickly realise why. Jay's head is buried in my shoulder, his arms fastened tight around me; and his shoulders are shaking. Is he crying?

What do I do? I shoot an alarmed look at Pan, but she's just smiling. What can I possibly say? Something sweet? Something charming? Do I tease him for crying so easily? Suddenly, I don't know what to do with myself. So I just draw my brother closer.

"I'm... sorry I was away for so long."

He simply tightens his grip.

That evening, Nate pulls a strange crate out from under his bunk. As he drags it into the Atrium and calls for me to help, I ask him what's inside.

"I've been keeping this stockpiled for a special occasion," he says, winking. I unlatch the crate and as I throw the lid open, the stench of dust and alcohol meets my nose. I must seem disgusted, because he laughs.

"Not much of a drinker?"

I grimace. I'm not entirely unfamiliar with alcohol; the Guards at the Mill often knocked back snifters of cheap whiskey while entertaining some particularly exotic 'company' in their bunkers. I'd woken to the stink of booze and throw-up more times than I'd like to admit – and the experience hasn't exactly endeared me to alcohol.

"Never tried it," I admit, "don't really want to."

"Oh, boo. You're an adult now, right? Nearly twenty. You can try a sip or two."

I really don't want to; but I suppose I should give it a try. I have to try to let go of the past a little, right? So I heave a sigh and promise to try some later.

The rest of the Atrium is dark now. As I glance up, I notice some strange black canopy near the ceiling. It blocks out the glass overhead, making it even darker.

"What's that for?" I ask, pointing. Nate just smirks.

"It was up the other day. You didn't notice it then?"

"No. What does it do?"

"You'll see."

The Atrium buzzes. With this new revelation, there's a new lease of life amongst the Clover. It's only been an hour since Jay addressed them, told them what had happened. He'd sworn them to absolute secrecy and promised that he would find a way to recover everyone who'd been lost. He'd promised that as long as their hearts were still beating, he'd bring them home someday. And to my surprise, everyone accepted it. While I'd half-expected them to run off and try to save their own loved ones from the Mill, they haven't. They've placed their faith entirely in Jay's hands. They trust him to see them through.

Still, they're excited. Many have lost people to the Cull, I'm sure – but now, there's an element of hope in everything they do. If one person was kept alive, who's to say that others weren't, too? Maybe I'm just the first of many.

Still, it's a leap. As Jensen warned us soon after the reveal, there's no guarantee that it happened again. The leaders could have kept me alive for the sake of leverage against our parents. They could have just forgotten about me. I could easily have slipped away from the Guards on the way to my execution and stumbled across the Mill.

Just because I'm alive, that doesn't mean the others are.

Still, it's something. Nobody's ever been recovered after being taken in the Cull. It's a death sentence – literally and figuratively. This could be a discovery of epic proportions. It could also be a one-off that has the chance to disappoint millions.

I've been thinking about the Mill since we found out. Thinking about Nel and Kane. If they really were born there and raised in Homestead. Or if they're like me, infants with stolen memories and a warped sense of their own existence. I never bothered to ask Nel if she could remember anything. I'd assumed that she was like me. That nothing in her life mattered except the Mill, and working as hard as possible every day for the entirety of her life.

Thinking back, though, that's not true. I recall the night she cried about the cows. How much it pained her to separate the calves from their mothers. At the time I'd dismissed it as foolish over-sensitivity, but what if it wasn't? What if she had some trace of memory from the times before that she didn't quite understand, and the parting of a family was enough to bring those memories rushing back? I called her a friend, and yet I never bothered to ask.

And now I'm staying here, I'll probably never get to ask.

My quiet self-reflection is broken by a heavy hand on my back. Nate grins toothily at me.

"Hey, cheer up. This is a good day, you know!"

"I know. But I have a lot of questions now."

"I know you do," he says warmly, "but let go of them for now. Just for tonight. The biggest question's been answered."

"But what happens next? There's so much more we need to do."

"Right now, we don't need to do anything except enjoy tonight. Tomorrow, I promise, you can worry all you like. But just for now, let it be. Try to have fun, alright?"

I watch him closely. I had assumed from the start that Nate was in his thirties, and only a little older than Jay. But Pan's story has me thinking. If Jay was eight when his - our - parents were killed, and Nate took care of him, how much older is he? It can't be by much, ten years at most. I can't imagine how hard it must have been for a teenager to take over the care of a kid that young. I feel a rush of respect for him.

At the Mill, I'd scowled and snarled at the workers who dared to have children. I'd considered it a cheap way of backing out of their obligations, or avoiding the work by taking the easiest way out. I'd felt betrayed by those who chose to do it, like they had made things worse for those of us who didn't run away. But that wasn't fair. Nate decided to raise a kid, and instead of anger, all I feel is respect. There's no difference – but then again, I'm finally starting to question everything I believed in before coming here.

As the blackness of night finally falls overhead, the lights come on. They're small, round, glowing things – and as we sit amongst them, bathed in their gentle light, I finally understand the point of the black canopy overhead. It must be to block out the light, so those above us can't see down into the Atrium. That would be a pretty stupid way of revealing ourselves.

We sit in small groups across the platforms, dozens of forms huddled around the little lights. Even from here on the bridge, I can see dozens of warm smiles illuminated softly by the lamps.

Jensen presses something cold against my arm and I jump; but it's just that bottle of alcohol, the same one they've been passing around for ten minutes now.

I open my mouth to refuse, but then catch Nate's eye. I did promise him I'd try. This is an evening of new experiences, right? I don't know exactly what Jay and the others have planned with this setup – they've refused to tell me – but I should jump in feet first. I take a swig from the bottle and gag.

"That's disgusting."

Jensen takes the bottle back, amusement playing on his features.

"It takes a little getting used to, I suppose."

"I'll take your word for it. Just tastes bitter to me."

Pan's leaning on Jensen's shoulder, one hand clutching her leg. As I quickly found out, it's a clean break. The helicopter had crash-landed behind us, throwing her off and into Jensen, who was driving in front of us. The two had woken together and looked for the rest of us in the carnage, but by that point Jensen's bike had already snapped her femur in half. The fact that she carried on searching is rather heart-warming.

From the sounds of it, everyone was up and about before me. They'd been darting through the flames, recovering the bikes, digging one another from the twisted metal before the fire reached them. Jay had run off to find me – only stumbling across me at the last possible moment. Gratitude wells in my chest. If I were them, I wouldn't have gone out of my way. It still scares me, the memory of being frozen against the burning ground and waiting for the bullet to hit me. At the time, I'd wondered why I couldn't fight back. Now I know. I was scared.

I was so terrified to die that I hadn't been able to move, or cry out, or do much of anything really. And though Jay brushes it off like it was nothing, we both know I'd be dead if he hadn't been there.

I've never thought I would die before. Sure, at times I've been scared or pained – running through the streets with Jensen on my back, or that time in the Mines when I nearly got caught in a cave-in – but before, there had been a rush of adrenaline to drive me forward. I'd been able to do something to fight the oncoming danger. This time, I couldn't. I'd been retired to the fact I was going to die.

Not the others, though. They were far braver than me. Even with a busted leg, Pan still busied herself digging the others out of the wreckage. Jay had cuts coating his body, and he still ran off to find me. I had a scratch on my forehead and was too scared to move, much less do anything of value.

Pan sees me staring and winks.

"You alright?"

"Yeah. I, er... I was just trying to figure out what's going on."

"Ah, I can't tell you that. Not yet. It's a surprise."

"I don't get it."

Jay sits down next to me, cross-legged on the ground, and shoots me a reassuring smile.

"You will."

A few minutes later, something shifts across the Atrium. It's the same screen they used to air the leaders' speeches before – but this time, there are no stern, angry faces on it. There's just static. Jay glances at Jensen.

"You got it working?"

"Yeah. Hacked the airwaves. This is going to be airing on every channel for the next ten minutes. No overlay, no nothing. Is that about right?"

He smirks.

"Perfect."

Those dusty eyes turn to me now, reminding me for the hundredth time why he seemed so familiar the first time we met.

"What's all this about, anyway?" I ask.

"You were taken when you were three," he explains, "the Cull only takes kids up to and including three years old, and the Cull took place just before your fourth birthday. It was the last possible time they could have taken you, and they did it. Just before it would have become illegal."

My chest tightens.

"Okay. So?"

"So... you never got to celebrate your fourth birthday. Let alone the fifteen that have come around since. You're not far off twenty either, are you?"

"Birthdays aren't really a thing at the Mill," I point out, "I didn't even know they were a common thing to celebrate."

"Well, they are. Now you're a little too old for a four-year old's birthday party, but I still wanted to give you a present."

I don't quite understand the words he's using, but I still feel a catch of excitement in my throat as he waves towards the screen, which is now crackling into life.

"You missed out on a lot because of what happened," he says softly, "and I can't ever give it back to you – but I can show you a bit of it."

The screen crackles again, and when the video finally forms, I gasp.

A young woman beams at the camera, laughing a high-pitched laugh. There's a man behind her – and as he leans forward to adjust the camera, I spot dusty blue eyes peeking out from behind his glasses. Someone wriggles to get into frame; a little boy, no older than seven, with a shock of dirty blonde hair and scraped up knees.

"James, come on. Sit still."

James? I open my mouth to ask the question, then stop. Oh. Jay must be short for James.

Young Jay shoots Mom a sheepish grin and pushes his head against her shoulder, eager to get more of his face in frame. She laughs.

"Okay, okay. James, do you want to say hello to Auntie Kath?"

"Hello, Auntie Kath!"

"I'm so sorry you couldn't be around for Ada's second birthday," the woman says, turning back to the camera, "but I understand you're... busy with things."

Her face falls suddenly, a hint of sorrow breaking the kindness in her eyes.

"After last year's Cull, I don't blame you for cutting us out. I know it's not our fault they took Toby. But I get it. It can be hard spending time around people who remind you of things you used to have. We won't try and force our way into your life, Kath. I understand that you need time. Nathaniel, too. It must be so hard for him to have lost his brother. But just so you know, we're always here if you need us."

I'm standing now, taking slow, measured steps towards the railing that stands between us and the screen. Her – Mom's – voice is soft and gentle, her eyes reproachful as she speaks to the person on the other side of the camera. Auntie Kath, she said. Her sister? Did she have a sister? How don't I know any of this? These are basic questions. I glance back at the others; Nate in particular seems oddly wistful. Could Nate be short for Nathaniel? Could this be how we're related?

There's something deeply frightening about Mom's voice. It's probably the first sound I ever heard, and yet it sounds as unfamiliar to me as Jay's did when we first met. Something that should have screamed home to me now echoes strangely, like an alien sound heard for a split second decades ago.

"Anyway, I know it's been over a year now, so we arranged for some flowers to be sent to you. Budded roses, your favourite."

"Tell her about the car!" demands James.

"Oh, yes. James has - very helpfully - put a toy car inside one of the flowers. Unfortunately he did this just before they went out, and I didn't get chance to stop him."

"It's lucky," the boy adds, "guess which one it's in!"

Mom loops a playful arm around James' neck and pulls him close, but there's hesitation in the movement. She's trying not to rub it in Kath's face. Trying her utmost to be considerate. Dad finishes playing with the camera and settles down on the back of the sofa. The two exchange small glances before Mom starts talking again.

"Anyway... listen, Kath. I know that flowers don't fix what happened. We can't change the Cull, no matter how much we may want to. With the chaos outside, you know there's nothing we can do. Trust me, sis. If I could do something - anything - to bring Toby back, I would do it in a heartbeat. And I know you would, too."

I rest my hand on the railing. I feel inexplicably moved by Mom's words - perhaps it's the knowledge that she did, in fact, do the only thing she could think of. She tried. Poured her whole damn heart into it. But it didn't work.

"But that's no reason to be so hard on yourself," she pushes on, "what happened isn't your fault. I know you blame yourself because you spoke against the leaders, but that doesn't mean you're to blame. It's an awful, evil system. I don't even know where to begin trying to change it; but I know the first step. It's knowing that this is outside of you and I. It may be our problem, but it's not our fault."

Huh. What's going on? My face is hot again, but this time I can't bite back on the tears. I'm suddenly glad to be facing away from the others.

Dad leans forward again and nudges the camera, his tongue poking out in a way I'd consider comical, if not for what's being said. Mom's eyes glisten with unshed tears - something shifts just below her and she leans down, scooping a small, blonde child into her arms. The girl's only a couple of years old, but already her eyes look just like her Dad's. There's a lump in my throat as Mom pulls the girl closer.

"I can never bring Toby back, as much as I may want to. But I will always be here for you, okay? Whether you want me around or not, I'll still be here. Both of us will be. No matter what happens, Kath, we're not going anywhere."

She turns to the camera and draws her lips back in a warm, if somewhat false, smile.

"Everything will be okay in the end. I promise."

As the screen dies, an uneasy silence falls over the Atrium. The others sit silently behind me, waiting for my reaction. I don't know what they expect. Should I be overjoyed at having seen and heard my parents for the first time? Should I ask questions about Kath and Toby and Nathaniel? Whatever reaction they're expecting, I'm bound to let them down.

Because I'm crying again.

I thought that time on the boat was the only time. After that, I'd vowed never to cry in front of someone again - if I allowed myself to cry at all.

But I can't help it. Suddenly, I'm thinking about all the years I missed out on. Going to school. Learning to read. Playing with my brother. Being scolded by Dad. Thanks to the Cull, every day of that life was stolen away like it meant nothing. And the days that did happen - learning how to walk and talk, falling asleep to my Mother's voice – are gone as well, because my memories have been taken away. I can watch this video a hundred times or more, and it'll remain the only memory of my parents that I have, because when they took me away they took my past and my future. Now it's too late. I'll never get it back.

The tears are hot against my skin. It would be almost funny if it weren't so painful. I turn away and head for the stairs, walking fast enough that they don't see my face. I stride past the other groups, who also sit in a reflective silence. Nobody speaks as I pass by, but I can still feel their eyes on me. Wondering where I'm going. Why I'm suddenly running. There are footsteps behind me, too – I recognise the clunky weight. But I don't want to talk to Jay right now.

I finally come to a stop in their memorial garden. That statue seems to scream out at me. The plain, insipid faces can't hope to mimic the expressive faces of Mom and Dad – but it's the closest I have to them. The nearest I'll ever have to them being here physically. I reach out and rest a hand on the marble, feeling the cool stone warm under my touch.

Jay steps up behind me, concern in his voice.

"Noah?"

I gulp hard, trying to bite back on the tears, but it doesn't work.

How could they? How could the leaders decide, as though it were nothing, that my entire existence could be easily reduced to little more than a political debate? That the memories I had were disposable, that they meant absolutely nothing? The sadness is suddenly replaced with anger. It's red hot, snaking through my veins and making the tears even hotter.

"Noah."

I turn to face Jay in the darkness, making no attempt to disguise the liquid on my cheeks. I'm so angry it's getting hard to breathe. As his face falls, I know he didn't mean to do this. He wanted it to be comforting, like some kind of replacement for the memories I've lost. Perhaps he thought this would make me happy. It didn't work. Instead, something unfamiliar struggles inside me. Rage.

"Are you okay?" he asks, his voice tinged with fear. I swallow hard.

"I will be."

He doesn't respond to that. He just steps up beside me and rests a comforting hand on my shoulder. For a little while, we just stand in the silence of the Atrium, staring up at the only reminder of our parents we have left.

CHAPTER TWENTY

We return to the others after about ten minutes. They seem to assume that my reaction was the result of intense sadness, that I couldn't stand to see the life I'd missed out on. And sure - that's part of it. But for the most part, I'm just angry.

Until now, I've been focussing on the world in front of me. Growing used to being here, getting to know the others. To me, it had meant more to know about them than to learn about the Cull itself. I guess I was trying not to think about it.

Not anymore. Now, I can feel the same ferocity building in me that I've seen in Jay. That immense anger at what's happened, and why - the uncontrollable desire to fix it, no matter what it takes. Any trace of guilt I felt about the helicopters fades in an instant. I don't care anymore. I'd do it again if I had to. The feeling is both frightening and exhilarating. I don't think I've ever felt so strongly about anything before.

Still, the rage compounding in my skull is easy to hide. I force my body to relax, leaning against the wall as we sit in our little circle around the globe of light. The others are laughing and lightly teasing one another. Whatever reaction they had to my outburst, it's gone now. Either they expected it, or they've mutually decided not to mention it. Either way is fine by me; I stretch one arm overhead and let out a long, dry yawn.

"Sleepy already?" teases Jay, "it's not been that long a day, has it?"

I consider this. Actually, it has. It must be the early hours now – it's been just over a day since we gathered in Jensen's room, eager to plan our actions. Since then, it feels like it's been non-stop. I could sleep for a week.

"Have the leaders said anything about our little stunt?" asks Pan. He nods.

"Just the typical stuff, from the sounds of it. Distrustful, chaotic children causing damage to civilised society. Supposed assassination attempt."

"She really said that?"

"You know Maynard. She always knows just what to say to make us seem like the bad guys. Though I have to say, maybe shooting down a fleet of helicopters didn't help."

I blush madly.

"It was not a fleet!" I insist, "it was three. I, uh, guess that doesn't make it better though, does it?"

"Not really. Bad, but necessary."

Jensen leans forward, intrigue in his eyes.

"I was surprised you even knew how to use a gun. Is that standard for the Mill?"

I shrug.

"Kind of. I was taught how to use a shotgun. It's a bit different from that explosive thing Pan had."

Pan and Jay exchange nervous glances, and for a moment I think he's going to yell at her. After all, she'd begged me not to tell him about that weapon. She'd tucked it against her thigh and only passed it over to me when we had no other choice. From that, it's fair to assume Jay doesn't approve of firearms. As she explained earlier, normal guns are hard to come by. Incendiary case launchers, though? Just owning one is a death sentence.

But then he smiles at her, and I know it'll be fine. Whatever bond those two share won't be broken so easily. Besides, by bringing that gun, Pan saved us. It might have been my finger on the trigger, but that wouldn't have been possible if she'd not thought to bring it along in the first place.

I bite back on another yawn.

"Alright, already," says Pan, "I get it, it's late. Come on, we'll head to bed."

"I'm fine," I insist, though my voice sounds like a small child refusing to put their pyjamas on, "I can keep going."

"It's been a really long day," says Nate, "I'm going to bed now, too."

The others quickly agree, and soon enough I'm tugging my torn shirt off in the relative privacy of Pan's room. I no longer care if she sees my back, unlike my first day here – and frankly, I'm too exhausted to care.

Still, she eyes me carefully from across the room. She's curled up on her little bunk, her blanket pulled around her shoulders and up over her head. Only her eyes watch from the tiny gap in the folds.

"Why are you looking at me like that?"

She shrugs.

"No reason."

Perhaps on another day, I'd try to draw her into a conversation to figure out what's wrong. But right now, I really don't care. I switch off the light and collapse into my bunk, pulling the sheets tightly around my body. When my eyes slip open again, though, she's still there. Sparkling green eyes glimmer even in the darkness.

"Okay. Seriously. Why are you staring at me?"

"Are you happy?"

"Huh?"

She leans forward, clutching the edge of her bunk like a small child.

"You know the truth, now. Are you finally happy?"

"Yes."

"And are you going to stay?"

"As long as you'll have me," I laugh. That seems to comfort whatever inane worry she seemed to have, and finally she flops down onto her bunk, exhausted.

For a moment, I stare at the rivets on the ceiling and try to imagine yet again that Pan's gentle breathing belongs to Nel. I wish I could tell her what's going on - what's happened in the time I've been away. I wish I could tell her that I found my brother, saw my parents. That I fought a dictator and got out alive. That I shot down some helicopters and fought off an armed Guard. That I finally understand why she always believed in family. How everything at the Mill is wrong, even though it's still home. How much I miss her. I imagine the conversation we'd have, the explanation I'd give.

Pan falls asleep quickly and I find myself sitting up in the darkness, rubbing blearily at my eyes.

"Atlas. Show me that clip one more time."

One more becomes two, then three. Soon it doesn't even stop between clips, simply looping my parent's faces until their expressions and voices are engrained in my memory. Sadness mingles with joy as I peer through the shadows at faces that seem both unfamiliar and yet incredibly meaningful. I catch myself wishing I could remember something more.

A week flies by quickly after that, and my days are filled with laughter. Whatever sorrow used to hang over the Atrium seems to have dissipated, and those few strangers who still regarded me with suspicion now greet me with smiles.

It's strange - to some degree, it doesn't matter what I do. My screw ups are forgiven almost immediately, my awkwardness dismissed without question. I wonder why for a little while, but then push it aside. It's pretty clear that the name Ada is enough to get me off most things. When we spar, I can see them holding back. Nobody wants to hit me anymore.

I take to waking in the middle of the night and pacing the Atrium with nobody but Atlas for company. Nobody has asked me to return the little device, and I'm happy about that. I don't plan to give it up any time soon.

Working the little crop patch takes up most of my time, but the more I do it, the more I feel like something's missing. There's something unpleasant about chopping wood alone - something weird about being the only one pacing the field. I've grown so used to having scores of people around me, and though I value those moments stolen for myself, I find a little hint of sadness threatens to break through during quieter moments.

Morning's still not broken overhead when I lower my spade, resting it against the spiked railing. I can't help but admire my handiwork - clean lines of newly sewn seeds, perfectly spaced, at the ideal depth. I smile, unable to disguise my pride.

"Looks good."

I look up. Jay's standing by, his arms crossed as he mimics me, looking up and down the rows with mild intrigue.

"You're up early," I say, "couldn't sleep?"

"I sleep like a baby just lately. I woke up early to work on my plan for the Cull."

"Oh, yeah. That's coming up in a few months, isn't it?"

He nods sadly.

"Yeah. I have to come up with another way to fight it. We have more people than ever, but there's still only a handful of us who are willing to speak out openly. When Mom and Dad were in charge, we were a public protest group. But they drove us underground and now, agreeing with us openly is basically confessing to a crime."

"What do you normally do?" I ask, realising that I should have questioned this weeks ago.

"We usually try to recruit people on the run up. The leaders always prepare for the Cull with broadcasts, but Jensen's become pretty good at hacking them. We replace their threats with messages asking people to join us."

"Does that work?"

"Not really, no. People don't think it'll happen to them, so they ignore us. It's only when the Cull happens and they do lose someone that they get in touch. But we still put ourselves out there and let them know we're here for them. We have contacts around Thorne who can bring people to us if they're approached – if they're trustworthy, that is."

I nod, deciding not to point out how easily they trusted me within a day. I suppose the whole 'Ada' thing probably swayed them – the Clover wouldn't have lasted very long if they were always so lenient. Jay leans back against the railing, clearly deep in thought.

"During the Cull itself we're out on the streets, protesting. It's dangerous as all hell and we always end up taking some casualties, but for the most part we try to fight off the Guards and protect some of the kids."

"You manage to save some?"

"No, never. Even when we manage to chase away the Guards, they just come back later when we're not around. The Cull isn't just one day, you know. They usually take between five and ten percent of the kids, but sometimes it's more. They can't do it in a day, and ever since we hacked their plan a few years back, they don't even have a strict method. There's no plan for where they strike first, and they don't warn us who's being taken; so it's nearly impossible to actually stop them."

I watch him for a moment. I hadn't imagined it would be that hard.

"I'm sorry."

He furrows his brows.

"For what?"

"All the time I've been here, I've been so distracted with who I am. It was all I cared about. But what I should have cared about was this. Stopping the Cull."

"Hmm, I noticed that. You've found your spark, haven't you?"

"I don't know about that. But I am angry. That video showed me what they took away - and they do the same thing to thousands of people every year. I didn't care all that much about the Clover when I arrived here, because it felt like there was a disconnect. It's easy to ignore something when it doesn't affect you. But now, it does. Now I realise just how sick this is."

I half expect there to be sympathy twisting on his face, but when I look up, Jay's smiling.

"What?" I ask.

"I knew you'd figure it out eventually."

I smile back. In the week that we've been siblings, I've started to pick up on the smaller similarities between us. Things I didn't notice before, things I probably wouldn't have cared about if not for everything that's happened. When Jay smiles, one side of his mouth curls a little more than the other. Just like me. Despite all my years away, I didn't even realise I did it until I came here.

But the warmth is broken, suddenly, as I think about what's coming. The Cull is close - less than four months away. We've not been able to come up with any way to stop it, so it's going to happen. I think about the children living right above our heads, about how their memories may not be the same in a few weeks' time. And that's only if our theory is true.

In an ideal world, I'm the rule rather than the exception. Ideally, every child that's been taken has had their minds wiped and their bodies put to work. It's still a grim, messed up theory, but it's better than the alternative.

"Maybe we should just tell everyone the truth," I say, "share what we know."

"No. We know that one person survived the Cull, but that's not enough. Like you just said, people only care about something when it affects them. We need to find a way to prove that this wasn't an exception."

"Maybe you need to have a little more faith in people. I'm sure this would be enough."

"Since revealing the truth to those within the Atrium, not a single person's stepped forward to join the main group. Even knowing what we know, people are still too afraid to step forward and risk everything."

His voice is hard now, bitter. I wipe a smudge of dirt from my face and push my hair back from my face. Pan took a pair of scissors to it last night, trimming it back as best she could; and though she apologised a dozen times for the state of the new, choppy style, I don't mind it. It's smoother and neater and doesn't feel so lank and heavy.

All things considered, I look practically the same. To anyone who knew me before, the changes are small and practically invisible; but to me, my reflection has never looked more different. My dirty hair is trimmed and tidied, and now that I'm not spending countless hours in the scorching sun, there's a quarter-shade difference in my tan. Whatever bruises I had from a hard day's work have faded now, little more than tiny shadows on my skin. In short, I feel better than ever. Just having a good night's sleep has made the world of difference.

But then I turn to my brother, to his troubled eyes, and the good feeling's gone.

"Can I do anything?" I ask, stepping closer, "anything at all, just tell me. I'd do it in a heartbeat."

"I know you would. But there's nothing. Don't worry so much. I decided to lead the Clover, so I'm the one who should be worrying about this stuff, not you. You just got home. Enjoy it, Noah."

His voice fades when he says my name, and there's a pang of guilt in my chest. He doesn't like calling me that. In his eyes, Noah is a false name given to me by the very people who tore me away from my home. Noah is a relic of the place I was held. Of the confused, angry stranger who showed up at his door. He'd much rather call me Ada - as would many of the others, I'm sure. But I won't let them. I can't help it. Even if we happen to be the same person, I can't think of myself as her. Ada is that sweet little kid on Jensen's screens. I'm Noah. I don't think that'll ever change.

Something clatters just behind us. Nate and some of the others, stepping into the Atrium. Several of them look our way and smirk, perhaps mistaking our shared concern for a sweet family moment. The notion's almost laughable; no matter how happy I am to be back here, I don't think I'll ever be one for a family heart-to-heart. Already, the grief that I'd felt after escaping the Guards is cause for embarrassment. That I cried at the screen, that I screeched my real name at Jensen in the street - all a source of humiliation. That's not me.

Luckily, the others seem to accept it. They don't remind me of those times, don't pressure me to say things I don't want to. Not that I sometimes don't want to talk about things like that; but they leave it to me. I'm grateful for that.

Nate waves.

"Jay, you actually doing some physical labour for once?"

Jay smirks.

"Don't be silly, Nate. I'm the brains of the operation, remember?"

"If you say so, buddy. Hey, Little Young?"

I bite back on a scathing reply at the use of that damned nickname. Since finding out the truth, Nate's taken to calling me Little Young at every given opportunity. It's awful, so instead of replying I just shoot him an irritated glare.

"Ooh, if looks could kill," he chortles, "anyway, come back over in a bit, okay? I'm in the middle of trying to build a new gauntlet for you and I need your thoughts."

I nod, though I don't know what kind of input he expects from me. I hadn't known just how good Nate was with his hands until I put that gauntlet to good use. Sure, I feel slightly guilty that I damaged it beyond repair in its first use, but it saved me from that shock baton, so I'd say it served its purpose.

"Just be careful," Jay warns me, "if he tries to get you to live test it, say no."

"Live test?"

"Yeah," he smiles, "a few years back, Nate decided to make me some electric-shock dusters. Just like the Guards' shock batons, only smaller. Innovative, he said. One punch and they go down. Easy."

"Was it?"

"Not exactly. He built them with the parts of an old shock baton, then decided I needed to live test them in a sparring match with him. Wrapped his limbs in rubber to try and protect himself. Of course, I'm a better fighter than him so I won easily; and as he tried to wriggle away, I accidentally caught him on a spot not covered by the rubber."

I wince, imagining the pain. While I've never been on the receiving end of a shock, I've been witness to their use. Perhaps the ones at the Mill are stronger, I'm not sure, but in my experience, a person's lucky not to die from the shock. Even if the first flash of pain's not too bad your body shuts down, going into shock from the injury. It's not pleasant to watch.

"Was he okay?" I ask, already knowing the answer.

"Of course. Eventually. Took a few hours to get back on his feet, but then he was fine. I was scared to death, though. I was certain I'd killed him."

"So it wasn't as strong as a baton?"

"No, though it should have been. I never could figure out why it didn't do more damage. It just knocked him out. You'd think he'd learnt his lesson after that, but no. He still tries to field test everything as much as he can."

I feel like I should laugh at that, to try to find the humour in his story. Instead, it just scares me. Unbidden images of Kane flash in my head. That kid's too loud mouthed to keep to himself – chances are, he's been on the receiving end of a shock at least once. That familiar guilt threatens to burst through again and I push it back. There'll be a time to deal with that. Now's not it.

"It's nice of Nate to rebuild the gauntlet, though. Especially after I destroyed the first one."

"The first one did what it was supposed to do, didn't it? Hopefully, you'll never have to use it. I don't plan to put you in a situation like that ever again."

I stare.

"But... I'm still going to help with the Cull, right?"

"We can't let them know who you are, remember?"

"There's something I can do. There has to be. I can drive the bikes for a quick getaway. I can set up more cameras for Jensen. I can help."

"No!"

Suddenly his voice is hard, and I take a step back. Regret mingles with anger in his eyes.

"I just got you back. I'm not risking losing you again, okay?"

Something stirs in my stomach, a horrible, sickening realisation. Am I not going to be allowed to help them? After all we've been through, am I really being cut out of this?

"That's not fair."

"What's not?"

"You showed me that video, remember? It made me angry - it made me want to help! And now you're telling me I can't?"

"It's too risky!"

"It wasn't too risky when I was just Noah! Before I was Ada, you trusted me to do things. You trusted me to help you."

"You're not going out there again, got that?"

Anger flashes in his eyes - perhaps another time, that might frighten me. I might step back and apologise, do what I can to fix things. Instead, I feel indignant.

"So you trust a stranger more than you trust your own sister?"

"We are done talking about this. If you're part of the Clover you follow my rules."

"By the sounds of it, I'm not part of the Clover!"

Oh, no. I can feel my anger rising – when I open my mouth, it's a shout that breaks out. For the first time, I'm raising my voice at him.

"I don't understand! You want me to stay, but I can't do anything? Then why am I here? To make your point for you, to prove you were right? Is that all you wanted?"

"Noah, that's not..."

"No! You can't make me care this much and then refuse to let me help!"

The Atrium's fallen silent around us, and I can feel a dozen sets of eyes settling on me. I know I'm yelling. I know this isn't okay. But I hate this. I hate it so much.

"Noah," he snarls, "this is not your fight."

I pause, suddenly breathless. All my indignation fades away, dissipating into nothing.

"W-what? Of course it is. I thought I was a part of this."

"Well, you're not. I'm happy you're back. We all are. But that doesn't mean you understand what's going on. It doesn't mean you're in any state to help us."

"But..."

"This fight's been going on much longer than just sixteen years, you know. It's big. Bigger than both of us, and certainly bigger than you. I know you want to help. I really do. But you still know practically nothing about this, and until that changes, I'm not going to put you at risk. It was different before – but if you're going to be a part of this, you need to understand everything, and right now you don't."

I feel deflated. It's only been two weeks. It makes sense he doesn't want me to help. Things are getting harder and like it or not, I don't understand everything. I look down at my mud-coated fingers, at the tiny scars and cuts there. At the physique that marks me out as little more than a Millchild. Just like I told Pan that first day. I'm not good for anything else.

He's right. It doesn't matter that I'm Ada. I'm not her anymore. A lifetime spent on a farm has left me utterly worthless to the Clover. I thought I'd done so well, that I'd been a big help to them; but what he's saying is true. This is bigger than me, and I can't pretend to understand what's really going on.

But then I meet his eyes, full of pain and stubbornness, and I can't stand here a moment longer.

"You're right," I say as I walk past, "I don't understand."

Pan finds me sulking in her room about a half hour later. Though they've offered me my own room I've turned them down, admitting that I quite like living with her. Pan seems happy enough for the company. But as she steps in to see me pacing angrily, her face falls.

"Oh, no. What happened now?"

"Nothing."

She settles down on a nearby chair.

"Is this because of what Jay said?"

"No."

"Yes, it is. Which bit bothers you? That he said you don't understand everything?"

"No!"

"Then what?"

For a moment I consider leaving the room, or barking at her to leave me alone. But then I catch sight of those pretty eyes again, and I know that even with my best effort, I'll never be able to turn her away. I heave a sigh and slump down in the chair next to her.

"I'm not even angry at him. I know there's a lot I don't really understand. But... there has to be something I can do."

"You know he's only trying to do what's right. Jay's wanted his little sister back for years and now he has you, of course he's a little scared of letting you go."

I sigh.

"That makes sense. I hadn't thought of it like that."

"He does trust you. He's proven that before. He's just using your inexperience as a reason to keep you here so you're safe. With the Cull coming up, he has a lot to worry about already. It's not that he doesn't trust you to do a good job out there. It's more that he's scared of what might happen to you if he puts you at risk."

"So everything's because he cares? There's not even a little bit of him that thinks I'll mess up?"

She considers this.

"Well, it's true that you don't know as much about the history of the Cull as the rest of us do. But that doesn't mean you're more likely to mess up. Those of us who were born and raised here have an advantage over you based on what we know. But you have advantages in your own way, too."

I pause.

"Seriously? Aside from being able to chop wood for twelve hours a day, what can I do that you can't?"

She pauses for a moment, like she's unsure what to say. With a quick glance behind her, she rubs a hand through her hair and sighs.

"There is... one thing. But if I tell you what it is, you have to promise not to tell Jay. If he knew I'd even mentioned this to you, he'd kill me."

"I won't say anything."

"Well, you know how we're trying to convince people that more than one person might have survived the Cull?"

"Yeah?"

"Jay's been talking about all these crazy theories," she says, "hacking systems that might not exist, tricking one of the leaders into confessing everything... but I think I've found a better way. How did we find out about you?"

I shuffle uncomfortably in my seat, not really wanting to recount the whole story.

"I ended up here because of Rian. You tested me on your system."

"Bingo. So logically, the best way to see if it's happened to more people is to do the same thing again, right? Get a bigger sample size. That way, we can put together statistics."

She's right. It would be easier to just scan more people through the system.

"But that won't work," I point out, "I'm the first person from the Mill in a while - how would we get more here to check? Wouldn't we need their DNA?"

"Yes, we would. I've thought this over, too. I requested more people from Rian, but he said it won't work. The last two people he sent never came back, as far as the other Guards know. If he sends anyone else, they might get suspicious."

"So what do we do?"

"Haven't you figured it out yet?"

She leans forward now, tilting her head at me. Whatever idea she has, she clearly thinks it's obvious. I shrug.

"I don't know! Like Jay said. I don't have a clue."

"Link it up, Noah. What can you do that nobody else can?"

Suddenly, it dawns on me.

"I can get into the Mill."

She claps loudly, her pretty face breaking into a triumphant grin.

"Exactly! Since you're already familiar to the Guards there, you're the only person who could get back inside and try to get more people."

"You're right," I gasp, "even if you guys went there, you look too much like city folk. They'd see right through you."

"You, on the other hand, blend right in. You know how it works there. Not only that, but you've not even been gone a month yet. You could go back tomorrow for all they know, and they'd never question where you've been."

I consider this.

"But what could I do from inside? There's security everywhere."

"That's the beauty of it. Jensen's already mentioned that he can create a transmitter; a tiny device you can take with you. If you scan someone's blood with it, the results can get sent straight here. We can find out the truth and get all the evidence we need, instantly."

"Wait, Jensen knows about this?"

"Well, yeah. I brought it up to Jay in passing and got an earful – that's probably why he got so defensive when you asked to help out. I'd already planted the idea in his head. As you might imagine, he's not a fan."

"No. I guess this plan doesn't work, after all. We can't really do this behind his back."

She nods, but I can see in her eyes that she wishes we could. I know. I wish we could, too. A thought occurs to me all of a sudden, and I wriggle uncomfortably in my chair.

"Hold up. Say that plan worked. What then?"

"What do you mean?"

"Like... how would I get back?"

She chews her lip.

"I guess... you'd have to wait until we came for you. After the three leaders had been brought down."

My stomach churns at the thought. It's taken Jay and the others nearly sixteen years to rebuild the Clover to this point. Even with all that information to help the cause, it could still be years before they finally manage to overthrow the leaders. I don't think I could deal with it for that long.

"Suddenly, I don't like this plan."

"Well, there's always a different way. You could break out. But I suppose it's hard enough to escape when you have a team behind you. On your own, it'd be pretty tough, wouldn't it?"

"Actually, no."

I reach for the nearest flat surface and start tracing the lines with my fingers.

"What are you doing?" she asks.

"I never looked around enough to think of an escape route before. If our theory's right, they wipe people's minds so they're more obedient. Since it's all anyone there has ever known, they're lacking in security. Here..."

I draw a series of squares with my finger, pointing to each one in turn. I talk Pan through it; the way in, the two Guard towers near the entrance that are always manned. I explain how they don't have much training – the Guards appear in their early teens, scrawny and spotty, and they're given a gun and put on watch. It would be easy to force my way past the Guard towers, since their aim is so terrible. It's about an hour to the docks. I could probably sprint if I had to. Take cover somewhere.

"But wouldn't they chase you down?" Pan asks, intrigued by my haphazard explanations.

"Maybe. But I'm just one kid, and there's nothing between the Farm and the Dock. As far as they're concerned, I don't stand a chance at getting past the gates at the Docks, or on the other side. There's a huge distance between there and Thorne, too – so even if they figured out where I was going, they wouldn't believe I could make it."

"And could you?"

I wink.

"I made it here, didn't I? I have friends at the Docks, and there's always a chance I'll run into Eagen again."

Pan doesn't ask who Eagen is. I don't mention to her that Eagen and Darus aren't like me. They're good people, sure, but if they knew they'd get in trouble for helping me, they might not. It's hard to imagine Darus turning his back on someone, and even harder to imagine Eagen leaving me in the dust; but I wouldn't blame them if they chose to do just that.

"There should be an abandoned cart partway down that road from the last guy who was sent with your delivery. Maybe I could take that and say I'm here to deliver something for you, just like last time."

"But that comes down to chance," she warns, "only a fraction of the Guard knows me. If you weren't lucky, you might end up being caught."

"Everything comes down to luck, you know. I still think that your plan could work."

She leans back now, unable to hide her smug smile. I can only imagine how good that must feel; it's not the simplest of plans, but she's got it. It works. But then her face falls.

"It's just a shame that Jay would never go for it. I mentioned it in passing and he practically blew his lid. If we went to him with all the details sorted out..."

"He'd be furious," I finish, "but you're right. This is the best plan we've got. Maybe it wouldn't hurt to ask him again."

"Not a good idea. You didn't see his reaction when I mentioned it. I know Jay can be a real prick at times, Noah. I'm not blind. But he really does care about everyone here. If he thought any of us were going to be at risk, he wouldn't agree to it. Especially not if that person is you."

"But that's just it. I wouldn't be doing some crazy stunt, would I? I'd just head back to the place I grew up. It might take a few weeks to get all the data, but once I did, I could be back pretty fast. Do you really not think he'd go for it?"

She stands now, pacing the room in a somewhat maniacal manner.

"He wouldn't, not if we just present it to him as an idea. But what if we got everything ready?"

"You think?"

"Yeah. Jensen and I have talked about it – what if I arranged your route back to the Mill, and Jensen pieced together the remote transmitter? Then, the day of, we'll drop the news on Jay."

I wince. I don't imagine him reacting well to that. Luckily, Pan seems fairly confident with the idea. I can't help but think she's done this before. If there's anyone who'd be forgiven for going behind his back, it's her. Still...

"Look, I don't know what's going on between you and Jay," I admit, "whether you're an item or whatever. It's none of my business. But would he really forgive you if you went against him?"

"It's not going against him. I know it seems unfair, but I know your brother. Better than you do, I dare say. I've spent years getting to know him, and though he's a great leader and person, he's stubborn. He doesn't know when to admit he's wrong. Even with this. If it was a stupid idea, he'd have forgotten about it sharpish. But the fact he brought it up to you, that means he's taking it seriously. And he wouldn't be doing that unless he knew it was our best shot. We're just going to make it easier for him to see that. Are you in?"

I bite back on my refusal. She's right. She does know Jay better than I do. If she says this is the right thing to do, who am I to refuse her? Sure, the thought of being stranded alone is terrifying, but I'm sure I can manage. Besides, I'll get to see Nel again. That alone is nearly enough to convince me.

"Sure. I'm in."

CHAPTER TWENTY-ONE

It only takes two days to get everything ready. Pan pulls a few strings with her friends in the Guard to arrange my safe passage back. As she talks me through it, I feel my irritation flare. The journey into the city had been fraught with danger, especially during the final leg. But Pan's description is much easier. I'll load the empty cart into a truck heading to the Docks, and from there I'll be placed onto a pre-selected boat. The trip between the docks and the Mill is up to me; but it's practically nothing. I can manage that part without any trouble.

Jensen summons me into his room and talks me through how to use the transmitter. It's a tiny hand-held thing, small enough that I can stow it away in my pocket. As long as the Guards don't decide to search me for any reason, I'm golden.

"How long will the battery last?" I ask him. I'm still surprised at how much I've picked up in the short time I've been here – two weeks ago, I didn't even know that batteries were a thing.

"That depends," he says, "to get a good sample size, you need to obtain blood samples from at least five more people. It's still going to be a fraction of a percent, but even that many will work. If you can get more, do it. A bigger sample size can only make it more accurate. The more you use it, the quicker the battery will go down, but even then I reckon it's got about six months in it. You won't be that long, will you?"

I scoff.

"No way. I'll be heading back as soon as I can. I'm not exactly eager to go home."

He nods and looks away, and I'm suddenly glad he wasn't listening too closely. I called the Mill 'home' again. I can't help it; in my head, it's still the place I grew up. If that wasn't enough on its own, I straight up lied. I am eager to go back. Not because I want to leave here. I don't. But then Nel's dark eyes and patchy carrot-coloured hair flash in my mind, and longing builds in my chest.

I miss her. I could happily go the rest of my life never seeing the likes of Wirrow or Rian again. But Nel's the only person I ever really cared about there.

Except Kane, of course. But he's in the Mines. Like it or not, I'll have to leave him there. Once we win this fight we can recover those who were lost, and maybe I'll be able to find him amongst the thousands. I don't know if he'll ever be willing to speak to me again, though. I wish I could speak to him again, even if it was only to apologise.

Jensen must notice that I'm deep in thought, because he clears his throat.

"Hey. Are you really up for this?"

I snap out of it and shrug, plastering a too-broad smile on my face.

"Sure! This is a piece of cake."

"You're going to be all on your own for a few weeks, you know. However long it takes you to get those samples. After that you can find your way back, but even so..."

"It's fine," I say calmly, "I grew up there, remember?"

"I know you did. But Pan's regaled me with the stories you told her about that place. It doesn't exactly sound nice."

"It's not. But I survived for eleven years. After a while, you just slip into autopilot. You learn to move your body without thinking. To look away when something starts going wrong. It's easier not to ask questions."

It's been a while since I've said that. Even longer since I've believed it. Jensen's eyes narrow at the phrase, too. His lips part as though he's about to say something, but then he just nods.

"If something goes wrong, anything at all, use the device on yourself, okay? Once your sample comes through, we'll know there's been a problem. We can find a way to get you out of there."

"Thanks, Jensen. I'll keep that in mind. Will you take care of Atlas for me?"

"Of course. I've got some work to do on it anyway, so I'll keep it safe and secure for your return."

"Thank you."

"One more thing…"

He nudges his glasses up on his nose, suddenly nervous. His gaze flits around the room, uncertain – but it eventually settles on me. When he speaks, his voice is low.

"Come home, okay? You have to. I don't think that Jay could deal with losing you twice. Even if he could, you're part of this thing now."

I laugh.

"Jensen, if you're going to miss me, you can just say so. I won't laugh."

I expect a firm rebuttal, perhaps a little teasing; but instead, he gives a solemn nod.

"Alright then. I'm gonna miss you."

Colour rushes to my face.

"Y-yeah. Right back at ya."

I stare up at the rivets on the ceiling, glaring like I could imprint the image into my memory. I want to remember everything – the bunk under my back, the feeling of being warm and dry and clean. My Mill clothes hang over a chair to my side. They're still utterly filthy, despite having been washed a few times. Dried dirt and blood have stained the familiar grey hoodie to within an inch of its life.

The last time I wore that, I met everyone here. Luse and her 'boys' had pinned me in the alleyway, trying to rob the cart. At the time, I'd known nothing. Only that I needed to get the stuff to someone called Pan. I remember questioning the name, wondering what kind of bizarre people might name their child after a piece of cooking equipment. I think I put it down to the unusual thoughts of the city folk. They'd seemed so different from those at the Mill. It was like they were from some different world, a universe far removed from my own. Stepping through the city gates had been deeply unsettling; everyone was tall and pale and bored. I'd never met a soul like that before. I'd felt alien as I walked the streets.

Now? Those streets are my secrets. I know the tunnels that run under Thorne. I know the symbols people wear to let each other know which side they're on. I know which streets have tiny, high-tech cameras recording remotely for Jensen's viewing pleasure. I've clutched onto Pan's back as we've raced down the roads, both in moments of delight and moments of utter terror. On these streets, I've never felt so scared, or so happy.

I can't believe I have to leave it behind. Even if it is only for a little while. I raise one hand toward the ceiling; it's well out of my reach, but I don't care. The sight of my own battle-damaged, worn hand next to the highly-polished metal makes me feel out of place and at home at the same time.

"What are you thinking about?"

Pan's sitting across from me, staring from her own bunk.

"Nothing."

It's true – I'm thinking about skin and rivets and clothes. Nothing of any real consequence, though they mean a lot to me. I drag myself into a sitting position.

"When's Jay getting here?"

"I asked him to come by at nine, so any minute now."

As if on cue, someone knocks at the door. But it's not just Jay that walks in – Nate and Jensen follow, along with both Hue and Nelson. Jensen and I exchange mildly alarmed glances, but it's with some confidence that Pan stands.

"Hey, guys. Listen, I brought you here because I – we – need to tell you something."

Suspicion instantly overtakes Jay's face, and he looks me up and down as though searching for clues. Finally, his eyes settle on the Mill clothing hanging nearby. The colour drains from his face.

"Oh, no. Pan, tell me you didn't."

"Just let me explain," she says, "everything's sorted. She'll be going at midday."

"No, she won't. And you!"

He rounds on Jensen now, anger flashing in his eyes.

"You were part of this, weren't you?"

"Y-yeah. But there's a good reason…"

"There's no good reason for this. I said no. I trusted you!"

Suddenly, my irritation flares and I stamp my foot. It's an unbelievably childish motion and rather unlike me, but that seems to work in my favour as Jay pauses to look my way.

"Stop this already," I snap, "this isn't their fault. They wouldn't be able to do anything if I hadn't agreed to it."

"I explained exactly why I didn't want you to do anything like this!"

"You told me I couldn't help because I didn't understand. I respect that, even if it's not what I want to hear. But I do understand this. I'm the only one who can do this."

His anger is building; but Nate rests a bin-lid hand on his shoulder.

"Maybe we should hear them out. If this is the plan Jensen explained to me before, it makes a lot of sense."

"No!" Jay cries, "why won't anyone listen to me? I'm not risking anyone like that!"

I take a long, deep breath, letting it out slowly to calm myself. As I found the other day, we're just too similar. We're both hot-headed and argumentative, and stubborn to boot. But I've already proven that screaming at him won't change his mind. Only reason can do that.

"Jay," I say, "please hear me out. I want to help. I know you're only trying to protect me, but I can do this. I'm the only one who can."

"It's a good plan," he admits, "but it's a huge risk..."

"I'm willing to do it. I trust Pan and Jensen. I trust that they know what they're doing. And I know you trust them, too. You know this is the best idea we have if we want people to fight back before the next Cull."

"But..."

"Please. You need to trust me. I can do this."

He meets my eyes now, blue against blue. To say he seems hesitant would be an understatement; he looks terrified. I don't blame him. If things were the other way around, I'd be inconsolable. But then, if things were the other way around, this wouldn't even be a discussion. Because I would trust him. Blindly, if I had to. No matter what he had to do, I'd hold out hope that he would manage somehow.

But then he sighs and steps closer, nudging a lock of hair from my eyes.

"I know you can do it. And I do trust you."

"Does that mean..."

"Yeah. If you're sure that you're up for this, I'll trust you. We'll go with Pan and Jensen's plan."

Delight fills my chest. Easy. Go back to the Mill, get the samples, come home. Then watch as the Clover fights back and makes everything okay again.

It's a small part to play, sure, but I'm proud to be playing it at all.

At midday I find myself loading empty containers into the cart. They've been keeping it in storage for me – something I find strange, considering they had no real use for it. The thought briefly crosses my mind that maybe they knew I'd have to take it back eventually, but I push it aside. They probably just forgot it was here.

As I move, my standard-issue Mill clothing scratches at my skin. It's not painful exactly, but a little itchy and uncomfortable. It's shocking just how quickly I got used to the soft, loose clothing Pan would present me with. Now I'm back to ripped, mucky jeans, my heavy boots and my grey hoodie. I brush a hand through my hair. It still looks too neat to be Mill standard. Too clean, too smooth. But I needn't worry. The ocean wind and intense heat of the road beyond the city will no doubt leave it a frayed, scorched mess by the time I reach the Mill.

I have to admit, it feels nice to be back. It sounds preposterous considering all that's happened, but I kind of missed the simplicity of being a Millchild. As I strap up the cart, instinct takes over. I know where it all goes. I know where to load things, how to lift the heaviest items in the best way. It's not a skill, not really. Not when I compare it to Nate's inventions, or Jensen's talent with computers. But it's something – and it's all mine.

The others watch in silence as I load the cart. I briefly consider asking them to help, then stop. This is a covert operation, after all. I need to know everything that's done. I need to know the sizing of every last buckle, the positioning of every last box. There needs to be nothing out of place except for my own thoughts.

Jensen steps forward and passes me the remote transmitter.

"Don't forget this. Use the chain to fasten it to the inside of your pocket so you don't lose it."

I take it, complimenting him on his ingenuity. I hadn't thought about it before, but that's a very real risk. When pacing muddy fields, it'd be easy to lose something so small.

He eyes me carefully.

"Are you absolutely sure you know how to use it?"

"Yeah. I've got it."

"Remember that any signal we get, we'll run against the database. We won't have any way of telling you if they're positive or not, which is why we need a sample of at least five people, ideally. If we get the signal with your own blood sample, we'll know that something's gone wrong and Pan will get Rian to report what's going on."

Right. Rian sent me here. It wasn't very long ago, but I'm already having trouble recalling that thin face and those slender shoulders. At the time, I couldn't tell if he was on my side or not. Now I know – but he's still a Guard. He showed zero compassion when they threw Kane into the Mines, or when the kid sent into the city before me never made it back. He might have helped us out once, but that doesn't mean I trust him.

"Ten minutes until your truck leaves," Pan reminds me, "and this is a big favour from the Guard. It's going with or without you, so don't miss it."

I gulp. This is it.

"I guess I need to go, then."

There's a moment of hesitation as I stare at the others, and they stare back at me. Nobody knows what to say. Not even Pan, though her face is already filled with sadness. I clear my throat.

"I'll be back soon, okay? I promise."

"You'd better be," Pan says, and suddenly she reaches out and draws me into a tight embrace.

"Gonna miss you," she mutters, "you'd better come back."

"Hey, this is your plan. Have a little faith."

"Hmm."

With that she pulls away, but there's a little emptiness as she does so. It wasn't a short embrace by any means, but it still feels like it was over too soon.

I glance at Jay. There's resistance in his eyes, and his arms are crossed in front of him as he nods and issues a short goodbye.

"Don't be like that," I joke, "I'm your sister. Is that really the goodbye I get?"

His expression falters, perhaps a little surprised at my attitude.

"O-of course not."

He opens his arms – and just like that day on the boat with Darus, I step into the embrace. This time, there's no awkwardness. I clutch my brother closely, taking in every aspect of him. His shoulders are broad. His hair is messy. His breath stinks faintly of coffee. Again, tiny details that mean very little in the grand scheme of things. Things most people wouldn't even notice, let alone care to remember. But for me, it's important. These are the memories I'll survive on until I can find my way home again.

As we break apart, I ruffle his hair.

"Wait for me, okay? I'll be back before you know it."

He smiles grimly.

"A few weeks, right?"

"A few weeks. Then I'm never leaving again."

"Good."

I strap myself into the bars of the cart, looping the leather strips with surprising ease. Someone pulls open the shutter door. The metal squeals as it opens, flooding the small space with blinding midday sun. I stare into it, half wishing it would rain just a little so I don't have to walk in this heat. But as I step forward, I hesitate. The others are still standing there, waiting for me to go. Their faces reflect my own feelings. Fear and hesitation mingled with cautious optimism. Suddenly, I feel like there's so much more to say. Thanks I never gave. Questions I never asked. Tiny, unimportant details I never bothered so disclose. But when my mouth falls open, I only manage one word.

"Thanks."

Jay smiles his familiar smile.

"Don't forget about us, okay? Promise."

"Promise."

I start walking, and a moment later, the garage door rolls shut behind the cart. As it does so, it crashes with a kind of frightening finality. The glories of the Atrium and the warmth of my friends fall away behind me as I step out into the stranger-filled streets of a city that's out to get me.

I slip through the main gates without being stopped or questioned. Apparently, the Guards care more about those trying to get into Thorne than those trying to leave. I'm waved through without a second glance, and feel rather grateful for it.

The truck Pan arranged for me is unlike Eagen's. This one is vast and black, made of some thick, matte metal. There are a half dozen Guards watching as I load the cart into the back - briefly, I wonder how many of them know who I am.

It seems strange that Pan would be able to arrange this 'favour' without telling them the truth. But the way they look at me is strange. It's stern and unyielding, like they either don't know why I'm here, or frankly don't care. I suppose they think the same as the Mill kids; that sometimes, it's easier not to ask the question.

"Sit in the back with the goods," a Guard tells me. His voice is hard, like he's biting back on his dislike for me. I can understand that. They don't normally regard those from the Mill as people deserving of basic respect, much less worth doing favours for. Still, they begrudgingly allow me into the back of the truck, where three step up next to me and sit down against the cold, metal insides. I open my mouth to question why I need three Guards plus a driver - but they're not looking at me. They've turned their backs on me entirely, in fact, and are now talking amongst themselves about some dock transfer. I see. The favour isn't a truck to get me back. It's my being permitted to catch a ride with the Guards already headed that way. I suppose that makes sense.

As the engine roars into life under me, I feel a pang of terror. Despite the bravado I'd shown to Jay and the others, I'm terrified to go back. I'm scared to be alone again after so long. I'm absolutely petrified of this weight on my shoulders.

Still, it's too late now. I stare into the distance as we speed away. Within just a few minutes, the gates are out of sight. Even Thorne itself seems to be oddly dimmed, like there's a half-layer of dust between the gleaming structures and my own eyes.

I can still feel the gaze of the Guards on me. While they talk between themselves, lounging in most of the available space, their gaze flits my way every so often. No doubt they're wondering why a Millchild has been added to their journey, negating the need for a car or other, more comfortable mode of transportation. It'll be a long journey with this tension in the air; but luckily, I'm past caring. I pull my knees up to my chin and lean against the back panel, eyes fixed on the city. I'm not going to move until it's well and truly faded from my sight.

Night's falling overhead. The bright, clear sky is turning periwinkle, and to my small delight I can see the first few tiny stars beginning to glimmer through. Despite the conflict in my chest, I can't deny it's nice to see the night sky again. It's the only good thing about this journey.

It doesn't take long before the Guards fall asleep, sprawled in the back of the truck like drunkards; I inhale deeply and sure enough, the stench of cheap whiskey hits me. But that's fine by me. With them asleep, and the cart blocking the driver's view of me, I'm able to steal a few minutes of precious privacy. I've grown used to being on my own; if I needed it, wanted it, I could take it. I remind myself that privacy doesn't exist at the Mill. Someone's always watching, even if they don't know it. I shiver in the cool evening air and suddenly miss Atlas' warning beeps. It would always alert me to a drop in body temperature, or a spike in adrenaline. But Atlas is back in Jensen's room, tucked away in the pile of computers. Only silence greets me.

As the sky darkens even more, I wonder what the others are doing. It might be too soon to sleep – but no doubt they're planning. Coming up with the perfect plan for whatever outcome I provide.

Hey, here's something. Nel will still be awake.

Suddenly, I feel myself smiling. I've missed her. Life at the Mill is hard enough; but she was the softness. She was the kindness and the understanding, even when she didn't mean to be. Without her around, who knows how I would have ended up. I wasn't angry like Kane, but I wasn't sad and wise like Nel, either. I guess I didn't really have much to me. Just work, sleep, work. Nothing else mattered.

Even though the notion frightens me, I still reach out to try and embrace it. I need to think like that again. It's hard to survive when you're distracted. If I want to go back, if I want to convince them that I'm the same as I ever was, then I need to hack back into that feeling. It was nice, I guess, to feel like I had a purpose, even if it wasn't what I might have chosen for myself. I never had to question anything, never had to worry – that may not have been a good thing, but it's how I survived for eleven years. If I go back like this, I'll either get caught or I'll snap like Kane did.

So I lean back, rest my head against the wheels of the cart, and watch the last glow of evening light vanish from the horizon.

CHAPTER TWENTY-TWO

It's several more hours before we finally reach the Docks and when we do, I find myself gaping. How could I have forgotten how beautiful it was here? The sun's rising on the horizon, tinting the ocean red-gold. I close my eyes, revelling in the soft hush of the tide. A deep breath and the sea air hits me hard, filling my head with memories.

It's odd. I've lived at either end of this peculiar journey, and yet my favourite part has always been the middle. The sight of the ocean is stunning – it glimmers gently under the sunrise, flashing bright white occasionally as the light hits it just right. Just below are the Docks. They're as busy as ever, with an alarming number of Guards milling around. As the truck passes through several people stare, perhaps unnerved as to why I would be here. I suppose a Millchild looks somewhat out of place riding with a couple of mid-ranked Guards.

Still, the moment I step down, tugging the cart with me, they're gone. As soon as I click the rear of the truck back into place the driver hits the gas, veering out of the Docks and turning back towards Thorne. It's been a long journey; I don't blame them for wanting to head back.

For a moment, I feel small and lost amongst the crowds. But then I remember what Pan said. She'd already arranged a route back for me. I quickly locate the boat in question, and when I give my name at the door I'm allowed on board. Again, nobody bothers to engage me in conversation. It's a far cry from the warm reception I received from Darus and his Dad the first time round. The thought occurs that I should try to look for them, see if I can speak to him one more time - maybe even run Darus through my transmitter. I'm sure he'd let me.

But then the boat shifts underfoot, and it's too late. We're off.

I spend the day perched at the front of the boat, ignoring the goings on around me. Several of the Guards are drinking again, but despite their inebriated calls my way, I don't move. Perhaps before, I'd have been feared a beating if I didn't obey, but I've become surprisingly good at knowing when I can push things. I guess that's Jay's influence.

The ocean is just as wonderful as ever. It's still the most beautiful thing I've ever seen - growing up I believed that nothing was lovelier than the sun setting over a well-worked field, or that sliver of moonlight breaking through the cracked ceiling of a bunker. In Thorne, I'd grown to love the underground glow of the Atrium, or the shadowed comfort of an empty alleyway. But nothing compares to the subtle shimmer that surrounds me.

I try to remember the last time I did this journey - how I'd eaten a peculiar meal of fish with Darus and his Dad, and tried to rest in a hammock. How I'd burst into tears for the first time in my life. How I'd rushed into the arms of someone who could never understand, but still wanted to help.

My heart hurts. I rest a hand on my chest as though I can soothe the pain there, but it's too late. I miss him. I miss everyone.

I've never been the type to need constant company. As far as I'm concerned, a stolen moment alone is precious. But suddenly, I feel very, very alone. Maybe it's the miles of water between us. Maybe it's the realisation that I'm nearly back at the Mill.

Tearing my gaze away from the ocean, I hang my head.

The walk from the Docks to the Mill is more tiring that I'd expected it to be; is it possible that just two weeks away has sapped me of my strength? Sweat runs off me in streams, and there's a burning in my legs I thought I'd outgrown years ago. Still, habit takes over. Muscle memory kicks in and I'm walking just as fast as I ever did, regardless of the new, fresh pain it creates.

There it is. The Mill looks strange from this angle – but then, I suppose I've never seen it like this before. Two Guard towers outside metal gates, and chain-link fences as far as the eye can see. I spy rolling hills of crops, and several large buildings I recognise as storage and where we keep the animals. In the distance, something thumps. Just beyond the Farm are the Mines, and beyond that, the Plant.

I didn't want to come back here. Even now there's trepidation in my heart, and a tiny voice is asking if there's any way I could go back to the city. Whatever anger I felt towards the three leaders is now mirrored onto the Guards; as I near and their hands find their batons, I feel like snarling. Someone steps down to meet me, and I measure him up. Note his weak spots. Estimate his weight. Yeah, I could pin him without much trouble.

"Where are you coming from?" he demands.

"Thorne. Rian sent me."

He looks me up and down now, perhaps not fooled by the dust in my hair and the mud on my clothes.

"That was weeks ago. What the hell happened?"

"I... I made the delivery. Got stuck on the way back. There's a long walk between the Docks and the city - I didn't expect it to take so many days extra."

His eyes narrow at that; clearly, he doesn't believe me. Nonetheless, he signals for them to open the gate.

"Come with me. You need to report to Rian."

"Ah, I remember you."

Rian's pacing the room, mild amusement in his eyes. I'm held fast by the first Guard and am desperately trying to maintain what little dignity I can while sprawled on the dirty office rug.

"So you did send her out?" the Guard asks. Rian nods.

"I did. Took a bit longer than I expected, but hey. The last one didn't even get there. Thanks for bringing this one in, Rod. I'll take it from here."

His weight shifts off me, and a moment later the door opens and shuts behind us. I can feel Rian's eyes on me as I sit upright, fighting to gather my composure. He shakes his head sadly.

"Oh, Noah. What are you doing back here?"

I wipe the dirt from my face.

"You told me to come back. After I'd made the delivery."

"Seriously?"

He sighs, pacing the room and spinning on his big office chair.

"Honestly," he whines, "I thought when Pan asked for more people that she'd got everything figured out. Clearly, they didn't even bother to test you!"

"They did."

"Huh?"

"We figured it out."

He watches me for a moment before opening a desk drawer and pulling out some matches and a box of cigarettes. Lighting one, he flicks the burning match onto the ground at my feet.

"Then my question still stands. If you figured it out, then why the hell did you come back?"

I bite into my lip, suddenly unable to meet his eyes.

"I... have my reasons. More importantly... you knew, didn't you? That's why you sent me. How did you figure it out?"

He shrugs.

"I'm familiar with Jay, so I had an inkling as to who you were. The two of you look so similar. Of course, I had no way of proving it – we don't know what happens after the Cull, really. As for our workers, only those at Homestead know what happens. We just get given an annual supply of slightly dazed kids."

"You never asked the question?"

He scoffs.

"Of course not. I might be a sympathiser, but I'm in no position to help Jay out. If I step out of line, I draw attention to myself."

"But you're a Guard," I point out.

"Yeah, and that doesn't mean much. I still have bills to pay and rules to follow, you got that? I came up with the same theory you probably have, but figured I wasn't able to do much without getting in trouble. So I decided that when you next stepped out of line, I'd just send you into Thorne."

He takes a deep drag and narrows his eyes at me.

"But you didn't want to act out, did you kid? You were perfectly well behaved. In the end, I took whatever chance I could to send you out. Happy to see that worked, at least. I am surprised you're back, though. Was my theory wrong?"

"No. I'm Ada."

"Hey! Shush with that. There might not be cameras in here, but Guards are nosey assholes. Whatever you do, don't say anything. Not to me, not to anyone. In fact, whatever little plan you're working on, don't tell me. I want plausible deniability if you fuck it up."

I hesitate at that. My initial opinion of him was right. He's not a rebel like Jay, Pan or Jensen – just a sympathiser, like the dozens of others who spend time in the Atrium. Yet another person who understands their cause but is too afraid to actually fight for it.

Just like that, I lose a shred of respect for him.

"I guess I should thank you for sending me there," I mutter, "or we'd never have known."

"Don't thank me yet. Don't you dare underestimate the leaders. You might be happy now, sure, but give it time and you might be wishing I'd let you carry on being ignorant."

I open my mouth to tell him no, that I'm never going to regret what's happened, but Jay's voice rings in my head.

You don't understand.

There's still a lot going on that I'm clueless about. Besides, Rian seems so solemn in his warning, those dim eyes even dimmer in the smoke of his cigarette, that I can't help but take him seriously.

"Thanks for the warning. But I'll be okay. I know what to do."

"You say that, but you still came back. Whatever you want to do, kid, you do without my blessing. I won't help you out any further, no matter who you are."

He fixes me with a stern gaze, and I meet it.

"Sounds fair. Should I go back to work now?"

"Yes. You're in the fields. Enjoy your stay."

Evening is already falling overhead; the others will be clocking off soon. So instead of sending me straight to the fields, Rian orders me to unload the cart and go to the bunkers. No dinner tonight, he says warningly. That's only for those who've earned it through a long day's work.

I obey politely enough, agreeing to his terms without argument. But inside, I boil. He might be a sympathiser - he might be soft and sweet inside - but when the outside is this much of an ass, it's hard to be impressed.

I enter the bunker just as the other workers are leaving the fields. I take a deep breath, expecting to enjoy the musk of dozens of familiar bodies - and gag. Apparently, it's easy to romanticise a scent. There's nothing 'musty' about the stench that hangs in the air around me. It's sweat and dirt and two dozen mouths worth of stinking breath.

But my bunk. My bunk's still there, with that little ray of evening light breaking through the hole in the ceiling. I take a seat on it and nearly fall through. Was my bunk always just a scrap of cloth stretched over a square of metal? Maybe I've gotten too used to the home comforts of the Atrium. It won't do to spend my time whining that things aren't up to standard. Two weeks of luxury don't outweigh the eleven years spent living here. So I fall back against the rough canvas of and fix my eyes on the tear in the metal overhead.

It's with immense relief that I finally start to hear the others. They bustle in after dinner, heaving familiar sighs. A few rub their aching muscles as they slump onto their camp beds. To my surprise, none of them look at me. Either they don't notice I'm here, or they've already forgotten about me. I wish I could feel offended, but I'm starting to realise just how little impact I've had.

I stare at everyone in turn as they enter, searching their faces for anything I might recognise as hers. That long nose, those dark eyes, that patchy orange hair. The smattering of freckles across her cheeks and forehead. Longing builds in my chest as I wait for her. When I see her, I don't know what I'll do - my instinct is to run up for an embrace, but I hold back. That's not allowed here, remember?

But the final handful of girls trickle into the bunker, and she's not among them. I turn to the closest girl, a lanky brunette who's scraping sawdust from under her nails.

"Where's Nel?"

She stares blankly.

"Which one's Nel?"

"You know, freckled, red hair? Shaved head?"

"I'm not sure who you're talking about."

I point at her abandoned bunk.

"She sleeps there!"

"Oh! I remember now. Yeah, she's not here anymore."

My blood runs cold.

"W-what? What do you mean, she's not here anymore? You don't mean she's..."

The girl narrows her eyes at me, clearly confused by my attitude. I bite back on my words, but panic is still welling in my chest. Oh no. Please don't let her be dead.

"It's alright."

The girl rests against the metal wall and heaves a deep sigh, like she's already fed up of my questions.

"She's not dead, if that's what you're worried about. About a week ago the Guards came by, remember? Took her away. How do you not remember that?"

Relief floods through me.

"I... I guess I wasn't here for that. Why did they take her?"

She shrugs.

"Beats me. Wasn't just her, though. They took a bunch of people. They've been talking about needing supplementary workers in other areas, so maybe it's that."

"Like where?" I urge. She looks closely at me now, suddenly suspicious.

"I don't know. Do I look like a Guard to you?"

"No. Sorry."

"Listen, I don't know how long you've been here - you don't look like a newbie - but I'd try to stop this behaviour if I were you."

That sounds familiar. I meet her dull eyes, frightened of how much they remind me of my own.

"I mean it," she warns, "if you keep digging around and asking stuff, you'll get a beating from the Guards. Just keep your head down and get on with it, okay? Quit asking questions."

At that, my heart sinks. Nothing's changed for the people here, even though everything's changed for me. They still don't know what's going on, and many don't want to. I remember that day in the field, when I warned Kane against the same thing. Don't fight back. Don't stand up for yourself. And most definitely, most vitally, never ever ask questions.

The room is quickly filled with the soft breathing of scores of Mill workers as they fall asleep around me. Some small voice tells me I should lie down too, that tomorrow will be a long and hard enough day without making myself tired. I fall back obediently, eyes fixed on the hole above me.

But then my eyes are drawn to Nel's empty bunk. Her scrap of a blanket is still screwed up like she always leaves it, only I can now see tiny specks of mildew showing through. With nobody around to air and hang it every day, her bunk is starting to rot away. The sadness wells in my throat. This was going to be the only good thing about coming back here. The only highlight to this horrible journey. I'd been looking forward to sitting together in the darkness, barely able to see by the light of the single bulb. I have so many stories I want to tell her – but now, I don't even know where she is. She could be in the Plant, perhaps. There's a chance they sent her to the Mines, but that's less likely. The Mines are a punishment, not an allocation.

Still. If I don't know where she is, then the chance of finding her again are slim to none. Even when this is all over and people can move freely again, I probably won't be able to hunt her down amongst the thousands of Mill kids from this section alone.

The last time we saw one another was unremarkable. It had been the start of another day, nothing special. We'd waved goodbye as we'd headed in different directions; though at the time, we hadn't known it would be a goodbye at all. It was more of a 'see you later'.

I reach out across the small space between our bunks, trying to imagine my hand clutching hers like it did before. When she was so upset and I couldn't think of a thing to do to comfort her. At the time, all I'd been able to do was be present.

I wish she could do that now.

Daybreak comes far too quickly for my liking. The jolt that hits me as the bunker door flies open is unpleasant – somehow, I'd even romanticised that rude awakening. I groan as I sit up. My back hurts from the bunk and I'm freezing cold and damp to boot. I can only imagine the chafing I'll deal with later.

Still, there's no point in whining. I lace up my work boots and throw on my grey hoodie, noting yet again that the sleeves are too short to keep out the chill. As I push my arms through, I check that Jensen's remote transmitter is still securely hidden in my pocket. Everyone else piles out, and I find myself slipping into the masses. Nobody talks to me – and while I know that I should try to corner some of the more rebellious types to talk them round, I'm simply too fed up. Being back here is disheartening enough; but not seeing Nel makes it worse. I'm just going to work. Whatever happens today, I'll just take it. No point fighting.

I trudge towards the field and briefly, my mood brightens. Here's one thing I hadn't romanticised – the sun is rising over the rolling hills, bathing everything in soft golden light. It's as lovely as I'd remembered. I pause to take in the sight, but a Guard walks by and pushes me back in line.

"Back to work," he sneers, turning his back. Hatred wells in my chest, but I push it aside. I have my priorities.

I strap the seeding bag to my hip, lining up behind my line's plough. I'm pleased I'm not the one pulling it. Years ago, we had oxen to do it for us. But then came an extra push from the city, an increased demand for meat. So we lost that, too. Now I realise that push was probably the result of a particularly lean Cull. More people, more problems. I wonder if Jay's thought of a solution to that particular issue yet.

As I walk, scattering the seeds into the soil, I try to make a mental list of everyone I could speak to. Jensen said he needed five minimum, right? There are tens of thousands of workers here – surely I can find just five willing to take a chance. But as I search the faces around me, I come up with nothing. I don't know anyone.

I'd been hoping that Nel would help me. She's always so friendly with everyone, even the Guard. I'd been sure that she would know who to talk to. Without her around, I'm starting to realise just how little I actually interacted with the other workers. Even that lanky girl from the bunkers. She sleeps two bunks down from me and is easily my age or older, but I don't know her name. Her face wasn't even familiar to me.

I can't risk just approaching someone – if I get reported to the Guard, I'm done for. They won't take kindly to a worker encouraging rebellion in their presence. If I want to find five people I can trust, then I need to talk to people. Sounds easy enough, right? But then I glance to either side. The workers are staring straight ahead. They don't even notice as I stare at them each in turn; they're all too focussed on what they're doing.

Suddenly, this task feels much bigger than before. It's not as easy as getting five samples and breaking out. As much as I hate to say it, this might not be a 'few weeks' kind of job. I'm on my own here – no friends, no family, nobody else on my side.

The thought physically hurts.

CHAPTER TWENTY-THREE

It's been three months.

Sometimes, I can't believe that's true. But then I recall the sorrow felt with every new moon, the notches I've tirelessly carved into the sides of my leather boots. In a way, it feels like a day or two. In another way, it's like I've never been gone. The days blend together in an unnerving way, so much that I risk losing track of time entirely. I never bothered to count the months before; I tracked the years by the seasons, and even then I didn't count too closely. It had only been Nel and her constant commentary on the changing weather that kept me in check.

She hasn't come back yet. Neither have any of the others they took away, and though I've asked the question many more times, nobody knows exactly where they were taken. If I had even an inkling of where she was, I could try to get transferred, too. They let me visit the mines all those years ago. I'm a well behaved worker, for the most part.

The work no longer means anything to me. It's not hard anymore, not a struggle to get going, nor to do a good job. But any trace of satisfaction is long gone – there's no pride in a hard day's work. Not now that I know it's all for nothing. Even the sight of the sun over the fields has long since failed to please me.

My memories are fading. What happened in Thorne often feels like some kind of fever-dream, some particularly lucid hallucination I might have once had on a hot day. Sometimes, I go a whole week without thinking about them. The realisation's usually followed up with sadness and anger, but there's little I can do to ease it.

More than once I've considered scanning my fingertip and begging with them to come get me. I'm sure they could find a way if they really tried. But when I think about it, I always change my mind. I haven't failed yet – not technically. I'm still looking for people to help me. I now realise how much I'd underestimated this place. The people here aren't just hard workers, motivated by a sense of daily satisfaction. They've been brainwashed and buckled, forced to only look ahead and never, ever question things. The few people I've spoken to about my device have seemed frightened, even angry at me for owning it; I'd thought it would be easy to find someone who was willing to fight back, even if it's only in the tiniest way. Apparently not.

It's a particularly dark evening when the sirens sound, telling us to leave the field. Good. I've been chopping wood all day and the muscles in my shoulders burn, and despite the floodlights, it's getting hard to see more than an arm's length away. Winter is getting closer; there's a distinct chill in the air, and as people move around me I can hear leaves crunching underfoot. I shoot a bored glance at the sizeable stack of chopped wood next to me. I've done a good job. Very productive. Before, that would be enough reason to be cheery. Not now, though. Now, I scowl at the pile as though it's to blame for all of my problems.

Why did I ever agree to this? I'd urged Jay to trust me, but that wasn't fair. I can't do this alone. I'm constantly walking the edge between snapping and being found out – and the punishment for both is the same. A sharp jab in the back of my neck, and a forced 'fresh start'.

"Not bad."

Wirrow. He's standing behind me in the now-empty field, smugness playing on his twisted face. As I turn to face him, I know my expression is grim. He doesn't seem to notice.

"You've been pretty productive since your trip to the city, ain't ya?"

"I suppose so."

I know I shouldn't speak this way. Logic and experience warn me to stay on Wirrow's good side. Though he may not be a high-ranking member of the Guard, he's certainly one with a lot of sway. Thanks to the cruelty in his voice and his vicious reputation, he can practically steamroll anyone who disagrees with him.

But he looks me up and down, regarding me with some modicum of interest.

"You seem unhappy, girlie."

"Of course not, I love it here."

I strain to sound believable, but it doesn't work. I just sound sarcastic.

"Is this still because of your buddy? That bratty little kid?"

Kane. Something clenches in my stomach, but I manage to straighten my body slowly; even though I'd much rather throw myself at the Guard's throat.

"What about him?"

"He attacked me, you know. You were there. Trust me, I take no joy from throwing people into the Mines."

He says it – but just like me, he's a terrible liar. There's a twinkle of pleasure in his eyes right now. He just adores taunting me. It takes all I've got to respond calmly.

"I know."

"You did well not to join in with that behaviour, girlie. I can't say I like you, but you're a hard worker. Noticed that before."

I don't say anything to that; there's nothing to say. He steps forward, and suddenly his hand is on my back. He's so warm I can feel the heat from his fingers through the back of my shirt.

"Um..."

"Take it from me, kid. Keep working. Your attitude's gone downhill lately, and if you step out of line I'll have no choice but to beat you myself. But if you behave..."

His hand sinks a little, grazing the base of my spine. I bite back a yelp.

No. Don't touch me.

But I can't say the words, and he leans in a little closer. His voice is barely more than a whisper.

"Good behaviour gets you rewarded. Remember that."

I can't breathe. My head is filled with the stink of his breath, all booze and gingivitis. My eyes are locked on his, that sharp, vicious gaze burning into mine. I swallow hard, my head swimming.

"I-I'll keep that in mind."

Wirrow departs soon after, tasking me with dragging the carts back to storage. It's going to rain tonight, he says. Can't have the wood getting wet.

As he heads back I shudder all over, as though mimicking a dog might shake some of the grossness off me. We're taught not to touch people, and his hand against my spine definitely felt wrong. Which is strange in itself; he wasn't threatening me. He didn't tell me anything I don't already know. There's no reason why I should feel so shaken.

I dutifully stack the logs into the cart, but by the time I'm done the handles are soaked from the incoming rain. I whip off my hoodie to pat them dry, then toss it over the logs in hopes of keeping them somewhat protected from the rain. It's not much, but maybe it'll help a little.

It's practically night now. I've missed dinner altogether, but I no longer care. If my stomach grumbles, then the sound is well and truly lost in the thunder rumbling overhead. I blink hard a few times, unsure if the flashes are lightning or just my imagination. Could easily be either.

There's mud building up underfoot, turning the dirt tracks into a slalom. I clutch at the cart to hold myself upright, as even my heavy work boots can't gather grip in the mess. I step into a particularly large puddle and promptly sink, slipping knee-deep into the muck. Fantastic.

I remember that this happened before. Not to me, though; some random girl had lost her boot in the mud, and while those around her had found it funny, Kane had hurried over to help. He'd reached shoulder-deep into the mud to recover her boot – and he hadn't even known who she was.

It'd be nice to have him around now. Or Nel. Or someone. Anyone.

But as I look up, casting a glum eye over the horizon, I see nobody. Sure, there are distant lights emitting from the Guard towers, the occasional Hoverbot on the perimeter, and a vague haze left over from the floodlights; but no people.

I heave a long, pained sigh and reach down to pull my leg out.

It takes a while to reach the storage unit, and by the time I'm done the Mill has fallen silent around me. Even the evening chatter of the Guards has died down, the only signs of life being the dull attentions of those on the towers. Even they seem to be dozing, though; as I strain my ears, desperate for a sign that something is happening, nothing reaches me.

Finally. A snippet of privacy. Sure, it's nothing compared to relaxing in Pan's room or sleeping in the grass of the Atrium's garden. There's nothing particularly pleasing about stealing a moment to myself in this way, hunched and gasping in the darkness of the Mill's storage.

I settle onto a pile of boxes and sigh. Everything hurts. It's not so bad when I'm moving around, but as I examine my hands in the dim light, I see scratches and scars that I'm certain weren't there last week. I run a hand through my hair. Despite Pan's best attempts to tame it, the new style makes little difference now. It's a frazzled, chaotic mess. There are even little twigs knotted into it. A glance at my clothes reveal a half-dozen new stains and tears, the kind of which I'd never get away with under Pan's watchful gaze. I know without looking that there's dirt smeared across my cheek.

Suddenly, misery wells in me.

Why am I here? I'd been so sure of myself when I first came back. It had seemed so easy; two, three weeks max. Then I could go home. Instead, I've slipped back into my old life without any trouble. Those two weeks spent with the others simply weren't enough to rewrite eleven years of instinct. My attempts at getting samples have not only failed, but nearly resulted in my capture. More than once I've had to lie to the Guards, acting as though my fellow workers were insane for their allegations. I don't know what else to do.

I think of the others. I promised Jay I'd only be a few weeks – but as I count on my fingers, I grimace. Thirteen weeks. I wonder if he's worried about me yet. I scoff. Who am I kidding? He was worried before I even stepped foot outside the city boundaries. I've been gone too long.

Some tiny, childish voice pipes up inside me. They've forgotten all about you, it says. You didn't come through when they needed you, so why should they wait? You're a forgotten relic to them now.

Over the past weeks, I've grown accustomed to hearing that tiny voice. Though Jay asked me not to forget them, I'm painfully aware that they never promised to remember me. I haven't even kept my promise – though I cling to whatever memories I have, the finer details are starting to slip away. I don't know when the Cull is anymore, if it's already been or if it's still to come. I've already forgotten the particular echo of the Atrium. The colour of Pan's eyes has faded from my mind.

But that doesn't change anything. Because I may not remember the exact shade of green, but I remember that they're pretty and clear and bright. I remember how they filled with tears and happiness and hope and pity. I remember how those eyes gleamed with trust as I'd strapped myself into the cart.

I need to come up with a plan. I can't let them down. They're counting on me.

A gentle breeze brushes through the storage unit, sending chills through me. I whip my hoodie off the cart and wrap it around myself, but the thin cloth does little to comfort me.

My mind swirls with half-formed plans that make little to no sense. I could demand Rian's help. He may have refused before, but maybe I can change his mind. But no. Each time I see him he walks by blindly, treating me like I'm not even there. I suppose he has to. He believes I'm working towards some ultimate plan. I could try to figure out where Nel was sent and go there, too. But nobody's told me despite all the times I've asked, and I've lost track of how many times I've been warned not to mention it. If I push too far, I risk being reported by the more zealous among us.

What else is there? I hit my palm to my head, once, twice, again, like I can knock some sense into myself and finally figure out how to get out of this mess.

I could just give up. I'm alone now, and it's a quiet night. I could slip over the fence and be gone before they notice. It would be easy. But that would mean returning to Thorne with my tail between my legs, and admitting to the others that not only could I not do it, but that they should never have placed their trust in me to begin with.

No. I have to find a way to get those samples. Even if it takes eleven more years. I either return with that data, or I don't return at all.

A sudden flash of pain accompanies the stress as multiple thoughts compound in my head, each one screaming out for my immediate and unyielding attention. I hate this. I hate this place. I hate these people. Jay's face flashes in the darkness, all faith and belief, and my hands curl into fists. I have to at least try, right?

I return to the bunkers under the cover of darkness. Everyone's already asleep. It's so late that even the stragglers who often stay up to talk are motionless in their beds. The room is still and silent, almost unnervingly so. As I pick my way between the bunks, nobody stirs. They're so utterly exhausted that they don't even flinch as I stumble around the room.

It's with some hesitation that I fall back onto my own bunk. I don't want to sleep just yet, but the sun will be rising soon – and without at least a little sleep, tomorrow's work will be infinitely harder. My blanket is damp, and as I lift it to my nose I realise it smells faintly of mould. I guess I haven't been airing it out properly.

I shove the blanket aside and pull my hoodie over myself instead.

I haven't check Jensen's transmitter in a long while. He may have said it would have a six month charge, but I'm frightened of the damage it might receive. Carrying it in my pocket isn't the best of solutions, even if it is the safest place. There's nowhere else I can stash things that the Guards won't quickly uncover.

I delve into the pocket of the hoodie. Nothing. I reach into the other side. Still nothing.

My stomach plummets. Oh no. Did I lose it?

I sit up and search frantically, even daring to rip at the lining of the jacket in hopes the device fell in there. All I find is the hook securely fastened to a seam, and a broken metal loop hanging loosely from it.

For a moment, I can't breathe. How can I have lost it? This is my most precious possession. If it fell out of my pocket, then it could be anywhere. In the bunker, on the dirt tracks. In the knee-deep muddy fields. Panic threatens to overwhelm me.

Wait. I took my jacket off to throw over the logs, didn't I? Perhaps the transmitter is still in the cart, or on the floor of the storage unit. If so, whoever unloads it in the morning is bound to stumble across it.

I'm on my feet in an instant, pulling the jacket on and lowering the hood over my eyes. I can't leave this. If it were anywhere else I might risk it until tomorrow – but it's going to be fairly conspicuous on the dirt floor of the unit, or against the wood of the cart. I can't leave it until morning. I need to go and get it.

I approach the door to the bunker slowly, treading as softly as I can. Creeping in after a long day is one thing, but if anyone happens to roll over just in time to see me slip out, I'm done for. It's one of the more ironclad rules at the Mill. Wandering around outside of hours is strictly forbidden and if they catch me, I'd consider a beating to be getting off lightly. A lengthy stint in the Mines would be a more likely punishment.

Nothing's changed outside. It's still pitch black and absolutely silent, save for the rain overhead – at least at first. A moment later, a strange, high pitched noise rings out from between the bunkers.

I follow the sound and quickly uncover two teens pressed against the side of the closest bunker. They're moving together in a curious manner, their lips locked tightly. In spite of myself, I scowl. Breeders. This must be how they excise their interest in the opposite gender; sneaking out at night for hurried courtship in the shadows.

Still, they don't notice me, so I keep walking. If it comes down to it, I can always use them. Claim I was out here to investigate a strange noise. Whether that would work is highly doubtful, but it's worth keeping in mind.

I reach the storage quickly without seeing anyone else. Heavy rain is still coming down around me, disguising the sound of my footsteps and heavy breathing. Although my leg still feels heavy from the thick coating of mud, I'm suddenly happy for the poor weather.

I push open the door to the storage unit, surprised at its weight. It hadn't felt this heavy when I was pulling it shut just ten minutes ago. As it slides on its guides, something catches, emitting a loud screech. I lower my head and wait for the sound to stop echoing. It's only when I'm sure nobody's around that I step inside.

Just as I thought. I see it. The remote transmitter is on the floor, lying near the wheels of the cart. It stands out like a sore thumb, but that's okay. I found it. I sink to my knees and reach under the cart, stretching out my fingers to scoop it up.

"Girlie."

Wirrow's voice is low and grumbling, not all that threatening, and yet it still sends panic shuddering through me. I jump at the noise and hit my head on the undercarriage of the cart - but there's no time to react to the pain though as I'm dragged out from under it and thrown hard against the wall.

The Guard looms over me. There's a strange look in his eye, like he's just smelled something particularly unpleasant. When he speaks, he sneers.

"I should've known you were up to something. Sneaking back here."

"I-I just wanted to..."

My head's spinning, fear running rampant in my veins. I can't think of any excuse that won't sound totally made up. My hand instinctively tightens around the transmitter. As long as he doesn't see it, I stand a chance of getting out of here relatively unscathed.

"I... thought I'd forgotten to shut the door," I say limply. He chortles.

"Nice try, kid. That explains why you're scraping around on the floor. Are you going to tell me what you were really doing, or should I just assume the worst?"

I swallow hard, my mind racing. There's nothing. No valid reason for me to be here in the early hours of the morning. I think of the two strangers embracing in the darkness, and the excuse I'd come up with when I saw them; but even that won't explain why I'm here now. And with every passing second, Wirrow's face is contorting. He's growing impatient.

"Not gonna confess, huh? Fine then."

In an instant he's grabbed hold of my arm, forcing back my fingers to reveal the transmitter tucked against my palm. His eyes narrow – but luckily, he has no clue what it is.

"What the hell is this? I'm pretty sure none of the Guards gave you this. Or did you steal it?"

"No! I didn't steal it."

"Then why do you have tech like this? Do you know what we do to thieves around here?"

My blood runs cold at that. Yes, I do know what they do to thieves. I've seen it happen. A lifetime in the Mines, plus a thorough beating for good measure. My fingers curl around the transmitter again. I need to call the others. I need help.

Wirrow tries to wrestle it from me, and though I cling on for dear life I can feel his anger building. His free hand sinks to his waist, and the shock baton that's threaded through his belt loop.

I wrench the transmitter from his grip and take off running, barrelling through the door and taking off down the mud track. It's still pitch black outside and the rain is obscuring my vision. The mud makes me slip and I'm not entirely sure whether I'm heading towards the Guard towers or deep into the heart of the Mill – but it doesn't matter. I just need to get somewhere, anywhere, so I can scan my own DNA and call for the others. I just need five seconds of relative peace; after that, I'll deal with whatever happens.

There's no time to rest. Already I can hear Wirrow behind me. He's a half-step out of reach and I imagine he daren't use the baton in this rain – but he's still there, his thundering footsteps making the ground shake underfoot. He shouts something. It's not for my benefit, though, as a split second later something whizzes by. They're firing. The

Guards at the towers have me in their sights as I sprint helplessly toward the fields. Why the fields? I'm not sure. Perhaps there's a slim chance of peace amongst the wheat. Maybe there's an abandoned tool I can snatch up to defend myself.

But even as I run, I know it's pointless. Even if I manage to send the transmission, they're still going to catch me. Pan might be a social genius, but even she won't be able to recover me from the mines. I'm done for.

One of the bullets grazes my side and pain blossoms across my ribs. It's not a direct hit, but the shock is still enough to make me miss a step and fall. I slip in the mud and roll down into the ditch near the dirt track, where I just about manage to prop myself up on my elbows before Wirrow catches up with me.

"Nice try," he sneers, "but it's over, girlie. Shame. You could've been a good one."

He bends down, snatches the transmitter from my hand, and throws it to the ground. For good measure he stamps on it - and with a sickening crack, it shatters. Nothing remains except shards of plastic and metal, indistinguishable from one another. I bite back on the insults that threaten to force their way out. I want to scream at him, hit him, demand he let me go.

But I can't. Because that transmitter was the only way of contacting the others, even in the most basic of ways. Now it's gone, and there's nothing I can do.

More Guards quickly arrive, and as they chain my wrists and feet, I don't bother to fight back. Even if I do, it won't accomplish anything. Even as they talk amongst themselves and decide to throw me into the Mines for the rest of my days, I can't bring myself to react.

It really is over.

CHAPTER TWENTY-FOUR

The Guards don't let me see my last glimpse of daylight. It's still pitch black outside when I'm thrown down the nearest tunnel entrance and the door's slammed shut behind me, immersing me in total and complete blackness. For a moment, panic overwhelms me. I don't know where I am. It's been so long since I've been in the Mines, and they're expanding their reach every day; I could be ten miles or more from the nearest person. Suddenly it hits me just how alone I am, tiny and helpless in the unending maze that surrounds me.

Everything hurts. My head hurts from the underside of the cart. My arm hurts from wrestling Wirrow for the transmitter. Moreso than that, my side hurts. The bullet may not have hit directly, but it's still done some damage. If I were in the city, I'd patch it up and carry on. But suddenly, it's painful. Perhaps because of the barely held-back sobs shuddering through my body. I curl myself into a ball and lock my arms around my knees, drawing them up to my chin like I can hide myself completely. Like if I could just squeeze a little tighter, then maybe I could fall into myself and vanish entirely. How I wish that were true.

How did I let this happen? Back in Thorne, I was in my element. Nothing was bad enough to make me give up. In that mind-set, I'd been so sure I could do this. A few weeks. In and out. But I was wrong.

Two weeks in the city hadn't been enough to rewrite a lifetime of habit. My fear of the Guard is so deeply instilled that I'm still shaking from the confrontation with Wirrow. The memory of his face twisted in anger is enough to send my heart racing. The daily grind is normal to me now. Even the threat of punishment suddenly seems ordinary, even a little mundane. Like I've never known any different. I look around, taking in the darkness around me and feeling like I deserve it for everything I've done.

It won't be long now. Soon enough the Cull will come around, and without the transmitter's data, Jay and the others will be helpless to stop it. They'll try, no doubt; I don't imagine they'd step back and allow it to happen. But because of my failures, it'll happen anyway. Thousands, maybe tens of thousands of kids will be snatched away. They'll have their memories wiped just like mine must have been. They, just like me, will end up as nothing more than blind, unthinking followers. Never asking questions, never wondering what's beyond the chain link fence. The thought makes me angry – but for once, the anger's not directed at the three leaders. Not even at Maynard, though the thought of her smug face makes me furious. The rage is directed at myself, at the fact that even after everything that's happened, I still haven't changed at all.

Faces flash in my head. Pan with her clear, pretty eyes. Jensen, clever and quick. Jay, who looked more and more like a mirror every day I knew him. They really trusted me, didn't they? And I let them down.

Jensen never explained how the transmitter would work if it were broken. Would they receive a message to say it was shattered? What about the battery? How long will they wait for me before they realise that I've failed at my task? I'd begged them not to come after me. I'd assured them that I knew what I was doing. I got over-confident – and now, I can't fix it. Now, there's nothing left but pitch blackness and a sore, aching body.

Something shifts in the shadows. There is something else. A lifetime of being trapped in the Mines. My greatest and until recently, only fear.

It's with grim acceptance that I climb to my feet, ignoring the stabbing pain in my side and the thumping in my skull. If the Guards catch me curled up like this, it won't end well. My legs quiver with the effort it takes to keep standing, but I ignore it. I can hear them now. A half dozen heavy footsteps echo their way through the nearest tunnel, moving slowly closer. Behind them, the sound of clattering chains. They echo the sound of my own. I'm shackled wrist and ankle, forcing me to shuffle along the rough, uneven floor. I won't have much chance to run – and with the entrance locked securely behind me, there's nowhere to go.

Small, handheld lamps light up the cavern around me, revealing a large, round chamber that splits off in several directions. The Guards eye me curiously, perhaps remembering my face from the last time I was here. For a moment they seem to think I've signed up for another stint – but then their eyes sink to the chains on my wrists, and their expressions change. Any trace of familiarity vanishes.

A broad-shouldered female Guard looks me up and down with impunity. Her expression softens a little when she sees that I'm bruised and bloody, but she shakes it off and pushes a pick into my hands. The tool is heavy, much heavier than the axes I'm used to using – but there's something familiar about it, too. I've done this before.

As I'm pushed into the rows of other workers, memories of the time before rush back to me. The unending darkness, barely being able to see ahead of myself. I swing the pick overhead and groan at how the weight rips at my shoulders. Suddenly, I remember the sixth month. Lying sprawled on my campbed, unable to move from the pain in my muscles. Something tells me it won't take six months to get to that point this time round. Back then, the Guards had allowed me some small amount of leeway. Perhaps they'd understood I was a volunteer. Maybe they just didn't care. But that won't happen this time.

I can feel eyes on me. Guards mutter amongst themselves, wondering what I must have done to get thrown down here. Nobody was told that I'd be coming. I suppose I didn't exactly allow them time for warnings.

I steal a glance at the Mill workers to my side. Even in the darkness, I can tell that their faces are thin and drained, their eyes devoid of all life. Many are little more than walking corpses working on autopilot - anything to distract them from twelve hours a day of constant, endless pain. I don't blame them, but that doesn't mean I want to be one of them. I try flashing a smile at the skeletal-looking man beside me. He doesn't even flinch.

Okay. Other workers, not so great in the way of company.

It doesn't even matter that it's the early hours. Down here, it's always dark. The world could be burning over our heads and we'd know nothing about it. They probably work shifts. I try to think back, try to remember if it was shifts the last time. But it was four years ago, and though I try, no clear answer presents itself.

It's several hours later when someone blows a whistle, and a great sigh goes up around me as the others lower their picks. I drop mine unceremoniously to the floor. We've found nothing of value, or at least nothing we can spot in the half-darkness. Realistically, I know that not every clump of dirt will contain something valuable - coal, gems, strange minerals used for science. But finding nothing of any remote interest makes it feel like wasted time.

As we slink deeper into the darkness, I remember that they don't sleep in bunkers. Some do, of course, but for the most part we're here as punishment; and that punishment is never being able to see the light of day again.

I step into a small cavern filled with camp beds – but unlike the ones I'm used to, they're not laid out in perfect rows, allocated and numbered. No, they're crammed into the space, each one taking up only a fraction of the space they really need. Workers slump down onto whatever seems to be nearest. I briefly wonder about food, then push the thought aside. Maybe they let us starve down here. I don't know. I don't really care anymore.

Someone catches my eye. She casts a diminutive figure, just a scrap of a child with wild-looking hair and wide, glaring eyes – but she still waves at a nearby bunk. As I watch, her cracked lips draw back to reveal a half-toothed smile.

She speaks as I sit down.

"Hey. You're a new one, entcha?"

Unbelievably, she has an accent; oddly clipped and lazily-pronounced, with a casual twang I can't place. I can only imagine it's intentional – I've been everywhere around here, and I've never heard anyone quite like her. Still, I'm happy to have someone to speak to, even if she is several years younger than me.

"Yeah. Just got thrown down."

"Betcha not feelin' good, huh? Noticed you limpin' around earlier."

Her eyes sink to my side, to the cut there. Now the light's a little brighter I can see a strong red line against my hip. There's a little blood around it, dried against my skin and matted into my jacket – I tenderly touch the area, then pull my hand back with a hiss.

"Hmm. Got grazed by a bullet."

She seems impressed. For a moment that unnerves me, but then I remember where I am. These people are mostly considered criminals in the eyes of the Guard – these are the people who've snapped in the past and flipped out, who've dared to question things. I feel a small rush of admiration for the kid.

"What's your name?"

"I'm Sara."

"Noah."

"Pleased ta meetcha, Noah," she grins, "Do you need some help getting patched up?"

I consider that. When I think about how much dirt is caked onto my skin and clothes, it's probably a good idea to do something about the cut. The pain's faded a little now, reduced to a dull throb that aches when I move too much.

"Yeah. That sounds good."

I fight to sit still as she wraps a length of unclean bandage around my side. She leans in close and I draw back – Mill workers don't do this. It's embedded in our minds from childhood that touching is bad, that contact is dangerous. But Sara seems blind to my discomfort as she reaches round me. I suppose that, to her, the teachings of the Mill have long since stopped mattering. She strikes me as someone who dances to the beat of her own drum, with little care for the 'proper' way of doing things.

When she's done, I thank her and lean back against the wall. To my surprise, nobody's asleep yet. Despite the exhaustion of the day and the heavy bags under everyone's eyes, everyone's laughing and talking. There's a strange sense of energy in the air. Still, it does little to comfort me. I pull my knees up again, like it'll somehow make me feel better. Perhaps it's the feeling of being smaller that helps.

Sara eyes me curiously, those wild eyes looking me over.

"If you don't mind me sayin', you don't look like the type we normally get down here."

"That's fine," I mutter, "I'm not really the type to fight back."

"You got shot at. Sounds like a fightin' type to me. Wanna tell me about it?"

I watch her for a moment, chewing on my lip. If I still had the remote transmitter, this could be a perfect opportunity. Sara seems like the type who'd be willing to test it out, even just for the hell of it. But now? Nothing good can come from telling her. All it'll do is risk the news reaching the Guards, and I can't take that chance. I may be done for, but for whatever it's worth, I need to protect the others.

I shake my head.

"Not yet. Sorry."

"Nah, I get it. You ain't ready. Wanna hear how I ended up here? Not a dramatic story, but it might be worth it just to get you laughin'."

I watch her for a moment. Sara seems to be different from anyone else I've met, more similar to Pan or Jensen than anyone at the Mill. There's a roughness about her - a readiness, like she's prepared to get her hands dirty at a moment's notice. She seems totally at ease around me, too. I should probably give her a chance. If I'm going to rot here anyway, I may as well try to find some company.

"Sure," I smile, "I'd love to hear your story."

As we nestle into our relative bunks, yanking the blankets as high as we can against the cold air, Sara glances my way.

"Are you sure you wanna hear this now? You seem tired. Don't want you fallin' asleep on me."

"I want to hear it," I say, surprised by my own eagerness, "if you want to tell me, that is."

"Can't say I ever get tired of tellin' this story, if I'm honest. But I love a captive audience, me."

I glance at the darkened cavern around us. In one corner someone's passing out bread - but beyond that, nothing's happening. A distant thud shudders through the ground, causing the gate to rattle and a clump of dirt to fall on my head.

"Well, you won't get any more captive than this."

Sara just smiles.

"Don't you mind the thumpin'. We can't get through rocks without using explosives, but they'll be used deep in the tunnels. Right now we're in the core, so there's no chance of a cave in."

I gulp.

"Do cave ins happen a lot?"

"Not so much, not anymore. See this?"

She flicks at something on her ear; a small, yellow tag with some kind of code etched into the plastic.

"What's that?"

"Trackin' tag. If we get lost in the tunnels, the Guards can find us. If there's a cave in, we know exactly who's been crushed and who's still movin' around on the other side. Not that there's much we can do when that happens – if you're stuck behind the rock, that's curtains."

I nod, hoping she doesn't notice the beads of sweat suddenly breaking out across my forehead. The last time I was here, I was so focussed on the weight of the pick and the pull of the cart on my shoulders that I never even noticed the explosions. The thought makes me physically sick.

Sara seems to find it funny, though.

"Don't worry so much! Explosions are controlled, we aren't stupid. Besides, I'm in your group. I'll make sure nothin' happens to you!"

She seems so confident that for a moment, I forget that I'm the older of the two of us. I do feel a little childish as I rip into my little lump of bread and cower from the shuddering in the walls around me. So I flash a warm smile her way in some small attempt to recover my dignity.

"Tell me this story, then. I'm dying to hear it."

She seems satisfied with that response and leans back, stretching her hands overhead with a sigh.

"First thing you need to know is that I'm a Plant worker. Or was, anyway. I loved it. It was actually kind of fun. The Guards always seemed a little less strict with us. The furnaces are tough, but where I was, it was less physical. More computers than shovels. And man, I love computers."

I open my mouth to tell her about Jensen – but she shoots me a look and I draw it closed again. I probably shouldn't tell her about Thorne. Not until I trust her a bit more.

"That doesn't sound too bad," I eventually say.

"It wasn't. But one day, we had word from up top. City population's boomin', they said. More demand than ever on power. Suddenly we had more coal brought up, more of a push. At one point, the Guards told us to double our output."

She looks me up and down, bemusement in her eyes.

"It's pretty clear to me that you ain't a power plant worker, so I'll just tell you. Doublin' the output is near impossible. So they started pushin' us. Double time. Triple time. You know the drill. Eventually, they were pickin' off the weakest of us and trying to convince them to work even more. Sometimes days at a time. It got to the point where people were droppin' like flies."

My chest tightens and she eyes me curiously, but I motion for her to continue.

"Anyway, I couldn't deal with that. Workin' is one thing, I don't mind doin' my fair share. But I'll be damned if I'm gonna be treated like a second class citizen."

"What did you do?" I ask, already dreading the answer.

"Just set some of the plant equipment off. Put some combustible material in places I shouldn't have. Made sure it wasn't traceable. I blew up one of the big pieces before anyone found out."

I don't mean to, but suddenly I'm laughing. I can't shake the thought of the Guards scratching their heads at the debris, wondering what happened.

"So how did they figure out it was you?"

Suddenly, I really want to know this story's outcome.

"They didn't! I managed to cover my tracks pretty well – but when the Guards were demandin' that someone step forward and confess, I slipped up. Started laughin'. To this day they can't prove it was me who did it, but they threw me down here for insubordination!"

She joins me in laughing now, like her permanent incarceration is just some trivial inconvenience. But it's not, and we both know it; when I think about the damage she caused that day, it's almost physically painful.

Blowing up part of the Plant would mean less power. That in turn probably led to a bigger Cull – anything to pull the population down to a manageable level. She'll never know it, but she played right into the hands of Maynard and the others. Momentarily I consider telling her, but then think better of it. She seems proud of herself; I don't want to ruin that.

But then the laughter dies a little, and I can feel her gaze shifting as she looks me up and down.

"You sure you don't want to talk about it?"

"I'm sure. Try me again tomorrow, though. You never know."

As others settle into sleep around us, I stare up at the rocky, muddy ceiling.

It's not as pretty as the stars, nor as meaningful as the riveted ceiling in Pan's room – but it's what I've got. I suppose I'd better get used to it.

I'm woken after what seems like only an hour or two – and in an instant, someone grabs me by the collar of my jacket. As the Guard tosses me aside, I realise I'm not the only one. They're pacing the room, tearing each person from their bunk and shaking them awake. To my surprise, the workers just compose themselves and carry on like they haven't just been torn from their slumber. It takes a moment to find the strength to move. I feel like I've not slept much at all, and as I reach up to my face, I can feel small creases forming in the purple circles under my eyes.

Sara offers me her hand.

"C'mon. You'd best hurry – sittin' around is just askin' for a beatin'."

I take her hand and she pulls me up. She's deceptively strong in spite of her thin frame and short stature; I make a mental note to remember that.

"What time is it?" I yawn.

"Probably early mornin'. I can never keep track of the time down here."

My stomach grumbles, reminding me that a chunk of bread doesn't really count as a meal. For a moment, I remember Pan's cooking. She might have whined about her lack of talent, but it had been enough to impress me. I'd had a tough time adjusting to the lukewarm sludge when I first returned to the Mill. Still, I get the feeling there'll be no more food incoming for at least a day. There's no point complaining.

As we leave the room, someone presses a rusted pick into my hands. As if on cue my shoulders begin to throb, and I realise I'm once again becoming accustomed to the familiar weight in my arms. Great.

After a few days, it feels like autopilot. Wake up, work, eat, sleep. Maybe slot in an hour or so of conversation, if I can. But for the most part, it's just digging. There's a strange sense of structure that comes along with it - if I hadn't known life outside the Mill, I'd probably feel some small degree of satisfaction. Even now, there's something mildly enjoyable about it, even though at the end of each day I collapse into my bunk and try to ignore the screaming in my muscles.

Talking to Sara helps. How she managed to remain so perky and happy down here, I'll never know. But when I'm aching and sore, she always offers to sit nearby and talk to me, even when I'm not in the mood to talk back.

She really does remind me of Pan, which is strange in itself. How can two people raised so differently have so much in common? But it's there - they share the same endless optimism, the same unyielding patience.

There's something else with Sara, though. While Pan does things because they're the right thing to do, Sara has an undeniable taste for chaos. On my third day in the mines she plants a small amount of explosive down the tunnel from us. When it detonates and sends the Guards running, she takes the chance to lounge against the tunnel wall.

"Why did you do that?" I ask, my voice harder than intended.

"For a five minute break. It's not a big deal – not unless they find out what happened, anyway."

"They're going to know one of us did it. That wasn't a smart move."

She just laughs.

"Oh, please. You think I don't know how to cover my tracks?"

Her lips pull back into a broad smile – but there are already footsteps in the tunnel behind us. The Guards are back already; and though Sara leaps to her feet and tries to look inconspicuous, it's clear they heard what she said.

"That's the one. Hey, you!"

In an instant she's pinned against the rock of the tunnel wall, a shock baton held to her face. For a moment my breath catches in my throat – but there's no shimmer of electricity around the tip of the baton. He hasn't switched it on.

"Did you do this?" he snarls, his face only a few inches from hers. Suddenly, Sara's bravado is gone. She strains against him, pulling back from the baton with wide, terrified eyes.

I can't move. This is just like what happened with Kane – only then, I didn't stop it. I'd been powerless to help. I recall crying on Darus' boat, sobbing in his arms like a toddler with a scraped up knee. I'd felt pathetic; I still do.

The Guard jumps back as I lay my hand on his arm.

"W-what the..."

"It was me," I lie, "I was playing a prank. I'm sorry."

He glares, his gaze flitting from me to Sara and back again.

"B-but she..."

"I helped to cover it up," Sara gasps, "I was scared she'd be punished for it."

His anger seems to dissipate a little at that.

"You stupid brats. You could have blown up the whole tunnel."

"I'm sorry," I say, "I swear – I didn't mean any harm by it."

"That doesn't matter," he snarls, his hand closing around my arm, "I can't let this go unpunished."

Sara and I exchange nervous glances. I half-expect to see anger in her eyes, but to my surprise, there's none. Instead, she shoots me a sheepish smile as we're dragged away.

In the depths of the furthest tunnel, far away from the others, she turns to me.

"Why did you do that? I've been caught before, you know. It's nothin' new for me to get thrown in here for a while."

"I couldn't stand to see you get dragged away," I confess. She seems pleased by that, if nothing else.

"Well, I'm kind of happy you did. Punishment up top is gettin' thrown down here, but if you're already down here, punishment's a week or so of hard labour."

I glance at the tunnel around us. It's tighter and darker than any of the others. The enclosed space makes my heart thump – but it's not so bad. Sure, it's claustrophobic, but there are no Guards this far in. Instead of carving out one of the other caverns, trying to excavate more of the known minerals, we're down here. Creating new tunnels, trying to find some more valuable stuff embedded in the dirt. It's harder work than I'd have thought – normally, every few hours will yield a small lump of something potentially worthwhile, and though it's a pathetic reward for the work, at least it's something. Down here, it's just solid rock and clay-like soil that jars my shoulders and fills the air with a rank scent.

"So it's this for a week?" I ask, half-hoping I heard wrong. She just shrugs.

"It's not so bad. Hard work, but at least there are no Guards. As long as you make a little progress each day, it's fine. We can relax a little."

I can't help but smile at that. I haven't relaxed for a very long time – in fact, the last time I felt calm was that sunny afternoon when I dozed in the long grass of the Atrium. It's a little harder to breathe down here than I would have thought, but if they're giving me even a minute to myself, I'm going to take it.

"I hope your little trick was worth it," I tell her. I suppose I should be feeling some resentment towards her for doing it, but oddly, there's nothing. I don't mind at all.

"It was. It meant everyone could stop, even if it's just for a minute. Plus, it's always funny to see the Guards trippin' over themselves in a panic. I carry out tricks like that every couple of months. It usually makes for a bit of interest."

"You're crazy. Blowing things up just for the hell of it."

"What about you? You confessed to somethin' you didn't even do just to protect little old me!"

"Yeah... don't read too much into that, okay? It won't happen again."

She smirks.

"Oh, it will. You're one of us, Noah. We just do this stuff. Sometimes just for a laugh, but usually because it's right."

My chest aches at that. Thanks to the influence of my friends, I can appreciate Sara's love of chaos – but I don't want to be lumped in with her as a do-gooder. Not when I think about how often I've screwed up. My guilt must show on my face, because she narrows her eyes at me.

"What?"

"Nothing."

"Don't lie to me. I'm not stupid. What's eatin' you? Other than the rats down here, I mean."

I bite back a laugh; it's been a long time since rats have bothered me. But as I meet Sara's eyes, gleaming in the dim light, I feel like I can trust her.

So I tell her. We sit cross-legged in the dirt and I tell her the whole story, from Nel crying in the bunker to Kane being dragged away. I tell her about finding my brother, and raiding Maynard's tower. When I tell her why I came back, her jaw drops.

"No wonder they shot at you. Did they figure out what you were tryin' to do?"

"I don't think so. But they knew it was something bad. It was enough of a reason to punish me."

She shakes her head.

"I can't believe it. You've had really bad luck, haven't you? And all this about a Cull, and about us... the idea that we might all be other people. It's incredible. Almost too incredible."

"I know it seems impossible."

"Oh no, I believe you. It's just a horrible story. You had everythin', and now you're stuck down here with me."

"There are worse places to be stuck, I guess..."

"It sucks. If I'd been up top, you can bet I'd have helped you out. But everyone who would is down here."

"I know. Every so often I think about Kane. I'm sure he would have helped me if I'd asked him... but thanks to me, he wasn't even there. I didn't help him out when I should have, and now he's down..."

I trail off, wondering how I hadn't realised this sooner.

"...here. Kane is down here in the Mines."

"Well, duh. Didn't you figure that out?"

I scratch my head, unnerved by how easily the thought slipped my mind.

"I guess I didn't think about it. But he is down here, right?"

"Of course he is," Sara chortles, "he's one of the carvers in the Northern tunnels. On punishment like we are."

There's a lump in my throat. Is she serious? Kane's alive - and not just alive, but here, in the tunnels?

"That's not far from here. Are you sure it's the same guy? He would have arrived about four months ago. Really tall kid, but skinny. Dark complexion, big hands. Probably only about fourteen."

"Yeah, that's the guy. I make a point to make friends with all the newbies around here. I remember him well."

Suddenly, I'm excited. I might be able to see Kane again. I'm not sure if apologising would help, but it's worth a shot.

"Do you think you could show me where he is?"

"Sure I can. There are some cross-tunnels we can use to get there without being noticed, if you really want to see the guy. I wouldn't recommend it, though."

"Why not?"

She hesitates at that. I lean forward, and when I speak, there's a hint of pleading in my voice.

"What happened?"

"He's okay," she insists, "he's just got a bit of a nasty scar. Not life threatenin' or anythin' – but he did seem really angry about it."

Dread settles in the pit of my stomach.

"A scar? He didn't have a scar when I knew him."

"I figured as much. I helped patch him up on his first night, like I did with you. Not sure quite what the Guards did to the poor kid, but nothin' I said would console him. Never seen someone so angry in all my time here."

I hadn't considered that he might be angry. I figured there'd be some tension left between us, maybe some unanswered questions, but pure rage hadn't been on my list of expectations. I don't blame him; after I turned my back on him, the Guards must have beaten him silly before tossing him down here. For someone like Kane, that wouldn't go down well – and I don't imagine that he'll be happy to see me.

Even so, the desire is still there. I believe Sara when she says she knows him, that he's alive; but I still want to see with my own eyes. I want to speak with him. I want to apologise, for whatever a four-month-late apology in the dirt is worth.

"Show me the way."

It easily takes twenty minutes to reach the Northern tunnels. In that time, Sara explains that Kane is also in the tip of the tunnel – permanently. When I ask what he did to deserve the most severe punishment the Mill can offer save for a total 'fresh start', she just shakes her head sadly.

There's trepidation in my heart as I near the entrance to the tunnel he's working in. He must be half a mile in, but I can hear the sound of metal against rock as he digs. I can tell he's working furiously – perhaps working off the anger.

It's been four months since we last saw each other. In that time, though things have changed a lot for me, they haven't for him. The last time we spoke was on that secluded road right before he kicked off. I'd scolded him for always challenging the Guard. I'd warned him I wouldn't help him if he did something stupid.

Sara bites her lip and looks me up and down, maybe questioning why I would want to venture into the darkness below. I've grown somewhat used to the unusual echo and cramped spaces of the mines, but this particular tunnel seems smaller than the others. I sink to my knees to wriggle through the entrance, nerves building.

I'm scared to know what Kane will do when he sees me. He might yell, or even lash out at me – and though I could overpower him with ease, I have a horrible feeling that I'd let him do it. I can't exactly punish myself, so if he chooses to punish me, I won't fight it.

What do I say? What greeting can I possibly give that will make up for our last encounter? How I stood silently by as he was beaten to the ground by the Guards? Nothing will fix that.

The tunnel opens up into a slightly larger cavern now – much too big for one person to have carved out alone. But there he is, scraping out one of the walls. He's got his back to me, and I'm unnerved by how much wider his shoulders look. I remember him being a scrawny, frail little thing. Now, I couldn't pick him out of a line-up.

For a second, I stand and watch him. As he pushes down the spade he lets out a growl, somewhere between a snarl of discomfort and a sound of fury. I briefly consider backing out of the tunnel and pretending I never came here, but I can't. Call it Pan's influence, but I can't turn away now.

"Kane."

He pauses, reaching up to wipe the sweat from his face.

"I'm working as fast as I can. Tell the Guards to stick it."

His voice is hard, unnerving – I take a pointed step towards him.

"Kane. Look at me."

As he turns, fixing me with a bored gaze, my stomach plummets.

CHAPTER TWENTY-FIVE

Kane's face is nearly unrecognisable. There's a horrific burn covering much of the left side, obliterating any shape in his cheek. His left eye is half-closed, narrower than the other, like it's been sealed halfway shut. He doesn't look like a child anymore; he looks older than me.

Still, it's Kane. There's still ferocity and defiance in his eyes, still that terrible posture. He's still there, behind the mud and scars. He stares for a moment, and then his face creases.

"Noah?"

I swallow hard.

"H-hey."

That's it?! Screams the voice in my head. Four months and one betrayal later, and your big reunion – and you kick it off by saying 'hey'? What's wrong with you?

"I thought I'd find you down here," I add.

He watches for a moment longer, his expression unreadable, and then turns away.

"Didn't expect you to end up here," he says, bitterness in his voice, "did you volunteer again?"

"No. I got caught doing something stupid."

He just snorts. I suppose I should be happy he's talking to me, or at least that he hasn't swung at me yet. I wouldn't blame him. But I can still feel his anger. It's simmering just under the surface, threatening to break out at any moment.

"So why did you come looking for me?" he asks, though his voice makes it clear that he doesn't really care to know the answer.

"I was told you were in these tunnels."

"And who told you that?"

"Sara. Maybe you remember her, she's the one who..."

"I know who Sara is."

His tone implies finality, that he doesn't want to speak to me for a moment longer - and under normal circumstances, I'd happily leave it be. But not now. I imagine Pan and how she would handle this. She'd throw her arms around Kane and pull him close, swearing that she'd never fail him again.

But that's not me. So instead, I wait until he draws the shovel back and grasp it, twisting it from his grip and holding it high overhead.

"What the hell are you doing?" he barks, anger flashing in his eyes, "give that back!"

"Not until you talk to me."

"We're not children, Noah. You can't just take things and expect it to be okay. If you don't give that back right now, I will take it back."

Emotion rises in my chest.

"Then take it back!" I cry, "fight me, or scream at me, or something! I don't care what you want to do to me, just do something! After everything that's happened, please don't treat me like a stranger!"

He just snarls and reaches for the shovel. I twist away from him, dancing just outside his reach.

"Noah, this is ridiculous."

"I don't like it any more than you do! But I came here to speak to you, and that's what I'm going to do. Whether you like it or not."

He opens his mouth to yell back, then stops. He's realised that I'm trying to draw him into a conversation.

"Keep it."

He pushes me aside and walks past, heading down another, darker tunnel. He clearly doesn't want to talk to me – but I pursue him anyway, despite the lump in my throat.

"Just give me a chance to explain!" I wail as we weave deeper and deeper into the labyrinth. I'm not entirely sure where I am or how to get back, so I stay hot on his heels. Kane's trying desperately to get away from me now, nearly running in some places. I try to explain myself as we run, but it just turns into a garbled mess as I duck, dive and crawl after him. More than once I stumble in the darkness, and there's a brief moment of panic as I realise I don't know my way back to safety without Kane's help. If I fall behind, I'll never find my way out.

Finally, though, he comes to a reluctant stop in one of the caverns. Perhaps he's run out of places to go. More likely, he's just realised that he can't outrun me forever. He rounds on me, fury on his face.

"Don't you see I don't want to talk to you? You're so annoying!"

I know. If someone did this to me I'd be furious, too. The feeling of being unable to escape, of not wanting to look someone in the eye after all they've done to you. It'd be like Wirrow chasing me through these tunnels – even if he wanted to apologise, I'd be too angry to listen.

"You don't have to speak to me again," I tell him, "just listen to me this once."

"Why? You're going to tell me that I deserved what I got, right? That my face is like this, that I'm stuck down here because I screwed up. Well, there's no point telling me that. I already know I screwed up – I don't need you to rub it in my face."

He thinks I'm here to taunt him. Was I really so smug before that he'd believe I would do that?

"I didn't come here to rub anything in your face. I want to apologise."

He pauses. That was the last thing he was expecting me to say.

"You want to apologise?"

"Yes. Everything that happened that day, it was a mess. I don't have any excuse for why I didn't help you – or why I didn't step in to calm things down when Wirrow turned on you. I should have done something to help."

He sighs.

"Well thanks for the apology, but you're kind of missing the point, aren't you?"

"I am?"

"I'm not mad because you didn't punch a Guard. I'm mad because you didn't believe me when I said it was important. It was important to me, and you dismissed it."

My chest tightens. Of course. He's not angry that I didn't jump in and save him. He's angry because I didn't trust him when he needed me. The guilt grows.

"You're right. I'm sorry."

"It's a bit late for that, don't you think?"

He points at his face, his lips curling into a sneer.

"See this? After I was dragged down here, they started beating me – I fought back, managed to beat one of the Guards down a hole. He ended up smashing his fucking head open on a rock, and as punishment, they use one of the cattle brands on me. Marked me property of the Mill, forever, right here on my face."

Horror flits through me. I'd assumed the scar was the result of some kind of accident, perhaps a mistimed explosion. I think about the brands we use on the cattle and wince.

"I can't imagine."

"No. You can't. So why don't you just leave me alone?"

What's this? My face is burning again. I slap at my cheeks, trying to stop the tears fighting their way out. I don't want to cry. I've already done my fair share of it.

"If I'd just listened to you, this would never have happened."

"Exactly. Do you understand now? You didn't listen to me. Why should I listen to you now?"

My frustration builds, and suddenly I'm very aware that I'm trapped. That there's nothing around me but tight spaces and pitch darkness, and I'm never getting out. I would do anything to be back in the cool, light Atrium or even the dirty city streets. The comfort of Pan's touch or Jensen's smile, or Jay's reassuring presence - I'd do anything to get that back.

What would they do now? What would Jay do?

Stupid question. Jay would never betray a friend. None of them would. I'm the only one who'd do something so ugly. Even now, Kane isn't yelling for the Guard, trying to get me dragged off. After everything that's happened, he still doesn't want to hurt me.

When I speak again, my voice is low, frightened.

"Do you remember what I said, the day we met?"

He scowls.

"I'm not in the mood to reminisce, Noah."

"I told you not to question things. Remember? I told you to keep your head down and just get on with it."

"What about it?"

I bite my lip.

"Turns out, I was wrong."

His expression briefly changes. Another thing he didn't expect me to say. I can't say I blame him - it's not easy to admit I messed up. It's almost physically painful.

"Wrong about what?"

"You should question things. You should question everything. Never trust blindly. I'm not going to apologise for not fighting with you. Blindly trusting you would have been stupid. But I didn't even try to find out why you wanted to do it. I didn't even ask."

There's conflict on his face now, logic warring with his anger.

"That doesn't change anything."

"After they took you away, they figured I had something to do with it," I push on, "I was sent to Thorne. While I was there, I learned how wrong I was."

He looks away, but there's a twitch in his eyebrow when I mention the city. I keep surprising him.

"I found a group of people hiding there. They're trying to fight their leaders. There's this... thing, every year, they call it the Cull. They take some of the children and execute them – or at least, that's what they say. Nobody ever questions it."

"Not that I'm not loving the story," he snaps, "but I don't care about what happens in the city. Why should I bother?"

"Because it matters. The leader of that group is my brother. Turns out I'm from the city."

He shoots me a disbelieving look, but remains silent.

"I mean it," I add, "I was taken away, brought here. And I don't think I'm a special case. I think it's happened a lot. I was sent back to see if anyone else at the Mill might be like me."

"This is nonsense, Noah. If anyone was from Thorne, they'd remember."

"Do you remember anything from before you left Homestead? Do you remember what your parents looked like, or what it was like growing up with them?"

He pauses.

"No. But that's normal. Nobody remembers."

"Exactly. The Guard have the power to wipe our memories at a moment's notice. Why do you assume they'd never use it?"

"Even if you're right, it doesn't matter. You're stuck down here. I've spent four months hating you; and even if you've had some kind of personal revelation, it doesn't change what you did."

"I know. I just wanted you to know that I'm sorry, and that you were right. We're not supposed to be here. We should fight back. For what it's worth, I wish I'd helped you that day. I wish I could help you now. But I messed up. I got stuck down here and now, it's over. I'm never going back. I'm never seeing my friends or brother again, and I'm never going to be able to show you the truth, either."

Misery grows in my chest, sending a cold chill running through me. I've known since they caught me that I wasn't going home, but I'm just now realising it. The months spent at the Mill have sapped me of my dignity and energy, as well as the finer details of my most precious memories. Already, the image of my mother's face is slipping away.

"This is the end, isn't it?" I choke, "this is forever. We're stuck down here. They can't save Thorne. They can't come for us. Give it a year and it'll be like this never happened. I'm already starting to forget."

Kane watches silently. Any anger in his face has faded to nothing now, replaced by a look of understanding. I can only imagine how much this must hurt him, reminding him of the misery he must have felt when they first dumped him here. I can imagine him now, some tiny, scrawny kid with horrific burns and bruises plastering his body, crying in a dirty heap in the corner. I imagine Sara sitting nearby, much like she did for me, only able to offer a gentle touch and warm words. She tries her best, but there's no way to change what's happened.

"Please," I beg, "I'll do anything to make this right again. Just tell me what it is. I don't care how stupid or dangerous it is, I'll do it. Just tell me what you want."

I know this is stupid. What I did was permanent and I'll probably never be able to make up for it; but I feel the need to try.

"What happened to you?"

Kane's voice is unnervingly soft.

"What happened to you, really? You're nothing like the Noah I remember."

"Did you know that Noah's not even my real name? It's Ada. I'm nineteen - nearly twenty. I'm from the Southern region of the inner city. I had parents, but they're gone. My older brother's James, and he's... well, I don't know. It's been too long."

"Will he be worried?"

"Probably. He didn't want me to come back. He wanted me to stay safe with him and the others. But I insisted I could do this on my own."

Kane sucks on his teeth. He's pacing now, circling me like a shark deciding whether or not to attack a caged diver. Doubt and anger war on his face - he doesn't know what to do.

"Tell me everything," he says finally, "that's what I want you to do. No lies, no tricks. Tell me exactly what happened after they took me away."

So I do. I relay the story to him in excruciating detail, making a point to omit the part where I cried on a boat. Somehow, I feel like that's crossing the line between repentant and pathetic. He just listens in silence, seemingly deep in thought.

When I'm finally done, he nods.

"That's one hell of a story."

"I know. When I told Sara, she could hardly believe it."

"You have to admit, it does sound kind of made up."

I consider that. I can see why he'd say that - it sounds like a ridiculous story one might tell to a frightened bunkmate on a thundery night.

"I don't blame you for not believing me."

"Oh, no. I believe you."

"You do?"

Delight dances in his eyes.

"Lots of ridiculous stuff happens. I've had vague dreams and flashes of weird things - things I couldn't possibly have seen before. Thing I don't even know the names of. Who knows, if your story's true, it could all make sense."

"You remember things?"

"Not exactly. Little flashes here and there. Images, faces. The memories don't link up to anything, but I must know them from somewhere. If you're right, I could be remembering my own family."

The thought fills me with joy and horror. Returning Kane to his family would have been wonderful. I'd have loved to know who he used to be, to watch as he steps right back into his old life like I did with mine.

But then I remember where we are, and my heart sinks. We'll never get to Thorne. I'll never see my family again, and he'll never even know his. There's no point thinking about how great it would be, since it's never going to happen.

"I'm just sorry I couldn't keep hold of that transmitter," I mutter, "we could have scanned you, then called for help. I don't know if they'd be able to do much, but..."

"You mean they'd come to save you?"

"If I called for help, yeah."

"It's been longer than they thought, though. If they could rescue you, don't you think they'd have done it by now?"

"Maybe. It's easier said than done. If I were on the surface, they could help. Hell, if I were up there, I could escape on my own. Find my way back. I could even take you and Sara with me if we were out there. Scan you back in the Atrium. But we're all stuck."

"Have you considered breaking out of the mines?"

"I thought about it. But it's not going to happen. The gates are too heavy to move and they're guarded at all hours. Not to mention it'd be impossible to get to the entrance when we're working so many miles down."

I huff, misery settling in me - but to my surprise, Kane's smiling again.

"What?" I bark, "what's so funny?"

"Not funny, exactly. Just… I've got an idea."

That night, Kane slips in with the rest of our group on the way back. The Guards either don't notice or don't care that he's in the wrong group; it's just that disorganised. Unlike the farms, workers aren't even separated by gender. On the surface that would be cause for alarm. The Guards would snarl at every lingering glance. But here? Nobody even looks up from the ground.

Even in the relative quiet of the bed-filled room, few people talk. They're more hushed than they've been the last few nights. Before, there were at least a few muttered conversations. Nervous whispers in the night. Now? Nothing.

"Everyone's exhausted," Sara tells me, perhaps predicting my next question, "they're upping the demand lately. Apparently there's some kind of event going on in Thorne, so they need optimal power. More coal."

Something squirms in my stomach. I'm willing to bet that this 'event' is the Cull. The extra power's probably for airing videos across the city. Showing people what happens when they dare to question, dare to speak up.

I just hope that Jay and the others can escape for another year.

Kane's expression shifts.

"Are you worried about them?"

For the first time in a while, I look at him. I mean, really look at him. Kane's no longer the lanky brat I met in the field, the one who struggled with swinging an axe for longer than an hour or so. The boy – the man – in front of me is solidly built, with scars forming a macabre patchwork on his face and arms. There are deep creases under his eyes, making him look much older than he actually is. That infuriating naiveté in his eyes has all but vanished.

Suddenly, I feel frightened for him.

"I hadn't seen you in the light."

He rolls his eyes.

"Yeah, I know. I'm told by the Guards that I look like some kind of fucked up zombie. Thanks for the reminder."

"That's not it," I say softly, "you just look... really grown up."

His immediate reaction is to laugh – but then he sees that I'm serious and shakes his head in dismay.

"You're nuts, did you know that?"

"What? It's true. You don't look like a kid anymore."

"That's what this place does to you, though I guess you already knew that."

I respond with a chuckle, then bite back on it.

"Actually, no. When I was down here last, it wasn't this bad."

He raises one eyebrow – or at least, what remains of an eyebrow.

"You volunteered last time, right? Maybe you just didn't realise how bad it was."

"No, really. It was back breaking work, sure, but it wasn't like this. Nobody was shoved down tunnels too small to walk through. Nobody starved. Nobody got their skin burnt off, either. It's a hundred times worse than I remember."

I glance around the room, at the tired, grey faces and limp forms.

"The last time I was here, there was some kind of life to the place. I remember wondering why everyone was so strange. They all acted like there was some big secret – creeping around, whispering. I'd thought they were going mad. But there's none of that now."

Sara sits back against me, her tiny weight pressing against my shoulder.

"Yeah, that would have been before the riot."

"The what?"

"Nobody's born a Mine worker, you know," she mutters, "we're all down here because we've committed transgressions against the Guard. Some of us have blown things up. Others have dared to not work as fast as they're told. There's a lot of anger bubbling just under the surface."

I look back at the pale faces that surround me, doubt building.

"There's no anger here."

"Exactly – not anymore, anyway. See, about two years ago everyone worked together. Tried to bust out. Of course it didn't work. They chained everyone up, and anyone who talked back or even mentioned the attempt had their memories blanked completely. They turned into the zombies you see around you now. Slowly, everyone forgot. Now there's nothing. People just accept that they're stuck here."

Something squirms in my stomach. How did I ever consider breaking out of here, when the focussed force of hundreds of Mine workers couldn't manage it?

"That explains it," I say glumly, "it's just like the leaders and the inner city Guard. They try to scare people out of talking back. When people are afraid, they become that much easier to control."

"They're clever," Sara agrees, "that's why there are so few of us still willing to fight back. And even then, we have to be sneaky. There's no standing up to the Guards now. At least, not directly."

Suddenly, I become aware of someone watching me. Kane rests his chin on his hands, watching with a strange combination of awe and confusion.

"Why are you staring at me?"

"No reason," he says, though the light dancing in his eyes suggests otherwise. I choose not to push the subject, instead fixing him in my gaze.

"So, you followed us in here for a reason, right? What's this brilliant idea of yours?"

As I speak, I try to inject a little of that hardness I used to use with him – the firmness that made him listen to me, even if it was only for a little while. It feels weird, though, and I quickly realise that the last time I used this tone, I was defending what the leaders had done.

Kane's leaning over the edge of the bunk now, trawling his fingertip through the dirt as though it were a pen on paper. It takes a moment for me to realise he's drawing a map.

"The tunnels, right?"

"Yeah. Obviously this is just the lower levels, there are more on top. Real world's 3D, you know?"

"I knew that," I insist, ignoring the flush in my cheeks, "why do you need a map?"

He points towards the centre with a smirk.

"Here's where we are right now. Over here is where I was working earlier and here... I think this is where you said you were allocated?"

Sara grunts her assent and he nods.

"Good. Think we can get over here?"

He moves his hand, pointing to an area somewhere close to where I was thrown in.

"Yeah," I say, "I know how to get there, I think. We can probably find a way through these smaller tunnels, right?"

"That's the plan. Half of it, anyway. The other half is... well, it's Sara."

Sara puffs out her cheeks.

"Somehow, I knew that would be part of it. What do you need?"

"Explosives. As much as you can get your hands on. I can get hold of everything else we'll need."

"Pfft. Easy."

Kane chuckles, and I choose not to ask how he knew she could get explosives. I suppose it's inkeeping with everything she's told me, though it's unlikely they'd just leave stacks of the stuff lying around. Still, she seems confident enough. I'm not about to question her.

"I don't understand," I mutter, "why would we need to blow something up? Is it some kind of distraction?"

"Nope."

"Then what?"

He leans in, but not before checking there's nobody listening in. He has nothing to worry about; everyone's dozing in their bunks, or trying to force chunks of bread down their throats. It's not that they're being polite. Nobody cares what we're talking about.

Still, I scoot forward and listen eagerly as he explains.

"Noah, you know that I came down here out of choice. The day I punched Wirrow, it was with the aim of getting thrown down here."

"I'd figured as much, but..."

"You didn't know why, right? I get it. I probably should have explained. I have a couple of buddies down here. One night, they had to come to the surface and I ran into them. They told me all about the history of the Mines, and that attempt from a few years back."

I stare. I hadn't known he was so social.

"I was sorry to hear about what had happened," he continues, "but I was excited that there were others who didn't want to be here. We got talking and eventually, they told me about the backup plan."

Sara gasps.

"I had no idea there was a backup plan!"

"Well, there is. The Miners were working together on a new access tunnel - right here, on the map. Since the mines are built under a risen piece of land, the idea was they could dig right out of the side of the hill. Outer edge of the Mill, no fence to jump. Easy."

But his face falls, and there's a hint of frustration in his eyes as he pushes on.

"They were only a couple of months away from breaking out. But things took a turn in the summer, and the Guards beat everyone down again. Nobody wanted to risk it anymore."

"You came down here to break out?"

The realisation almost hurts. The day he'd pleaded with me to join him, he was trying to help me. He'd figured the Mines were his best chance to get away, and for some reason he'd trusted me enough to want to save me, too. Even though he knew I'd be resistant.

If I'd helped him that day, we'd be out by now. We wouldn't have reached Thorne and we certainly wouldn't have ever learned the truth - but we'd be free. And Kane wouldn't have that snarling voice or horrific scar.

The guilt swirls in me. Kane doesn't react, but it seems he's trying hard to keep his expression neutral. Perhaps he can see the agony in my eyes.

"That was the plan," he mutters, "but it was too hard to do alone, and frankly I was too angry. I don't even know what I'd have done if I got out."

That doesn't do much to relieve me of my guilt.

"It won't work anyway, right?" I say, "if they were months away, we won't be able to dig that. Maybe eventually, but not before the Cull."

Sara guffaws, then slaps me on the shoulder.

"Come on Noah, I thought you were smart. What do you think the explosives are for?"

"You can't be serious! A detonation that big will summon every Guard in the place! We won't be able to get away."

"There's not much we can do about that, is there? We'll just have to run and hope for the best. You know where we're goin', right? Show us the way."

She winks.

"Team effort, right?"

I glance at each of them in turn, feeling simultaneously sick and empowered.

"This is really the best plan we have?"

"Looks like it," Kane smirks, "unless you'd rather stay here forever?"

I watch him for a moment. Even in the dim light, I can clearly see his scar. I think about the pain it must have caused him, the terror he must have felt. My fault, no matter how I dice it. I can't let him stay here. I can't let my family and friends slip away and become a memory, either. My fingers tighten on the edge of the bunk.

"No. Okay, you're right. Let's do this. Tomorrow."

He just smiles in response.

I don't know how she did it, but she did. As I stand waiting at the entrance to the escape tunnel, Sara jumps into sight with a load of explosives strapped to her back. There's a surprising amount, enough to unnerve me.

"That's going to be one hell of an explosion," I mutter. She drops the pack into the shadows and flips back a lock of hair.

"It needs to be done. These tunnels haven't been worked for years, so the soil's not going to be easy to dig through. There'll probably be a lot of rocks to blast aside, too. Have you sorted it out?"

I nod. I've spent the last few hours hidden away in here, carving large crevices in the walls where we can hide from the blast. It made sense; I haven't been tagged yet, so I can sneak around much longer than the others can without being noticed. I'm plastered in muck and a little breathless from the hard work - but for once, I'm satisfied. There's something pleasant about working hard when it's for something you actually care about.

Sara glances up and down the tunnel; I can see the nerves building in her eyes.

"Where's Kane? We need to get movin'!"

"Nobody's going to notice we're off our post," I assure her, "and even if they do, by the time they figure out where we are, we'll be long gone."

She ignores me.

"He needs to hurry up."

"Hey. What's wrong with you?"

I try to sound nonchalant, but her attitude disturbs me. I may have only known her a few days, but it's not like her to seem so panicked.

She bounces on her heels for a moment, shooting me awkward sideways glances.

"I'm just worried. It's not like Kane to be late. Do you think somethin' happened?"

I move to shake my head, but then stop. I really hope not.

"I'll go check," I say – but as I step into the tunnel, he's there. Kane barrels into me, sending both of us crashing into the dirt.

"Ow! What the hell?"

He doesn't apologise; just grabs my hand to pull me up.

"We need to move now."

"What? Why?"

Suddenly, his face grows dark. There's genuine fear lurking behind those youthful eyes, contorting in his features. It's enough to make my own heart beat faster.

"On the way here, I had to cross one of the bigger caverns," he explains, his voice hard, "they had a bunch of surface Guards down here. I don't know why. But Wirrow was there."

My blood runs cold, and suddenly I share the same fear as him. Neither of us want to encounter that man again – ever, if we can help it.

"Is he close?" I whisper.

"He saw me with the wires. He's not thick; he knows I stole them. He's coming after me."

I open my mouth to object, to tell him he wouldn't chase Kane for no reason, but the words die in my throat. This is the same man whose touch on my back was enough to terrify me. The same man who chased me through the darkness for the hell of it. Would he abandon his post to pursue Kane through the tunnels on a hunch? Absolutely.

I whip around to Sara, who's staring blankly at us.

"We need to move."

"I'll need a few minutes to set up the explosives…"

"No time," Kane barks, "I can hear someone coming. Just blow the lot."

She seems frightened at that – and I can see why. She's never been in this situation before; so close to getting out, so close to getting captured. It's easy to see why she's scared. Still, to her credit, she doesn't let it show. She throws everything into place, quickly determines the weakest part of the wall, and starts linking up wires. I don't have a clue what she's doing and I don't wait around to find out; I'm too busy staring into the depths of the tunnel.

Kane's right. Someone's coming. And though it might just be my own fear speaking, I'm sure I recognise the weight of their footsteps, and the huffiness of their breathing.

"It's him," Kane breathes, and the panic sets in.

If we're caught now, there's no way out. Wirrow won't rest until he's destroyed us. We exchange nervous glances. Before, I hadn't been afraid of the Guard at all. Wirrow had seemed like a slightly harsher-than-average enforcer – but nothing to fear. Now? Knowing how mercilessly he tortured Kane, how easily he beat me down? The last thing I want is to face him again. I'd rather have a fist fight with Maynard at this point.

I close my eyes. Think of a plan, think of a plan. Something, anything.

It's too late. A hand reaches from the shadows and clutches at Kane, pulling him round by his shoulder. He yelps and jumps away, but Wirrow's grip is too strong. In an instant he's pinned him up against the wall, those beady eyes filled with malice.

"I knew you'd be up to something," he snarls, "stealing, this time?"

There's a frightening degree of hatred in his voice as he speaks, tightening his grip on Kane's collar with each word. The younger man's face turns red as the air is squeezed from him.

"Kane!"

My own voice echoes in the darkness – and as Wirrow's head snaps toward me, I realise he hadn't seen me until now. His face contorts with rage at the sight of my face.

"You too, Girlie? What are you planning?"

I gulp, instinctively stepping back. What's wrong with me? Why does this man scare me so much? Knowing what he's done, knowing what he's willing to do... my heart pounds at the thought of the punishment he might inflict on us. And that's before he's even figured out what we're doing. It's taking all I have not to turn and run.

Kane catches my eye – and I see all my own fear reflected back at me.

I can't go.

I take advantage of the momentary distraction and dart to the side. It's not enough to make him release Kane, but Wirrow twists to watch me and his grip loosens a touch. The younger man inhales sharply, drinking in what little air he can as though it were the most precious thing he's known.

Wirrow whips back around to tighten his grip but in a moment I'm on his back, locking my legs around his waist as best I can. He's a damn sight taller than me and just as broad, but he still staggers as I loop my arms around his neck and kick off from the wall.

He releases Kane and the two of us tumble to the ground, rolling into the narrow ditch alongside the pathway. As I shift, though, I feel his weight on me. Knees press into my stomach. Heavy hands dig into my shoulders.

Suddenly, it's hard to breathe.

Wirrow's eyes are fixed on mine, black into blue, anger into fear. His fingertips sink into my shoulders, hard enough to hurt – I strain against him, but I'm pinned.

"Nice try, girlie."

Despite the nickname, there's no familiarity or warmth in his eyes. Unlike that first day with Kane in the fields, there's no hint of pride in his expression. I'm no longer a hard worker, worthy of some small degree of respect. Now, I'm a criminal. A traitor.

But then his eyes roll back in his head – and a moment later, he slumps against me.

"Are you okay?"

Kane is standing over us, rusted shovel in hand. There's a little blood on it – for a brief moment I panic, fearing he's killed Wirrow – but then the Guard groans, and I realise he's not quite out.

"Thanks," I say as I wriggle out from under him, "I was starting to panic."

He shrugs as though it were nothing; but there's a hint of colour in his cheeks, a tell-tale sign of how proud he feels. He's likely wanted to knock Wirrow out ever since that first day, when the older man had threatened him in the field.

I try to smile back, but I'm surprised to find it doesn't work. There have been plenty of times I've thought I might die, and they've all been frightening; but I've never seen bloodlust in someone's eyes before. Not like that, anyway. The look in Wirrow's eyes was different from Maynard's cold, calculated anger, or any of the other Guards and their brutish mannerisms. I suddenly remember what the others told me about the Guard; they're all psychopaths. All insane. At the time I hadn't been sure whether to believe them. Now? I don't doubt it.

Kane pokes his head into the tunnel.

"Sara? You still there?"

"Yeah," comes the breathy reply, "what the hell happened?"

"We sorted it. But we need to hurry, before he comes to."

As I follow them into the tunnel, I'm surprised how quickly she's got everything set up. The explosives are set up in a strange order that doesn't make much sense to me. She seems a little confused; her hair is an unruly mess around her face, and she looks at each of us with concern in her eyes.

"Are you guys okay? You look like hell."

I reach up and gingerly touch my shoulder. There are a multitude of sore spots that I'm sure will form impressive bruises, but it's not too bad. Kane's neck is the same. Wirrow must have put a lot of force behind his attack. He really was trying to kill him.

Another groan emits from the passageway behind us.

"We need to go," I say, "how long?"

"Just a minute longer."

"Hurry."

Sara does as she's told and finishes quickly.

"Timer's set," she mutters, "get into the hides, quick."

We obey immediately, sinking into the ditches I'd carved earlier. They're somewhat tighter than expected – I should have made them larger – but they'll serve a purpose. I squeeze myself in as deep as I can and listen to the hushed, building beeps of the timer. In the crevice next to me, Sara counts under her breath.

"Fifteen, fourteen, thirteen..."

My throat feels tight. Perhaps I'm nervous about the upcoming explosion and the chaos that we'll experience straight after. More likely, it's hope and trepidation and excitement. I can't wait to see the sun again, to step outside and feel some kind of freedom.

Somehow, no matter what it takes, I'll make it back to the others. I might have failed my mission – but I'll go back, and I'll take the others with me. Jensen said he needed five more people. I don't suppose for a second that two will be enough, but it's all I can do.

"Nine, eight, seven..."

Something shifts behind me. Wirrow steps into the end of the tunnel, all teeth and eyes and ferocity. There's blood streaming down his face and mixing in his mouth – he looks like he shouldn't be able to move and yet, there he is. He snarls something that sounds like my name, quickly followed by Kane's. He doesn't see us, but he's looking.

"Five, four, three..."

We duck down as the explosives detonate.

CHAPTER TWENTY-SIX

"Is everyone okay?"

Sara's voice breaks through the silence. There's too much dust and dirt around for me to see her clearly, but she sounds unharmed. Kane responds with a coughing fit.

"Y-yeah. Did it work?"

I don't answer. I'm too busy staring at the bus-sized hole we just blew in the wall. At the sunlight streaming through. At the sight of hills and sky beyond it. Suddenly, I don't care about the mud in my hair or the dust catching in my throat. We did it. We're out.

Kane steps up beside me as the dust clears, planting a hand on my shoulder.

"I can't believe that worked."

Sara just laughs.

"You mean you doubted me?"

"We don't have time to wait around," I tell them, "there's no way the Guards didn't hear that. They'll be here any minute."

They both nod, but still wait for me to head out first. To some degree, I don't blame them; I'd do the same in their position. Still, it's with some trepidation that I step towards the light.

"Girlie."

I whip round, terrified that he's right behind me – but he's not. Wirrow's voice seems disembodied, floating up from somewhere near my feet. It sounds pained, stressed. Like the speaker is barely conscious.

My gaze sinks to the pile of rubble and dirt in front of me – the remnants of what we just blew up. Even in the dim light, I can see something alien within the mess. Something moving. Wirrow's buried in the rubble, encased up to his ribs. His skin is pale and it's clear that he's injured – but he's still straining to reach for something. I follow his gaze to his shock baton. It lies only a few feet from him, an inch too far for him to grab.

I scoop it up, then immediately regret it as his eyes widen with fear.

"Going to kill me, are you?"

My heart is in my throat. I hadn't intended to harm him; but I could. I've done it before, right? I was able to forget that. I could forget this, too. There's no doubt in my mind that he'll come after us. He'll chase us to the ends of the Earth if he has to. Now we've beaten him so thoroughly, his pride is on the line. My fingers tighten around the baton, index coming to rest on the button. It's just like killing a particularly troublesome fox, right?

Memories of that night in Thorne flash in my head. Aiming Pan's gun into the sky, feeling horror in my stomach as the helicopters had plummeted to the ground. At the time, I'd pushed aside how awful it was because if I hadn't done it, we would have been killed.

But now, I don't have to do this.

And I don't want to.

Instead, I toss the device aside. Wirrow stares.

"I'm not going to kill you," I scowl, "I'm not like you."

His mouth twitches, the corners turning upward.

"Big mistake. I'll track you down, you know that."

Kane steps up beside me, a familiar hand resting on my shoulder – assurance, if it were needed, that I'm doing the right thing. I look from one man to the other, then return Wirrow's smile.

"I know you will. And we'll finish this then. But I'm not going to attack while you're helpless. Whatever would my parents say?"

He doesn't answer, but anger flashes in his eyes. There's a slight ringing in my ears, perhaps a remnant of the explosion; Kane's saying something now, addressing Wirrow, but the ringing is loud and I can't quite make out the words. But there's something akin to fear in his eyes, so I'm sure Kane's threatening him. Warning him what will happen if he comes after us. It won't stop him. We both know that. Wirrow's pride won't let him be beaten without recourse. He'll do anything to catch us now. As we gather what few belongings we have and exit the Mines, I feel satisfied with the look of failure in his eyes.

I'm not sure how long we've been running for. I know the general direction of the Dock, and there's the definite scent of sea in the air, but it seems like it's taking much longer than normal to get there.

I glance back; nobody's following us. They haven't been for miles. Upon leaving the Mill we'd heard a few stray gunshots and had taken off running, but either the shots weren't for us, or they'd realised rather quickly that they couldn't keep up.

I stick my nose in the air and inhale deeply. I can still smell the ocean; we're near. The dirt underfoot is mixing into sand, making it a little harder to keep up the pace. I can hear Sara and Kane straining to keep up with me, so I slow down. They've been in the Mines a lot longer than I have. It's been a long time since either of them have had to run flat out like this.

"Okay," I say as we slow to a stop, "I think we're near the Dock."

As if on cue, a ship blares its horn. Sara yelps and ducks behind Kane, much to his amusement.

"W-what the hell is that?"

"Calm down. It's just a boat."

Kane smiles broadly at her naiveté, but his expression betrays him. He's exhausted, too, and doesn't know quite what's going on. It suddenly sets in that out of the three of us, I'm the only one who knows where we're going. The thought is intimidating at best. Sara runs a hand through her coarse hair, tugging at the roots like she could understand what's going on with just enough pain.

"I-I can't believe we did that. We're out."

She turns her eyes to the sky now, inhaling deeply. She's taking in everything around her with cautious optimism, as though frightened it could be snatched away at any moment. It's only in the bright, open space that I realise how tiny she is. Shorter than most, with stick-thin arms; unusual for the Mill. Most of us build muscle through everyday work. But Sara looks more suited to life in Thorne than anywhere else. Her eyes have grown so used to the darkness that now she draws her hair over them to shade them from the blazing sun.

Kane seems less shaken, though knowing him, he's just putting on an act. There's something in the way he's moving, some hesitation behind his bravado, that tells me he's more frightened than he'd like to admit. I guess we've all been conditioned to follow the Guard, whether we like it or not. It's still there, in our heads. The fear of what might happen, and the instinct to obey.

I'm still a little shaken myself. I've fought off Guards before and thought nothing of it, but this was different. This wasn't some random, faceless Guard taken down in a fight. It was Wirrow. A face I've spent years around, a voice I'd recognise anywhere. I don't feel sorry for him. He deserved everything he got – he's just lucky I left him alive. But there's still guilt there. Like I've destroyed something important. But then Kane wraps a slim arm around Sara's shoulders, turning her away. She gasps.

"W-wow."

"What is it?"

I follow their gaze into the distance.

There it is. The ocean, just as gorgeous as last time. It's silver-blue in the growing light of morning, illuminated by just the tiniest hint of gold on the horizon. The sun's coming up. I take another deep breath through my nose, revelling in the salty air and distant sound of waves. I know that Thorne is my home, but the ocean always takes my breath away. It's definitely my favourite place in this whole messed up world – and already, I feel calmer. My breathing slows and all the tension drops from my shoulders as I step up next to Kane and Sara.

"Beautiful, isn't it?"

My voice is soft, unusual for me, but they don't seem to notice. To them, it's a reasonable reaction. Quiet reverence is the only appropriate way to handle this sight. Suddenly, I'm happy we did this. That I'll likely see Wirrow's harrowing expression in my nightmares doesn't matter; as long as I can feel this freedom every day.

After several minutes of staring, Sara rubs at her face.

"Well then, what's the plan?"

She pulls back her lips into a smirk, and I feel somewhat taken aback by her sudden shift in attitude. She's moved past her fear in a matter of minutes, bouncing back much faster than I would have. Or indeed, faster than I did. I choose not to question it.

"Thorne's across the ocean," I say, "so we need a boat."

Kane shoots me a pained look.

"Sure thing, let me just pull out the raft I keep in my back pocket. There aren't any boats, Noah!"

"Oh, really? I hadn't noticed. I figured we'd just float across on a cloud. Of course there aren't any boats! They're not allowed to cross anywhere except between the Docks."

He raises his eyebrow at that, and in his eyes I catch a lingering sense of loathing; but he pushes it aside. For a brief moment I wonder if I should address it. If I should bring his anger out and try to face it somehow. But there's no time for that. Besides, he's willing to put his frustration aside for the sake of our goals. I can't fault him for that.

"We need to head towards the Dock," I explain, "it should be... this way."

I take off in my chosen direction, certain it's correct. The way the beach curves up over there is both familiar and tempting, so I decide to go for it.

"Won't we get caught the second we go in?" Sara asks.

"No. The last time they asked me where I was going, but that was it. The only security we should have to worry about is the outer city limits."

"But," Kane points out helpfully, "won't the Mine Guards have let the Docks know they've got some escapees? There's no way they won't be on lookout."

I pause.

"Okay... good point."

He just stares, as though waiting for me to pull the answer out of thin air. The expectation is unnerving and I fight the desire to remind him of my own inexperience, that I'm playing this by ear just as much as they are. But that won't help anyone.

"As I remember, there were chain-link fences all around the Dock," I mutter, "if we can get there quickly, before it gets too light out, we can vault the fence while they're loading up the boats. The Guards will be too distracted to notice us slip on board."

Sara gives a small nod, clearly satisfied with my answer – but yet again, Kane seems unsure.

"Won't the people manning the boats notice us? If we try to sneak on, we'll get caught."

"It's okay. The Guards don't go on every trip – just the big ones. The cargo transporters and such. We just need a small boat."

"And will there be a small boat?"

I stare out into the ocean, familiar voices and faces flashing in my head.

"I really hope so."

We approach the Dock under a cover of half-darkness. There's a general sense of chaos in the air as we duck around to the side of the gate, staying low in hopes that the Guards won't notice us. For a few moments we stand in the shadows just beyond the chain-link fence, watching the bustle of another normal day.

"They don't seem too agitated," Sara says hopefully, "maybe they don't expect us."

"Not likely," Kane grumbles, "there's no way the Mines wouldn't have told them. Maybe they just don't think we'd be likely to get away."

Sara lets out a small whine of concern, but I ignore them both. I'm watching the movements of shadowed silhouettes, trying to determine which are Mill workers and which are Guards. It's nearly impossible to tell; but then I spy a familiar device hanging from the belt loops of some figures and wince. I hadn't noticed it last time, but Dock Guards have those ridiculous batons, too.

Though I'd insist I was playing lookout if they asked, I do have an ulterior motive for watching so closely. I find myself half-hoping that every strapping young man pacing the sand will have that familiar gait and those long strides. A little part of me wants to see Darus' easy smile and kindly eyes again. I remember coming here the first time, unsure and frightened. He'd been the only person willing to reach out. I'm relying on that kindness to help me again; and though guilt twists in my stomach, serving as a painful reminder of the risks, I'm quietly confident he'll help me. Whether I tell them a half-truth or explain everything has yet to be seen, but I don't imagine he'll turn me away if I ask for help.

There's a distant splash as something – or someone – slips into the ocean, causing a small ruckus. The few Guards still nearby head down to deal with whatever situation is unfolding, and I decide to snatch the opportunity.

"C'mon, this way."

As I clamber up the fence, I realise how misleading my idea was. 'Vaulting a fence' seems to imply some subtlety, some technique. Instead, the chain link rattles and creaks in an effort to hold my weight, and as I throw one leg over the top I wince at the unpleasant sensation of barbed wire against my thigh. Still, as I drop down onto the other side, there's silence. Nobody noticed me. I motion for the others to follow and as soon as they land beside me I take off, delving into the crowd with a renewed sense of purpose.

Just like the last time, I receive one or two curious stares from the workers. I'm reminded of how little I resemble them, how much I stand out. But cowering from their gaze isn't going to help, so I pull back my shoulders and try to seem like I belong. Eventually, the stares seem to lessen.

Sara and Kane exchange nervous glances.

"T-this place is huge."

"Do you know where we're going?"

"Course I do," I growl, but something squirms in my stomach when I speak. I have a theory – if it doesn't work out, I don't have a backup plan – but they don't need to know that. As we walk, I can still feel fear coming off them. I don't blame them, either. I had been just as frightened when I first arrived. At least they have each other.

I step down onto one of the piers, unnerved by the creaking underfoot. At least I don't have a cart with me this time.

"Huh."

Something about this feels familiar. I look wildly from side to side. Why does this particular corner feel so familiar?

Then, I see it; a small boat in the distance. It's rusted half to hell and doesn't look like it should be able to stay afloat, much less travel the whole sea – but I don't care.

Because it's familiar, too. I make a beeline for it, relief filling me. They're here.

Two figures stand nearby, arms crossed as though their work is done and they're just awaiting their orders. As we near, I start to pick out details; broad arms and a rugged face on the older man, and a strange gentleness on the younger's, despite his large shoulders and muscular physique.

Darus.

A wide smile splits my face and I fight to remain calm as I walk towards them. I don't want to make too much of a fuss, don't want to draw any attention; but I'm happy to see them. Not just because they could help us, but because the last time I'd seen them, I'd felt an uncharacteristic sadness at seeing them go.

Darus glances up as we approach, and I spot the slightest glimmer of recognition in his eyes. I wouldn't blame him for not remembering me; I look different from back then, and it was several months ago. If not for everything that's happened, I'd have forgotten them by now, too.

But then his face breaks into a warm smile.

"Noah, you're back."

There's an undeniable hint of warmth in my face as he steps closer, regarding me closely. His dark eyes sweep up and down the lines of my body, drinking in the changes. It must be unnerving to see me like this – I glance down and tug at my shirt, making sure to cover the blood stained bandage still wrapped around me.

"H-hey," I eventually manage.

Behind him, his Dad winks; but it's not a threat like when Wirrow did it, or a joke like Pan's. It's almost a bizarre kind of greeting, an acknowledgement. I don't know how to return such a message, so I just nod.

"I didn't think I'd see you again," Darus says. I stuff my hands into my pockets, doing my utmost to seem casual.

"I didn't think I'd ever have to make this journey a second time. But at least they didn't send me alone this time round. These two are Sara and Kane."

He peers at the others, who've been standing silently behind me as though afraid to speak or even move. If he recognises Kane's name from before, he doesn't show it. Just extends his hand in greeting.

"Hey. Any friends of Noah are friends of mine."

Kane clicks his tongue.

"Sorry, who are you?"

I shoot Kane a glare, preparing to scold him - how dare he jeopardise this for the sake of idle curiosity? But before I can speak, Darus chuckles.

"Ah, she didn't tell you about me? I'm Darus. This is my Dad."

"Pleased to meet you," says Sara, stepping up to grasp his hand. Kane doesn't motion for the same, or even respond to his greeting - but the older man isn't offended by it.

"So what do you think?" I ask, "can you take us across?"

"Sure, we're just about to head out. No cart this time?"

I bite my lip.

"No. We're going for some routine maintenance. Nothing exciting, but you know city types. Can't do anything for themselves."

I try to laugh it off, but the laugh is too mirthless and my smile is too fake - and though Darus steps aside to allow us onto the boat, I can feel his eyes on me.

The man's not stupid. He knows.

CHAPTER TWENTY-SEVEN

As midday hits overhead, I sigh. Since we set off several hours ago, I've been standing at this same spot towards the front of the boat. I've no idea what the others are doing down below, and I've still not busied myself with helping out even though I know I should. But I can't seem to shake this strange feeling, and I can't seem to tear my eyes away from that spot on the horizon that might just be Thorne.

"What are you thinking about?"

I don't need to turn around to know who's asking. Darus watches me with renewed curiosity, and though I wish I could ask him what's so different, I fear drawing attention to it. I want to trust him implicitly, but it's not so simple. All I know for sure is that he's bent the rules once before - that doesn't mean he'd willingly break the law. He's already had one 'fresh start'. It's better for him if he doesn't know.

I'd been excited to find him and tell him everything that's happened. I'd imagined his face as he learned the truth about the world, dreamed about him begging to accompany us the rest of the way. I enjoy his company; he'd be a relaxing presence if nothing else, bringing a sense of serenity to the ghastly affairs of the city.

But as I look at him now, I can't do it. Darus has never fallen victim to the cruelties of the Mill. His life is the ocean and his family and this wonderful sensation that seems to fill the air around us.

So I just smile serenely in response. He doesn't buy it.

"You can't get off that easily. I know you better than that. Remember? People don't stand out here unless they've got something on their mind."

He really does remember me. I try to throw together some nonsense idea in my head. Any excuse will work, anything that sounds halfway plausible. Nothing comes to mind.

"I'm going back. That's what's wrong."

He grimaces.

"Was it that bad?"

"No. Not really. I kind of loved it."

"Then what's the problem?"

I open my mouth to reply, then bite back on the words. I'm just scared I won't be the same when I return. I'm scared I'll be too afraid to fight alongside the others. I'm scared they'll reject me. I'm scared that Kane won't ever forgive me, or that I'll somehow fail and let both him and Sara down.

Even so, I can't wait to return home. I want to bury my face in my warm, familiar pillow and gulp down plentiful servings of Pan's home cooking. I want to build with Nate and see whatever incredible thing Jensen's doing on his computers. I want to wrestle with the others and watch videos with my brother. I glance back, half expecting to see Atlas hovering there, ever present. Nothing.

Suddenly, it dawns on me just how much I miss them.

"I want to go back."

"Then how come you look like you're about to cry?"

"Because..."

I bite my lip.

"...I should never have left in the first place."

There. I said it. The words linger in the air, both prominent and meaningless. Those words are my confession that I was wrong, that this was harder than expected and that I've failed in my mission. But though the words hurt me, Darus' expression doesn't change. When he does speak, his voice is low and gravelly.

"That kid you brought with you, the one with the attitude. Is that the same Kane you told me about last time?"

"Yeah. I'm sorry about him. Things are still kind of tense. We're kind of on an, um, impromptu trip right now."

He smirks.

"I knew you were running away."

I swallow hard. Suddenly, I remember how it felt to sob like a child in the arms of a perfect stranger. I'd figured we'd never meet again. But there he is, watching me with kindly eyes. I don't want to tell him everything. He's the only Millchild I've ever met who's been happy. But those clear eyes demand the truth. He's never lied to me before. Perhaps I should return the favour.

"How did you figure it out?"

"Easy enough," he says, "yesterday, we were told to look out for three escaped Mine workers. Nondescript. The Guards didn't seem to know their names and it was pretty clear nobody took the risk seriously. Then the next thing I know, you're asking for a ride."

"So they did warn everyone."

"Yeah, but nobody cared. If they did, you'd have been ratted out straight away. If anything, people were impressed someone could escape the Mines."

That explains the uncomfortable stares at the Dock, as well as the eventual silence that emerged. The other workers knew exactly who we were; but they were on our side. Something about that makes me smile.

"So why are you running away?"

His voice is soft now. It's not a demand, but a request. I can't refuse him.

"I'm going back to Thorne so I can help overthrow the leaders there," I say bluntly, "but I needed some Mill worker DNA to do it, so I had to go back. But I messed up, got caught and thrown into the Mines. I found Kane down there and he doesn't hate me quite as much anymore, so we blew up a Guard and came here."

Darus' mouth hangs open, and I can't help but laugh.

"Sorry, I guess that was a lot of information, huh?"

"N-no, it's fine. Why... why do you want to overthrow their leaders?"

My hands tighten against the railing.

"They've done some pretty awful things to innocent people, including me."

"So you're out for revenge?"

I hadn't considered that before. I search my feelings, ask myself whether I want to see the leaders hurt or executed for all they've done. But I'm disgusted by the hypocrisy of it.

"No. I don't want revenge. I just want them to stop."

"You really don't want to tell me, do you?"

I laugh.

"You're better off not knowing. It'd ruin everything for you."

"If it's going to affect me, don't I have the right to know?"

Damn. Good point. I shoot him an irate look, but his eyes just sparkle in response. He knows he's got me.

"So that's what happened."

Darus is staring at his hand now, slowly clenching and unclenching his fist. Perhaps it's the sheer volume of information I just unloaded onto him, or maybe it's the exhaustion of a long day. Most likely, I've just made him realise how little he understands – and consider who he might be.

"I'm so sorry," I beg, "I never wanted to hurt you."

He looks my way and for the merest ghost of a moment, I could swear I can see anger in his eyes. I wouldn't blame him. But then he draws his lips back into a small smile, and whatever frustration still lingering in his gaze dissipates.

"Can I come?"

"What?"

He turns to face me, a wild look in his eyes.

"Let me come with you to the city."

"Are you crazy? Why would you want to make that trip? It nearly killed me the first time round. Not to mention the chaos we'll be starting back in Thorne. Besides..."

I wave at the boat around us, at the golden waves below.

"Why would you ever want to leave? You have the boat. This amazing sight. Your Dad."

"But he's not be my Dad."

"He is. You said it yourself, remember? When you had your mind blanked, he was the only one who looked out for you. Wouldn't he be heartbroken if you left? Wouldn't you miss him?"

He hesitates at that, conflict warring on his face.

"O-of course I would. Maybe you're right. This is my home, I can't just take off on some ridiculous adventure."

His shoulders slump. I hadn't thought he'd be so eager to help us, let alone join us. But despite his broad build and endless bravery, he's not cut out for the city. It sounds strange, but tearing him away from this haven and taking him to the chaos of Thorne would be nothing short of cruelty.

"I'm sorry. I really am. It's not that I don't want you there – I do! But this place is amazing and you're happy here, and I can't take you knowing how much it would hurt you both. I finally understand how important family is, and you can't abandon yours."

"I know. It would destroy my Dad."

Something shifts behind us. The older man is standing by, just beyond our last line of sight. A set of wizened grey eyes are fixed on Darus' strong form. The younger man flushes red.

"Dad. How much did you hear?"

"Enough," comes the muttered reply, "and I think you should do it."

"Huh?"

"Go. Find out the truth. If that's what will make you happy, do it."

Darus stares, hurt flashing in his eyes.

"B-but, what about you?"

"Easy. Oh dear, my son fell into the ocean. No point searching, we're just workers, right? I can cover for as long as you need. And if you ever choose to return, I'll cover for you then, too."

"But I can't leave you alone!" Darus cries, "don't you want me around?"

"Course I do. But I heard what that girl said just as clearly as you did. I believe her. Do you really think you'll be able to forget about her stories if you stay behind, or will it drive you mad knowing you didn't snatch the opportunity while you could?"

Darus falters at that, his expression dropping. I feel awful as I look between them, knowing the part I play in tearing this unit apart. But there's no hurt in his Father's eyes, no anger; just understanding. He's more than willing to let the boy he raised leave, just as long as he's happy. Suddenly, I understand what it is to have a parent. His Dad glances my way, a sudden hardness in his eyes.

"Will you take care of my boy? Make sure he doesn't get hurt?"

"Absolutely."

"Then Darus, what are you going to do?"

He looks between the two of us for a moment, perhaps waiting for a flash of anger or the merest hint of a demand; but he receives nothing. We won't force him. Finally, he heaves a sigh.

"Dad, I'm sorry. I'm happy here, I really am. But you know I've always wondered if there's something else. Things have never added up. I need to find out why."

His father nods.

"Then, you have to get ready."

"Huh?"

"The walk into the city is ridiculous. You kids won't last long without supplies. The cargo hold is packed to the brim with stuff inbound for Thorne. Take what you need, and we'll write some off as having being destroyed in a small fire."

He winks at me, and I find myself wondering if he intends to set a small fire aboard his own ship to serve as cover for his son's escape. Man, what a parent. Mom and Dad's faces flash in my head, and I wonder if they'd do the same for me. But I stop. Of course they would. They died for me and Jay. What more could anyone do for their kids?

I step a little closer and grasp his Dad's hand tightly.

"Thank you for everything, sir."

It's getting dark by the time we reach the docks. Darus doesn't move to share farewells with his Dad – I can only assume they've already said whatever needs to be said. As he passes me a pack and instructs me to put it on, I notice his eyes are red. Has he been crying?

"Are you sure you want to come?"

"Yeah. I'm sure. It's just, uh, harder than I expected to leave home. I do want to come back again, eventually."

I nod. That's one feeling I can certainly understand.

"For the record," I smile, "you're really brave for doing this. Not many would – that's why we're a band of just four."

"Making history, right?"

"Exactly."

We vault the fence as night begins to fall over the Dock, and quickly find ourselves on the endless stretch of highway that leads to Thorne. I'm surprised at how quickly we traverse its length – alone this had been days of walking, but without the weight of the cart straining at my shoulders and the impending sense of isolation, everything moves much quicker.

Having food and water helps, too. I'd been frightened of tackling the journey without supplies, but Darus has brought plenty from the boat. They're little more than bottles of water and a few packs of hard biscuits, but for where we are and what we need, it's plenty. As I bite into yet another semi-solid lump of food, I catch myself drooling. They taste like nothing, but what I would have given to have these during my first journey! Still, it's a long way. I feel my limbs growing heavier with every few miles we walk, and each time a truck passes by, we're forced to jump aside and lower our heads to our chests in hopes they don't notice us. They never do; just like before, nobody cares. We're of no consequence to them. But I still catch myself tugging the filthy rim of my hood over my eyes. I can't risk being recognised. After all, Maynard did air footage of the whole helicopter debacle.

After several hours, Sara groans. It's the first sound any of us have made since leaving the Dock, aside from heavy breaths and the occasional muttered curse word.

"You okay?" I shout. She's only a few steps behind me, ambling along as best she can, so I don't really know why I'm yelling – but she just whines in response.

"I'm tired…"

"Newsflash," Kane snaps, "of course you're tired. We're all tired."

"It's okay," I say, trying to inject some sense of reassurance into my voice, "I think we're about a quarter of the way there. We're making this journey much faster than I'd have thought."

At that, they stop. I can feel three pairs of eyes shooting daggers at my back. I turn to face them, but I feel sheepish as I do so.

"What?"

"We're not even close?" Sara wails.

"This is ridiculous," says Darus, "we can't make this journey - even with food and water, we'll drop dead from heat exhaustion before we even reach halfway!"

"It's okay," I urge them, "it's not that far, I swear..."

"You got driven most of the way! You have no idea, do you? This is impossible!"

Sara falls to the ground now, and all the resistance in her seems to break; she pulls her knees up to her chin and buries her face in them. After a few moments, her body shakes and I wonder if she might be crying.

"I should never have left," Darus is saying, scraping a hand through what little hair he has, "this was stupid. I abandoned my Dad, and for what?"

"It'll be worth it," I say, "It's amazing, trust me. You won't regret it."

"Too late for that," Kane mutters. He's no longer smiling, no longer putting up that thin veil to hide the hatred in his eyes. My stomach twists.

"But..."

"Just let it go, Noah. This journey is impossible, and we're not going any further."

"There's nowhere else to go," I retort, though I know I'm clutching at straws.

"That doesn't matter. You've failed, Noah. Just accept that."

There's a very pregnant pause as we stare at one another, each side facing down the other in a battle of will. But try as I might, I can't win; I'm just one person. My mind is suddenly filled with images of turning and leaving them here - I'll make this journey alone if I have to. I even shift my weight back, ready to run ahead before they can stop me.

But I can't. As much as I wish I could throw out a mirthless laugh and take off running, I won't. It wouldn't be fair to these friends of mine, and I don't even want to imagine the disappointment on Jay's face if I told him I'd left people behind. He'd never do that.

"No."

I drive my booted foot down into the dirt, sending up a cloud of dust.

"I'm not... I'm not going to accept that. If I accept that, then they win."

"Noah..."

"No! Listen, I know you're tired. I know it's hard, and believe me I know how scared you are. But if we let them win, then this keeps happening. They'll keep taking people, and taking everything away..."

Heat builds in my face, grief and anger compounding with the fear in my veins.

"I hate that damn Mill. Knowing what happened, why we were there – everything I lost out on. Things should have been different. They could still be different."

Their anger seems to fade as I stamp my foot again, this time choking on the dust cloud that rises.

"But nothing is ever going to change if we don't do this!"

"I know what you're saying," says Sara, "but there's no way we can complete this journey. You know that as well as I do."

Sorrow builds in my chest, and I fight the desire to spit. I'm sick of the taste of failure. I glance at the road ahead – the city's not even in view yet, and it won't be for many more miles.

But then something glimmers in the corner of my eye. A truck. Instinct compels me to cover my eyes, but this time, I don't. Because the truck is slowing down, red lights flashing to indicate where it's stopping, right next to us.

"Oh, no."

I step in front of the others as the truck door flies open. The vehicle's the same long, sleek metallic type as the others. Nothing spectacular. As something shifts within the cab, my mind races. This thing could be filled to the brim with Guards. They might have recognised me. They might be out to catch me, to take me into Thorne and proudly hand me over to Maynard. I swallow hard, fearing what they might do to us.

So when I spot a man with grey hair and whiskers, the relief is so strong I nearly fall over.

"Eagen?"

He smiles.

"Hey, Kiddo," he grumbles, "I finally found you."

My stomach plummets and I step pointedly away, spreading my arms over the others. Making it clear that I won't let him touch them.

"You were looking for us?"

"I was looking for you," he corrects me, "I heard you decided to run off."

"That's not..."

"It's alright. I'm not going to drag you back to the Mill. But someone mentioned they'd noticed a blonde girl on these roads, and I figured it might be you. So I thought I'd keep an eye out on my way up this road. I hoped I would run into you."

My stomach clenches; behind me, Kane sighs.

"Great. They know we crossed the sea. They'll catch us any second."

"None of the others did," I point out, "so maybe not everyone knows yet. If we hurry..."

"You kids had better get off the road," says Eagen, "or you'll get found sooner or later. Hop in, I'll smuggle you into Thorne."

"But what would they do to you if they found out?"

He just shrugs.

"There's nothing they can do to me that I can't take," he answers simply.

For a moment, I hesitate. I don't know for certain that I can trust Eagen - it all seems a little convenient to me - but do we really have a choice? I glance back at the others, at the sweat dripping from their chins and their paling faces. I don't have it in me to compel them much further than this. And if they're not on board with it, I don't stand much chance of dragging them the full way.

"Are you sure about this?"

My voice is hesitant, fear showing through – but he seems nonplussed as he steps aside, waving us into the cab.

Rain begins to pour about an hour into our journey, and I'm relieved when it finally starts to batter at the windscreen of the truck. Its pounding seems to break the awkward silence that's fallen over us as we sit cramped in Eagen's cab. I'm pressed between him and Kane, and it's strange to feel both Eagen's coolness and Kane's simmering rage beside me. At least the greying sky and the water streaming down the windows serve as a momentary distraction.

I shoot the older man a curious look. I'm not sure why he'd risk everything to help us. Unlike Darus, he didn't have a rebellious fibre in his body, as far as I could tell anyway. Maybe I was wrong. Finally, he breaks the silence.

"Bet you're wondering why I kept an eye out for you, huh?"

"Yes," I confess, "I hadn't expected it."

"Don't worry about it, Kiddo. I helped you out the last time. I'll do the same now."

I open my mouth to ask the question, but nothing comes. I don't want to know why – and maybe it's better if I don't ask.

"What's the plan once we get there?" asks Sara. She's calmer now, her face pressed against the cold glass of the window pane.

"You kids will come in with me," smiles Eagen, "past the gate. I'll get out to sign the papers, tell them you're with me. Then I'll let you off a little further in."

"Are you sure about this?"

"For the last time, yes. You kids just rest up. It's a long way to go."

After what seems like hours in the driving rain, we reach the city. I glance at the others, expecting to see trepidation in their eyes, or the same sense of deep-seated fear I'd felt when I first arrived here. But instead, there's just excitement. I catch myself smiling. I don't know why, but I had somehow expected Thorne to look different. But no. It's still tall glass buildings that form spires and seem to soar up into the clouds. It's still breathtakingly huge and, even after all that's happened, still beautiful.

Eagen nudges the brakes as we approach the gate, shooting us a warning look.

"You kids just sit here quietly while I talk to the Guards."

He leans out of the window as we pull up, tells them he's got a delivery. They wave him through the first gate, exposing Thorne to us - but there are Guards here too, and despite the beauty of the inner city, we're too nervous to speak. I tug my hood over my eyes and motion for the others to do the same. It doesn't hurt to be safe.

The truck stops again just inside the gate, and Eagen slips from his seat. He glances back as he goes, familiar eyes lingering on mine, and my stomach churns. Why do I feel so uneasy?

I don't understand this feeling of concern filling my chest. I have no reason to distrust Eagen, but as we sit holding our collective breath, trying not to inhale the scent of the musty cab, there's real fear in my throat. I know where we are now. The closest entrance to the Atrium is only a few streets away. We're almost there - I can feel the pull of it, like a magnet. We could just go, right now. Slip out of the passenger side and take off running.

"What's wrong?"

Kane's staring at me. I shuffle in my seat.

"I'm not sure about this."

"Me neither," he mutters, "is this guy for real?"

I bite my lip, then scoot across into the driver's seat. From here I can see Eagen talking to the Guard - but there are no papers in his hand. He talks in an exaggerated manner, waving his hands as though he's telling a story, rather than just relaying his orders. As I watch, he points back at the cab, then punches one hand into his other. A clear threat.

My blood runs cold.

"Open the door," I hiss. Sara flinches.

"B-but he said..."

"I don't care what he said. Open it."

She does as she's told and I glance back at Eagen – he's noticed. The click of the door echoes across the entrance to the city and in an instant, there are Guards moving towards us. Something glimmers in their hands. Panic flits through me. These are city limit Guards – they have guns.

"Run. Get out!"

I push the other three out of the vehicle, and though we land in a chaotic mess on the floor, we recover in time to see several Guards moving our way. Eagen steps around the vehicle, conflict in his eyes. For a split second, I meet his gaze – and I see reflected back at me everything I used to be. All the blindness and ignorance, all the unthinking loyalty.

He sold us out.

"Run!"

I bellow the words, and it's enough to set the others into motion. They jump to their feet and step in line behind me as I push through the line of Guards. To my surprise, they don't try to grab us as we race by. Perhaps they're thrown off by our uncharacteristic behaviour. They probably haven't seen Mill workers fight back before.

But as we race down the main street, I can hear them behind us. The Guards, while clueless, aren't stupid; they know they'll never find us if we manage to slip into the labyrinth of the city. I'm surprised I don't hear bullets whizzing past us, but then I look around and understand.

Citizens line the road, watching with dropped jaws as some unknown chaos unravels before them. Like before, they're frightened by the appearance of strangers in their domain, but then they spot the Guards chasing and their fear builds. One woman clutches a small child closer to her leg, all but clutching at her pearls as we run by. No wonder they can't shoot. They can't risk hitting someone else.

I can feel the others panicking behind me. They're following blindly, suddenly lost somewhere that's scary and unfamiliar. For a moment that frightens me, but I push the feeling aside. I know what I'm doing. As we run, building space between us, I try to map out Thorne in my head. Suddenly, I wish I'd spent more time poring over the maps in Jay's office. I know the main streets, and several of the Atrium entrances. But while they're so close behind, there's no way we can head there. We can't risk them finding the others.

"This way!"

We turn sharply and race down an alleyway, hoping we might lose them somehow – but as we emerge on the other side, we hit a wall of people.

"W-what the..."

CHAPTER TWENTY-EIGHT

We're near one of the leader's buildings - so close that it seems to loom overhead. I'm not certain which building it is - it's not Maynard's - but it doesn't matter. Hundreds, if not thousands of people are packed into the tiny space, forming a mass of writhing bodies. Many jump and cheer.

Others slink awkwardly through the masses, guilt playing on their faces. None of them look this way; their attention is fixed on something at the front of the building.

This is our chance. I reach back for the others.

"Everyone grab hold of each other," I say firmly, "we're going in."

For a split second they seem alarmed; but then Darus steps forward and clutches my wrist. The others follow suit and I pull them forward, delving deep into the terrible crush of strangers. It's worse than I'd imagined. City folk don't smell even half as bad as Mill workers, but there's still something unpleasant about being smothered by the body odour of so many people. One woman screams in my ear - I don't know why - and it sends a wave of pain through my skull.

But it's working. Already we're lost within the masses, and I can no longer hear anyone coming after us. We're hurrying through the crowd faster than they could with their bulky armour or intimidating frames, and they inevitably fall behind.

We stop once we're close to the front of the crowd, taking a second to catch our breath.

"W-what the hell was that?" Kane gasps. He's breathless from the run and seems deeply unsettled - his eyes flit around as he tries to take it all in, trying to piece together what just happened.

"Eagen sold us out," I explain, "he wanted to be the one to hand us in."

"Why would he do that? I thought you guys were friends."

I look away.

"So did I. I think there's an entrance to the Atrium nearby. Keep your hoods up for now. We'll go as soon as this crowd dies down."

"What's this crowd even for?"

I shrug. I don't know. But I'm curious, too - those around us seem to be torn between celebration, indifference and dismay. Whatever's going on under the mumble of the crowd, it's big. I push a little further towards the front, my head low, eager to see what's going on.

To my surprise, it's not the leaders. Instead there are a number of trucks parked up outside the building. Long, black, sleek things like those that drive up and down the highway, except these ones are open along the side, revealing row upon row of benches locked into the metal wall - and a number of tiny shackles, too small for an adult.

I don't need to ask what they're for. The Cull is closer than I thought. They're preparing to round people up, to drag them away in those things. Suddenly, it makes sense that there were so many trucks heading this way.

They're prison vehicles, intended to drive the stolen children back to Homestead to be raised there. It dawns on me that, most likely, that's what Eagen was going to be doing. Whether he realised it or not.

For a moment I feel sick at the thought – but then my attention is drawn to the figures standing atop the trucks. They're swathed in black, standing motionless as their leader speaks. From this distance I strain to pick up on any of the finer details, faces or words, so I sneak forward a little more. I know this is reckless, that I may lose sight of the others or stumble into something I can't escape. But I need to know.

When I finally slip into the front row of the crowd, the leader's voice finally comes clear. When I hear it, it's all I can do not to run forward and call out.

"These are what they'll use!" Jay cries, "to steal them away. One week from now, they'll do it. They're going to take them, and nobody is safe. You can't reason with the Guard, don't fool yourselves that you'll be the exception!"

Jay's standing to the front of the group, and suddenly I can see all the detail in his face. There's something there that I've seen before – a ferocity, a sense of fury. I'm reminded of after the crash, when he plunged a bullet into a Guard's shoulder to defend me. At the time I'd been frightened by the barely-concealed rage in his eyes, but now it comforts me.

They're fighting for their cause.

"This doesn't have to happen! Trust in us, and we can stop it. Come find us, you'll know where! We can stop this together."

Despite the anger in his face, his voice is a little pleading. It's unusual for him; has something happened since I've been gone?

Something shifts nearby. A small collection of Guards filter through the crowd, pulling towards the others. It's not enough to pose a threat to them, but it confirms my fears. They've raised the alarm, and if we don't move quickly, we'll get caught up in the upcoming chaos.

I race to the others, who are still standing frozen in the midst of the crowd. As I near, they seem perplexed by my expression.

"What happened?"

"Things are getting hairy," I shout over the crowd, "we need to get out of here. Follow me."

Catching just a momentary glimpse of Jay and the others is all I need. It would be stupid to try and approach them now – and with Guards on their way, I can't distract them. I consider staying to try and help, but think better of it. They've been in tougher scrapes before. They know how to get out.

Besides, as we slip from the writhing masses, the half-formed map in my head suddenly makes sense. There's an entrance about two miles from here, hidden behind a dumpster in the side of an abandoned bank. While the Guards are distracted, we can reach it. The thought of returning to the Atrium before the others, to be sitting waiting for them when they arrive, is almost humorous; but there's no time to stop and plan. We need to keep moving.

We slip down an alleyway behind the protest. I can hear building shouts of shock and anger as the Guards try desperately to reach the others – but I'm momentarily distracted. A little further down the alley, tucked into the half-shadow, are the bikes.

"What are those?" Darus asks. I open my mouth to laugh, to ask him if he's never seen an ATV before – but dimly realise he probably hasn't.

"These are their bikes. This must be where they're hiding them. They'll be coming this way."

We should probably move. The chaos in the square is building now, Jay's tone more ferocious than ever. I reach out and glide a hand softly across the handlebars of the nearest bike, memories coursing through me. In the months I've been gone, they've rebuilt them; some minor damage still remains but for the most part, they're shiny and new. I try not to think about the last time I was on one of these, how I'd taken hesitant aim at the helicopters. I shake the thought from my head.

The others stand impatiently behind me. I get it. They're terrified, and want to reach the haven I told them about before something else happens. I can already feel a hint of resentment in the air between us – something I choose to ignore. They'll forgive me later.

"Who the hell are you?"

Jay's voice is firm and steady as he steps up behind me. The distant sound of chaos has faded now, something I'd been too distracted to notice. The others are behind me, too, and clearly don't recognise me in my near-black, filthy clothes.

My heart hurts. After missing him for so long, he's so close I can hear his breath in my ear. I reach up, pulling my hood down and shaking my hair free.

His eyes widen; clearly, I was the last thing he expected to see. I don't blame him. I think I'd feel the same. I open my mouth to say something, anything. Comforting, funny, stupid. It doesn't matter, I tell myself. Just say something. Nothing comes – as usual.

Jay lets out a sound akin to a hiccup, and suddenly he's pulled me close. His grip is tight but mine is tighter as I return the embrace, burying my filthy face in the cloth of his collar. If I'm getting dirt on him, he doesn't seem to care. He's warm and familiar and safe.

A moment later he loosens his grip just enough to meet my eyes – I can see my very own shade of grey-blue reflected back at me, a family resemblance so strong I can't believe I ever questioned it.

"Where have you been?"

It takes all the strength I have to respond.

"I... got lost for a little while. But I'm home, now."

His smile broadens, but then he spots the others and his eyes narrow.

"Who are they?"

"They're my friends. From the Mill."

His lips part, perhaps to scold me, perhaps to congratulate me. But then something bangs in the main street behind us, and alarm flits through the group.

"You can tell me everything when we're safe," he splutters, "you guys hop on."

Pan's sitting on her bike already, a broad smile dominating her tiny face. She waves for me to get on the back - I do so immediately, instructing the others to do the same. As hesitant as they seem, my sudden mood shift seems to reassure them that there's no immediate danger, and they soon follow suit.

I'm surprised that Pan hasn't said anything yet. The others behind them seem to vaguely recognise me, but seem to realise they shouldn't get involved. But as we take off speeding down the road, I can feel Pan smiling. She speeds up a little and we jolt; my hands instinctively lock around her waist and she laughs.

"I thought you were too prudish for that."

"So you are going to speak to me."

"I figured you two needed your moment. But I really am happy to see you. I'm happy you came back."

"What do you mean?"

He expression falters momentarily, but that split second seems to compound all my most deep-seated fears.

"What is it?" I demand.

"Nothing, really. It's just... it's been a while. We were scared that something had happened to you."

Her voice sounds strained when she says that, she's frightened to say it, and I can see why. I've been gone so long without a signal from the transmitter that they must have thought something horrible had happened. I look towards the front of the group. Jay leads as he always does, his shoulders back proudly, his head lowered into the wind. For the last few months, did he assume I wasn't coming back? That I'd changed my mind and decided to stay at the Mill? Perhaps he thought I'd betrayed them somehow. The thought is almost painful, and I heave a long, strangled sigh.

"I'm sorry," I whisper, "I never meant to be gone for so long. Things happened, and…"

"Don't worry about it. You're back now. Heck, you even brought friends. That's all that matters – we can figure out the rest."

She glances back at me, those clear, beautiful eyes lighting up with her smile, and some childish part of me smiles back. She's right. Everything that's happened up until now doesn't matter, or at least diminishes in importance in the light of day. It doesn't matter that Kane still hates me, or that I've ripped Darus away from his family. Leaving Wirrow injured in the dust and being betrayed by Eagen is awful, but it's fine. Now I'm back amongst the glass spires and familiar streets, I know that everything will be okay.

We arrive at the tunnels under the cover of darkness. Judging by the look on Jay's face, they didn't intend to be gone so long – everyone within the Atrium will be fast asleep by now.

As we dismount the bikes, he turns to me. The initial rush of the reunion has started to wear off and while I'm still overjoyed to see him, my tiredness is starting to catch up with me. I glance at the others. Their faces reflect my own feelings, and the desire to curl up and get some much-deserved sleep.

"You guys look exhausted," says Jay, "I suppose you don't want to sit down and go through everything right now?"

I shake my head, much to the others' approval.

"Can we talk in the morning?"

My voice comes out much softer than I would have expected, much weaker. I'm so thoroughly worn out that I can't even bring myself to speak at full volume. I clear my throat and try again.

"Please."

"Of course. We'll go over things then."

Jay shoots the others a concerned look; he doesn't know who they are, doesn't know why they're here. It makes sense he'd feel threatened by their presence. But as I take a step towards them and place a hand on each of their shoulders in turn, he seems to settle.

"I assume your friends will need some clothes and a bed. I think there's a spare room opposite Pan's – we can keep you all close that way."

For a moment I move to object, to insist I'll stay with the others. But then I remember the unending cosiness of my bunk, and realise that after everything, I want nothing more than to return to the same room.

"Are you guys okay with that?" I ask. They nod, hesitant, as though afraid to speak out loud. I laugh.

"It's okay. These are my friends. This is Pan, and this is my brother, Jay."

They look up, glancing between us as though searching for that tell-tale sign to confirm it.

"Oh yeah," mutters Darus, "I see it now. He looks like you."

For some reason, it makes me happy to hear that. I look back at Jay, tracing his face for more of those familiar signs. The same dark brows, the same mid-blonde hair. If not for how dark my tan is, nobody would question that we were related. It's almost funny.

Jay just smiles.

"We're pleased to meet all of you. I understand you've had a long journey – please, come with us. We'll set you up some beds and find some clean clothes for you."

They set up the others in the room just across from us. They seem a little hesitant as they pull the door shut, but I quietly assure them that it's safe here. That everything is going to be okay. Darus and Sara seem to believe me at least, even if Kane shoots daggers at my back as I leave.

"Perhaps I should stay with them," I mutter. Pan shakes her head.

"Just let them rest for now. You guys have been through a lot, I can tell."

"That's an understatement if I ever heard one. There's a lot to tell you."

She watches me for a moment, torn between asking what happened or letting me explain when I'm ready. My throat aches with the desire to tell her everything; but then I remember how heavy my eyelids are, how overwhelmed everybody seems to be. I allow her to pull me into our old room.

For a moment, I take everything in. It's surprising just how much I've missed such a nondescript room. But there it is, metal sheets and rivets lining every surface. There's a small table and a collection of chairs, and two beds with a number of colourful blankets piled high. In my absence, Pan's even strung a few fairy lights across my bed. There's a small, stuffed toy tucked against the pillow.

"Miss this place?" she asks. She's got that nervousness on her face again, like she doesn't know what to say. I give a small nod and peel off my damaged clothing before collapsing into the bed.

"I've kept the bed made for you," Pan's saying, "the others weren't so sure, but I figured you'd be back soon..."

She's still talking when I fall asleep.

CHAPTER TWENTY-NINE

I wake to the sensation of several pairs of eyes watching me. It's strange how, even in a daze, I can tell someone's standing near the bunk. Sure enough, when I open my eyes there are figures standing in the room. They're not facing me, not staring at me - but their eyes linger on me as I lie curled into a ball, blanket pulled up over my head.

"I can't believe it," someone says. I recognise the voice as Nate's - but there's something strange in his tone. Something unsure. They haven't noticed my eyes flutter open. They think I'm still asleep.

"Have the others woken up yet?" asks Pan. He shakes his head.

"No. They're so tired."

"Who are the others, anyway? Has anyone checked?"

"They're locked in for now, while they sleep. They won't do any harm - we'd best wait to hear the full story."

That was Jay. He stands just inside the room, his back to the wall. His face is bathed in shadow.

"Stop panicking," he says, "Noah will tell us everything."

"I know. I just... I wonder what took so long. It's been months. No signal from the transmitter, no contact from Rian. Nothing – and then she just shows up. I'm sure something awful must have happened."

At that I force myself to sit up, pulling the blanket around myself as I do so. I'm still wearing my vest and undershorts from the Mill, but they're torn to shreds and probably aren't doing much to hide my modesty. I don't feel quite as well-rested as I'd hoped, but at least yesterday wasn't a dream. We really did come home.

For a moment, nobody speaks. They eye me curiously, their expressions unreadable.

"Okay," I say, "this is getting annoying now. You've all been weird since yesterday. What's with you?"

"We're sorry," Pan replies, "it's just been so long. We were worried you'd got hurt. Or... something."

I look between them, and finally understand the look in their eyes. It isn't betrayal or anger or mistrust; it's fear mingled with relief. I sit up slowly, swinging my legs over the side of the bed. Suddenly I don't care who sees my legs or stomach. It doesn't matter.

"Hold up. Did... did you guys think I wasn't coming back?"

My question is met with silence, but as I meet Pan's eyes she looks away. I'm right. They did. When I hadn't come back after all those months, they assumed I had changed my mind. That I'd betrayed them. Back at the Mill, I'd been frightened of slipping back into my old way of thinking. I'd been sure that when I arrived home, I'd tell Jay how he was right for not wanting me to go – because I couldn't do it. Because I hadn't changed.

But I have. The old Noah likely wouldn't have survived all this. She wouldn't have tried to escape the mines. Wouldn't have blown up a Guard or snuck across the ocean or escaped from someone hoping to betray her. She would have lowered her head and been afraid, and apologised to those in charge because it was easier than daring to rock the boat. She would never have questioned anything – but me? I would. I do.

"I can't believe you guys!"

I intend to sound angry, but it doesn't work. Instead, laughter bursts forth. I can't even explain why; perhaps it's that nobody expected this, not even me.

Jay stares.

"Y-you're not mad?"

"No! I don't blame you! For a while there, I figured I'd never get out. I had planned to apologise and tell you I should never have gone, but you know what? I did it!"

I wrap a hand in my hair, pride and laughter mingling in my chest.

"I did it. It took three months, and I got thrown in the mines, and I ended up getting shot at by the Guards, but I still did it!"

"You what?" cries Pan. Jay steps forward, concern in his eyes.

"Are you hurt?"

"I'm fine. I'm just… realising how insane it's been. The transmitter broke, and Nel wasn't there, and there was this explosion…"

"It's alright," he tells me, "just tell us everything from the beginning."

Despite their hesitation at the start, it doesn't take long for the others to feel involved. Soon enough they're sitting on the bunks with me and Pan, eyes wide as they listen intently. Jay wraps a protective arm around me, and though I can feel his worry rising during the more dangerous parts of my story, he also seems proud. When I finally finish, they all shake their heads.

"That sounds awful," Pan coos, "but I'm so glad you're back. Are you sure you're all okay?"

"We're fine. But they're nervous, you know. Scared of what might happen. I hope it's okay that I brought them back."

I turn to Jay now, who nods.

"Of course. Without the transmitter, bringing them here physically was the next best thing. We can run their DNA through Maynard's system later today and find out if they're citizens, too."

"I'm just sorry there are only three of them. I know Jensen needed five."

"I'm sure it'll be fine. This will still help to confirm whether our theory's true or not."

Even though I smile at that, a frightening thought occurs to me. What if the theory is wrong? What if I really am the exception to the rule? I've dragged the others halfway across the world, assuming it was worthwhile. Darus left his family. I don't even want to know how Kane will react if this turns sour.

Jay seems to notice my hesitation, and squeezes my shoulder playfully.

"Even if they're not, you know we won't turn them away. We'll never turn anyone away, especially not someone who helped us out."

"I know. Let's just hope it works out. We'll have to get Jensen to set everything up."

At that, Jay's jaw drops.

"Whoops."

"What?"

"Uh, nobody told Jensen you were back. It was so late last night that nobody's spoken to him yet, and he was probably too busy monitoring the Guard activities to notice anything."

Somehow, the thought excites me.

"I'll go pay him a visit then, shall I? Let me just get cleaned up and talk to the others first."

I feel like a new woman as I stride down the metal hallways of our little base. A quick shower and some fresh clothes have left me feeling wonderful. The others are on a tour with Pan, just as I did during my first day here – and though I feel I should have gone with them, there's little time to waste.

Jay's already versed me on his plans. We'll hijack the Feed during one of the leaders' pre-Cull speeches. Jensen will air all the data we have, all that he's collected over the past few months. About how the Cull might be a lie, about how there have been no signs of the war outside our borders in years. All the truths about their lies. He'll make it available on every system, every device. Everyone will know.

Then, we'll go all out. We'll run into the streets and encourage the citizens to fight back by whatever means necessary. But to get to that point, we need Jensen and his computers.

As I nudge open the door to his room, I spot him in his usual position. He's got his back to me. His shoulders are hunched, casting a stark silhouette against the white of the screen before him. Half-built devices litter his room, including a particularly sad-looking crimson Hoverbot I never noticed before. He doesn't seem to hear me enter.

For a moment, I just watch. I remember when he asked me to help him with his cameras. At the time I hadn't questioned his motives, but now I do. He probably wanted to check who I really was, and figured that catching me alone for a few minutes would be enough. I remember the story he'd told me about a rebellious teen who gave up everything to sit at that screen and work. The way he'd smiled told me he considered it more than worthwhile. At the time I'd thought he was crazy but now, not so much.

"You'll damage your eyes if you sit that close to the screen."

He whips round at the sound of my voice, and those intelligent eyes widen in shock.

"Noah!"

He stands in a hurry, moves towards me, and promptly trips over his own feet. I bite back on my laughter.

This is a serious moment. He regains what little composure he can and lurches towards me.

"Y-you're back!"

"Looks that way, huh?"

"Where the hell have you been?" he barks – but though there's a hint of anger in his voice, he still wraps one arm haphazardly around me. Heat fills my cheeks.

"You really did miss me, didn't you? And here I thought you were teasing."

"You know something, so did I. Guess I called my own bluff."

I puff out my cheeks in mock offence, but he just smiles that awkward smile. Suddenly, I realise how much I missed that funny face of his.

"For what it's worth, I missed you too."

At that he averts his eyes, glancing at the ground like I've just scolded him. But then he shakes it off, regarding me with renewed interest. I glance down at myself too; I'm wearing jeans and a soft grey t-shirt, and my trusty boots have been replaced by some oddly comfortable slip-ons Pan pushed onto me. My hair is pale again now that it's free of dirt, and seems to fall back into the style she had so meticulously carved it into. If not for the dull ache in my ribs, I'd wonder if the whole thing had been a dream.

"I have something for you," he says suddenly. He darts past and begins digging in the pile of computers propped against one wall. He pulls something out; and I feel my face split into a grin as he places a familiar-looking green Hoverbot in front of me.

"Atlas!"

It awakens instantly, a half-dozen lights flashing across its surface. Its camera lens narrows and opens as it takes me in, and a moment later, I hear those familiar beeps. It takes off and spins around me, and it takes all I have not to reach out and embrace it. I know I never really understood the point of Hoverbots, but I've missed its constant presence these past months.

I beam at Jensen.

"You kept it for me."

"Of course I did. Put it back into stasis – right after I linked it to Atticus, that is. Now the two can work in sync. Never know when that might be useful."

He seems so happy that for a brief moment, I almost forget all that's still ahead of us.

We don't wait around. I tell Jensen everything as we weave our way through the tunnels – and though he seems just as enthralled as the others were, I'm growing sick of the story. I'm ready to forget it ever happened. There's something nice about being back here, striding down these corridors with him. It's hard to believe he'd hated me so much on our first meeting.

I nudge the door to the Atrium, and we're blinded by blue-silver light.

It's just as beautiful as I remember. Soft daylight filters through the glass overhead, lighting up the various platforms and open spaces. People work and chatter and shift around us. When I close my eyes I can hear running water from the stream, and a deep breath fills my nose with the scent of freshly cut grass and evergreen trees.

Jensen chuckles.

"Did you miss it here?"

"You have no idea. Where are the others?"

We quickly find them – Pan's just finishing up the tour for Sara, Kane and Darus. Nate stands by, too, his booming laugh echoing across the Atrium. They wave when they see us approaching, and it takes a moment for me to realise who I'm seeing.

Without crud layered on their faces, they look younger and brighter and larger than life. Sara's dirty hair is actually soft and springy, and now I realise her eyes weren't just sparkling in comparison to her dust-coated face. They really are that bright. Kane's scar appears somewhat worse in the pale light, but he no longer seems to care. There's a broad smile on his face that makes him almost unrecognisable. Darus looks much the same; if anything, his hair seems a little longer without salt air swilling around it.

"Wow. You guys look great!"

Sara beams.

"I know, right? And look at you! Much better without dirt smeared all over you."

"So what do you think of the place?"

It's strange how easily my voice comes now, how normal it feels to talk casually when it seemed so impossible before. They watch me curiously; they're picking up on the change in my demeanour, the confidence in my stance.

"It really is amazing," Darus says, "I can see why you love it so much."

Kane's eyes float across the room, eventually coming to settle uneasily on Jensen. His mouth twitches.

"Who's this? Your boyfriend?"

"Nope," I say simply, "and don't forget what I told you when we first met. You've got more important things to focus on than girls and romance. We all do, so don't even start with me."

He opens his mouth to speak, but then bites back on the retort. I'm quietly pleased to discover that despite his hatred, he still respects me, even if only a little.

"This is Jensen," I explain, "Jensen, this is Sara, Kane and Darus."

He greets them in turn, asking where they're from, what their roles were. Even though everyone knows that he's already heard the entire story from me. They just answer as politely as they can, though Kane's delight seems vaguely diminished by my outburst.

Nate catches my eye and smiles broadly. I've missed him, too. Jensen shoots the others a confident look.

"Are you guys ready for DNA testing?"

He's met by nervous glances. Sara shuffles a little closer to me, as though I can somehow protect her from the inevitable. Pan sidles up on her other side, laying an arm across Sara's shoulders. What's intended to be a casual and comforting motion is somewhat awkward as she catches her watch on Sara's ear tag – but the point gets across.

"You don't have to do it now, if you don't want to."

"Actually, they do."

Jay's voice rings out across the Atrium, and with it comes a firm demand for our respect. I don't question that feeling as he nears – both sibling and leader, friend and commander. A strange cocktail of respect, admiration and affection.

Pan sighs.

"Why do they need to do it now?"

"Because we've got six days until the Cull," Jay says firmly, "and we need to know the truth. Our plans drastically change depending on the outcome of these tests, so we need to know and we need to know now."

He glances at the others, a hint of sorrow in his eyes.

"I'm sorry to hurry you, but this is important. I really need you to do this for me now."

Sara shoots me an alarmed look.

"W-what if it's not what you're looking for?"

"It's alright," I tell her, "there's no right result."

"You want us to be from Thorne, don't you? Like you are."

I consider this for a moment. It would make everything so much simpler if they're like me – if I'm the rule rather than the exception. Everything points to that, so I've not been too worried until now. I'm sure we've cracked this.

"It doesn't matter," I insist, "it's not the end of the world."

I can tell she doesn't believe me, but she nods nonetheless and steps forward to greet Jay. The two briefly shake hands and he moves on to the others, introducing himself just as Jensen did. Like he doesn't already know everything about them.

"I've got the testing equipment with me," Jensen says, "we can get set up wherever you want."

Jay nods.

"My room. Come on."

The others walk off, led by Pan – but as I step forward to follow them, a strong hand grasps my shoulder.

"You guys go on ahead," says Jay, "I need to talk to Noah."

There's a ball of unease in my stomach as I turn to face him. This is it. The scolding I've been half-expecting since I arrived home. I gaze into his eyes, certain I'll see anger and disdain staring back at me. But he's just smiling.

"They're just like you said. I don't know why I'm surprised."

I swallow hard.

"I'm just sorry I couldn't do more. What happened back at the Mill... it was awful."

"It sounds it. You took a beating or two, didn't you?"

"It isn't that. I mean, it was. But I... I slipped right back into things. I'd started to forget who I was."

His mouth twitches.

"That's understandable."

"But not forgivable," I snap, "I feel terrible about it. I should have done everything in my power to get back to you. I really wanted to. But I just felt..."

I trail off now, and his hand tightens on my shoulder.

"What is it?"

"I felt... lonely. Which is weird. I've never felt lonely before."

His face creases with unspoken sympathy. I push on.

"I shouldn't have said I would go. I had no idea what I was doing. No wonder I failed."

Shame compounds in my chest, the result of three months of constant failure. I'd been happy with what I'd done, how I'd found my way home when things had seemed so bleak. But now, standing in front of him, I feel like I let him down.

"Don't be stupid."

Jay's brows sink, settling into a hard expression on his face.

"I thought you were smarter than that, Noah. I thought you knew me. I'd never think you failed."

"But I did!"

"You did not."

His voice lowers, morphing into a half-growl.

"Noah, I've been a wreck for the past three months. I didn't know where you were. No signals, no news. Nothing. The others thought you might have been killed. They said that I should accept it. But I had faith in you."

"I should have come back sooner. I should have found a way to let you know I was okay."

"By the sounds of it, you did all you could just to stay alive. What's more, you kept your wits about you in that chaos. You think I don't know how afraid of the dark you are?"

I wince.

"W-what do you..."

"The Mines. I know how much they frighten you – but you still survived. You broke out, you found your way home. You even managed to bring three people back with you. You might very well have saved their lives."

He pushes my shoulder a little, in a motion that's half-playful, half-comforting.

"You didn't fail. Far from it. I'm proud of you. Mom and Dad would have been, too."

I stare up at my brother's face, blinking a little in the bright sunlight. There's a smile on his face again. I close my eyes and inhale deeply, enjoying the scent of the stream water and the garden in the distance, the scents that remind me of home. When I open my eyes again, there's a smile on my face, too.

CHAPTER THIRTY

We're about half-way to Jay's room when a deafening crack breaks the silence.

"What's that?"

I look up, towards the source of the sound – and freeze. The delicate glass ceiling has shattered. We duck just as it falls around us, forming tiny shards of razor-sharp rain.

When the tinkling of glass finally stops, I stand up and brush the tiny pieces from my hair. My scalp stings and there's blood on my fingertips. Beside me, Jay's looking at the floor.

"T-this is bad. This is our cover. They could find us!"

Fear courses through me.

"It's too late for that."

He follows my gaze and gasps. Countless black-clothed figures are sliding down ladders and ropes, through the now-empty ceiling and into the heart of the Atrium. I don't need to look too closely to recognise the city Guard.

They're armed to the teeth as they land around the Atrium, ferocity in their eyes. I can hear the familiar buzz of three dozen shock batons bursting into life.

"Oh, no."

I stare wildly at Jay, who seems just as stunned as I am.

"How did they find us?"

He grits his teeth then grabs my arm.

"It doesn't matter. We need to get out of here."

He doesn't wait for my response before taking off running towards his room. Initially, I question why - the glass walls and non-existent security won't help at all - but I quickly figure it out. Even in this, the worst of circumstances, his first thought is warning the others.

As we run, I try not to wince. His grip on my hand is almost painful, and with each step he nearly pulls my arm out of its socket. The severity of the situation starts to set in as we approach the room.

If they've found us, we're done for. They'll have figured out it's the old transport system - there'll be Guards at every entrance, blocking our escape. They'll trawl every tunnel in this place if they have to. They'll arrest us - and I don't want to think about what will follow. The flicker of fear in my chest threatens to grow to full-blown terror. I bite back on it.

We fly through the door of the office and slam it behind us; I press my back against it, eager to hold back anyone who might try to force their way in. I wasn't aware of anyone behind us on our way here, but there are plenty of Guards. I can't rule out the possibility that one or two are pursuing us.

The others are crowded around a computer, Jensen at the helm - but they pause as we enter.

"What's wrong?" asks Pan, "we heard a big crash."

"The Guards found us. They came in from the roof. The whole place is crawling with them."

Panic flits across each of their faces.

"W-what do we do?" Jensen yelps. His gaze is fixed on Jay – a reminder, if it were needed, that he's their leader. Just like he told me. He's to blame for whatever happens next. For a moment, he seems clueless. Perhaps he's realising what I did on the way here, that there's no way out. Nowhere to go, even if we could escape.

But then his expression sets.

"We need to get to Jensen's room. Barricade ourselves in."

"Why there?"

"His computers have all our records, all our camera links. We can monitor things from there."

"What about the others?" I cry, "there are dozens of people here! We need to protect them!"

Pain crosses his face.

"They all agreed to this when they came here. We can't save everyone."

I open my mouth to object, to tell him that we need to save as many as we can, but Pan nods.

"You're right. The four Mill workers might be the key to saving everyone. We need to protect them."

"Are you crazy?" I snap, "we're getting everyone out of here. We can't just leave them!"

Jay locks eyes with me and for a moment, I can see all my own terror and unbridled fear mirrored back at me. He doesn't want to do this. It's killing him. It's taking all he has just to hold it together. Knowing he has to sacrifice so many. I can't imagine that pain. Nate sidles over and rests a huge, comforting hand on Jay's shoulder.

"We have no choice, Noah. The Clover… the Clover comes first."

Slowly, I nod.

"Okay. Okay! I understand."

Jensen stands up, tapping a few keys on the computer.

"There. I've wiped all the computers in the place except for in my room. They won't be able to find anything out from here."

"Good," says Jay, "we're going to need to make a run for it. You all know the way?"

Kane shakes his head.

"Not really, no."

"Okay. You three, stick to Pan like glue. If something happens, she'll show you the way."

They nod, though I can feel trepidation in their every movement. My heart sinks, a sick realisation squirming in my gut.

"Wait."

I step up to Sara, regarding her closely. She seems unnerved by my closeness – but in an instant I've snatched up her ear tag, twisting and breaking it in between my hands. The thing shatters surprisingly easily, revealing a mess of wires and flashing lights.

"What are you doing?" she shouts, clutching at her bloody lobe.

"I thought so. Look."

I push the shattered remains into Jay's hands. He stares at them for a moment before his face creases. Rage and understanding war in his eyes.

"What is this?"

"The trackers used in the Mines," I say, my voice hard, "they put them on all the mine workers so they can find them in the tunnels. They must have tracked us down. Followed the signal here and found out what this place is."

"You knew about these?"

"I did. But I had no idea they could work out here. We had to cross a freaking ocean. I didn't even think."

He grits his teeth tightly.

"Never underestimate the Guard, Noah. You should have known that."

"I'm sorry."

And I am. Guilt is swirling in me, tightening in my gut. A mere minute after being so proud of me, now he's angry – and rightfully so. How could I have missed something so important?

His hand tightens on the remains of the tracker, curling until the pieces crack under his grip.

"There's no use pinning blame. Not at this point. Kane, get that tracker off. Now."

He does so immediately, not even blinking as he rips it from his flesh and stamps hard on the device.

"Sorted."

"Good. Look, it doesn't matter how they found us. They did. That's what we have to deal with. We need to move before they find this place."

I swallow hard. He's right. We may have let something obvious slip past us, but no good will come from moping about it. I can hear chaos building outside. I near the door, daring to slip my hand through the crack, and glance through.

The Atrium is a disaster. The moment the door seal parts, the sound is almost deafening. Figures race around, in the tunnels, over the broken glass on the floor. Shouted commands echo through the empty spaces – followed quickly by a number of muffled explosions. Pained screams ring out across the Atrium. When I breathe in, I can smell gunpowder and blood.

I look back at the others; their faces are full of fear, and they can't even see what I can.

My fingers tighten against the doorframe.

"Okay. Let's go. Atlas, go ahead. Light the way."

We take off running through the Atrium, trying to remain calm despite the chaos around us. I shoulder barge a Guard aside to clear a path, throwing him into the wall in hopes we can be gone before he recovers. It works this time, but it won't always be so easy. We're a big group. A big target.

A Guard throws his weight towards me, briefly sending me sprawling. I recover quickly and in a split second Nate is next to me. He reaches out a hand to help me up – I take it gratefully and fall into line beside him.

As we follow the others, I briefly imagine targets on everyone's backs. The largest on Jay's.

He's the leader of the group. The spokesperson, the one who steps up more than any of the others. Say they catch everyone else – will they leave without him? Is there anything I can do to make sure they don't come after us?

"This way!" Pan cries, waving towards the nearest door into the tunnels. I map out the path in my head. We're not far from Jensen's room. It'll be easy enough to barricade ourselves in; but how long will we have to wait before we can come out? How many people will they kill to get to us?

As I reach the doorway, there's a blinding flash. The explosion in front of me is so strong that I'm thrown backwards, rolling into a heap on the floor.

I sit up, gasping from the dust in the air. Something's detonated nearby; the doorway has collapsed. Rubble fills the available space, and terror flickers in my chest. Everyone else was already inside – save for Nate, who's already standing, his frightened eyes fixed on the blocked doorway.

"Nate! What happened?"

He glances back, momentarily confused; he didn't realise I was here, too.

"Are you okay?"

"Yeah. But the others..."

He bangs on the doorframe.

"Hey! Is anyone in there?"

A moment's silence makes us both hold our breath.

"We're here," comes the muffled reply, "Noah, Nate? Are you okay?"

"Yes!" I shout, stepping up to the rubble wall, "is anyone hurt?"

There's a scuffling sound, followed by a pained yelp.

"Guys?"

"I-it's fine," Jensen barks, though it's clear it's not. I recognise his yelp from that night in the city. He's hurt. How badly, I don't know. But I can feel my fear flickering into panic.

"Everything's fine," Jay shouts, "you two will have to use the service duct to reach us. Meet us at Jensen's. You know the way?"

I swallow hard. I know the tunnel. It doesn't connect directly, instead going under Jensen's room and up the other side. Even here it's used as a service duct; dark and cold and frightening. Not to mention, across the other side of the Atrium. My skin crawls.

"Is there any other way?"

"No! Hurry, before they see you!"

He's right. Whoever set off the explosion is still here somewhere – and for all we know, they could be aiming a gun at us right now. I grit my teeth and motion for Nate to follow.

The heart of the Atrium is a disaster. Guards litter the place, many struggling with members of the Clover. I'm surprised and pleased to see them fighting back so well – I'd worried that they might roll over and surrender when faced with the consequences of their crimes.

I form a mental map of where we need to go. Down the steps, across the gardens. A short sprint, but if we stumble across a number of Guards, we may find ourselves in trouble. I step forward and promptly slip on something wet. When I look down, I spy a long, thin string of blood across the tiled floor. Like someone was wounded and running. Suddenly, I feel a little sick.

"Come on," says Nate, and his hand locks around my arm. He doesn't seem quite as frightened as I am. Instead, his expression is hard. He knows what to do – and suddenly, I feel he'll do anything to get us there.

But then we reach the top of the steps, and are met by several heavy-set Guards. They round on us with malice in their eyes and batons clutched in their hands – and even as I punch the first one aside, I worry that there are simply too many. One Guard armed with a shock baton is dangerous enough. This many, even in an open area, are too many to handle.

Nate's wrestling with holding off two Guards at once. How he's doing that, I'll never know. But as I round on the next one alone, that familiar sensation is back. Adrenaline. It pumps through my veins and makes everything seem fast and slow at the same time.

The Guard looks me up and down, a sneer playing on her lips. She's never seen anyone quite like me before – but that's not about to stop her. She swings wildly towards me and I jump aside, trying to sweep her legs out from under her. But I'm not as graceful as Jay and the motion is sloppy at best. She leaps away and I'm forced to throw my weight at her.

For a brief moment, I'm certain we've both fallen. The steps are right there, after all. But when I open my eyes, it's just me still standing at the top. The Guard is sprawled across the bottom of the steps, groaning. Satisfaction briefly fills me.

Nate is finally free, too, though he's only been able to push the two Guards aside. He cries for me to head down the steps, presumably to help clear that area while he keeps watch.

My feet hit the bottom of the steps and I'm face to face with a Guard who looks, frankly, like he couldn't fight his way out of a paper bag. A long, narrow face seems to taunt me. I take a step forward with the intent of pushing him aside – but then he catches my wrist and throws me back towards an open doorway. Something beeps just behind me, and I catch sight of a sly grin before that door explodes, too.

Immediately, I consider myself lucky to be alive. Even though I'm surrounded by rubble and pinned by a particularly large chunk of rebar, at least nothing hurts. Except my chest, where the rebar is pushing down and making it hard to breathe. I briefly wonder what that ringing sound is, then realise it's just my head reeling from the shock.

I turn my head as best I can. Nate is standing across the Atrium, his face a picture of horror. His normally-jovial attitude vanishes altogether as he races towards me, my name echoing from his mouth.

He throws a punch at the skinny Guard, sending him cowering to the ground. Not so much of a tough guy when he has to do the fighting himself.

"Noah, you okay?"

There's untold pain in his eyes, but I can't tell why. He seemed so fearless just a moment ago.

"I'm alright. I can't... move this thing, though."

I push on the rebar as best I can. It doesn't budge. He grits his teeth, conflict in his eyes. Is he thinking of leaving me here? But then he shakes his head sharply, takes a deep breath, and grips the rebar with both hands.

"You'll have to help me," he says, "push from below."

It takes a minute or so to push the rebar off, and as soon as it moves, I can breathe easily again. Amazingly, I'm unharmed. The only pain is a mild ache in my chest. Nate drags me upright and pushes on, nudging me ahead as we run. As we head into the garden, it's surprisingly empty. Perhaps they don't know this place is here. But that deafening chaos is still there, still raging in our ears. Still, I can see the entrance.

"We're almost there!"

I glance back, hoping to exchange a joyful glance with Nate – but he's not there. No, he's a little further back, lying in a heap on the grass of the Clover's memorial garden. Even from here, I can tell his breathing is laboured. He clutches at his torso; and as I near, I see why.

There's a clean bullet wound through Nate's stomach. Blood streams from it and mixes into the grass, more blood than I've ever seen come out of one person. It sends panic flashing through me.

"Nate!"

As I collapse next to him he falls into my shoulder, agony contorting his features into something unrecognisable. When did he get shot? I didn't see any guns. Was it when I was pinned? Did the ringing disguise the sound?

The wound must be agony, and yet he fights to keep his face straight as I stare down at him.

"It's okay," he lies, "really, it's... it's fine."

"It is not."

I feel like I should say something more; to comfort him, to ease his pain. But instead, I'm just frightened. I don't know how badly he's hurt or how to begin treating it. This isn't a bullet graze like the one in my side. This is a direct hit deep into his core. Grief mingles with the panic as I realise he might die.

The thought is too painful to stand.

"Come on. We need to get to the others. Put your arm around me."

I try to lift him, to toss him over one shoulder like I did with Jensen when he was hurt. But Nate's far too big and his injuries are far too deep. When I move him, he just cries out in pain.

"Please, Nate. Just try. The others, they're waiting for us."

I'm pleading now, clutching his hand tightly in mine. I always forget how large his hands are; but right now he seems so small, curled up against me. His eyes plead with me, but he doesn't seem afraid. Just pained. My stomach churns.

I can't carry him. What do I do now? Tears fill my eyes as I consider the logical option. Leaving him here. He's probably going to die. Moving that rebar would have been difficult enough even without such injuries – and now, it's that much worse. If I'm being purely logical, I should run ahead. Leave him here and hope he bleeds out before the Guards find him. But of course, I can't. Forget for a moment that the others would hate me for it. I wouldn't forgive myself if I left now.

"M-maybe I can find something to carry you on. A pallet, or something. There's bound to be something... hold on while I look, okay?"

But then I look down, and my blood runs cold. Nate's eyes have slipped shut. His hand feels cooler under my touch, too. The pain has faded from his face; he looks terrifyingly calm.

No. No!

I grab his shoulders and suddenly I'm screaming, but my cries are lost in the discord filling the Atrium. I feel sick and terrified and angry, and Nate is dead and even though I shake him he's not moving and the screaming means nothing because nobody's coming to help.

CHAPTER THIRTY-ONE

I step into the service duct with a heavy heart.

Here, the endless chaos of the Atrium falls away. Now it's replaced by unnerving silence that's punctuated only by the occasional thud overhead. I stretch out a hand in front of myself, but see nothing. It's too dark. I wish I had Atlas to light the way – but I sent it ahead with the others.

You'd think that, after everything, I'd be happy to be away from the Guards. That I'd steal this moment to myself in an effort to remain calm. I'd have thought so too; but instead, my blood runs cold. Because Nate is still outside, motionless in the grass. Because I couldn't save him – but I'm still dimly aware that I need to save myself. Even if I no longer feel I deserve it.

I turn a corner and freeze.

Wirrow stands in the service duct, his eyes searching in the shadows. There's something purposeful about his movements, and though he's barely lit by the torch on his belt, I can see fury in his eyes. Nasty scratches cover his face and arms. When he sneers, several teeth are missing.

Why is he here? I'd known he would try to come after us – he would chase us to the ends of the Earth if he could. It makes sense he'd come to Thorne. But why here? Why in this tunnel, right where I am? Why so close that I can smell his putrid body odour?

His eyes snap towards me, and those thin lips twist into a sickening grin.

"I thought I'd find you here, Girlie."

I curl my hands into fists, then loosen them. Don't turn to violence. Not yet. Grief builds in my chest, but I swallow it back. Time for a little bravado.

"I'm surprised you tracked me down," I say lightly, "though I must ask you to stop calling me Girlie."

"You're right. Noah, isn't it? I remember that boy saying your name. Before his punishment."

He's doing his utmost to remind me of his actions, of what he can do – what he will do – to cement his legacy within the Guard.

"How did you find me?"

He walks forward, every step slow and menacing. I do my best to look indifferent as he nears.

"Followed the kid's tracker."

"I know that. I mean, how did you find me here?"

"I figured you'd come to the darkest, dirtiest hole there was. Something about Mill workers always sends them to the best hiding spot."

That explains it. I suppose I should be happy; he didn't track me down. He just took a guess that happened to pay off. Lucky bastard.

I back up as he reaches me, swallowing hard. After our last encounter, I'd been sure he wouldn't frighten me. When I consider all the chaos I've seen in the last few months, all the fear I've felt even in the last few minutes, this one man shouldn't unnerve me. But he does.

It's not the ferocity in his eyes that does it. I've seen that before; all the Guards regard me with a similar sense of disgust and hatred. I don't care about that. If this were anyone else, I'd be fighting him already. If it were anyone else, I'd have put an end to this back at the Mill.

But it's not just any faceless Guard. It's Wirrow.

He's always been there, a constant presence for as long back as I can remember. For many years I'd felt nothing but respect and admiration for him – and even now I know he's the enemy, my instinct is to lower my head and obey.

So it takes all my strength to raise my head and look him in the eye. My back promptly hits the wall.

"I'm not coming back with you."

He lets out a laugh, but there's no real humour in it. It's mirthless and hateful and full of contempt. When he smiles, it doesn't reach his eyes.

"I'm not here to bring you back."

He reaches behind himself now, pulling out a long, thin device that I instantly recognise as one of the city Guard's shock batons. It's sleeker and glossier than the clunky ones he must be used to, but there's delight in his eyes as he turns it over in his hands.

"Once the Guard found out what this place was, they declared a state of emergency. Their weapons network was increased to max. Every single baton in Thorne is set to a lethal level. That means that with just one touch of this..."

He flicks a button and the body of the baton crackles. Several jolts of electricity jump from its surface, lighting up the darkness between us. My heart races.

"It's over."

For a moment, I can't breathe. Terror threatens to overwhelm me; I try to take a step back, but the wall's still there, blocking my path. Wirrow meets my eyes, beady black meeting dusty blue – rage and hatred meeting fear. I bite my lip, and a moment later something warm streams down my chin.

I don't know if I can do this.

The day Kane attacked him, I remember measuring Wirrow up. I remember thinking I could probably pin him, or at least throw him down for long enough to run. But that was before. Before this rivalry, before the horrors between us. Brute force won't work. I give him the once-over, looking for weaknesses. Just like Jay told me. A trick knee, a weak ankle. Anything that might grant me even a split-second advantage. Nothing. He's just a wall of muscle and fury, and I don't know if I can win.

Still, I curl my hand into a fist and take aim at his jaw. I have to try. If he kills me here, at least I'll have given it my all. Nobody can criticise me for that.

He clicks his tongue just as I pull my arm back.

"Don't get cocky."

I try to land the blow, but he's fast. Much faster than me. He snatches at my arm and pulls it, sending a jolt of pain down my shoulder. I yelp, but it doesn't stop him; he whips around and throws me hard against the metal wall. Pain explodes across my face and the world turns black.

CHAPTER THIRTY-TWO

"Noah!"

Dimly, I become aware of someone shouting. The voice is strangely familiar, but I can't place it.

As feeling returns to my body, I realise I'm on the floor. There's a lock of hair covering my eyes. I take a long, slow breath, inhaling the scent of blood.

"Noah, wake up!"

A hand finds my shoulder, shakes me; and my body finally starts to wake up. Pain blossoms across my head again, pulsing in my brain. I groan, The voice comes again.

"Come on... please."

It takes an immense amount of strength to force my eyes open. The speaker is kneeling next to me, their face overcome with worry. That's why I recognise the voice. Of course.

Jay's eyes are filled with panic. Figures move behind him, standing, watching. Everyone sounds a little breathless. I wonder what happened.

Hands find me, help me to sit up, but the world still spins.

"Are you okay?" my brother asks, and his voice is warm and familiar and wonderful. I lean into him and rest my head on his shoulder. It feels safe here. The spinning slows.

"W-what happened?" I eventually manage.

"We heard a crash," comes the reply, "it had been too long so we knew something had happened. When we got here, we saw you... and him..."

He grits his teeth at that last part, hatred seeping through. I let out a long breath. I suppose he's angry. Seeing me unconscious and Wirrow looming nearby must have been a shock – especially as he'd been so sure the service tunnel would be clear. For a brief moment, I'm certain he's going to be mad. But then arms loop around me, pulling me into a protective embrace.

"Let's get you into Jensen's room. We need to clean you up."

We stand, him still supporting my weight – but as we turn towards the end of the tunnel, I stop. Kane stands with his back to us. His hand clutches a stolen shock baton, and his shoulders are hunched with barely-held rage. But what draws my eye more is the darkened heap in front of him. It's disgustingly familiar; a pale, bloody hand catches the light. I step forward and place a shaky hand on Kane's back.

"D-did you..."

"I'm sorry."

For once, there's no edge in his voice, no sarcasm, no attitude. He gazes at Wirrow's prone form with sadness in his eyes.

"Back at the Mill, you didn't do it. I know you think it's wrong."

I wait for the world to stop spinning to reply.

"He didn't leave much choice. I get it. I've done the same thing. I just..."

He turns to me, and in his eyes I see my own regret mirrored back at me. All the feelings I've bottled up since the incident with the helicopters come rushing to the surface. Remembering what I did. Wishing I hadn't had to do it. Knowing I had no choice. Kane stares.

"Just what?"

"I just... I thought you hated me."

He blinks.

"I never said that."

"But after what happened..."

"Being mad at you is one thing," he mutters, "letting that bastard kill you is another. You really think I'd sink so low?"

My hand tightens on his back.

"Of course not."

Pan, Jensen and the others are already in his room when we step inside; Pan gasps when she sees me, waving for me to sit down. I briefly wonder why; the initial dizziness is now fading, and though I'm still unsteady on my feet, I'm not too badly hurt. I'm more concerned about Jensen, who's sitting in a heap on the corner of the bed, clutching a bloody leg. He looks nothing short of traumatised.

But then Pan presses a towel to my cheek, and it comes away red.

"What the hell happened?" she cries.

"It's okay," I say, but my mouth is swollen and the words sound distorted and strange.

"It was Wirrow," Kane mutters. He and the others are now working to barricade us in, shifting several of Jensen's larger computer units towards the sliding door. I notice they're leaving a sizeable gap. They probably haven't realised that Nate's not with me yet.

Pan grimaces.

"The Guard from the Mill? What's he doing here?"

"He tracked us down. We should have expected it."

Pan makes a small, sympathetic noise and turns back to me with a frown.

"Look at you... I hope you lot beat the hell out of that Wirrow guy for this."

"He's not a problem anymore," Kane says. There's a certain finality in his voice as he says it, as though to confirm that the Guard lying in the hallway is dead.

Suddenly, Jay speaks from the doorway.

"Noah. I know you're in pain right now, but just answer me one thing."

I meet his eyes - they're a little bloodshot. He's stressed again.

"Nate," he mutters, "he's not with you."

The others pause, as though they've only just noticed. I shiver.

"No."

"Captured or dead?"

His voice is dull and heavy as he asks, as though neither answer would surprise or disgust him. Suddenly, I can't bring myself to meet his eyes a moment longer. There's no point trying to hide it - even if I wanted to, I can't.

He's gone, isn't he? Nate's familiar smile, his heavy movements, his booming laugh. All gone. Lost in the chaos. One more person screaming in agony amongst a dozen other screams. Another river of blood across the floor of our home. Nate has been one of the unshakeable pillars of the Clover, always present, always laughing - and now, he's gone for good.

"Shh, it's okay."

Pan dabs at my cheek, trying in vain to stop the flow of tears streaming down it. My body is wracked with sobs that only exacerbate the pain in my head. I can feel Jay's eyes on me as I fall into Pan's embrace and start wailing.

It's been three hours since the glass ceiling was shattered.

Three hours of listening to the chaos upstairs, which is showing no sign of slowing down. Three hours of hushed grief. Three hours of sitting in relative silence, punctuated by the occasional pained whimper from Jensen. His leg was crushed by some rubble when the doorway collapsed before, leaving the bone in a state. Still, he powers through, showing remarkable bravery considering the size of the injury.

I sit uneasily on Jensen's chair. The spinning has long since stopped, but as I turn and catch sight of myself in the darkened screen, I grimace.

I'm a mess. I've got a cut on my head and a bloody lip; my nose is definitely broken, and although Pan was able to push it back into position, it still looks purple and swollen. At lease it's not completely malformed. The pain has faded, but there's still a certain heat under my skin, pulsing like some bizarre, inhuman heartbeat. My eyes are bloodshot from crying. I still hiccup every few minutes.

Nate's death has left everyone shaken. Even Kane and the others, who barely knew him. It's starting to set in that this is serious. Pan had me explain what had happened in excruciating detail; but Jay had simply turned his back as I'd spoken. He didn't want us to see him cry. I can understand. It's more personal to Jay than anyone else. Nate practically raised him.

A particularly large explosion overhead sends tiny bits of plaster raining down from the cracks in the ceiling. Instinctively I wince away from the noise, pulling into myself and wrapping my arms tightly around my chest. This is awful.

I had thought this was something to scatter and frighten the Clover. But this... it's not a warning. This is all-out destruction. There's no telling from the screaming overhead whether people are being killed or arrested, but I'd rather not know. I remember all the people I've met during my time here. Nelson, Hue, Marla. I can't stand to think of them being hurt.

The others aren't dealing with the chaos any better than I am. Their heads hang, misery dominating their faces. Jensen's the only one who's still calm, and that's only because of the painkillers Pan scraped together. He's leaning back against the pillows, his eyes half-closed. Not asleep, but not completely awake, either. Envy flits through me.

My eyes are drawn to Jay. He's standing in the centre of the room, the only one of us who has the strength to remain upright. His hands are clenched in anger, and his eyes are still red from the tears he refused to show us. I know this is hell for him.

Hell because he's left behind all the people he promised to protect. Hell because he should be out there, fighting alongside them. Hell because he's afraid to stay and afraid to go, and hell because he won't be able to forgive himself no matter what he does.

A particularly loud scream sends a jolt of pain through my still-sore head and a whimper escapes my lips.

"You okay?"

Pan glances over, her face awash with sympathy.

"Y-yeah."

"You sure?"

She doesn't believe me. She's already tried pushing the painkillers onto me, too. But the thought of not being aware during these moments is unbearable. I want to remember this.

"This is horrible," I eventually say. I don't really know what response I expect; there's nothing anyone can say or do to make this easier. But it's almost physically painful to be trapped in here, and I can hear my voice cracking when I speak. I don't want to be here anymore.

"What do you want us to do about it?" Jay snaps.

"I'm sorry. I didn't mean..."

"It's fine. You're right. It is horrible."

Suddenly, I can't stand it anymore. I push the chair back and stand unsteadily. It takes a few attempts, but I eventually manage to take a good step forward, crossing over to the shoddily-made barricade. I reach out to move the first piece.

"Where do you think you're going?"

"Out," I mutter, "I'm going mad in here."

"There's nowhere else to go," says Pan, "what do you plan to do?"

My hand tightens against the edge of the computer.

"I don't know yet."

"Don't be stupid," Jay says, his voice hard, "you can barely stand up. You're not going anywhere."

"But we need to do something."

My voice sounds weaker than I'd have expected. I smack my lips a few times, realising we've not had food or drink since walking down the road to the city. No wonder my head hurts so much.

Jay takes a step forward, conflict warring on his face. I can tell that he wants to go, too. Wants to fight, even if it doesn't result in a win. But he's smarter than me. He knows we won't win. Knows we'll all be killed, one way or another.

"They'll catch us, Noah. You know that."

"I don't care."

"At best, they'll shoot us on the spot. At worst, they'll make a spectacle of us. Right out there, right on the doorstep of Maynard's tower. Just like they did to Mom and Dad."

I pause. I've seen the clips; two youthful figures cuffed at the top of the steps. Maynard herself, surrounded by Guards, talking nonsense to a number of Hoverbots and the small crowd of citizens who came to witness the demise of innocent people. I remember how she'd swung a shock baton around like it was some kind of performance. Just before she'd set it to max and shocked my parents to death. I hadn't been able to watch that part.

"But..."

I turn to Jay, saddened by the agony in his eyes. His face twitches and I know he's taking in the cuts, bruises and broken bits of my face. A timely reminder, if it were needed, of what the city's willing to do to everyone he cares about. He sighs.

"You're right. Guys, help me clear the barricade."

Pan objects loudly, but he ignores her. Darus, Kane and Sara move forward to clear the computers – they don't question his sudden change of heart. Neither do I, at least out loud. I don't believe for a moment that he'll actually let us fight. But he's allowing the barricade to be cleared, and that's the first step.

Finally the door is clear, and Darus presses his ear to it for a few minutes before declaring this particular piece of tunnel to be clear. I feel a small rush of relief at that. Despite the big talk, I don't want to fight anyone. Jay's right; I'm in no condition. But we have no choice.

Jay stares at the door for a moment, then sighs. That singular sigh seems to encompass all the horror we're feeling, all the fear of what we may yet face. But then he glances back at Pan, a warm smile playing on his lips.

"Pan. You'll look after everyone, won't you?"

She nods – but her face fills with sorrow as she does so.

"I understand. Of course."

"What?" I ask, "what's going on?"

He just looks at me; and in his face I see guilt and deception in equal measures. The sense of dread grows.

"Y-you've got to be kidding me," I blurt, "you have a plan, right?"

"Yes. The plan is to walk out there, and let them do whatever they want to."

"Why would you…"

"Listen, Noah. They're here to destroy the Clover. Do you really think they'll stop without finding the leader? Because they won't. Maybe if they have me, they won't need to search so much for Pan, Jensen and the others. Maybe if they have me, they'll leave."

Suddenly, my mouth is dry. Even more so than before, if it were possible. I can't let my brother – my only family – go to his death. Not like this. Not without a fight.

As he heads out into the tunnel, I follow on unsteady feet. It's dark out here and the place sets my heart racing, but I can't let him just leave.

"D-don't be stupid," I say weakly, "that won't work. We can fight our way out together. If we can just get to the bikes..."

He comes to a stop a few feet away and half-turns to face me.

"It won't change anything. You're in a state, and there's no way we can move Jensen right now. He needs medical attention, and we can't get to our supplies while we're stuck in here."

I bite back on my retort, shooting a concerned look back through the doorway, at the dazed figure on the bed. He's right. This is the only way to clear the Atrium of Guards. Until we can do that, there's no way to treat his leg properly.

"Then I'll come with you."

"That won't work. You and your friends might be the secret to unlocking this thing. You need to stay here, where it's safe. Maybe one day, you'll figure out a way to stop the Cull. But for now, you need to stay safe."

"But..."

"Look down, Noah."

I do as I'm told, and instantly regret it. Wirrow's corpse is still outside. His face is almost unrecognisable, the pain of his death still etched into every line. I stumble back, unreasonably afraid of him even now. Jay shakes his head sadly.

"That's what those weapons do to people. I can't let that happen to anyone else, least of all you."

"But I just..."

The sentence fizzles out in my throat. He's right. He's right about everything. This is the only thing that makes sense, the only way to make sure everyone stays safe and alive. Except him. He said so himself. If he goes out there, they'll kill him. Maybe immediately. Maybe later. Maybe Maynard will try to make a spectacle out of his death. But it doesn't matter how they do it; he won't survive long outside of this room. Something hot pricks at the back of my eyes.

"But... I just got you back."

A warm, heavy hand finds my shoulder, just like it did earlier – like it did when he'd smiled and told me how proud he was. He's got that same expression now, all love and sadness and goodbyes.

"The Clover collapsed before, you know. Back when Mom and Dad died. It needed a member of the Young family to bring it back, better and stronger than before. You might not like the name, but no matter what you say, you're still a Young. Even without me around, I know you can do this."

And then he smiles. He pulls his hand away, and for a moment I consider grabbing it. I could wrestle him back into the room. I consider screaming at him, threatening all kinds of horrible things if he dares to leave. I could cry. I could tell him he's abandoning me. There are things I could do to force him to stay.

I can't.

He turns towards back into the darkness. It's taking all his strength to keep up the illusion of confidence – and as much as it pains me, I can't break that.

"Stay safe, Ada."

His footsteps fade away.

CHAPTER THIRTY-THREE

It's another half hour before the Atrium and tunnels finally fall silent. When they do, there's little reaction from within our sombre group. Jensen's asleep now, oblivious to the horrors of today. At one point I consider slipping into the bed beside him and trying to get some sleep – but there's no point. I'm too tense.

It's been hard to keep from crying since Jay left. If I were alone I wouldn't hesitate. But when I think about what he said, I need to at least create an impression of strength. Pan's hands have been trembling for a while now, a sure sign she's on the brink of tears again. But when I gaze questioningly at her, she looks away. She doesn't want to be comforted.

We wait another full hour. Silence.

"Anyone else goin' stir crazy?" mutters Sara. She's stretched out on the floor, head in her hands, plucking through one of Jensen's magazines. For her, the chaos and fear has fallen away to boredom. Jay leaving means less than nothing; he's just a stranger who happened to leave the room. She doesn't quite understand what that means.

I close my eyes and let out a long, slow breath. The spinning has stopped, giving me chance to stand and move around. I touch my face gingerly; it's bruised and beaten, but that's all. Nothing I'm not already familiar with.

I tap open the door with a hesitant hand. The others watch nervously as I poke my head out into the hallway, but all seems quiet. The lights flicker slightly overhead, making me wonder if they did something to the electric – but it seems safe enough. I beckon for the others and we steadily make our way towards the Atrium. Along the way, I catch myself wincing at the signs of struggle in the tunnels; deep gouges in the floor, darkened splatters on the walls. I feel slightly sick at that, and catch myself hoping that the stains are something else. Anything else.

"I don't want to know what's up ahead," Darus mutters. I'm suddenly happy that Sara stayed back in the room with Jensen. She'd be mortified if she could see this. Pan walks silently by my side, her expression oddly neutral. Considering how much of a bleeding heart she is, I don't doubt this is hurting her. But she's the second in command. Now, it's up to her to guide us. Even though I'm physically leading, we both know she's in charge.

As we push out the rubble in the doorway, the Atrium opens up to us.

It's awful. Worse than I'd have thought. The ground is coated with layers of shattered glass that crunch under our feet as we step inside. Those same vile bloodstains litter the area, marking out corpse-like shapes on the tile. Oddly there are no bodies, Guard or otherwise – Maynard's men must have cleared it up. It makes me slightly sick to think about Nate's body and what they might have done with it – but at least it's a sure sign they've moved out.

I step up to the bridge, casting a cursory glance over the rest of the Atrium's platforms. The crop patch is destroyed, months of work burnt to a crisp. Any furniture, any shelters – they're all shattered, broken into splinters and strewn around the open space. My eyes are drawn to the garden below the bridge. The bushes are scorched there, too, and still smoking a little. A twinge of pain flickers through me when I see Mom and Dad's statue. It's been broken, too, as though by explosives. The once-mesmerising shapes are now just shards of ugly concrete sticking up from the ground. Jay's last vestige of normality, the last trace of his parents... gone just like that.

I stand motionless at the railing until the others eventually wander away. I feel no desire to chase them down or drag everyone together – even if I did, I'm not sure what I'd do.

I take a slow walk around the now-familiar areas of the Atrium. The kitchens. The open space where people spar. My precious crop patch. Ruined. Even Pan's room has been ransacked; the beds overturned, seemingly for no reason other than to inconvenience whoever might be left. Pan's precious fairy lights are broken on the floor, causing a weird churning in my gut. To destroy something so incredibly harmless, how much hatred must have been behind the Guards' orders?

Finally, I wander into Jay's office. It's surprisingly unharmed despite the carnage elsewhere, making me think that they may have missed this room. Perhaps they noticed us running out and assumed there would be nobody left, and that ransacking this particular room would be pointless. Either way, I don't question it as I sink into Jay's chair. It's red and leather and soft to the touch, and there's a comforting smoky scent to it. I glide one hand over the cherry wood desk, marvelling at how out of place it is in the dark, metallic tunnels. It serves as a momentary distraction from the grief building in my chest – but then I pull open the drawer.

Inside is a photo frame. In it is the same photo that Nate showed me after I first arrived here. Mom and Dad embrace in frame, kindly smiles dominating their faces. They're younger than I seem to remember; perhaps I've aged them in my mind. But it suddenly strikes me just how similar Jay is to Dad. They have the same nose, the same jaw.

I take a moment to focus on Mom. Nate had insisted I resembled her, that the similarities were uncanny – but at the time I hadn't seen it. Now? There's something there; the upward arch of our eyebrows, the thin lips. Details so tiny I'd likely never have noticed them if not for Jay. I'm starting to understand now.

I tenderly touch the glass with the tip of one finger, feelings welling in my chest. It's strange. I cried that day when I saw the clip of them, but since then I've not given them much thought. I suppose things have been a bit chaotic – not that that's a good excuse. I gaze into their eyes and wonder how they'd feel about me now. Jay insisted they'd be proud, but how could they? I just let their only son walk to his death.

In a flash I remember the look of pain in Mom's eyes on that video. The intense sorrow she'd felt at the thought of someone – anyone – being taken away. I consider how hard they fought after their child was taken. How much harder would they fight for the one that remained?

I inhale sharply and shake my head, trying to force the tears back. I don't want to cry. Crying will mean accepting he's gone. It's not fair. I'd been so happy. I'd finally found the strength to fight, only to have all the power snatched from beneath my fingers.

What do I have left?

Three mill workers who barely understand what's going on. One woman so distraught at losing her lover that she'll be unreachable for days. And one computer whiz with a shattered lower leg.

I'd told Jay I'd never felt lonely before I returned to the Mill. Who'd have guessed that, mere hours later, the same feeling would be building inside me again?

I throw the frame back in the drawer, hearing the glass shatter, and slam it shut.

When I finally return to Jensen's room, he's awake. He seems more alert than before, though he's still bedridden. I glance at his leg as I enter. Still bound, still bloody. I clutch the med kit from Jay's room a little closer to my chest. I don't know what good it will do, but I'll try.

Sara sees me approaching and shrugs.

"It's about time. I want to see what's goin' on, too."

"Sorry about that. You head out, I'll take care of things here."

She obeys immediately, relief apparent on her face. Clearly she felt uneasy at being here alone with Jensen, and I can hardly blame her; to her, he's still a perfect stranger. It can't be comfortable to be sitting in here with him.

As the door slides shut, an uneasy silence settles over us. I can feel Jensen's eyes on me, tracing the lines of my body. I heave a sigh and sit near the end of the bed, beckoning for him to move his leg closer.

I pull back the bandages, trying to hide my disgust. The wound is terrible. I'm sure there are several patches of bone showing through. But as I dab it with a clean cloth, he just sucks in a lungful of air and remains remarkably still. As I work his eyes are still fixed on me, but I ignore it. It's not that I don't want to talk to him. I just don't know what to say.

Finally, he speaks.

"You look awful."

It shouldn't strike me as funny that he said that. But it does. Perhaps it's because he'd say it any other time, if none of this had happened. Maybe it's just a hint of normality in the chaos of this day.

"You don't look great, yourself."

"I feel better now. Painkillers have kicked in."

"Good. There are more here when you need them."

He bites his lip as I finish wrapping his leg.

"Noah. Have you treated your face?"

I shrug. The cuts are clean enough and my nose has been pushed back into position - beyond that, I don't care.

"It doesn't matter."

"Yes, it does. Come here."

He reaches into the med kit, and presses some kind of cold pad onto my face. It smells vaguely medicinal and I doubt it's helping at all, but I let him do it. Whatever makes him feel better.

Already I'm wondering how much he remembers. How aware was he when the others dragged me into the room? When Jay left? When did he go from dazed to unconscious and back again?

There's something strange in the air as I close the lid on the med kit. I haven't moved from the foot of Jensen's bed. He's still sitting forward, his face only a few inches from mine. In any other situation, I'd back away and complain about the closeness. I'd feel discomfort squirming in my gut, base desire warring with everything I've ever been taught about intimacy.

Now? I don't care.

Several minutes pass in silence before he finally speaks again.

"He's gone, isn't he?"

"Which one?"

"Jay."

I nod.

"Did he leave willingly?"

Another nod.

"I thought so. Sounds like something that idiot would do."

"Hmm."

I look away, but he doesn't.

"Listen, Noah. I'm sorry."

"It's fine."

I intend for the words to seem nonchalant, full of bravery - but my voice cracks a little, betraying me. I clear my throat.

"It... it had to be done."

"I know. That doesn't make it easier, does it?"

He reaches out and places a hand on my knee. It's a tiny motion, meaningless for the most part, but when I meet his eyes, pure compassion smiles back at me. It's remarkable, the change between us. When Jensen first set eyes on me in the tunnels, he'd regarded me with as much respect as one might grant a spider, or a cockroach. Now, there's a tenderness in his face. An undeniable goodness. Something pulls me inexplicably towards him, - but I tear my eyes away. There's no point.

"I heard about Nate. Kind of. What happened?"

"Gunshot," I reply glumly, not wanting to relay the whole story again. His face settles into a grimace.

"I'm sorry. That must have been awful."

"Yeah. It was."

He clears his throat, then pulls his hand away.

"Have you checked to see what's happening now?"

"No. I think we're all a bit nervous about heading up to the surface."

"You don't have to. Just switch on my computer. I'll show you how to check the Feed - if they've got Jay, we can find out."

My stomach swirls at the thought. I'm not sure I want to know what's happened. But that's not fair to anyone, so I give a small nod.

"Okay. Let me get the others."

As I boot up the computer, I can feel several pairs of eyes on my back. The same trepidation I can feel in my chest is filling the room around me. Nobody really wants to see. Nobody really wants to know.

Jensen leans over, wincing from the pain of remaining upright. He taps at the screen, instructing me in a low voice. I obey without thought. I've never understood computers; feeling the metal and plastic shift and click under my fingers is alien, almost unpleasant. Any other day, I might have let Pan or even Sara do it. But they're both watching closely, barely concealed panic in their faces. I have to at least act like I know what I'm doing.

Darus leans by the door, his expression grim. He's supposed to be on lookout, ensuring no stray Guards find their way to us. It's unlikely, though, so his attention is mostly turned to us.

"What makes you think this will tell you anything?" he asks.

I swallow hard.

"The three leaders are awful, but Maynard in particular is an ego-maniac. It was her Guards who ransacked this place, so if Jay's still alive, she'll have him."

I glance back at him, mirroring his glumness.

"Trust me, if Maynard has him, she'll want the whole damn world to know."

He gives a small nod then turns away, looking back into the tunnels. There's nothing he can say to comfort anyone; all he's ever been able to do is be there for people, and right now, that's not going to help us.

For a brief moment, I catch Pan's eye. She's standing in the centre of the room, close to where Jay stood earlier. But unlike him, her hands aren't clenched into fists. They're hanging loosely at her sides, as though she's already given up. Her expression is somewhere between carefully indifferent and utterly bored. All the sweetness I've grown used to seeing from her has dissipated into nothing.

The computer finally flickers to life and I tap the buttons I'm told to tap. After a few minutes of Jensen's frustrated growls, the static on the screen comes clear. The Feed's showing live. A familiar face graces the screen.

Maynard stands atop the steps of her tower building, an arrogant smirk playing on her lips. Her face is so smug and self-assured that I find myself wishing I could punch that smarmy mouth of hers; but then the camera pans out and another figure comes into view.

My blood runs cold.

"Jay!"

Pan darts forward, pushing us aside and leaning into the screen. Seeing him alive seems to grant her a moment of clarity – but then she sees the state of him, and her face falls.

"Why…"

My brother is chained and bound, on his knees in a crowd of Guards. They sneer at him as he looks up at Maynard – but to his credit, he's keeping a calm exterior. I can tell he's fighting to keep his face neutral, looking fed up by the whole thing. There's rain coming down overhead, no doubt sending a chill across the patches of his skin that are still exposed, but he seems bored by it. I'm not sure if that's the best course of action, but he can't really be so calm. I know him better than that. He's likely just as scared as I am watching him.

Maynard's talking, brandishing a shock baton as though it's some kind of trophy. Every so often she glances at Jay, wiggling her eyebrows. Rubbing it in. Rubbing his nose in her victory. It's infuriating. There's a painful ringing in my ears; I shake my head hard and try to focus on her words.

"…following some traitors from the Mill, we were able to locate the Clover's headquarters. Buried underground, if you can believe it. They must have thought they were safe there."

She chuckles at her own sick joke.

"Well, we soon put an end to the whole operation. May I introduce to you, my citizens, Mister James Young. The so-called 'leader' of the treacherous group known as the Clover."

The Guards jeer loudly, nearly drowning out the crowd of citizens nearby. Several let out a half-hearted cheer, but even more remain utterly silent. Nobody boos. Nobody cries out in his defence. My gut clenches at the thought. People are still so afraid.

Jay doesn't react to any of Maynard's words. He's got the same look about him as he did when he left. He's sad and frightened, but defeated. He's resigned himself to his fate. Heat builds in my stomach at the thought. Anger. Hatred. I tear my eyes away from his face, instead focussing on Maynard.

She's pacing the length and breadth of the little platform, reaching out a long, skinny arm to touch the tall glass doors of the building. In the other hand, she twirls the baton. She's taking far too much joy from this moment. From tearing down the last vestige of freedom in her crumbling city.

"Nearly seventeen years ago, I was forced to do the same thing to poor James' parents. They, too, decided that their own personal wants should come over the needs and safety of everyone in Thorne."

The briefest flash of sympathy crosses her face.

"Don't mistake me for a villain, James. I'm not the bad guy here."

He simply glares.

"I mean it," she pushes on, "everyone else seems to understand. Why can't you?"

She addresses one of the many Hoverbots now, and I notice they all have cameras embedded into the front. This must be how she's airing her manic speech. As if on cue, Atlas beeps beside me.

"The world beyond our borders is in chaos," she explains, "war has overtaken everything outside of our safe bounds. We have immunity, our own brief reprieve, based purely on our self-sufficiency. Those beyond our walls won't seek to destroy us unless we prove that we can't manage ourselves. The Cull is just a symptom of that. A difficult truth."

She's plastered a serious expression on her face, but somehow it still sounds like taunting. I can feel the hair on the back of my neck standing on end, like a wild animal sensing a predator nearby.

"There are too many people. As unjust as it may seem, our choices are either the Cull, which is a humane system of control, or…"

She takes a moment to breathe in deeply, as though she's about to cry. I don't buy it.

"…or we can hand over all control to those outside our borders. If we do that, I won't be able to protect anyone. Not a single soul will be safe. That's why I need to do this, James. I can't have you speaking lies to the innocent folk of Thorne. I can't have you messing with their heads, filling them with untruths. I have to destroy you tonight, and I have to make it clear that traitors are to be dealt with swiftly in my city. Your comrades are stored within my private cells. Once you're out of the picture, I intend to make a public example out of each and every one of them."

Suddenly, I can't stand it anymore. I tap a button and the screen turns black, immersing the room in a silence that's punctuated only by Pan's unsteady breathing.

"Tonight, she said. She's going to kill him tonight."

I glance at the clock. It's just turned five. Assuming she'll be aiming for the evening, that doesn't leave much time. Much time to prepare the others for what will be coming. Much time to prepare myself for losing the only family I've ever known.

There's blind rage fluttering in my chest, burning through my veins. I hate this. I hate her.

"Is there nothing you can do?" asks Kane, turning his attention to me.

"I... I don't know. There aren't enough of us to fight back. People's perceptions are going to be shaken, too. I don't know if we'll be able to rebuild."

"Maybe if we left Thorne? She said there are people out there. Maybe they can help."

It's Jensen who replies, his voice hard.

"That won't work."

"It won't?"

"No. A few years back, we ventured out on a hunch. We had a theory that the whole 'war' story might have been a lie concocted by Maynard to keep people down. It wasn't. We went to the next city over, according to some old maps... but when we reached the site, there was nothing but a crater. Still smoking, but it couldn't have been recent."

"So the war's still going on?"

"No. I hacked into their scanners a while back - they've not traced any activity for over a decade. The war's over. Has been for years. They just haven't told anyone."

"Why not?" I ask.

"It could be a way to keep people scared. It could be that the system relies too heavily on the Cull and the Mill to keep the city afloat. I don't know. But she's lying through her teeth every time she mentions the 'danger beyond our borders'."

I click my tongue.

"So we need to do this on our own. Without any citizens, any outsiders. Just the six of us."

Until now, I'd been working on the basis that there was something I could do. Some way that I could stop this, or even just delay it. Some idea that would pick at the weak spots in Maynard's plan. But there's nothing. It's starting to dawn on me just how impossible this task is. My hands tighten on the edge of my seat.

"So it's useless?" Kane asks, and his face is a picture of sympathy. He may not understand the way things work here, but he's not stupid. He can read the look of defeat on my face. He knows there's no way out of this. Jensen chews his lip for a moment, then nods.

"It... looks that way."

There's a sudden crash from behind us - I whip round just in time to see Pan darting from the room. One hand is clapped over her face to keep us from seeing the tears in her eyes, but she's always been bad at faking. Sorrow flits through me and suddenly I'm on my feet, chasing her down.

"Pan!"

She ignores me altogether, instead racing into the Atrium. She runs down the steps, towards the little underground river and garden. This time, I hesitate to follow her. It's not like her to reject company or comfort. Maybe I shouldn't force myself on her.

But then I notice rain pouring from the hole in the ceiling and realise I can't leave her. She'll catch her death of cold if I let her hide out here. For a brief moment, I ponder my next action. She'll be crying, no doubt about that. I don't blame her. I would cry, too, if I were her. It's all I can do to bite back on my own tears.

I find Pan standing motionless by the shattered statue in the garden. She's drenched through entirely, her normal shock of red hair now a burgundy mess plastered to her forehead. She doesn't look up as I approach; perhaps she doesn't hear my footsteps in the downpour.
She's crying. Maybe she thinks I won't notice her tears if her face is already soaked. But there's no mistaking her reaction. For the briefest of moments, she reminds me of Nel. I remember that night in the bunker, how she'd wept about the cows. They'd reminded her, oddly, of the importance of a family she couldn't even remember. At the time I'd been slightly irritated by her reaction. I'd wanted to scold her and tell her she was being stupid. But I'd been able to rein myself in just enough to show a sliver of compassion.
"I wish you'd never come here."
Pan's voice is measured, deceptively calm. She glances at me.
"If you hadn't come here, things would be okay. We wouldn't have taken this so far."
Her eyes narrow. Her mouth twists into an uncharacteristic scowl.
"If you'd just stayed at that Farm, nothing would have ever changed. This place would still be home. Nate would still be alive. And Jay... he wouldn't be about to die."
She inhales deeply.
"Why couldn't you have just stayed dead?"
Her words hurt; but what she's saying is true. If these words were coming from anyone else, I'd likely be distraught. But instead, they glance off me. It's true that Jay would still be safe if I hadn't come here - or if I'd done any number of other things to avoid this situation. If I hadn't come here, Nate would still be pacing the Atrium with a

broad smile on his face. But there'll be time to hate myself for that later.

I step into the downpour and place a hesitant hand on her shoulder.

For a brief moment, we stare at one another. Surprisingly, I'm not angry. Instead, I'm sad. Pan never had much before she met Jay. He was the one who gave her a home. In her eyes, he's the embodiment of everything good in the world - and he's been snatched away. It might not have been my doing, but I'm a convenient fall guy. I've done just enough to justify her hatred of me.

But then her face falls, and she takes a pointed step back. Recognition glimmers in her eyes as she picks up on the bits of my face that resemble his, the broad shoulders, the dusty eyes. In a moment, she seems to remember who I am. Her face drops as she realises what she said.

"I'm sorry... I... I didn't mean..."

She buries her face in her hands and lets out a pained sob.

I think of Nel again. How my words had done nothing to help when she was hurt. At the time, I'd reached out across our bunks to hold her hand - a bold move considering the circumstances. Just like when I was in tears on Darus' boat and he dared to hold out his arms to me. He couldn't fix my problems. Couldn't even start. But he knew enough to just be there.

Pan watches as I unfold my arms, holding them out to her.

"W-what?"

"Come on."

I beckon her forward, calling her into the embrace, but she seems hesitant.

"But I just said... that was awful."

I laugh.

"I got my nose broken earlier today. Nothing hurts more than that. Now come on."

She doesn't seem to believe me, but then her chest swells and her eyes shine with more tears. She takes a step forward and throws herself into my arms, where I pull her even closer. She buries her face in my shoulder. Her body is racked with sobs and I tighten my grip, wishing I could squeeze hard enough to get rid of her pain.

That twinge of anger I'd felt earlier is growing now. How dare they? How dare they attack us, kill Nate, take Jay away, hurt her like this? I allow my eyes to slide shut for a moment, and ask myself a question.

Am I going to let them get away with it?

My fingers tighten around her.

"It's okay," I breathe, "I promise I'll bring him home."

It's with a strange sense of ferocity that I burst into Jensen's room. Pan enters meekly behind me, a sheepish look on her face - but everyone's too distracted by my entrance to notice her slipping through the door. Jensen stares.

"Noah? What's going on?"

"Jensen, I need your help. We're going to get him back."

He stares. I can feel the eyes of the others settling on my back, too, and wonder if they think I've gone mad.

"Don't be stupid," he warns, "I want to get him back as much as anyone, but we don't have the manpower."

"We don't need manpower."

"Do you have a plan?" he asks disbelievingly.

I hesitate.

"Not... exactly."

"Well, let's break it down. We need to save Jay, but he's surrounded by Guards and Maynard, so we need manpower to try and break him out."

My gut squirms.

"Not manpower. Firepower."

"You mean the incendiary gun? I suppose that could work... but they could just hold the others at ransom to stop us acting."

"Then you guys need to break in and let them out. I'll take the gun and cause a distraction."

Pan steps up beside me.

"Are you sure about this?"

I shrug.

"You'll need someone who can force their way in. Someone who has a reputation for not respecting lives. I'm your girl. Once Maynard realises who I am and what I did to her Guards, she'll be plenty distracted. It'll allow you guys chance to save the others. Then, you can storm the area and pluck Jay out of there."

Her face creases with concern.

"What about you?"

"I'll deal with it. Maynard's not much of a threat on her own - hopefully that ego of hers will keep her from setting the Guards on me."

Jensen frowns.

"But as long as she has that shock baton, she is a threat. All it takes is one hit."

Right. Just like Wirrow said. Maynard declared a state of emergency. Their network's set to a lethal level - I was lucky to avoid the blow from his shock baton in that cramped tunnel. I don't know if I can do that again when faced with dozens of them. Maynard's in particular is going to be set at a frightening level, since she intends to kill Jay with it.

Wait. Wirrow. What were his exact words?

I step out into the tunnel and collect the abandoned baton from beside Wirrow's motionless form. I turn it over in my hands, the Guard's final words echoing in my head.

A strange thought occurs to me - and the idea is so stupid, so ridiculous, that I can feel a trace of excitement in my chest.

CHAPTER THIRTY-FOUR

The others take off before me, riding off on some of the more well-hidden bikes. How the Guards didn't find them is beyond me, but I don't bother to question it as I straddle a particularly glossy machine. Idly, I run a hand over the metallic surface, revelling in the tiny sparks of static that bounce off it. The electricity matches the feeling under my skin. I tug on the earpiece Jensen gave me and twist the dial on the side; after a few moments of crackling, the line comes clear.

"Guys, can you hear me?"

It's Jensen that replies.

"Loud and clear."

His voice echoes strangely, and there's a strain at the end of each word. I realise it's because we left him sitting upright, parked awkwardly in front of his computer. He's in no fit state to be moving around, but we need him. The background is filled with the sound of tapping keys.

"How is it going?" I ask as I venture out into the alleyway. The streets are deathly quiet tonight. Everyone's watching to see what happens.

"It's a tough system," he replies, "but I think I've got it. If you can give me fifteen minutes, twenty tops, I can get it done."

My chest tightens at that. I'm only ten minutes away.

"Keep me updated. You can watch through the Feed, right? Try to gauge the situation. Pan?"

"Yeah?" comes her breathless reply. She's terrified, and I understand why. She's leading three clueless individuals into a practical warzone. I don't envy the job - until I think about what I'm going to do.

"Let me know when you reach the back of the building," I tell her. For a moment, I'm surprised by the level of control in my own voice, the degree of authority there. If I'd spoken like this even a week ago, I'd have expected to be laughed from the room. But now? Remarkably, the others are not just listening, but obeying, too. Pan promises to let me know what's going on - and then I hear Kane's voice on the line. It's lower than it was when we first met, a sure sign he's grown up since then. The thought makes me sad, but I push the feeling aside and listen to the words.

"Are you sure about this, Noah?"

I swallow hard. No.

"Absolutely. It's the best plan we've got."

That seems to be our usual course of action. We don't always have a good plan. But we always go with the best we've got and usually we wriggle out with minimal damage. I have a terrible feeling that won't happen this time, but right now, I have to take charge. Jensen's in no state to do so, and even now I can hear a familiar crack in Pan's voice. Like she might burst into tears any moment. Even though I'm scared half to death and my heart is hammering in my chest, I need to at least seem like I can handle this.

I need to try.

I rev the bike and take off at top speed down the street. I'm surprised just how easily I'm remaining upright on this thing; it's nothing like the ATVs back at the Mill. Luckily, adrenaline seems to be forcing me to go faster than I'd like, and my balance is oddly working out.

I glance around the streets as I go. People line the streets, just as they always do – but they don't seem drunk and dazed tonight. Instead their eyes are drawn towards the massive screens projected onto nearby buildings. I don't need to look at them to know what they're showing. Besides, I'm worried that my resolve will break if I'm forced to look at my brother's face again. Still, it's comforting to see how many people are drawn to the chaos at Maynard's headquarters. I wonder how many of these people would fight back if given half a chance. Maybe it's time to test that.

I turn a corner and suddenly I'm on that same road again, the one with the fairy lights. Maybe it wasn't set up for a parade, after all. Once again I'm tempted to reach up and hold my fingertips up to the glowing orbs overhead, but I just speed up instead.

If this ridiculous plan works, I'll have all the time in the world to look at lights.

It's still raining. The tyres of the bike catch the water and sends it in a wide spray behind me. The constant motion does little to calm my racing heart, so I reluctantly turn my head towards the nearest screen. Maynard's still talking – but with every step she nears him, and with every word her grip seems to tighten on the shock baton in her hand.

Hold on. I'm nearly there.

I turn the corner to Maynard's building and run into a crowd of Guards – but I expect them. They're not looking my way, but I flick on the lights and cup one hand around my mouth.

"Move unless you want to get run over!"

The reaction is immediate; they fall over one another to get out of the way and I'm able to drive through the clear space. As I do so, my gaze is fixed on the top of the steps.

Maynard still hasn't noticed me. Still hasn't noticed the chaos going on below. Good.

"Guys," I shout into my earpiece, "this is it!"

Above me, Maynard pulls back her arm. There's a broad, vile grin on her face as she swings the baton down.

I kick her arm away when it's about three inches from his face. Maynard gasps, but before she can react I twist and punch her aside. In an instant, the world around me seems to slow; the Guards turn their attention towards me, and Maynard crumples into the concrete at my feet. When she looks up, I'm pleased to see one of her teeth has fallen out.

Behind me, Jay sighs. His relief is apparent – but it's not over yet. Maynard's scrambling to her feet now, fixing me with a stern gaze.

"Seriously?" she barks, "I knew we'd missed some people from the raid, but I didn't think for a moment that anyone would be stupid enough to actually try a rescue!"

I don't respond; I'm not sure she would care anyway. Pan and Jensen are both yelling in my ear, too loud and panicked to make much sense at all. I grab the earpiece and rip it off, throwing it aside in frustration and lowering my hood.

"Fuck, that thing's annoying."

In an instant, all eyes settle on me. It's the same sense of bizarre intrigue that every citizen has when they see me – only now, it's tenfold because I'm committing a crime right before their eyes.

Jay growls behind me.

"Noah! Why did you come here? I told you to stay safe! Why would you come out here?"

A growl escapes my throat.

"Because you didn't say goodbye. You called me by the wrong name. Because you're an idiot and I care about you! Reason enough for you?"

He falls silent at that, though I can still hear his heavy breathing. There's no way to respond to that little outburst. I'm not about to say something soppy and heartfelt in front of the whole city. My skin crawls at the thought.

Maynard reaches up and wipes a little blood from her chin. It's remarkable how quickly she's bounced back – I'd expected that punch to knock her out cold, at least for a minute or two. But no. She's upright again, pacing the length of the platform in her skyscraper heels. Cold, merciless eyes give me the once-over.

"A Millchild? Huh. I'd known James had some in his ranks, but I certainly didn't think they would be so reckless as to try something like this. But wait..."

Her eyes narrow, and I can almost see the wheels turning in her head as she tries to place my face.

"You seem familiar," she eventually says. There's a strange edge to her voice as she speaks – she doesn't know whether to try to frighten me off, or whether she herself should be frightened. I take advantage of her confusion and plaster an arrogant smirk on my face. I even add a tiny, mocking bow.

"I'm honoured you remember me. You must have seen me on the videos where I took down your helicopters."

Her faces folds at that, creasing with fury. If it were anyone else, I'd feel sympathetic. I'd think she was angry at the lives lost and the injuries incurred that day. But that's not it. As far as she's concerned, those men were her property. And I took them away from her.

"Oh, you're that Millchild. One of my men insisted that he'd seen you in the rubble. I've been wanting to meet you since that day."

She shoots a curious glance at Jay, but his expression is unreadable. He's not giving her any clues. Not letting on to who I am, or what relevance my presence here has. When I glance his way, he shoots me a knowing look. The choice is mine.

But then Maynard laughs.

"A little young for you, isn't she James? Not to mention that face. Nose is a little bent, don't you think? Though I suppose you probably don't have very high standards for your concubines."

Concubines? Yuck. My skin crawls at the thought, and my face settles into a scowl.

"Insulted by that, are we?" she scoffs, "then clear things up, Millchild. Who the hell are you and why are you here, tracking mud in my precious town?"

I bite my lip. She's taking this a little too well, a little too much in stride. I'd expected rage, confusion and fear - not suave arrogance. My plan was to distract her, to give the others chance to break out. I'd expected at least a twinge of fear. Instead, she meets my gaze directly. And despite my best efforts, I'm the one who's unnerved.

This is the woman who ordered her Guards to snatch me away. The woman who wiped my memory and put me to work against my will. It's Maynard who executed my parents for daring to speak against her - and it's Maynard who's staring me down now, all arrogance and superiority. I look for any trace of regret in her eyes, any sign that she's not as bad as she seems. Nothing.

I swallow hard. It doesn't matter. Just like with Wirrow, I have to try. I can hear Jay's laboured breathing from behind me. He's terrified. This must be his worst nightmare, to be bound and tortured by the same person who murdered his parents. I can't let this slide.

So I take a deep breath and walk towards Maynard, fixing my gaze on hers.

"I'm upset, Maynard. I'd have thought you'd remember me."

"Am I supposed to?"

"You should. After all we've been through. Look again, tell me what you see."

She does as she's told, casting a cursory glance over my body, but there's no hint of recognition on her face. She doesn't know who I am. Surprisingly, I'm a little hurt by that. You can't destroy a person's life and not be able to recognise them afterward.

"Come on," I urge, "you're supposed to be better than this. How could you forget me so easily?"

"I don't remember every mudhorse that steps foot in my town."

I step closer, until our noses are only a few inches apart. Guards ripple around us, moving closer - but to my surprise, she signals for them to back up. She's curious. She wants to know who I am. And that means the distraction is working.

When I speak again, I fight to keep my voice low. I want Maynard to hear the truth; but just her.

"Look at him."

"Who?"

"You know damn well who. Look at him."

She does as she's told, fixing Jay in her sights. I try to inject just a little of my anger into my voice when I next speak - but in truth, it's taking all I have not to grab her by the throat and hurl her down her own damn steps. I step a little closer and breathe in her ear.

"Do you see the resemblance?"

Her eyes widen, and in that moment I know she recognises me. Maynard stumbles backward and stares, taking in all the details of my face that she hadn't noticed before. The eyes. The brows. Even the curve of my jaw, so similar it hurts. For a brief moment, I see all the fear and shame I had wanted to see. It dominates her face, and I wonder if this is the first time she's been faced with the result of her own cruelty.

"Y-you're not..."

She steps back again, panic in her beady eyes. She knows who I am now, but she doesn't know how to deal with me. In a world controlled by her, I'm a loose cannon. A wild card.

"You can't be," she eventually manages, "the chances of that..."

"...Are surprisingly high," I tell her, "you'd be surprised the lengths people will go to for the truth. You'd also be surprised by the reaction you'd get, being told your whole life was a lie."

She grunts.

"Y-you're lying. He called you Noah. This is some kind of trick from the treacherous Clover."

"No trick," I smile, "Noah is my Mill name. As much as I like Ada, I do rather prefer the name I grew up with. Besides, it's not like my parents are around to be bothered by it. Thanks to you."

There it is. The little twinge of anger breaking into her calm, like a crack in an eggshell. Breaking the perfection of her pale face.

"Nonsense! Listen to me, whatever they've told you, it's not true. It's impossible."

If it were anyone else, I might actually consider listening. I've never been totally convinced that Jay and the others were the heroes; there are too many flaws worth considering, too many weaknesses to be addressed. But gazing into the face of the woman who's killed before - willingly, and without reason - I don't believe a word she says.

So instead, I laugh. The sound echoes strangely around us, sending nervous shudders through the Guard. I must seem crazy right now. So why is nobody stopping me?

"Why are you laughing?" she cries, "you have no way to prove these ridiculous claims!"

"I'm all the evidence you need. Blood and bone, right in front of you. And as long as I'm breathing, Maynard, you'll always be on the losing side."

She stares. Of course, I could tell her about the database. I could tell her that I've proven my identity twice over. I could let her know about the other Mill workers, and how they also showed up on Jensen's computer mere minutes ago. The truth hangs on the tip of my tongue, tempting me to tell Maynard everything. But I can't. I want to give her a chance.

At the Mill, I never questioned anything. It wasn't that I wanted bad things to happen; I just didn't realise that they were bad. I allowed the Guards to drag Kane away. I allowed Nel to cry in the night. I allowed hundreds of people to suffer for years on end because I was too afraid to question the way things were. Maybe Maynard's the same.

The Cull has been going on for much longer than she's been alive. If the rules were already in place when she adopted her role, maybe she carried on in that vein because there was no other way. But now - knowing there's no way out - she might start to ask.

"You have a choice," I whisper, "tell them the truth. You can still save face if you do it now."

Her lips part, and I half-expect her to curse me out - but instead, she extends a shaky hand. Relief floods through me. Maybe she's willing to listen.

"Fine," she replies, "have it your way."

"I knew you weren't totally unreasonable."

I try to smile brightly as I reach out and grasp her hand in mine. I hadn't expected this would be so easy. I'd expected fist fights with every available Guard until the others succeeded. But maybe that won't be necessary. Maybe, for once, I can use words to solve a problem. Maybe nobody else has to die.

But then her hand locks around my wrist, and her face twists into a manic smile.

"As long as you're still breathing... right?"

Before I can move she's pulled out the baton, flicking a button on its side - electricity jumps from its surface, filling the air between us with an intense heat. Just like before. Just like Wirrow.

She swings it toward me and I move instinctively, blocking the baton with my left arm. Nate's gauntlet does little to defend me from the shock - but I grasp at Maynard's arm and we both soar backwards.

"Noah!"

Pain prickles through me as I lay sprawled on the floor at Jay's feet. I can hear him above me, fear apparent in his voice. From the panic around me, it's only been a matter of seconds since I turned the baton on one of Thorne's leaders.

I take a deep, rattling breath. There's a terrible pain in my wrist, but it's fading fast. In a matter of moments I'm able to roll over onto my front, lifting myself up onto my elbows. Maynard sits in a frazzled heap on the ground, surrounded by concerned Guards. Her black hair stands on end and her eyes are bloodshot, but she seems otherwise okay.

By all rights, she should be dead.

By all rights, I should be too.

Jay stares at me.

"H-how did you..."

I glance at my arm. The second gauntlet Nate made for me has fared better than the first, but it's still destroyed. There's a deep scar in the metal where it's melted, and as I tug it off, the rubber on the bottom sticks to my skin a little. I rub at the red patch of skin and sigh.

"Damn, Jensen was right. That does hurt."

Jay stares disbelievingly for a moment, his jaw hanging. It's almost laughable; or at least, it would be, if it weren't so frightening. I suppose that, in his eyes, I just shrugged off the shock of a lethal attack. But he doesn't know. Of course he doesn't. I draw my lips back into what I hope is a reassuring smile.

"It's okay. Jensen worked his magic. They won't... they can't kill anymore."

A moment later, Jay mirrors my smile back at me. Realisation is dawning on his face; realisation that we haven't just jumped in without a plan. I know what I'm doing.

Back in the tunnel, Wirrow had warned me. Maynard had declared a state of emergency – and the shock weapon database had been updated. Whether they'd liked it or not, every baton had been set to lethal. A necessary evil, no doubt; but that meant there was a master control. Where there's a master control, there's a computer. And where there's a computer, Jensen can work miracles.

I stand again, a little more easily this time. Knowing that our plan is working, even in the tiniest way, is all I need to fill my chest with confidence. I draw myself up to my full height and pull my shoulders back. For once, I don't feel out of place in this body. I feel strong. Intimidating.

And as Maynard clambers to her feet again, that's exactly what the look in her eye tells me. She's scared. Scared that I would dare to go up against her. Scared that I would turn her own weapon back on her. Absolutely terrified that I managed to survive.

Her hands shake as she stares me down. Any trace of her sizeable ego has faded away, leaving her looking exactly like what she is; a frightened, angry, somewhat dishevelled maniac. Knowing what's coming next, I pull up the corners of my lips. A confident smile can only help to make her look less sane in comparison.

"What did you do?"

Her voice is high-pitched now, tinged with pain. I get the feeling she's never been on the receiving end of a shock before. It's frazzled her nerves. She doesn't wait for me to answer. I don't think any reply I could give would suffice, anyway. She waves at the Guards around her, pointing at me wildly.

"Get this thing out of my sight! Now!"

They start forward, but stop about a half-step in. Slowly, everyone's eyes sink down to my hand. There's a strange sense of power filling me as everyone realises I've plucked the incendiary gun from my belt – and that power only grows as I aim it directly into the sky.

"What are you doing?" hisses Jay. His breathing is even heavier now. For him, not being able to help is pure torture. I wish I could tell him to hold on. That it'll be over soon.

"Maynard."

My voice rings out across the silence, loud and clear and oddly captivating. It doesn't sound like me. There's too much sanity, too much authority. This is the voice of someone who knows what they're doing; someone who's entirely unafraid.

She doesn't respond – she just shoots daggers in my direction. If looks could kill.

"I didn't come here to hurt anyone," I explain, "not even you. But I gave you a chance. I turned off the shock batons so I could explain. You could have told everyone the truth and ended this calmly, but you didn't. Now, I'm forced to play my hand."

I gesture towards the gun in my hand, trying to ignore the way my fingers shake against the trigger.

"Unlock the code on Jay's restraints. Now. Or I'll do it."

A hint of that smugness reappears on Maynard's face – but only for a moment.

"If you pull that trigger, nothing will happen. You're aiming at the sky, Millchild."

I smirk.

"You always tell the people of Thorne that there's danger outside our borders. That one disaster could summon a whole army to our doorstep. If that's true, then this incendiary shell will draw them just fine. Unless, of course, you weren't telling the truth about the big, bad war?"

For a moment, we meet one another's eyes. I can tell she's mad; there's barely-concealed fury in her eyes. She's looking for a chance, even a half-second opportunity to send her Guards at me. Her bloodlust is so strong it's almost palpable. But then her eyes lift to the gun in my hand, and she grimaces. She'll do anything to keep up her lies.

"Unlock it," she mutters.

They release Jay and he steps up behind me, one strong hand resting on my shoulder. His chest is swollen with pride; but I can tell he has his doubts. I suppose it makes sense. We're still trapped, after all. Still vastly outnumbered.

He takes the gun from me and holds it up even higher. This is one hell of a bluff, even for us. Still, I've done my job. I've got Jay out of his binds. I've distracted Maynard. Jensen's done his part, too. So where are Pan and the others?

"I sure hope you have a plan," Jay breathes. I don't respond. Instead I let my eyes slide shut and listen to the death-like silence that's fallen over Thorne. Every citizen is watching with baited breath, still clueless as to the true nature of this scene. Waiting to know what's going on. Waiting to find out what to do.

Now would be a great time for the cavalry to arrive.

CHAPTER THIRTY-FIVE

The sound starts out quiet at first, a dull roar that blends into the sound of the wind and rain. But then it begins to build, a strong, repeating sound - like the chanting of a hundred furious voices in perfect unison. I quickly realise that's exactly what it is. Pan hasn't just rescued the others. She's whipped them up into a fury. She's given them words to scream into the chaos. She has - single-handedly - brought the Clover back from the brink.

And suddenly they're among us, racing up through the glass windows of the building. For a brief moment, the world is awash with shattered glass and excited screams; and then there are people surrounding me, and their faces and voices are wonderfully familiar.

Jay turns to look at me, and his face is the most familiar of all. A pair of hands find me in the crowd, and Pan's beaming face is all I can see.

"We did it!" she cries, throwing both hands over her head. Jay's face breaks into a smile and he plants a kiss on her head – but the joy in my stomach vanishes.

We're not done yet.

I turn back to Maynard with a heavy heart. Her Guards have been pulled away into the crowd, or have fled from the sheer numbers. More will be arriving shortly to come to her aid, but for the moment, she's alone.

She stands in the broken glass of her own building, arms hanging limply at her side. Her face is a picture of defeat; but when she looks at me, there's nothing but hatred there. She's lost the battle, but as far as she's concerned, the war is yet to come.

I realise with a start that she's right. Even if we worm our way into the shadows tonight, the Cull will still happen next week. And we'll have to keep on fighting it, every year until something finally changes. The idea both saddens and sickens me. In a matter of minutes we can be gone from her sight, and her Guards will return in full force. What then? What changes?

I pluck at Jay's sleeve.

"W-what?"

"Here."

I lean down and collect the now-broken gauntlet from the ground. I push it into his hand and he obeys immediately, fastening it around his own arm just like I did.

"What's this for?"

"We need to do this now," I say, my voice hard, "before the Guards get here."

"Do what?"

I pluck the earpiece from the floor and jam it on. It's twisted a little in the chaos, but after a moment of static, it comes clear.

"Jensen? Do you hear me?"

"Hell yeah, I do. Nice going out there!"

I turn towards the building. Maynard's ego has paid off. There's a large, holographic screen projected up there, too, bathing the entire building in blue light. I take a deep breath. This had better work.

"Put up all the evidence on the Feed. All the DNA matches, all the info on the war."

"Everything?"

"Everything. And do it now."

"On it."

When I pull the earpiece off, Jay's still watching me.

"What's the plan?" he asks, "what do you need me to do?"

A smile plays on my lips. This is dangerous. Perhaps we shouldn't do this. But then I catch Maynard's eye again, and my decision is made.

"You're going to address the whole city. You're going to tell them the truth."

He doesn't seem convinced, but I smile. Somehow, I know this is going to work. One speech, one explanation, and Jay will win them over. He's fought for these people for sixteen years - they won't fail him now. And while the shock batons are harmless and the Guards don't pose much of a risk, it's the best time to rise up. This will work. It has to.

"Trust me. You can do this."

As Jay steps forward, a solemn silence falls over Thorne. Even the sound of distant traffic seems to fall away into nothing. He eyes the multitude of Hoverbots around him, perhaps nervous about their closeness - but then his eyes settle on a green one floating nearby and he smirks.

"Is that Atlas?"

"I had it hiding nearby. It'll keep filming no matter what," I mutter, "you've probably only got a few minutes before more Guards arrive, though, so make it count."

I push him a little further forward, something warm stirring in my chest.

"This is what you wanted, right? Do it."

For a brief moment, I see fear in his eyes. I get it; for sixteen years, he's fought to help these people and now he's asking them to help themselves. Jensen's made it easier than ever, but it's still down to them. But if anyone can convince them, it's Jay. It has to be him.

But then he turns to the crowd still gathered around him, and glances up at Atlas, who's still circling.

"You know me. Even if sometimes, you wish you didn't. I understand being frightened of the leaders and their brutish Guard – but the time has come to say no."

As he launches into his tirade, Pan steps up beside him. The pain is gone from her eyes now; her face is once more filled with joy as she loops her arm through his. The other members of the Clover stand by with quiet confidence. They don't doubt him, either.

In the moment of reverence, I realise that nobody's watching Maynard. She's still standing in the broken remains of the glass doors, tiny cuts covering her arms. Along with the missing tooth and frazzled hair, she looks insane.

As I walk up to her, she meets my gaze with vitriol.

"You stupid girl."

Her voice is weak and afraid – perhaps she thinks I'm going to kill her. I must admit, I'm tempted.

"Stupid?" I chuckle, "I had a fantastic education at the Mill."

"Don't you understand anything? How do you plan on fixing this?"

"What?"

"If your precious leader manages to overthrow my Guard... then what? You have nearly a billion people in the city alone, and about a quarter of that number at the Mill. You bring those people back, you'll be throwing us into chaos."

For once, it seems like she believes what she's saying. She's even ignoring Jay's ongoing speech, instead staring me down with distraught eyes.

"Where will you home those millions? Who will generate power and grow food and keep Thorne alive? These people can't provide for themselves."

That's it, then. She knew the war was over; but she couldn't find a way out of her situation. She thinks there's no way for us to survive without the Mill – and for a moment, I worry there isn't.

But then someone strides past. Darus, a confident smile on his face as he steps a little closer to hear Jay talk. Darus was never a slave. He never hated where he was. Even now, he plans to go home someday. And I don't plan to leave the Mill behind forever, either.

So I just laugh.

"You need to have a little faith, Maynard. The people around here are stronger than you give them credit for. We'll find a way. I'll work the farmland myself if I have to."

And I mean it. As she sinks back and lowers her head in defeat, I'm surprisingly unafraid. I will go back. I will chop wood and work fields, for as long as it takes. I'll fish and dig and even scrape my way through the mines to help this city.

But this time, it'll be my choice.

CHAPTER THIRTY-SIX

"Are you sure about this?"

Pan brushes a lock of hair from my eyes.

We're standing at the edge of Thorne, where the chain-link fence used to be. We tore it down on the first day, mere hours after Jay's stirring speech to the masses. At the time, I'd been too amazed to do much more than sit in awe as he addressed them. I don't even remember his exact words – but it doesn't matter. All that matters is how the whole city had burst into life minutes later. Reports had come flooding in about people tackling Guards. Tying them up. Taking whatever weapons they had. All in all, the whole thing lasted less than two days. The Guards had been surprisingly unprepared for any kind of uprising, which I suppose is a testament to Maynard's level of control. Not everybody had immediately agreed with the choice to overthrow the leaders, but it doesn't matter. Thorne's in good hands now. The leaders sit in cells far cushier than they deserve, awaiting trial. Some call for their execution.

Others sow empathy, asking for their release. Still others think they should be on the receiving end of a memory injection - a 'fresh start' of their own. Nobody's asked what I think yet, but personally, I think a few years chopping wood would do wonders.

I glance up at Atlas. It's hovering overhead, ready to follow me the whole way. Jensen linked it up to Atticus, right? I should be able to get updates pretty easily.

"Yeah," I finally reply, "supplies are dwindling fast as more Mill workers are brought in. I did volunteer to go and help out at the farm. Besides, Jay needs to go and oversee the workers being shipped across, so it makes sense for us to head out together. I'll help him out at the Dock and then carry on the rest of the way alone."

"What a shame. We need you here, too."

She smiles; and the sight is marvellous. It's so good to see the life returning to her face. After the chaos that we've been through, I'd been scared she might never smile again.

The others stand behind her. I move to address them, but stop short. It's not acceptable to use their old names anymore. Kane is Shaun. Darus is Michael. Sara is Daisy. Such simple names that don't seem to link to all the chaos we went through to find them. All three are still in awe at the sights and sounds of the city. To them, this is all new. All incredible.

But then Kane - Shaun - glances my way, and I feel like all might finally be forgiven. Jensen leans unsteadily on him. He looks so strange now, with his hair trimmed and his leg mostly healed. It helps that he was seen by an actual doctor. When he smiles, his face is round and healthy. More alive than ever.

"Hey, I hope it's okay but I... made this for you," Jensen says, "for the journey. Just in case."

He digs in his rucksack for a moment before passing me a small, metal object. I stare at it for a moment. Sleek metal, thick rubber, and a number of straps form a familiar object – and immediately, I feel warmth flickering in my chest.

"A new gauntlet."

"Yep. I found Nate's old designs. I'm not as good with my hands as he is, but…"

I lock the little device over my arm. It's strangely comforting to have it on, like a little sliver of home. Like I'm carrying Nate with me. We've still not found the bodies of those killed in the initial chaos, but we've held funerals anyway. I'd never been to one before. It was actually somewhat comforting to say goodbye – especially as I didn't get to say it in time.

Jensen smiles broadly.

"You seem happy with it. I don't know how durable it'll be, though."

"I'll tell you myself when I come back in a few weeks."

"Alright," he teases, "as long as I still get to take you out for that drink."

Discomfort squirms in me. He's been asking about that for a while now, and each time something seems to come up. I still don't have much interest in romance – I haven't changed all that much – but as I meet those dark eyes in that handsome, intelligent face, I can't bring myself to say no. A smile plays on my lips.

"That sounds nice."

With that I turn away from Thorne, straddling my bike. Jay sits beside me, already on his – but as I roll up beside him, he shoots me a curious look.

"What was that about?"

I roll my eyes.

"Don't even start with me, Jay. It's not like I'm marrying the guy."

"Hmm. Have you thought about what's going to happen once we get there?"

I consider this. All he's doing is overseeing the receipt of Mill workers from the docks. We don't really have to get involved; we just have to be patient and understanding, and answer questions where we can. We're finally bringing the Mill workers back. Several thousand citizens are working to set up places to live and clearing farmland around the city; within a few months, everyone will finally be reunited.

But I'm not stupid. Just as I didn't easily adapt to my new life, neither will they. I'm expecting a lot of anger from those who've been ripped from their homes, plenty of sadness at the lives they've been forced to leave behind, and a great deal of doubt when we tell them what happened. If it had happened during my time at the Mill, I wouldn't have believed it either. I'd have felt betrayed and furious at being pulled away from all I've ever known.

That's why I'm going with him. Maybe if they hear the truth from someone like me, it'll be easier. Perhaps I'll be seen as a little more approachable. The notion is almost laughable. Approachable isn't exactly how I'd describe myself; if anything, this whole debacle has left me saltier and more sarcastic than ever. Still, I have to try.

"It won't be easy," I mutter, "but we can do this, right?"

"I'm not worried about that."

"Then what?"

"Are you sure you want to be introduced as Noah?"

I click my tongue at that, irritation flaring. Jay's been hinting for a little while now that I should use Ada, rather than my chosen name. I can see why - things are changing and he wants to feel some semblance of normality. But I can't do it. Using that little girl's name would be like finally connecting the two of us together, and though he claims otherwise, I feel like that would cancel out everything we've been through. Like nothing ever happened.

"What's wrong with Noah?" I ask, venom in my voice.

He shoots me a sheepish smile.

"Nothing at all... but you do realise Noah's a boy's name, right?"

I poke out my tongue – he reaches out for it, but I pull it back at the last second.

"You do realise that Jay's just a letter, right? Hypocrite."

He laughs at that. The sound is wonderful.

"Fine, fine. Come on then. Let's head out."

We reach the Dock rather quickly. I'm more than happy to hop off the bike, which is now scorching hot under my touch. Perhaps the journey's a little too long for such a small vehicle. I tug off my helmet and toss it aside. It isn't really necessary on a long, straight road, and yet Jay insists we use them. Personally, I find his newfound protective streak to be hilarious.

The Docks are busy; much busier than I've ever seen them before. The Guards were removed from their posts several days ago and taken into the city to await trial. Now the boats are being used to ferry people, animals, and supplies across to the mainland. I cast a nervous glance at the crowd of people heading towards Thorne. They're waiting for more trucks, to be loaded in and taken back to their homes and families – not that they know it yet. Their faces are grey and sunken, but there's an unmistakable tinge of fear as they gaze into the distance. They pull together, moving as one, an unending, hundreds-deep crowd trudging hesitantly towards their new home. Several drag carts or animals behind them, and still others carry rakes, hoes and shovels, as if they had no chance to prepare before coming here.

Atlas soars overhead, scanning the crowd curiously.

Jay steps up beside me, his face a picture of dismay. I don't think that even he imagined the sheer numbers that would be heading back from the Mill. He draws his lips into a glum smile; but I fire back with a genuine one.

"It's alright," I tell him, "it'll be okay."

"What makes you so sure?"

"Trust me. This is just the first group, remember? There are more to come, so we'd better get used to it."

He nods curtly, turning his attention back to the crowd. They shoot us the occasional nervous look, but seem too afraid to approach. I don't blame them. I'd have kept my head down, too. Jay sighs.

"I don't even know where to start. What about you? Recognise anyone?"

I move to shake my head – but something catches my eye. A single, bold colour in the midst of the crowd. Someone's patchily-shaved head bobs in the chaos, a glowing shade of orange. My chest swells with excitement.

It can't be.

Suddenly I'm darting through the masses, worming my way through the crush of bodies around me. It probably isn't her. The chances are slim to none, but still...

Jay calls after me, but I ignore him. He'll understand once I tell him what I've seen. What that little dot of orange means. I break into a momentary clearing, and there she is. Patches of carrot-coloured hair, a long nose. Dark, pretty eyes meet my gaze.

Nel stares at me, her face blank. For a second, I worry she might have forgotten me. Heaven knows I haven't forgotten her. Even with everything that's happened, I've been so worried.

But then there's a glimmer of recognition, and her lips part in shock.

"...Noah? W-where have you been?!"

I stand breathless, delight filling me. She's here. Nel – my Nel – right here in front of me. The weight of the past few months is suddenly lifted in her presence, but curiosity is still apparent in her eyes.

Finally, I can tell her everything. About Kane and Darus and Pan and Jay. I can tell her all the places I've been and all the horrible, wonderful, chaotic things I've done since last we met. And with Nel by my side, any trace of fear left in my chest fades. I'm not afraid anymore.

I take a deep breath and smile.